AFTER THE FALL

Laura Jordan was thirty-two years old and everything in her life was falling apart.

During the endless wait in the hospital where Jack had been taken after the plane crash, Laura paced restlessly. Just for something to do, she bought a cup of coffee from the machine. It was lukewarm, but it burned into her stomach like guilt.

Why had Jack taken such a reckless gamble, she wondered. What made him fly across the mountains in a blinding snowstorm? The unidentified woman in the plane with him—who was she?

The unanswerable questions went around and around in her mind, tormenting her so she couldn't sit still. The one thing she knew for sure, she thought, her heart sinking, was that Jack had disappointed her again. Whatever he set out to do, he had fallen short.

(Cover Photograph Posed By Professional Model)

DENNIS
HIGMAN

Laura Jordan

LEISURE BOOKS NEW YORK CITY

A LEISURE BOOK®

Published by

Dorchester Publishing Co., Inc.
276 Fifth Avenue
New York, NY 10001

Printed in the United States of America.

1992 Edition
Leisure Entertainment Services Co., Inc.

Chapter 1

The airplane came in low over the log cabin, drowning out the old man's benediction. "Bless this food, and bless this house," he went on, raising his voice. It was a small plane, single engine, and the old man knew it must be in trouble.

Three generations waited for him to finish. Only his wife kept her head bowed and eyes closed. The grandchildren peeked at him between fat little fingers, and his son and daughter-in-law glared at them across the dinner table.

The smell of roast beef was overpowering in the small room. The children shifted in their chairs. The faster they ate, the sooner Grandma's homemade peach cobbler would come, a specialty she always served the night before Easter. In the morning, there would be hard-boiled eggs and chocolate bunnies hidden around the cabin.

The plane turned at the end of the lake, coming back, lower this time, its engine cutting out in quick, desperate, staccato bursts. The whole family stirred uneasily and turned toward the sound, alert like wolves disturbed by an unexpected noise above their cozy den.

"What kind of fool would try to fly over the pass on a night like this?" the son said, putting down his napkin.

"Come on." The old man stood up and went striding for the door. His Black Bear work jeans hung on his spare frame, held up high on his flat stomach by wide green suspenders. The son followed, a meatier version of his father.

The children, sensing excitement, were on their feet.

"Sit down," the old woman ordered them. "Grandma will show you how to properly carve roast beef."

The blond daughter-in-law watched her husband pull on his snowmobile boots.

"Be careful," she called after him.

The two men hurried through the pelting snow toward the lake, sinking up to their ankles in the mud. It was just above freezing, and the snowflakes, huge sloppy prisms that fell straight down, dissolved into a gray mush on the ground. The bottoms of the overturned aluminum boats, lining the shore, shone under the old man's flashlight beam.

The airplane engine had stopped. "Where the hell did he go?" the son asked. Just beyond the end of Cougar Lake was the icy black barrier of the Cascade Mountains. In back of them, acres of fir and hemlock fell away to the Seattle suburbs fifty miles to the west. The old man swung the light out across the lake and held it steady when he caught a glint of metal.

The plane rode straight down the beam, rushing at them, propeller silently windmilling, wing lights flashing. Just short of the beach, one wing dipped, caught the water, and the airplane cartwheeled into the shallows in an explosion of spray.

They rushed down the beach and into the water as the plane settled back, hissing and gurgling, its flimsy aluminum back broken. The old man hauled himself up onto the wing and pulled at the door, cutting his hand in the process.

"Here," the son panted, coming up beside him. He grabbed the top of the sprung door with both hands and began working it back and forth. The plane shifted under them as he yanked the door until it gave way and popped open.

Stale cigarette smoke and the unmistakable smell of whiskey poured out as the old man pushed the light inside. The pilot was jammed up against the shattered windshield, and a passenger wedged next to him in the narrow cabin. Water was already seeping through the floor.

"Get that one," the old man said, pointing the light at the passenger.

The son leaned into the cabin and lifted. It was a woman. If she had been pretty once, she would never be pretty again.

Her face was crushed. Ribbons of blood, black in the flashlight beam, ran down her bare white torso. The nipples on her breasts stood up like ripe red raspberries. Her legs were hopelessly pinned in the wreckage.

"Papa, this one's got no top," the son protested in a childish strangled voice.

"Never mind, she's dead. Help me with the man."

He continued to stare at her in the wavering beam. The old man gripped his son's arm. He'd seen too many boys paralyzed by fear, overcome by things they would never be able to accept. That was a long time ago. The naked woman reminded him of Italian girls he'd seen in the Mountain Corps, just little girls really, naked and bloody in the snow.

"This one's alive. Help me get him out," he ordered.

Together, they dragged the pilot over the girl and eased him onto the wing. The old man was sorry his son had to see this, but there was no helping it now. "Get down in the water. You have to carry him."

Obediently, the son slid off the wing into the freezing water. As he released his grip on the plane, it groaned and shifted. The sides of the alpine lake were steep and dropped into a bottomless blue hole.

"Get off there, Dad," he warned his father, taking the pilot in his arms. At any minute, the plane might slip, and the naked woman would be gone forever. The man was surprisingly heavy, and he gurgled with each breath as the son splashed to shore.

When they came into the house, the children stopped eating, their greasy faces shining in the bright light. A Sesame Street record was on the stereo to keep their minds off what was happening out in the snow. The son, staggering with his load, ducked under the "Happy Easter" streamer over the door.

"Go in the bedroom," the grandmother told the children.

Reluctantly, they backed away from the table, watching, fascinated, as Daddy and Grandpa lay the bloody man on the couch in front of the hot cedar fire that snapped and popped.

"Call the ranger, Son."

Carefully, the old man unzipped the leather flight jacket, looking for wounds. His wife helped him ease the coat back. The pilot was a big fleshy man.

The children closed the bedroom door to a crack and kept watching. The record played on. "OK, now everybody, it's time for a game. Rub your tummy just like this, one . . ."

"Shut that off," the old man ordered savagely.

The blond wife, grateful for something to do, went over to the record player and pushed the black reject button. The turntable shut off automatically, and then she came back and watched her father-in-law probe along the man's neck.

The pilot had an ugly pockmarked face, so ugly, the blond wife thought, he was handsome in a sort of bizarre way. Suddenly the eyes flicked open.

"I'm Jack Towne," the man said, "tell her I love her."

They were the most startling blue eyes the young wife had ever seen. They seemed almost electric and entirely out of place set in the heavy middle-aged face. She leaned over the couch, feeling a strange compulsion to look closer. She blushed with shame as she felt the touch of her husband's hand, drawing her back.

"I don't know," the old man consulted with his wife. "I don't think we can wait. We'd better take him down in the jeep."

She nodded in agreement and sat down beside the pilot while he went to get the keys. The blue eyes were closed, and each breath sounded like the last. The old woman took his left hand and held it between hers. There was a heavy gold ring on his third finger. It was a big powerful-looking hand but soft to the touch.

"Tell her," the man said, his lips barely moving.

"She was in the plane too," the son whispered to his mother as if confessing a sin, "but she was dead."

The children silently watched their grandmother from the doorway while the jeep cranked over out back. She was no stranger to death, and she was not afraid.

"God loves you, mister," she told the pilot, "and he loves your wife too."

Chapter 2

Laura Jordan paced across the Emergency Room at Lincoln Memorial Hospital in Seattle, her running shoes squeaking on the linoleum tile. It took her exactly fifteen long paces, thirty round trip. Time after time, it came out exactly the same no matter how hard she tried to change the count. So this is how it's going to end, she thought, giving her long, tangled blond hair a nervous shake and pushing her hands deeper into her raincoat pockets. It was two A.M., Easter morning. She ran her tongue around and tasted sourness.

The telephone had awakened her out of a sound sleep. "Miss Laura Jordan?"

"Yes." The call was so matter-of-fact it sounded like a business contact. Hell, Laura thought, rotating her neck to relieve the tension while she continued to pace the waiting room, it was business—the living and dying business.

And the message was as clear as if Jack had called himself. "Laura, I wouldn't bother you for the world and if you can't make it, fine. But if you could come down for a minute, just drop by, I'd really appreciate it."

Unconscious, he was reaching out for her help one last time, and Laura could not deny him. So she put on her maroon running suit and black poplin raincoat and came, forgetting to see if the cats were in or out, not waiting to comb her hair or brush her teeth. The cats would survive. They would go off to visit other houseboat cats until she got back.

Laura rubbed her eyes, pressing against the lids until she could see kaleidoscope flashes of light in her mind. It was no good dwelling on it, she told herself, and strode purposefully over to the coffee machine. She didn't want a cup of coffee, but it was something to do. She inserted a quarter. It fell through into the coin return tray with a clatter. She scooped it out and tried again. This time the coin made a hollow clunk and the red "Please Make Selection" sign flashed on.

Laura selected the fourth button "Coffee, Light, No Sugar," and the cup dropped. She watched the mixture rushing down, and listened to the clicking of the meter inside. It was all so scientific and exact. Somebody had the profit figured down to so many drops of heated water, so many grams of coffee.

Why had Jack taken such a reckless gamble? she wondered. What caused him to fly across the mountains in a blinding snowstorm? While Laura hoped it might be a noble last-minute gesture aimed at winning Shirley back, she knew better. She knew there were other, more devious possibilities.

What does it matter now, she chastised herself, sampling the lukewarm coffee. Whatever he was coming to do, he'd fallen short once again.

The coffee ate into her stomach like guilt. Laura Jordan was thirty-two years old and everything in her life was falling apart.

"Mrs. Towne?" the nurse called from the front desk. There was a doctor standing beside her. He was short, Jewish, and pale with fatigue. "Is this the wife?" he demanded.

Laura whipped a strand of blond hair out of her eyes and pulled herself up to her full five-foot-eleven-inch height.

"I'm not Mrs. Towne," she said.

The nurse arched her eyebrows in surprise, a willowy vibrant woman with perfectly coiffed silver hair.

"But you are here in regard to Mr. Towne, aren't you?" she asked pleasantly.

The doctor cut off her answer. "It has to be his wife or a blood relative," he snapped at the nurse. "Where the hell is the wife anyhow?"

"I told you. I notified her. Shirley Towne; she lives in West

Seattle," the nurse countered, not at all flustered by his brusque manner. "There are also two daughters, but only one has a phone—Christina, a student at the University of Washington. I called her, but she's only eighteen."

"She has to be twenty-one." The doctor angrily slammed his hand down on the counter top.

The nurse consulted a sheaf of papers. "His father lives in Kentucky. He said he would come on the first available flight."

"Terrific." The doctor threw up his hands and marched in a nervous circle. "Terrific!" He had a heavy black beard and a bald spot on top of his head.

"Excuse me," Laura said, "maybe I can help."

"Not unless you're a damn good surgeon or God," the doctor said abruptly. "Who are you anyway?"

"Laura Jordan. I'm a counselor, a friend of the family."

"No good," he said, turning his back. "I want to see the wife the minute she comes in," he ordered the nurse.

Laura felt two burning red spots of anger coming out on her cheeks. "What's his condition, Doctor?" She put a hard edge on the question.

The doctor turned back to her, a hint of recognition followed by contempt crossing his aggressive dark face. She knew that look. He recognized her. "The man is critical. And he's going to die unless I take some extraordinary measures which I am not going to do, Ms. Jordan, until I get a signed release."

"Thank you."

"Right away, understand?" he told the nurse. "As soon as she gets here." And with that outburst, the doctor exited, leaving the two women facing each other in the deserted room.

"I should apologize for Dr. Fisher," the nurse finally said, still standing in front of the counter. "He gets very rude when he's under pressure. Actually, he's a good surgeon. But he's young, and he's very, very tired."

"I understand."

"He means well. He hates to have people die on him. It makes him angry, I guess. But your friend Mr. Towne couldn't be in better hands."

"I'm glad to know that." She watched the rain fall outside the high windows fronting on the empty street. Shirley would come soon, and that would be a very hard time for Laura.

"I know who you are now," the nurse said suddenly, "you're on television. The Laura Jordan on television. I knew. I recognized you from somewhere. It just came to me."

"That's me." Laura waited uncertainly in front of the counter.

"Say, how would you like a good cup of coffee? The machine stuff is awful."

"That would be nice."

"I read your book too," the nurse said, going around the counter. She poured coffee from a pot on the desk into two porcelain mugs stenciled "Love a Nurse" in wide red cursive. "I'm absolutely terrible about titles, but I do remember the cover—bright pink. Pink is my favorite color. It was a good book too."

"Thank you." The nurse smiled and handed her the steaming cup. The name tag read "P. Washburn, RN."

"I'm going crazy trying to think of that title. It's right on the tip of my tongue."

"*The Femme Factor,*" Laura told her.

"That's right. *The Femme Factor.* Isn't that something? I knew I recognized you." They sat facing each other in the waiting room. Laura noted that P. Washburn, RN, had beautiful legs encased in white nylon stockings and was probably much older than she appeared. The clue was around her eyes, a hollowness that showed only in the bright overhead lights and up close.

"I'm sorry, I didn't get your name."

"Oh, Penelope—Penelope Washburn."

"That's an unusual name. I really like it."

"You do?" The nurse smiled again and her serene face gave Laura a moment of hope. "It was my great-grandmother's name, but I've gotten used to it. I grew into it, sort of like this job." She sipped the coffee and made a face. "Boy, that'll make your hair curl."

Laura tried hers. "It's good—really good. I like strong coffee." A pile of magazines lay on the table between them. There were some *Better Homes and Gardens, Sports Illustrated,* and one called *Rocky Mountain* with a picture of Robert Redford on the cover.

"It's hard, isn't it—the waiting I mean?"

"Yes. Do you get used to it?" Laura asked her.

Nurse Washburn took a sip of coffee. "I've been doing it for twenty years. I suppose you do get used to it. A person can get used to anything."

"Do you like it?" It was habit that made Laura ask. She made her living finding out what people liked and disliked, what they felt, what they wanted or dreamed of, why they were happy or unhappy. But it was also because she desperately needed to talk to someone.

"Like isn't the right word. This isn't something you like," the nurse said, indicating the empty room. "I don't like pain and suffering. But it's satisfying work. It's a job where I can help people. I think that's important, don't you?"

"Helping people?" Laura asked her.

"Yes."

"I don't know. It is to some people."

"You help people. You help them get along. You help families."

"I'm beginning to wonder if I really do."

"That's silly. Of course you do," Penelope Washburn insisted. "I've watched you. I don't know how you come up with ideas so fast. I could never think of ways to solve those problems. I'd sit there and be so confused I wouldn't know what to do."

"I get confused too," Laura said, but the nurse wasn't listening.

"I just have to tell you this. I have a friend who watches "Family Line", and she wants to call you about her husband, you know, but she can't get up the nerve. Every week she says she's going to call, and I wait and wait, but she can't make herself do it."

"Maybe it's not the right thing for her to do." Laura knew about the agonizing indecision between wanting to confess and wanting to keep it all inside, between wanting to trust someone with your innermost thoughts and the fear that once revealed, that person might strike at your most vulnerable point.

"But you're not a stranger; everybody knows who you are. It's like you're a friend. They trust you; they really do."

They trust false images, Laura thought sadly. False images created by lights and camera angles and a particular tone of voice with a special intimacy. People always wanted to tell Laura Jordan everything.

The telephone rang across the room, and the nurse excused herself to answer it, her white nylon uniform swishing as she walked. She punched the flashing button and picked up the receiver.

"I can't give you that information," she said after listening for a few moments. "Only the doctor can give you that information."

She paused again, listening. She stood very straight in front of the desk, her legs slightly apart. "Of course, the patient is here, but he's in surgery. He will be in surgery for several hours and only the doctor can tell you that."

Watching her, Laura realized one reason she felt comfortable with Penelope Washburn was her height. She was almost as tall as Laura. "Unfortunately, the doctor's in surgery with the patient," she told the caller with flawless logic. "My name is Mrs. Washburn. W-A-S-H-B-U-R-N. I'm the head nurse."

She listened attentively to the unseen caller. The control was marvelous. Nobody got around P. Washburn, RN, and Laura liked that in a woman.

"Well, it couldn't have been his wife. I talked to her not ten minutes ago on the telephone. I also talked to the youngest daughter."

Laura sat up suddenly, her heart pounding against the top of her throat.

"It doesn't sound like her either. The oldest girl is only twenty-four; her name is Wendy. She lives in Eugene, Oregon," the nurse said crisply.

Laura felt the bands tighten across her chest.

"Of course, you can come and wait," Nurse Washburn said, cocking the telephone receiver away from her ear and shaking her head at Laura. Laura could hear the tiny voice of the caller across the room.

"It's a free country, young man," the nurse smiled. "You're very welcome." She hung up forcefully. "That was the FBI," she said. "Is Mr. Towne in some kind of trouble?"

Laura massaged her face with her hands. "I don't know." She kept her head down. "What did they want?"

"Apparently there was a woman on the plane with him. She was killed instantly. They're trying to identify her. They said she was around forty so it couldn't be the oldest daughter."

"No," Laura exclaimed, "it couldn't be." Her voice was shaking. She hadn't known about the woman.

"Are you all right?" Nurse Washburn asked, coming over to her.

Laura took a deep breath. "No, not really." She felt sick. She could guess why the woman was there.

"Is there anything I can do?"

Penelope Washburn was a complete stranger, but Laura knew she would have to trust her. There was no alternative.

"Yes," she said quietly, "there is. You could listen to me. You could let me tell you something about Jack and about the whole family."

"Well, I'm a good listener," Penelope Washburn said, sitting down in the opposite chair and crossing her beautiful legs.

"Four months ago, I didn't even know the Townes. I'd never heard of them." Laura knew she was talking too fast and made a conscious effort to slow down, to explain clearly what had happened and how it had happened. "I was skiing in Sun Valley last Christmas with my folks. It's sort of a family tradition with everybody in our neighborhood on Birch Bay. That's over on Lake Washington."

"One of our doctors lives there; it's a beautiful place."

"It seemed like pure chance at first. I mean there were thousands of people there, and I got on the same chairlift, the same chair, with Shirley, Jack's—Mr. Towne's—wife. The

Upper Warm Springs Chair. It was unbelievable."

Nurse Washburn put her chin in her hand and gave Laura Jordan all her attention.

"And after I talked to her for a minute, I had the feeling I knew her from somewhere, that I'd held the same conversation with her. It was the most uncanny feeling."

The nurse smiled. "There's a word for that, but I'll be darned if I can remember what it is. I know what you mean though. It's an eerie feeling, like you're watching yourself in a movie."

"Exactly. That's it exactly. But the thing was, you see, I had talked to her before, actually talked to her and heard the same story. That was the strange part."

"Quite a surprise," Penelope Washburn remarked, sipping her coffee. The rain whipped across the windows with a low rattle. Nurse Washburn held herself very still. She wanted to know all the details.

"Well, as it turned out, it was a little more than a surprise," Laura said, looking away out into the rain. "I'd talked to her on my TV program, 'Family Line.' Shirley Towne had called me for advice."

"I see."

"I have no idea what the statistical chances of something like that happening are. I'm coming down a mountain and out of a hill full of people from all over the world, and I end up sharing a chair with Shirley Towne."

"Pretty remote, I imagine."

"I was ready to write it off as one of those million in one chances until I saw the boy."

"The boy?" Nurse Washburn said, folding her hands. She sensed Laura was on the verge of telling her an intimate secret and waited patiently to learn what it might be.

Chapter 3

Tiny slivers of snow were drifting down in the clear stillness. High on Bald Mountain, the snow groomers pushed upward, their dull yellow headlights probing the night. Below, Hailey, Ketchum, Sun Valley, and Elkhorn lay like a wandering string of twinkling Christmas lights in the folds of the white velvety hills.

At the Elkhorn pool, the fat girl kept her eyes on the stopwatch and the gutter where her sister would finish the 200 meters. It was very important that she punch the silver watch stem at exactly the instant she touched. That was why the fat girl didn't watch her sister plow into a powerful flip turn at the opposite end of the pool and come back toward her.

The sister drove for the finish line, her blue swim cap low over her forehead, arms slicing, curving, pulling; the kick steady as a heart beat. She imagined herself to be a speeding boat, planing over the water. She ordered the boat to pick up speed. The red band widened across her back as the pain spread.

Huddled with a wool blanket over her ski clothes and almost invisible in the blinding steam generated by the hot pool and the freezing air, the fat girl was still very cold and her shaking hand almost slipped when her sister touched the tile gutter. She punched the button hard, fearful she'd missed the exact time by a fraction of a second.

The sister fell back in the water, slowly dipping up and down. "How—did—I—do?" she asked, gasping for breath.

"Uh, 2:01.5, I think," the fat girl answered, unsure of herself.

In the distance they could hear the sound of laughter and clinking glasses. The smells of suntan oil and broiling steaks were in the air.

"Oh, damn!" she swore, rolling her head around to loosen the tension in her shoulders as she waded for the edge of the pool. "Damn!" She knew her sister missed the exact time, but it didn't matter because 2:01 or even 2 flat wasn't good enough.

"Let's try it again," she said, pulling herself up and out of the pool on the chrome ladder. Her body gleamed like white marble under the lights. She was shapely but somewhat big at the shoulders and had a high powerful rump. The red band across her shoulders faded to a dull glow, and the steam rose off her like smoke.

"You've got to stop, Chris," the fat girl said, her voice tiny and childlike even though she was almost six years older than her sister.

"What I've got to do, Wendy, is beat two minutes, " she said, stripping the water off her arms and puffing her cheeks out to calm her breathing.

"But you're going to hurt yourself. Please don't hurt yourself," the fat girl begged, shivering violently.

Chris smiled at her sister and put her arm around her. "Tell me what we're going to do at the Queen City Invitational, Wendy? What's going to happen?"

Wendy laid her head against her sister's shoulder, feeling the heat of her body. "We're going to win the Queen City Invitational 200-meter freestyle," she recited as if recalling her favorite bedtime story. "You're going to get a scholarship to the University of Washington and be a doctor."

She paused and looked at her sister for approval. Chris nodded at her and gave her a squeeze. "And then what's going to happen?"

Wendy looked off through the steam into the stars hanging like pinpricks in the blue-black sky over Sun Valley. "And then you're going to take care of Rob and me, and we can do whatever we want. We'll all be a happy family again. I can write poetry and . . ." she trailed off.

Something awful had just occurred to her. She couldn't swim, and if Chris should flounder in the pool she couldn't save her from drowning. And then there would be no one left to love her.

Her sister gave her a reassuring squeeze. "So you've got to be my helper," she said cheerfully. "You've got to help me train and work hard so we can all do it—together—you and me and Rob."

"But Chris, what if you sink? What do I do?"

Chris sighed. She was afraid for her big sister. It seemed to be getting worse every year. She loved Wendy, but ever since their mother left, her sister had not been the same.

"You can throw me that life ring. See it? Over there on the lifeguard chair." She pulled her blue swim cap down even with her eyes. It helped her concentrate.

"I see it." Wendy smiled, and when she smiled, Chris could see the face of their mother, and it hardened her resolve.

"Now make sure you punch that stopwatch the instant I touch," she directed her sister kindly and climbed up on the wooden starting block.

"Oh, I will, Chris."

She looked down the lane slowly, cocking her arms back and up, feeling the strain. It would be worse at the Queen City Invitational.

"Swimmers, take your mark," Wendy called obediently, her voice ringing across the deserted pool.

Chris narrowed her eyes, sighting the exact mark where her hands would touch the calm flat water.

She was only seventeen and she had to take care of them. There was nobody else. She would explode out of the blocks, feel herself reaching for the surface, being the speeding boat, the boat that never tired. Somewhere a band started to play.

"Go!"

Chris Towne launched herself out over the water with the grim determination of someone who had to win. Wendy kept her eyes on the ticking watch. This time she would get it right. Chris was counting on her. It was her last chance.

From the third floor window of the Sioux Condominiums, he could look out across the golf course and see the steam rising off the Elkhorn pool where his sisters were swimming. Beyond were the colored lights of the outdoor skating rink. The band was playing and the ice skaters moved smoothly with the live music.

He drained the beer can and ran his tongue around the inside of his mouth. Numb. Good as a dentist. He snorted and cleared his sinuses.

"Hey," he said, "let's go skating."

"Naw." William Blue didn't look up from the TV movie. He was still wearing his royal blue neoprene racing suit that clung to his wiry body like a second skin.

"Come on." Rob stood up and stretched his bare torso. Although he still had the smooth skin of a young boy, his sixteen-year-old arms were heavy with bunched muscle that tied in roped knots across his back. He liked to watch the smooth flowing rhythm of the skaters. He was a very good skater himself.

"It's cold out there, man." Blue kept his eyes glued to the screen. "You should rest. You gotta race."

"I don't have to do anything." He squinted hard at his watch. Weird. The digital face came up at him like some boiling green chemical. 9:45. It was the beer and the pills.

Rob stood up and the sudden movement sent a starburst of light flashing across his peripheral vision. He pulled on a shirt. It was a cowboy shirt, bright pink with a yellow bird sewn on the back.

"Come on, let's take a walk." He wanted to get out, to move, to forget about the race.

"No," Blue replied petulantly, still staring at the screen. "I wanna see this." He squinted at the flickering movie, pressing his thin lips together in irritation. He wanted to stay in the nice warm room and trip along with a rerun of *Centennial*.

"Hey, I'm not gonna sit here all night, OK?" Rob snapped, tucking the shirt into his pants. His sisters would come back and want to do something he didn't want to do. His stepmother might show up. She might want to take him out for a hot fudge sundae or something. She was like that. "Hey, you comin' or stayin'?" He ripped the zipper up on his ski jacket.

Blue turned his hard eyes on the younger boy. "I told you, Robbie, I wanna watch this program."

"So watch it." Rob Towne stomped into the kitchen, threw open the refrigerator, and extracted three half-quarts of beer. Two of these he put in the pockets of his ski jacket, one in each pocket. He opened the third with a noisy pop.

"Why don't you settle down, man, try a little grass?" Blue called through the kitchen door. "The store's open." He'd never seen Rob so nervous before a race. "Why are you so uptight?"

"Me? Uptight?" Rob took a long swallow of beer. "I'll tell you why. This is big leagues, man, I don't belong here."

"You're good, Robbie, one of the best."

"Bullshit. You been listening to my old man. The Super Salesman. That's all bullshit."

"Have it your way."

"Yeah, Blue, I think I will have it my way."

"Take it easy, don't get so mad. I was trying to help for chrissake."

"I'm going."

"Don't do anything stupid, Rob."

"Don't sweat it." Rob Towne slammed the door behind him. Someday he was going to dump Blue. Before his father found out.

But he didn't want to think about all that now. The floor slanted to the left, he leaned to the right and by the time he got to the stairwell, he was in full control. He had the talent. He even had the nerve. What he didn't have was the experience to win a race like the Miller Downhill.

The cold outside hit him a stinging blow across the face as he left the condominium complex and started down the highway. He walked fast, avoiding the plowed shoulder, going through the deep snow along the side. It was easy for his old man to enter him in a big-time race so he could get all pumped up standing alongside the course with his damn stopwatch. That was one thing.

It was something else to be in the gate, looking down the hill. He felt the sweat starting to come and lengthened his stride. It was crazy. He didn't like to race. He hated it. His breath came harder. He drove himself along, charging through the untracked snow. But maybe tomorrow would be his day. If he could hang on the edge long enough to place, his mother might see it in the newspaper.

He remembered her sweet, flowery smell, the soft feel of her breast. He imagined how she would pick up the newspaper, maybe at the store where she did her shopping or at her house on the front porch. She would open it, thumb through, humming to herself like she did and see his name, maybe even his picture.

And she would smile and forgive him for all those bad things he had done, forgive him for failing so badly she had to leave him.

Laura Jordan kept the Hoot Gibson hat with the eagle feather in the brim pulled low over her eyes as she watched the after-ski crowd whoop it up at Snorting Elk. Her skin-tight Levi boot jeans pulled up hard on her clitoris as she leaned on the railing and swirled the last of her J&B in the oversize glass and swallowed it. She felt wired; her skin tingled. Laura wasn't sure it was the jeans or the whiskey. Probably both. Something felt good. She wanted another drink, but it was a long trip to the bar. Her legs ached; her face burned. She felt marvelous.

She'd also worked off enough calories to treat herself to steak and potatoes and a big piece of chocolate cheesecake, but for the moment, she was content to drink whiskey and observe the natives of Birch Bay, young and old, indulge in their annual Sun Valley Christmas fling. Her father, carrying his paunch with dignity, stood out like a bald eagle among the lesser birds. Her mother's fifty-year-old body that looked thirty was somewhere in the steam of the hot tubs that lined the outer deck rim.

Laura had been making this trek since she was six or seven years old. They used to drive, gathering in caravans of Buicks in front of their homes lining the shores of Lake Washington in Seattle. Now they flew over each year to spend the holidays under the clear Idaho skies.

Laura privately referred to it as the Hot Tub Scene at Snorting Elk, but it was a place to get away from the office, the weekly television program, the book writing, and a thousand and one other commitments. It was a place where she was comfortable and where she could ski.

More than anything else in this world, Laura Jordan loved to ski, and she waited for the day when an interviewer would ask her about it. But nobody ever asked. Instead, they wanted to know what was becoming of the family in this modern world and did she really believe the American people would elect a woman president who promised to dismantle the armed forces while the Russians had nuclear missiles aimed at New York?

Laura saw him coming and shifted uncomfortably on her perch. No matter where she stood, she was never alone for very long. Somebody always came. There was no graceful retreat, and Laura at all times tried to be graceful. This one was red-faced, middle-aged and dressed in at least eight hundred and fifty dollars' worth of Will Bogner's finest. She watched with steady cool eyes. She was used to it. Laura was a very tall, very striking, very blond woman alone. His walk had a slight weave.

"My God," he said loudly to her, "excuse me, but you are the biggest woman I've ever seen."

Laura Jordan didn't blink. The problem with the Birch Bay crowd these days was that every year there were more and more newcomers. Californians came in droves, and they thought nothing of paying a quarter million and up for the waterfront homes that lined the gentle curve of Birch Bay. She eased her jeans away from her crotch. The electricity was gone.

"You know, I could use a drink," Laura told the intruder, noting the wedding band and tremors in his blotchy hands. "Would you get me a whiskey, J&B, no ice, no glass?" She gave him a smile. He blinked. "That's a joke." He looked confused. "On second thought," Laura said kindly, "forget it. I'm really not all that thirsty. Are you having a nice time?"

"Oh, I'll be glad to," he replied hurriedly. "J&B you said?"

"Yes. Thanks very much."

Laura watched him rushing off toward the bar. Somewhere, she knew, he had the little woman stashed and, of course, three or four darling children. It was hard to be nice to them when she was off duty. She could always introduce herself as Gene Jordan's daughter, that would set him straight in a hurry. But it wouldn't be fair to the fiery-faced little men of the world. All they wanted was a quick ego stroke. It wasn't a difficult thing for Laura Jordan to give.

She stepped down and hooked one high-heeled Frye Early American boot over the rail. The heels brought her up to a little over six feet. The irritating thing was, she thought, that after mending broken relationships seven days a week, she deserved a little relaxation where she could be herself. And if she wanted some extracurricular attention, sex or otherwise, she could always get it from Jim. Unfortunately, Jim McClay was in Washington, D.C., this Christmas, trying to keep some of his political clients out of jail.

"Here we go, here we go," he chimed. He was back, drinks spilling over the rough flooring. Proudly, he extended the remains to Laura.

"Cheers," she said and downed the drink in one gulp.

"My God," the man chuckled uneasily, "you were thirsty."

"Like you said, I'm a big girl. Thanks very much. I really appreciate it. Enjoy yourself." In one fluid practiced motion, she handed him the glass, pushed off the rail and into the flow of the party. It was time to go.

She had one more day before heading back to Seattle. One more precious day.

"Hello, Laura." A hand reached out. She shook it and kept

moving. "Hi, Bill." The trouble was the people in her parents generation were all familiar and dull. They lived in the same houses, held the same jobs, and, oddly enough, they even looked the same. It was as if they were preserved indefinitely by the good life on Birch Bay in perpetual, tanned, middle age.

Her father was engaged in a lively conversation with several women who looked a lot younger than he was. She paused to kiss him on the cheek.

"Stay and keep me company," he joked.

"Got to turn in. See you on the mountain tomorrow."

She walked along the deck by the hot tubs, trying to find her mother lounging in the steam and then gave up. Suddenly, she felt very tired. The whiskey settled in her stomach, killing the hunger pains and leaving only a vague loneliness.

The cold evening air felt good, and in the distance, the town of Ketchum glowed in the darkness. She walked down the steep hill beside the golf course, the dry snow creeking under her boots like old saddle leather. A hard glittering moon hung in the star filled sky. The band at the skating rink was playing "Moonlight in Vermont."

The people at Snorting Elk were nice enough, but somehow they brought out the rebelliousness in her. She didn't want to live the way her parents lived. Laura turned onto the deserted highway, pushing her hands deeper into the sheepskin jacket pockets. There was a man striding along the edge of the road, coming toward her in the darkness. For some reason, he had chosen to walk in deep snow. She could hear his breath rasping in and out. He was moving fast.

"Hello," she said, as they drew abreast of each other.

He didn't reply at first, but she heard him stop. "Hey," he called after her, "do you have a match?"

She turned carefully. "No, I'm sorry, I don't."

"Oh, well, I was gonna ask you if you had a cigarette too," he explained awkwardly.

"Sorry, I don't smoke." He looked very young and strong. His face was beautiful, almost feminine, but it was mounted on a massive neck. The heat steamed through the back of his jacket.

"Oh, well," he said, "I guess I'm out of luck."

The boy seemed to be on the verge of saying something else, but then he abruptly turned and went striding off in the deep snow. Laura watched him go for a minute, wondering what his real purpose was in starting the conversation. Overhead, a jet plane streaked silently across the sky.

At the Challenger Motel, Laura found a message from Jim McClay. As the desk clerk handed her the pink slip of paper with the box "Wishes you to return the call" checked in pencil, she felt the sharp sense of urgency that always gripped her. Laura hurried down the quiet hallway, her boot steps muffled by the thick carpet. She went straight to the telephone and dialed while unbuttoning her jacket. The room smelled of pine-scented disinfectant.

It was late in Washington, but Jim was wide awake. "How are you, Laura?"

"Fine. How are you?" A faint hum on the line made her talk louder than normal.

"OK. The snow's not very good."

She laughed. "You missed a great day here," she said wistfully, throwing her sheepskin jacket on a chair.

"You had a good time, huh?"

"Fantastic. All that's missing is a man in my bed."

She could visualize him sitting in his hotel, probably stretched out in a chair the way he liked to sit, surrounded by legal papers, his tie loosened, his white shirt rumpled.

"I'm working on that case right now. I think we can resolve it early next week."

"Good." She ran a hand through her long blond hair and brought it around across her throat.

"How are your folks?" he asked rather formally.

"Fine. They're having a great time. It's the usual crowd. I miss you." She moved her mouth close to the cold receiver. "I want you here right now," she breathed, "right now."

"I wish I was there, honey, believe me."

She straightened up. She was keeping him from his work.

He would be dead in the morning if she didn't let him go. But Laura didn't want to let Jim McClay go. "Doesn't it ever occur to you that the more successful you and I become the less we see of each other, the less fun we have?" she asked him, feeling the surge of whiskey and a sexual anger putting a bite in her voice.

"You've got a point there." He coughed and covered the receiver on his end. "I know a good way to solve that problem, Laura."

She waited for the answer she knew was coming.

"Laura?"

"Yes."

"Did you hear me?"

"Yes." She heard the strain in his voice. Jim McClay was paying a high price for success. "I don't mean set up housekeeping, I mean put some quality in our lives. Some closeness. We used to find time to come over here. It seems like we're missing something—oh, hell, I don't know. I'm tired, I guess."

"Me too. I'll be back in a couple of days, honey."

"Don't stand me up," she laughed, "I'm horny as hell."

"Don't worry, I wouldn't miss it for the world."

"Me neither. Good night, Jim."

"Goodnight, Laura. I love you."

Laura carefully hung up the phone. She was crying and it was ridiculous. She wiped the tears out of her eyes with her shirt sleeve, went to the window and pulled back the curtain.

Jim McClay didn't know what she was talking about. Laura wasn't sure she did either, but love wasn't enough.

She was filled by a desperate longing. The moonlight was like white fire on the mountain; it glistened in the frozen night. There had to be something more.

Chapter 4

Through the smoked lenses of her glacier goggles, the incandescent blaze of the morning sun spread from the white hot center out into pale concentric rings tinged with blue. The virgin powder hung deep and sparkling on the face of Willy's Wall.

The ski patrolman bent down, cranking his boots tight. The acne scars made trails across his mahogany face. He finished with the boots and stood up, running his skis back and forth. He carried himself with the arrogant grace of the very young and highly coordinated.

Behind his rose-colored goggles, Laura knew, would be eyes with the faraway look of a fanatic. She punched the start button on her tape.

He gave her a grin with cracked greased lips and said something. His hot breath puffed into the frozen air. The deep-blue vault of the Idaho sky stretched from horizon to horizon. Laura couldn't hear him. Waylon Jennings on stereo tape howled out of the Astraphone pack strapped across her stomach into each earphone. "Mama, don't let your babies grow up to be cowboys," he sang. She grinned back and gave the patrolman a thumbs-up sign.

He moved his skis restlessly, like a bull pawing the ground, anxious to get on with the attack, watching her carefully, observing the trickle of sweat on her brown taut cheek, the hard curve of her ass under the funky wool trousers. Everything about this babe was completely outrageous, he thought, from her purple gaiters to her ten-year-old jacket covered with wax. And the hat. He'd never see a White Stag billed hat except in the brown faded photographs hanging in the Lodge. Laura's was bright red and looked new. It had a little white ribbon on the front.

The ski patrolman liked her. She was as big as a giraffe and skied like a ballerina. He didn't know how old she was and didn't care. Any woman who could ski The Wall was good enough for him.

He could probably put out all night without breaking into a sweat, Laura thought idly, but skiing was something best done alone, and the patrolman was getting to be a pest, racing around her like a honeybee. He was a fast skier, but she was better. And like a lot of men, he didn't know the difference.

Without saying goodbye, Laura kicked off the top, dropping like an elevator with a broken cable down the vertical side of Willy's Wall.

The trick was to keep your body forward while your stomach sucked into your throat and every survival instinct screamed "Get back." Laura Jordan stayed forward, the dry snow exploding over her knees with each quick check turn, trailing behind like fine talcum. A sensuous charge ran through her, the flying, mesmerizing feeling of absolute weightless freedom.

It was over soon enough, the slope flattened, and she swung into wide arcs, breathing hard. "Oh, I've had loves and I've had lovers, but they never seem to do. I'm lookin' for a feelin' I once had with you."

He was pressing now, darting in and out, showing his stuff. Laura tried to maintain her own pace, but he was hard to ignore, and then the tape ran out. He grinned, cut in front of her and did a "360" off a packed mogul. It was time, she decided, to end her relationship with this young man on the flying trapeze who'd been dogging her ever since the first run of the morning.

As they approached the lift line, Laura saw her chance and took it. A short woman in yellow had been dumped while boarding and was struggling back into position for the next chair. She was alone.

Without slowing, Laura went down on her haunches, ducked under the safety rope and came shooting up the entrance ramp in time to gracefully sit down next to the woman as the chair cleared the loading area.

"Made it!" she gasped.

"My God," the woman whimpered, hanging onto the center pole as the chair went swinging into space.

"I'm sorry, I didn't mean to scare you." She had frightened deer eyes. Vulnerable eyes, Laura thought.

"Oh, it wasn't you," the woman explained, trying to muster a smile. "Everything about this place scares me."

The chair crossed over a deep gorge, and Laura could see her tracks coming down the ridge, clean and fresh in the undisturbed snow. The ski patrolman had crossed her turns into figure eights.

"It helps to look up the hill," she suggested, seeing the woman watching the ground drop away behind them.

"If I make it to the top, I don't know how I'll ever get down," the woman said in a quivering voice. She was about Laura's age. Short black hair peeked out from under her knit hat.

"Is this your first time up?"

"Yes, I mean no. I've been skiing on Dollar Mountain. The only reason I came up here is for the race."

"The Miller Downhill?"

"Yes, my son is in it. Actually, he's my stepson."

"He must be good."

The bright orange lift towers started their march up the hill, and the chair swung gently as the narrow cable pulled them up the face of the mountain.

"He would have died of embarrassment if he'd seen me fall getting on." The woman managed a genuine smile, and there was a touch of humor in her voice.

"I've fallen off a few chair lifts myself," Laura assured her. "It happens to everybody."

"But I feel like such a klutz," the woman replied almost enthusiastically, warming to the conversation and forgetting her fear. "These people here, they're so continental. And here I am, a little Catholic girl from Seattle. I feel like I'm in a foreign country or something."

Laura took off her White Stag hat and shook her long blond hair free.

"Nobody ever accused me of being continental," she laughed. "And here I am from Seattle like you."

"Really?"

"Born and bred. I'm afraid I'm not a Catholic though."

"You know there is something about you that's familiar," the woman mused, looking at her carefully. "It's your voice. I know you from somewhere."

Laura extended a gloved hand. "I'm Laura Jordan."

"I'm Shirley—Shirley Towne," she replied, reaching cautiously over the bar to shake Laura's hand. Shirley was blushing.

"I'm glad to meet you."

"You really are Laura Jordan, aren't you?" she exclaimed.

"Yes," Laura laughed easily.

"I didn't recognize you at first, but I knew your voice. You look different than you do on TV."

"Maybe it's my clothes."

"Yes. Maybe. Oh, Laura, this is really something. I called you once on your show right after I got married."

"Really?" She didn't remember Shirley Towne or her call.

"Yes, I married into a family with three older kids. Their mother'd walked out on them, and I was having a heck of a time adjusting. My gosh, this is absolutely unbelievable."

Laura smiled. "It's quite a coincidence isn't it?" There were so many calls from women who needed someone to talk to Sunday night.

"Wait until I tell Jack; that's my husband. He's waiting for me at the race."

They were over Willy's Wall. It was odd, Laura thought, looking down, how flat and safe the slope looked when you weren't on it.

"You really helped me, Laura." Her eyes glistened with grateful emotion. "You said I needed to give myself permission to take care of myself, and that by doing that I'd get along better with my kids."

It was sound advice. Women tended to take care of everybody but themselves.

"I hope things have worked out for you," Laura said, seeing the top of the lift ahead.

"To tell you the truth, I was thinking of calling you again."

"Better get your ski tips up, Shirley, "Laura advised her, "we're about to unload."

Shirley put her ski tips straight in the air. "Already? What do I do?"

"Same thing you do on Dollar Mountain. Ski down the ramp," Laura assured her.

"OK." Shirley twisted nervously in her seat as the chair went over the safety net.

"Watch yourself," Laura warned as their skis plopped onto the snow. The attendant glared at them through his plexiglass window and reached for the kill switch. He knew what was going to happen next.

The chair caught her under the rear end, lifted her up, and dumped her down the ramp, skis trailing by their safety straps. Laura skied back to help her.

"That wasn't quite the same as the Dollar Mountain lift," Shirley laughed nervously, climbing to her feet."It's a lot steeper."

Laura steered her over to the side and straightened out her skis.

"You go on, Laura," she said. "I can take care of myself."

"Let me show you how to get down to the race course."

"Oh, I couldn't do that." Shirley looked around hopelessly, her expressive liquid eyes clouded with confusion.

"Come on, it's right over the hill. We can ski down together."

Gratefully, Shirley fell in behind the taller woman and they eased down the gentle rolling trail. Laura sideslipped easily, Shirley edged for all she was worth, knees bent, leaning back and into the slope. Laura showed her how to keep her shoulders away from the hill. Shirley tried, succeeded, and then fell heavily.

"Oh, Laura, it's so steep. I'm absolutely hopeless," she said self-consciously. "I can't do anything right."

"Sure you can," Laura insisted firmly. "It's a matter of practice. Like the first time on a new job, you never think you'll get it but you do."

If Shirley was nothing else, Laura thought, watching her try the hill again, she was persistent, and this time she went much farther before embracing the safety of the hillside.

"Darn it!" Shirley exclaimed in disgust, "I'm such a coward."

"You're looking good, Shirley. Don't be so hard on yourself. You made it twice as far; that's progress. Don't measure yourself against what everybody else does."

Shirley Towne sighed. "Oh, you're right, Laura, you're so right. I feel better just talking to you. You help me see things differently." She struggled to her feet.

"That's important. You should feel good about yourself." The words came easily to Laura.

"The truth is I'm not doing very well at home," Shirley suddenly blurted, turning to her. "I was going to call you to see if I could come in for counseling."

"What seems to be the problem?"

"Oh, it's still me. It's probably all my fault."

"I'd be glad to talk to you," Laura offered, brushing the caked snow off Shirley's jacket. "Why don't you give me a call when you get back to Seattle. I'm in the book."

"Really?"

"Sure. There'll be a charge, of course," she said, laughing, "but the ski lesson's free."

Shirley Towne's eyes lit up. "Oh, that would be wonderful, Laura, absolutely wonderful."

"I'll look forward to it. Come on, we'll miss the race. And keep those shoulders parallel to the hill."

This time Shirley stayed up, bobbing precariously but forcing herself away from the slope.

The crowd stretched along the flag barriers on each side of the steep course, their murmur rising and falling like surf as each racer flashed by, skis clattering on the hard ice.

Laura saw him before Shirley pointed him out, a great bear of a man, stylishly attired in charcoal wool mountaineering pants with a liberal stain of wine around his wide mouth. He stepped out to meet them.

"I knew you'd make it," he exclaimed to Shirley, folding her in an enthusiastic hug. "I knew you could ski down here."

"Jack, you'll never guess who this is," she said breathlessly, pointing to Laura.

He had the most marvelously ugly face Laura had ever seen.

"Laura Jordan," he said, triumphantly, holding out a large hand and releasing his wife. "Laura Jordan of the 'Family Line' show. Am I right?"

"Yes," she admitted, "that's me." His big hand was surprisingly soft.

"It was the most remarkable thing, Jack," Shirley said, "we ended up riding the same chair. Isn't that something?"

"Wonderful!" He released her hand. "Wonderful!" Jack Towne had the face of a ruined Russian prince: big, fleshy, and pockmarked. And between the folds of ruddy skin that bunched up when he smiled were eyes so blue Laura was sure they must be colored contact lenses.

A skier topped the rise above them, completely airborne in a racing tuck, landed with a sharp slap and was gone straight down the hill.

"My God!" Shirley gasped. She paled. "Jack this is dangerous."

"Jeff Springstein, Stowe, Vermont, in the starting gate," the loudspeakers boomed. They all glanced up the course. Jack Towne had a stopwatch poised.

"I'm getting some sample times on these first guys so I'll know how Rob is doing," he explained. "He's in some fast company."

Somewhere above them, Jeff Springstein poled out of the starting gate.

"It's not as dangerous as it looks," Jack assured them.

The racer popped over the hill, going flat out, never wavering off the line. Laura watched him, a crouching missile in a gold-flecked helmet. She heard his grunt as he landed. What was the point of it all? she wondered. He was like the ski patrolman. One speed. Fast and hard.

Jack Towne produced a boda bag from under his coat.

"How about a shot of Ernie Gallo's finest?" he offered. Shirley wasn't enthusiastic, but obediently opened her mouth and leaned back while Jack squeezed the bladder.

Laura declined. "I never drink when I'm driving," she explained.

Jack threw back his head and barked appreciatively. "Christ almighty, that's good, Laura."

"Has your son taken his run yet?" Laura asked him.

"Oh, hell no. Rob's in the last seed." Jack tracked another speeding racer with his stopwatch. "It'll be a while yet. Listen, he's lucky to even get in this race. He's only been skiing competitively for a couple of years."

"Really?" Laura knew enough about ski racing to know that most of the racers in the Miller Downhill had been training since they were in grade school, many of them full time in various racing programs around the country. Jack Towne was either modest about his son's training or the boy was an extremely gifted athlete.

"Yeah, all of a sudden, he took off. He's worked his way up in a little local racing program. This is the first big shot." His face was flushed with pride and wine.

"Maybe it's too soon, Jack." Shirley lit a cigarette and looked up the hill.

"He's OK, honey, not to worry. Heck, the course at Crystal was a lot tougher than this. Really, you watch. The guys from Washington are gonna show these hotshots a thing or two." He pulled up his pants, adjusting the waist over his stomach to emphasize the point.

"Hey, Blue," he called loudly, "we're gonna clean their clock, right?"

A thin boy in a royal-blue neoprene racing suit, his dark hair pulled into a pony tail, turned mirrored silver glasses on

Jack Towne. "All the way, Mr. Towne," he grinned slowly.

"Hey, bring the girls over here. I want them to meet somebody." Jack explained to Laura under his breath as the boy approached with two girls. "Blue didn't make the traveling squad, but he and my son Rob are good buddies."

Jack motioned the young people forward until they stood in a ragged line for review. "Laura, this is William Blue and my daughters Chris and Wendy." They all nodded. Chris, tanned and very blond, had her father's eyes. She nodded and looked straight at Laura with a cool inspector's gaze. Wendy—heavier and ill at ease—smiled, blushed, and turned her eyes away. She couldn't tell where William Blue was behind his sunglasses.

"I'm very glad to meet you," Laura said politely, sensing the silent discomfort of the three young people. "It's a great day to ski, isn't it?"

"Laura's the Laura Jordan on television," Jack explained loudly, glancing around at the spectators. "You guys should ask for an autograph."

"Oh, Jack," Shirley protested, "not now. They want to watch the race."

Above them a rippling trill of excitement rose from the spectators, and Laura saw a cloud of snow and the windmilling skis of a falling racer. "Clear the course, please, no spectators on the course," the loudspeaker crackled.

"Somebody ate it up there," William Blue said quietly.

"See?" Jack told Shirley, giving her a reassuring hug. "Not all those guys in the first seed are that good. I wouldn't want to wish the poor bastard any bad luck, but that's one more space Rob can move up."

Shirley nodded grimly and exhaled, looking away from the scene of the crash. Cigarette smoke hung over them in the still air.

"Did Rob fall?" Wendy asked plaintively.

"No," Chris assured her, putting an arm around her older sister, ignoring the adults. "It was somebody else."

High above them, the sun moved behind a thick bank of clouds. It blazed angrily for a moment in the gauze streaks along the leading edge and then succumbed, casting a cold shadow across the mountain. Spectators reached for jackets and hats that had been piled in the snow. Laura zipped up her old blue parka.

"Sure I can't interest anybody in some of the red grape?" Jack Towne asked gaily. "Everybody but you, of course," he said to Chris. "Chris is in training—swimming," he explained to Laura.

"A competitive swimmer?" she asked, but Chris had turned her attention back to the race.

"Yes, Takes it entirely too seriously too," Jack added quickly to cover his daughter's rudeness. "I don't know, Laura, kids these days are too achievement-oriented it seems to me. Heck, a little wine never hurt anybody."

"Girls that age tend to be serious, Jack," Shirley put in. "Isn't that right, Laura?"

"I think so."

"What the heck," Jack Towne said, wiping his mouth with a coat sleeve. "Us old folks can have fun, can't we? What brings you to the Valley, Laura, business or pleasure?"

"Pure pleasure." It was hard for her not to stare at his electric blue eyes.

"Well, it's the best Christmas I can remember here. The snow is fantastic and the chutes are in great shape." Jack Towne looked toward the top of Baldy.

"Yes, it's been a terrific week."

"I don't ski myself," Jack Towne explained. "Bad knee. Old high school football injury. Kid stuff. Wanted to be the hero, you know? Damn foolish and permanent unfortunately. I do have a very keen interest in the skiing business, however."

Shirley Towne dropped her cigarette in the snow. "Jack's involved with a group that's trying to put a new resort over in Wyoming," Shirley explained proudly.

"Well, it's hardly off the drawing board. Early Winters, across the Idaho border at Wilson. We want to make it a destination resort. There's been a small place there for years, know it?"

Laura knew it well. "Early Winters? You bet. It's got the best powder skiing in the world."

"Our idea is to expand, build a lot of condos. It's a tax write-off for the guy who owns it now."

"That's a great idea."

"Jack met a man last night who's really interested in investing," Shirley prompted. "Tell Laura about T.R. Timberlake, honey."

Jack smiled, his craggy face breaking into furrows. "There isn't much to tell, at least not yet. We ran into this guy at a party down in Ketchum last night, a little function for the race officials. Anyway, his name is Timberlake, T.R. Timberlake. Heard of him?"

Laura admitted she hadn't. "Well, he's one of the biggest potato brokers in the country. He's rich, and his hobby is skiing. He says he's interested in the project." Jack slapped his gloves together. "I have a little public relations firm in Seattle, Laura. I'm in with a couple of local guys on this deal, politicians—Jack Howland and Frank Greenway."

"Oh, yes," she nodded. The names were vaguely familiar.

"They're the big money people; I'm the organizer. We could really go places with a guy like Timberlake in the group."

"Sounds good. I hope he puts some money into it," Laura told him, swinging her arms to stay warm. The racing had started again.

Jack glanced at his stopwatch. "Boy, these guys are good." He shook his huge head. He looked worried. "I don't know whether Rob can beat that or not."

"Hey, Mr. Towne, they're starting the last seed," William Blue called to him.

They moved closer to the course. The thin band of evergreens running along the opposite side looked black in the subdued light. First came a boy in orange, skidding and sliding. Jack Towne eyed his watch with satisfaction. "He can beat that. I know he can. Come on, Robbie!"

He crouched in the gate, loose and ready. Hands clapped

him on the back. He hated backslappers. Somebody was saying something, yelling at him. He didn't listen.

"Rob Towne, Seattle, Washington."

He coiled, sighting down the course. Lots of creeps waving their arms like ragdolls. They'd never know what it was like to feel the cold, cold fear twisting and shriveling.

He pushed off, taking two, three long skating steps and dropping into his crouch. Go! Go! Go! they yelled at him. Forward, forward, forward, he repeated over and over to himself, the chant that would keep him on his feet.

He hurtled down the hill, wind tearing at his face. He felt a hard bump, but kept his balance. The faces were blurring, dissolving. He aimed himself down the course. No more turns. Go for it!

Somewhere out there they would be waiting—his father, Blue, Wendy, Chris, and Shirley. All counting on him. He was airborne. They were howling at him like wolves. The fear gripped him. I'm going to fail again. Forward! he screamed at himself.

He glanced off the first hay bale, but stayed on his feet, sitting back on his heels, dragging his poles. His legs would not lift him up.

Rob Towne sliced into the crowd going seventy miles an hour. They melted in front of him, diving left and right. Finally, he regained his feet, but too late, pitching on his head, going end-over-end into the trees in a cloud of snow.

And then the silence. A frozen peace settled over him. He moved a foot, an arm. He was still together. He tasted salt. It was defeat. Still holding one ski pole, Rob Towne staggered to his feet. There was a dull ache in one leg. It was bad.

"You all right?" the patrolman asked him.

"Shit!" Nobody would read about it in the paper. There were two patrolmen now and everybody else—his dad, sister, Shirley, Blue, and the tall woman that looked like his mother. She had cat eyes.

"Sit down, son," the patrolman said. "We're going to give you a free tobaggon ride."

"I'm OK." He lunged forward, trying to get past them so

they wouldn't see him. The tears welled in his eyes.

The patrolman grabbed him by the arm. "Take it easy."

"Fuck off!" They were surrounding him, pressing in; he turned his head away.

"Rob, stop talking like that," Shirley scolded.

The tears ran hot on his face. He ducked his head and let them put him down on the toboggon, allowed them to wrap him in white blankets and fold a tarp over him. Teeth clenched, he cried very quietly so nobody would hear.

Jack Towne hobbled alongside the sled, his face beet red with anger.

"That course isn't safe," he berated the patrolman. "My son could have been killed."

"Sir, it's a dangerous sport," the patrolman answered politely, struggling to turn the toboggan in the deep snow. "He went out of control; he fell."

Laura noticed Jack's knee and thought he'd probably twisted it as they all ran down the hill to where Rob had fallen.

She'd gotten one quick glimpse before they folded the tarpaulin over the boy to protect his face from the needles of snow that were starting to fall. Enough of a look to see he was crying and to realize that Rob Towne was the same boy she'd met on the road the night before. The boy with the beautiful face who'd turned away so suddenly.

Chapter 5

The tabby cat's half-closed yellow eyes watched the bright lights of Seattle sparkling across Lake Union. Occasionally, the sweep of headlights from cars probing down the hillside on the opposite shore made darting paths out onto the lake. His alert ears heard the ping of metal rigging against aluminum masts close by. Far away, a siren howled in the night. Crouched on the window sill between a Christmas cactus and bougainvillea, he was perfectly balanced on his padded feet against the light bumping sway of the houseboat in its mooring.

At the first ring on the telephone, he turned his head sharply. On the second, he got up, and giving his back a quick arch, leaped silently to the carpeted floor.

"It's only the telephone," the woman said to him, stopping the ringing, but he stalked off into the darkness, tail high.

"Hello," she said in a whisper.

"Hello? Is this Laura Jordan? Laura?"

"Yes." She raised her voice slightly, glancing at the sleeping man in her bed. She had not been asleep; she had been watching the cat.

"I know it's late, but I just got in. Am I disturbing you?"

"No," she said with a throaty laugh. "Who is this?" The man turned restlessly in his sleep. She'd guessed the identity of the caller.

"This is Jack—Jack Towne. Look, if it's inconvenient, I can call you back in the morning."

"Jack, what a nice surprise!" She swung her bare legs out of bed and sat up, holding the covers around her body. "It's fine, look, let me, uh, get to another telephone here." She glanced at the alarm clock glowing on the bedstand. It was eleven o'clock.

"You sure I'm not bothering you?" There was a faint touch of humor in his smooth voice.

"No," she whispered. "No, just a minute." As she stood up, the bed creeked and Jim McClay gave a groan and turned his back to her, exposing one freckled shoulder.

Laura Jordan, completely naked, took the telephone and cautiously moved across the room toward the window. "Hang on. I've got to undo this damn phone cord."

Laura had decided not to go all the way downstairs to her office. That was silly. Besides, when Jim McClay got to sleep, he slept like a log.

"There," she said, clearing her throat. "Now, how are you? How's Rob?"

"He's fine. Some torn ligaments, that's all. Listen, I really am sorry I called so late. When I get all wound up, I forget other people keep regular hours."

"That's OK. I was up anyway doing a little heavy thinking." She tried to laugh quietly but was alarmed by the involuntary girlish trill that came out. She'd been expecting a call from Shirley not Jack. Laura rubbed her stomach and felt down to the stickiness of Jim McClay's semen in her pubic hair.

"Well, I don't want to keep you up, but I did want to talk to you before I went to Boise tomorrow. I'm going over to see Timberlake, the guy I told you about, the big money man."

"That's good, fire away."

She straightened up and looked out over the dark lake, surrounded by a curious mixture of industry and residences. Laura could see the dim lights of the America's Cup restaurant on the other side and the dark shapes of the World War Two Liberty Ships chained together, rusting at their dock.

"I've been talking to Shirley, Laura, and I was surprised, uh, quite frankly, uh, that she was considering, uh, consulting you. Professionally, that is. I mean I had no idea she was so upset over this thing with the kids."

Laura ran her hands down her thighs. "Oh, I don't think

she was all that upset, Jack," she replied smoothly. "It's more like she's very concerned about being the best wife and mother she can be."

Laura smiled to herself. She used to get a tremendous sexual thrill when she was in high school by standing stark naked in her room talking to Jim McClay on the telephone, feeling the hardness of her nipples as she talked.

"Oh, I realize that. I want you to understand that I'm willing to go along with whatever Shirley wants to do, and I'm perfectly agreeable to the whole thing. In fact, we had a nice talk about it when I got home tonight, and she wanted me to give you a call."

"Great."

There was a tug at the far end of the lake, its red and green running lights on the mast bobbing gently. Far behind, the lanterns on the tow moved slowly across the backdrop of the city.

"The thing of it is, Laura, we—Shirley and I—thought it might be better if you talked to our daughter Wendy. She seems to be the one who could really use the help." Laura visualized Jack Towne's magnificent ugly face, the rough skin, the dazzling, mysterious blue eyes.

"Well, I hadn't really considered that. I was expecting to hear from Shirley." She twisted the telephone cord absently around her finger.

"Oh, I know you were," he said quickly, sensing her confusion, "but when we really sat down and looked at it, it seemed to us that Wendy ought to be our first priority. Shirley's in full agreement. I don't know whether she told you about Wendy?"

Laura stopped twisting. "No, no, she didn't."

"Wendy lost her job recently. It was kind of a traumatic experience for her, I'm afraid. Shirley got her on as a mail girl at the telephone company. Shirley's been with them a long time; she's a supervisor in the billing department."

"I see."

"Anyway, Wendy walked out. She just left one day. No explanation, nothing. She won't talk to us about it. The girl has some real problems, Laura, and Shirley and I would really appreciate it if you would see her."

"Of course, I'd be glad to talk to her. But in a situation like this, I do like to discuss it with the parents first. It wouldn't take long, and I think we'd all benefit." A cat rubbed against her leg. It was one of the two females, Puss Puss.

"Oh, I agree completely, Laura, completely, but I've got a problem. This business with Timberlake could literally take off. Once it gets rolling, it can really go, and I won't have time to sit down. I can feel it, Laura. We're right on the edge of big things with the Early Winters resort, very big things."

"That's good, Jack. I'm happy for all of you." The Early Winters project excited Laura, and she found herself wanting to accommodate Jack Towne against her better judgment.

"Apparently, Timberlake always wanted to get involved in a ski resort, and he's raring to go. I am very hopeful we can get a commitment tomorrow."

"Really?"

"Yes. And I'll tell you what I'd like to do if I could suggest it, Laura, is drop Wendy by in the morning. We've already discussed it with her, and she's agreed to talk to you. In fact, she's looking forward to it."

"I don't know. I've got a busy schedule." Laura had no idea what her schedule was, but it was always busy. Barbara Adams, her secretary, made it up. Of course, Barbara could always change it too.

"Now you tell me if it's inconvenient, Laura. I don't want to push you on this thing. You're the expert."

The cat put her front paws on Laura's bare leg and began to methodically sharpen her claws. "Come on, knock that off."

"Pardon?" Jack sounded alarmed. Laura held her reply for a second in order to think about what he was trying to do.

"It's only my cat. She thinks I'm a tree stump," she finally said.

"No kidding," Jack Towne laughed with relief, and then went back to the attack. "How about it, Laura? We'd really like to have you see Wendy, and it would be a big load off my mind. I want to concentrate on getting T.R. Timberlake's name on that dotted line so we can all ski a little powder next winter."

He was a mover, and he did it all so smoothly. For a moment, Laura Jordan hesitated. She recognized the technique. She did the same thing herself. Take the direct approach. If you want something ask for it. All they can do is say no. Never assume something can't be done. Lessons from her father, Gene. Why not, Laura thought? She liked Jack and she was interested in Wendy.

"How about ten o'clock?"

"That's terrific, terrific. I'll drop her by on the way out to the airfield. You've really taken a load off my mind, Laura, and Shirley will be so pleased. We were both concerned, you know, and this way we know everything's in good hands."

"I'll look forward to seeing her."

"Great! You know, Shirley really, really admires you, Laura. She's sort of reserved in a way, but I've never seen her so high on somebody before."

"I liked her too. You're a lucky man, Jack."

The cat was back, looking for more attention. Laura bent down, rubbing the arching neck, thinking how silly she must look wandering around her apartment in the dark, naked, with a telephone, petting a cat.

"You're telling me? Shirley's made my life mean something again. I haven't felt this good about things in years. I have a feeling it's going to be my day tomorrow. I know it's going to be good flying weather. Do you fly, Laura?"

"You mean like a pilot?"

"Yes. I just got my license, strictly for business, of course, but what a great way to go! It's not only efficient as hell, but it's fun."

"I never tried it. It must give you a great sense of freedom."

"Oh, it's even better than that. You feel like a bird. We'll have to go up sometime."

"I'd like that. Give my best to Shirley, Jack, and tell her to give me a call."

"I sure will, and Wendy and I will see you at ten."

"OK, been nice talking to you."

"Oh, Laura?"

"Yes?"

"Thanks for everything. I mean it. You've taken a heck of a

load off my mind. I'm really pleased you'll be helping Wendy. I'll give your best to Shirley."

"OK. Thanks. Goodnight." Laura set the telephone on the floor and sat crosslegged on the rug, rubbing the purring Puss Puss behind the ears. "What's the matter, little kitty," she crooned, "isn't anybody paying any attention to you?"

"Why don't you use your answering service at night?" Jim McClay asked her, his voice muffled by the covers.

"Too impersonal," she replied, still petting the cat. "I only use it when I'm not here."

He rolled over in the bed until he was facing her, his square freckled face heavy with sleep. Jim McClay's tousled red hair made him look like a little boy.

Laura smiled. "I'm sorry, I didn't mean to wake you up."

"I feel like I'm in the middle of a soap opera," he groused, stretching. "You got anything to eat in this place?"

"Sure, the refrigerator's open. There's a pork chop or two in there."

He swung out of the bed fully awake and hit the floor with a purpose. He was a big powerful man, and Laura had always been fascinated by his body. He was wide at the shoulders, narrow in the hips, and his legs were laced with fine nets of long lean muscles that flexed gracefully as he walked.

"You know, Laura," he called from the kitchen, "I'll never understand why you don't like to stay at my place. I never get telephone calls in the middle of the night from strange men."

"Because I like it here, because I like to screw on my terms, because I don't like to be given the once over by the damn security guard at the gate of your fancy condominium when I leave at two in the morning. Because my kitties would miss me." She scratched Puss Puss. The tabby, Fat Cat, wandered by, pretending not to care that he was being left out.

"You want some of these pork chops too?" Jim asked.

"Sure."

"I need my seven hours a lot worse than you need yours," he said, handing her a cold pork chop. "I've got to be in court at nine-thirty. What time is it anyway?"

"I don't know, eleven-thirty, something like that."

Jim McClay went back and sat on the bed. Laura gnawed off a big piece of pork chop and vaguely considered going over to sit beside him. She wondered what would happen if she dropped the pork chop on his limp penis. Fat Cat circled closer. "Come here, you stubborn cat," Laura called to him.

"I've go to run ten miles. That means I've got to get up at five-thirty. Oh, God," he groaned.

"I know how we could knock off a quick seven, buddy boy."

He snorted. "Oh, sure," he said with his mouth full.

It was an old joke. Jim, with his penchant for precision in everything he did, had read that the average sex act consumes calories equivalent to running seven miles.

"You could stagger in there with pork chop on your face and your pants unzipped," she kidded him gently, "and you'd still beat them hands down, lover."

"Sez you."

"I have complete confidence in you, counselor."

"Laura," he said, finishing the pork chop, "I'm going to have you arrested for sexual harassment under section 601 of the Penal Code."

"The Penal Code," she howled, sending the cats scattering. "I always wondered what that meant. What's a 601?"

He smiled indulgently. He enjoyed watching her laugh. He thought she was at her most beautiful when she laughed.

"That was Jack Towne," she finally said, controlling herself, "of the most interesting Towne family. Those people I was telling you about, the ones I met at Sun Valley."

"Oh, yeah, the guy that looks like a fat Russian prince."

"Ruined, not fat, ruined. Like he lives in an old battle-scarred castle, the last of the czars." She stood up and stretched, still holding the pork-chop bone in one hand.

"OK, ruined then." The soft girlish curves had hardened into a statuesque figure. He liked to watch her move. She was so graceful and uninhibited.

"Am I getting old and ugly?" she asked, seeing him looking at her. Laura gave him a brief bump and roll.

"No," Jim McClay said seriously, "you're the most beautiful woman in the world, and I love you."

"But do you think I'm sexy? Do you want to ravish me?"

"I already ravished you," he pointed out calmly.

"But again and again."

"You find the time, I'll find the energy." He stood up and came to her, but she could tell he wasn't serious. Laura Jordan tried hard not to show her disappointment. She held him tight, the familiar rough body.

"I love you," he said quietly.

"Me too."

She supposed it was true. And if it wasn't, it should be. She'd known Jim McClay all her life. He was her best friend, a kind and considerate lover, an honest, very successful, highly paid criminal lawyer.

"Do you really?" he asked quietly, and with a jolt Laura realized they'd been together so long he knew what she was thinking.

"Of course."

It was not quite a lie, but it served to hide the wild, reckless streak in her that rebelled against the conventional way of doing things.

"I've been thinking," he said, stroking her long blond hair, "that you and I should get away for a vacation. I mean a week, maybe even a month."

Laura closed her eyes and kissed his shoulder. She knew it was a prelude to another serious proposal, the kind that had been coming gently but steadily ever since that first night in the boathouse. To Laura, sex seemed a natural extension of their growing friendship. It awakened an exciting new dimension in their relationship.

For Jim McClay, however, it meant an obligation to try and do the right thing, and the right thing was marriage. Laura almost agreed in her junior year in college, but at the last minute, she backed out. The truth was, she thought, as she pressed into his shoulder, she was basically happy with the relationship the way it was. It suited her.

"Sometimes, I think we're going to be this way for the rest of our lives, rushing around, passing each other, saying hello when we have time. Sometimes I feel we really don't know each other all that well. Do you ever feel that way?"

"Sometimes." She laughed quietly in spite of herself. With the exception of a brief fling with an Austrian ski instructor during a European vacation, Jim McClay was the only man Laura Jordan had ever slept with.

"I'm serious, Laura."

"I know you are. What did you have in mind, big boy?"

She wrote him everyday when he was in Viet Nam, and when he got back, they went on as if he'd never been gone. Actually, Laura knew Jim McClay very well. There were no secrets.

"I want you to come up to the San Juan Islands with me for a long trip."

"And pray tell, what is the objective of this generous offer? Do you intend to have your way with me night after night, trapped on your ship?" She playfully pushed her pelvis into him.

"Come on, Laura. To be together, to talk, to get away from all this." He did not push back.

"I don't know, Jim. I can't leave, not just like that. I have obligations, you know. For one thing, I'm going on a tour to promote my book."

"How long will you be gone? Three weeks, right? You'll be back in plenty of time."

The San Juans, hundreds of tiny islands stretching north into Canada, were a cruising paradise with deserted deep-water inlets where one could catch Dungeness crabs and sleep on the beach by a fire. Back in the days when Jim's father Angus McClay was alive, the families took summer vacations there together. The islands were a Robinson Crusoe kind of place, and Laura had wonderful memories of running half naked, brown and free, along the beaches.

But she knew Jim McClay never took a real vacation, and so she pushed him away and went over to the bed. She let herself fall with a plop on her back and spread her arms and legs wide as if staked down.

"When do they run that big blue water race off Vancouver Island? What's it called, Race Light?" she asked innocently, talking to the ceiling.

"Oh, in a couple of months," he admitted sheepishly, "but

that's only two days. We could have the rest of the time to ourselves. That's early in the season. There wouldn't be any tourists."

He came over to sit beside her. She'd cut through to his one selfish motive. His forty-two-foot racing sloop was named in her honor, the *Laura J.*, but it was also the defending Class II Champion.

"Oh, God," she laughed, sitting up to hug him. "You're incredible. A nice intimate time with your jolly little crew. What's that guy's name, the one who plays the harmonica?"

"Cat Stevens?"

"Oh, yeah. A little heavy-weather sailing and then a roll in the hay with four other guys two feet away."

"I didn't mean then. We'd go after the race," he said angrily.

"I know," she soothed him. "I wouldn't change you for the world. I love you the way you are, honest."

"I am the defending champion," he pointed out.

"I knew you were going to say that. Never let it be said Jim McClay got beat."

"Not very often," he said stubbornly.

"I'll think about it, Jim. I really will."

"OK. God, I'm sleepy. Did you set the alarm?"

"Yes. Five-thirty, right?"

"That's it." He swung into bed and pulled the covers over them. Laura reached over her head and shut out the lights. Moonlight filled the room.

"You won't be disappointed if I don't join you on your run, will you, hon?" she asked.

"No, that's OK."

Laura didn't like running before dawn. Neither did she particularly enjoy running with Jim anymore. It hadn't always been that way. In college, it was fun, like playing, and they were never in a hurry. Once on a whim, both hot and sweating, they veered off the path and plunged into the cold lake in the middle of November.

But since he'd come back from Viet Nam, Jim McClay was always in a hurry, pushing himself harder and harder, looking straight ahead, never wavering off his chosen route. His job became an obsession, the leisurely runs became races, and the fun turned to pain. Laura absolutely refused to trail along after him, trying to keep up. She liked the peace and solitude of running alone with her own thoughts.

"What are you doing Saturday night?" she asked, moving close to him. He was so solid, so reassuring. Maybe she did love him after all.

"I hadn't planned anything. I've got to take my mother to the doctor in the afternoon. I'm going to Washington again, but it's a turnaround. I'll be back that morning."

"Is your mother all right?"

Laura liked Myra McClay, a big raw-boned Scottish woman who always looked out of place among the sleek tanned Junior League ladies of Birch Bay.

"She's fine. It's only a physical. I like to go along to let her know I'm there."

"How much do you love me?" Laura said suddenly, sitting up in bed and leaning over him.

"I'd do anything for you, Laura."

"Anything?"

He looked at her suspiciously. "What's the deal?"

"Well, partner, it so happens I have two great tickets to the Waylon Jennings' concert Saturday night, and I'd jest love to have y'all by my side, Tex." She slapped him hard on the shoulder with an open hand. Her breast brushed against his chest. She let it brush back and felt the tingling sensation start between her legs. Damn, she thought, maybe I'm a closet sadist, and she whacked him again.

"Stop that, goddamn it," he sat up irritably and grabbed her hands firmly.

"Well, you comin' or not? 'Course, I can always find another fella."

He lay back defeated. "I suppose. What is this, some kind of loyalty test? I don't understand what people see in him. He's such a surly son-of-a-bitch. He acts like he hates the audience."

"He does. You're finally beginning to appreciate old Waylon, Jim. After all these years of listening to every one of his records, you finally know why I love him."

"I'll go, OK, Laura, I'll go. Now I'm going to sleep."

"Yahoo," Laura whooped at the top of her lungs.

"For chrissake," Jim complained, burying himself under the covers.

Laura Jordan fell back, giggling to herself. She was really awful. She knew Jim was serious about his seven hours of sleep. Without it, he felt vulnerable. But the thing was, she had never seen Jim fail at anything, seven hours of sleep or not. He never looked tired, and he was always in control.

Laura's three cats gathered in the moonlight on the floor. Puss Puss was officiously cleaning off Christabelle, her little female kitten, while Fat Cat stood by looking bored. Laura patted the covers gently.

All three cats turned. They watched her with unblinking eyes. Fat Cat finally stood up and walked away. A fine thing, Laura thought, you say "come" and he goes. He was an independent little cuss. They all were. They did as they pleased. If you were nice and it pleased them, they were nice to you. Puss Puss, having finished her nightly cleaning job, pranced over and leaped onto the bed in one fluid glide, landing directly on Jim McClay's protruding bottom.

"That's another goddamn thing I haven't got at my place," he complained sleepily as the cat walked the full length of his body, daintily sniffed his ear, and curled up to sleep next to his head.

"She loves you," Laura said.

"No, she doesn't," Jim growled. "All she wants is my warm body."

Chapter 6

All that was left of Jim McClay was a trough-shaped depression in the unmade bed where the three cats lay, lazily licking each other and watching Laura struggle through ten repetitions of exercise twelve—the leg lift—of *Arnold's Bodyshaping for Women.* A light rain was falling, and the cats stayed in bed when it rained.

"What's this note about a ten o'clock appointment with Wendy Towne?" Barbara Adams scolded over the intercom connecting Laura's upstairs apartment to the first-floor office on the houseboat. "You already have a ten o'clock appointment with Susan Litche."

"Susan will have to wait, Barb. These are the people I met at Sun Valley. Wendy is one of their kids. Look, never mind, it's a long story." The sweat poured down Laura's naked body. She liked the feel ot it.

"What do I tell Susan?"

Laura had done her last leg lift. "Your usual perfectly plausible excuse, OK? I'm sorry, I can't help it."

Good old Barbara, Laura thought, picking up her five-pound dumbbells and launching herself into the last exercise. "You do know it's nine-forty-five, don't you?" Barb laughed.

"Yes. Thanks."

Barbara walked out on her husband after thirty years of marriage and physical abuse. Her children were grown. At fifty-two years of age she had never held a paying job until Laura offered her one. Barbara Adams didn't know it, but she was the prototype for the balanced woman in *The Femme*

Factor. A prime example of the untapped potential in the female species. Laura was convinced Barbara could run AT&T if she put her mind to it. Probably a lot better than the emotionally crippled man who held the job, whoever he was.

She dropped the weights and rubbed herself down with an oversize orange towel and threw it on the floor. Dishes from last night were still on the table. Her clothes from yesterday were on the chair. She considered it creative chaos. It drove Jim McClay crazy. By now he was in court, doing his thing.

Laura went to the closet, breathing deeply as she walked. She slipped on a pair of white jeans, no panties, sandals, no socks and a clean cream and earth-brown running jersey, no bra. She didn't want to come on like a cold professional head shrinker with Wendy Towne.

She took the stairs two at a time, her sandals slapping, and dashed into the reception room. "Is it ten yet?"

"No. You have at least two minutes for a cup of coffee." Barbara Adams handed her a steaming mug. "How's Jim?"

"You're a real detective, aren't you?"

"No, but I'm a very observant lady. I always know my neighbor's business. The only thing that ever caught me by surprise was myself—when I walked out on Harold. Thanks to you, Laura, that turned into a very pleasant surprise."

"But how did you know?" Laura persisted playfully. She had few secrets from Barbara Adams.

"The little sports car shape in the parking lot, the dry place right next to your car."

"Oh, God, Jim must have had a fit. His pride and joy got all wet," she laughed. "Did I ever tell you that right after he got that thing he actually wanted me to take my shoes off when I got in?"

"You did."

"The virgin Porsche," Laura laughed. The rain dripped off the covered eaves and splattered into the lake. The jumbled roofs—tin, shingle, composition—made a crazy pattern of shapes and colors around Laura's two-story houseboat. They were connected by a series of floating piers and a long gangplank that ran to the shore.

Laura's houseboat, mounted on a cement barge, was shingled in cedar with wide blue-tinted windows facing the lake and small, clear round ones in the rear. The top was flat and landscaped with evergreens in a combination garden-sun deck. The official owner was Family Counseling Service, Inc. Laura was the president, her father Gene was the treasurer and Barbara Adams was the secretary.

Jack Towne was impressed. The houseboat stood out like a modern sculpture among its squatty odd-shaped neighbors, many of them lopsided in the water.

"Boy, that's really something," he told Wendy as he pulled the rented black Lincoln Continental into the parking lot. Wendy didn't say anything.

Jack rented the car to impress his partners with his own importance in this scheme even though he wasn't putting up any of the money. The car was a visual sign, a symbol, to show them he was the one who knew T.R. Timberlake, a very rich man.

Wendy Towne sat low in the front seat, her chin resting on her right hand. She was watching the rain. It seemed to come down in wavy lines, and it made her slightly dizzy.

"That is strictly first class, Wendy," he said enthusiastically, setting the parking brake.

Laura's houseboat would have been an imposing building on land. On the water, it was totally unique. A small carved wooden sign at the head of the ramp read "Laura Jordan, Family Counseling."

Jack appreciated good graphics, and the sign was well done. Not too much, but very classy. It was a nice touch. That was what counted—appearances. Jack knew appearances were all important.

That's why he insisted they charter the plane. Because when they landed in Boise, it would show T.R. Timberlake they were not a bunch of yokels from Seattle. And being at the controls himself would demonstrate to T.R. that he was competent to arrange finances for and promote the successful opening of the Early Winters Resort. Jack Towne knew people had great faith in airplane pilots.

He clapped a hand on Wendy's shoulder and guided her across the swaying ramp.

"I don't want to," she whined under her breath. "Do I have to?"

"Yes," he said, and seeing Laura opening the door, smiled widely. "Laura, how are you? You remember Wendy? This is a great place, really marvelous. I was telling Wendy, this is the nicest houseboat I've ever seen."

"Thank you. Come in. Can I take your coat, Wendy?"

The fat girl shrugged and looked at the floor.

"Maybe you want to leave it on for a while, it's a little chilly in here." The girl showed no sign she'd heard her. Wendy Towne was wearing unironed blue-denim carpenter coveralls, oversize tennis shoes, an old wool sweater, and a faded yellow windbreaker. Her uncombed brown hair hung in tangles.

"Barbara, this is Wendy and Jack Towne," Laura introduced them. Jack shook Barbara's hand; Wendy reluctantly shook too. He looked absolutely radiant, Laura thought. And very stylish. The light-blue belted raincoat was top quality. The rough tweed pants hung perfectly over the soft calfskin Wellington boots. His thinning golden hair was slicked back against his massive head.

"I've really got to run. I'm the pilot; the pilot can't be late."

"We're going to have a nice talk," Laura said, trying to get Wendy to look at her without success.

"Wendy's a little shy, Laura. Once she gets started you'll have to shut her off. She's really been looking forward to this."

Laura could see that Wendy was looking for a way out, but it would be easier to talk once Jack was gone.

"Have a nice trip. The weather played a dirty trick on you."

"Weather doesn't bother us. I've got an instrument rating. We fly right through it."

"Well, good luck with T.R. Timberlake."

He had a spring in his step and for such a big soft man, he positively pranced over the swaying gangplank to the parking lot. There was no trace of the limp, Laura noticed, after Rob's fall at Sun Valley.

Wendy was looking past Barbara into Laura's conference room behind the receptionist's desk.

"Wendy, would you like to come in and sit down?"

Wendy Towne gave her blank look and walked in. She's plodding, Laura thought, listening to the slap of her tennis shoes.

"Feed the cats, will you, Barb? I forgot—again."

"Those pussy cats won't know who their real mother is if you don't remember soon," the older woman chided her and shut the door.

Laura Jordan and Wendy Towne were alone in the spacious room with the wide bay windows looking out over a lake full of activity. A seaplane droned noisily by, struggling to break the last sticky pull of the choppy gray water. The harsh flash of a welding torch flickered from the shipyard on the other side. A Hobie Cat skittered back and forth, tilting dangerously up on one pontoon as it caught the gusting wind.

Wendy Towne stood at the window. Laura let her stand and sat down in one of the swivel armchairs. There was also a wide overstuffed couch and two beanbag chairs. All the furniture was leather.

"Pretty, isn't it?" Laura said.

"Yes," she replied in her tiny child's voice.

She looks like a big unhappy teddy bear, Laura thought, standing so forlornly with her hands deep in her pockets.

"Have you ever been on a houseboat before?"

"No."

The rug was thick and oriental. There was a huge color photograph of the *Laura J.* under full sail on one wall, a very fine Calder print on the other. Behind the desk was Laura's degree in education and a framed certificate of appreciation from Harrison Junior High for the four years of service it took her to decide she was a counselor and not an English teacher.

"You know, I'd never been on one either until I bought this. My dad talked me into it. I was afraid it might rock in the waves."

Wendy turned and looked straight down at the floor. "Can I sit down?" she said.

"Certainly. Would you like something to drink, a cup of coffee or anything?"

"No—thanks." Wendy sat heavily in one of the beanbag chairs. Her knees stuck up above her chin, and she looked extremely uncomfortable.

Laura swung around and faced her. "Did your father force you to come here, Wendy?"

"No." The reply was barely audible.

"But he persuaded you, didn't he? You really didn't want to come?"

"I don't mind."

"Well, I don't want you to feel you have to stay. Really I don't. Did your dad and Shirley explain who I am, what I do?"

"He said you were a counselor." She looked up for the first time, and Laura could see pain in the dark shifting eyes.

"Yes, I try to help people know themselves better, so they can communicate their needs to others. So members of a family can work together."

Wendy Towne looked at the floor. Laura was trying too hard. There was never any structure to these initial conversations, she reminded herself. When she tried to use stock questions, apply technique, invariably the results were poor.

"How did you like Sun Valley?" she asked, trying a new tack.

"It was OK," came the muffled reply.

"It's one of my favorite places. Where's yours?"

"Pardon?"

"Do you have a favorite place? A place you like to be?"

"My room."

"You know, that's funny. I like my room too. I feel safe there. It's peaceful," Laura said kindly.

Wendy looked at her for the second time that morning. A trace of a smile crossed her bloated face. "So do I."

There was a flash of beauty in that brief smile, evidence of the same prettiness that both her sister and brother had. But in Wendy, it was buried under a layer of fat and hidden in the defensive crouch of her body.

Wendy Towne turned away from her and looked out the window onto the lake.

"I never get tired of that view," Laura said quickly. "It's always different."

The girl didn't reply. Laura leaned forward, resting her chin on folded hands. "Do you have a view from your room, Wendy?"

"No."

Laura waited, listening to the steady tick-tick of the grandfather clock on the opposite wall. Wendy sat perfectly still, a miserable lump who wished she was somewhere else. Shirley had said she was what—twenty-four years old? Laura was beginning to realize that Wendy Towne had some very serious problems.

Still, Laura waited. If she continued to grill this poor girl like a policeman, Wendy might pull back completely.

Fat Cat the tabby came silently across the carpet in his long bouncing stride like a little tiger, ever alert for danger or opportunities to pounce on anything that moved. He ignored Laura and jumped up on the low window ledge in front of Wendy, looking at her with his unblinking, cold yellow eyes.

She looked back. He tucked his head down and rubbed the corner of his mouth across her thumb. He drew back and did it again.

"He likes you," Laura said very quietly.

Wendy Towne reached out timidly and touched the big cat. He pushed into her hand.

"You're very, very fortunate. Fat Cat doesn't like strangers," Laura added.

"He's purring," Wendy said.

"Of course, you've made him happy."

The cat walked into Wendy's lap, turned around twice and, satisfied with the arrangements, plopped down. She gave a startled giggle.

"He doesn't trust most people. He's very suspicious."

"He's nice," Wendy said, carefully petting him across the

head and down the back. The cat flexed his needle-sharp curved claws into the denim trousers.

"I'll tell you a funny story," Laura said, leaning back in her chair and looking out the window. "I didn't find Fat Cat. He found me. He was the only surviving member of a family of cats that lived over by the parking lot. One by one they got killed, even the mother, until one day there was nobody left but old Fat Cat. He came wandering down the dock, a little kitty meowing at everybody he saw until he saw me, and then he came right up like he did with you, Wendy, and he sat down. And he stayed."

"Really?" she turned and looked at Laura.

"Just like that."

"I wish I had a cat," Wendy Towne said wistfully.

"They're nice. They can be good friends, providing you're nice to them."

"Oh, I'd be nice."

"Of course, they're kind of quiet. They don't talk much. I like to have somebody to talk to. Don't you?"

"I guess," the girl said, lavishing attention on a grateful Fat Cat. He was so happy he was salivating tiny beads that ran out the corner of his mouth.

"I like to talk to Barbara, the lady you met out in front. She works for me, but she's also my good friend. Who do you talk to, Wendy?"

Wendy stopped petting. "I used to talk to my mother," she replied, looking down.

"Your real mother?"

"She went away to Oregon."

"Do you know why she went?"

"No." She looked down at the cat, lowering her head until her forehead rested on his protruding furry stomach.

Laura watched her carefully. She could sense the thin, thin line that tied Wendy Towne to reality, and it scared her. I'm like a chiropractor faced with a crushed spinal column, she thought desperately. There's nothing to manipulate and if I try, it might be fatal.

A trawler was chugging by the window; its graceful black

hull gliding through the chop without bouncing or slapping. A big gray-and-white sea gull was standing on the piling directly in front of the window looking in at them. His feathers ruffled up in the breeze.

"Look here, Wendy, I want to show you something," Laura said, pointing out the sea gull. "That's Sam—Sam the Sea Gull."

She went to the door and motioned Barbara to hand her the soda crackers.

"How's it going?" her secretary whispered.

"It isn't," Laura said grimly, taking the crackers and returning to the room.

Seeing her come, the gull hopped down onto the window ledge and rapped smartly on the pane. "He wants something to eat, see? He's knocking."

Wendy watched as Laura opened the lower window and handed the gull a cracker. He bobbed his head as if to say thank you and was gone, gliding over the lake toward the far shore, clutching the square cracker in his yellow beak.

"Wait, wait," Laura said, and the two women sat and watched as the gull skimmed over the water until the beat of his wings blended with the low waves.

No sooner had he disappeared than he was coming back, rising as he approached the houseboat, making straight for his perch at the window.

"Here," Laura said to her, "you give him the cracker."

Wendy Towne hesitated, but Laura had already made the transfer. Timidly, Wendy extended the cracker out the window. Politely, the gull took it, nodded his thanks, and flew away. Fat Cat watched in alert fascination.

"That's it," Laura said, "he won't be back. Sam's not greedy. He takes only two crackers a day."

"He's neat."

"He's quite a character. Sometimes I think he's a person or was a person, you know, and now he's in another form. Maybe somebody I knew coming back to visit me."

"You really think so?" Wendy's dark eyes went wide and steadied.

"You never know, could be. I don't take any chances. I

feed them. In fact, I don't like to hurt anything that's alive," Laura told her. "Not even spiders if I can help it. You never can tell when you might need a spider."

"What could a spider do for you?" Wendy asked, faintly suspicious.

Her voice was stronger and seemed to contain a mild challenge. Maybe Wendy Towne wasn't as close to the edge as she imagined, Laura thought.

"Well, I might want him to spin a beautiful web for me in the fall, you know, right outside my window where I could see it in the morning light with the dew on it."

"I like spider webs too," Wendy Towne said enthusiastically.

"People can't make anything that pretty. That's why we need spiders."

"I wrote a poem once about a lady bug," Wendy ventured.

"I'd like to see it. Why don't you bring it when you come back?"

"I never show my poetry to anybody."

"But why not?"

"I don't know. Because it's no good, I guess."

"But you have to share it to make it good. You have to let others understand how you see things. Then it would be good poetry."

"I guess."

"Why don't you bring it with you next time. Would you like to come back?"

Wendy picked up the cat in her arms. "Yes, I like it here. You have nice—friends."

Laura laughed. "Yeah, they are nice. I'd like you to meet my boy friend sometime. He's a good friend too. He's kind of busy, but he's very nice. His name is Jim. Do you have friends to talk to, Wendy?"

The girl looked suddenly alarmed; her eyes went back to the floor. She held the cat against her tightly.

"Sort of," the girl said vaguely.

"Do you and Shirley ever get a chance to talk?"

"Not much," Wendy said, staring at the floor.

"Do you have somebody to talk to when you need to talk, Wendy? Is there somebody in the family?"

"I used to talk to my mother. Now I talk to Chris."

"Your sister?"

"Yes." Wendy looked back up at Laura. "I like Chris."

"It's nice to have another woman friend, particularly when it's your sister."

"I like Grandpa too," Wendy suddenly volunteered, "but he lives in Kentucky."

"Is that your mother's father or your dad's?"

"My dad's. He sends me money sometimes to buy things."

"That's nice."

"Chris is going to take care of Rob and me," Wendy said.

"What do you mean?"

"That she's going to take care of us like she did when Mom left. Before Shirley came."

"Oh, I see. She did the housework and cooked?"

"Yes. Chris told me she's going to take care of us again as soon as she gets a good job."

"You had a job didn't you?"

"Yes, but I got fired. They said I was stupid."

"You're not stupid, Wendy."

"That's what they said," she protested, tears in her eyes.

Laura was about to probe further to determine if Wendy had actually been fired or had quit when the girl went on.

"But Chris told me not to worry, she was going to take care of me—and Rob too."

Laura glanced at the brass clock on the wall. It was past eleven. "You like Chris very much don't you?"

"Chris is going to be a doctor."

"That's wonderful. What do you want to be, Wendy?"

The fat girl stared at her with sad dark eyes. At least she's looking at me, Laura thought, that's major progress.

"I don't know," she said miserably, putting the cat on her lap. Methodically, she ran her hand down his back, smoothing the fur until it shone under the lights.

"What would you be, what would you do if you could be anything you wanted? Anything in the world."

The girl looked up at her, still stroking Fat Cat. "Loved," she said in a whisper.

Laura smiled. "That's a good answer, Wendy. We all need love." It was also a good place to end the initial interview. "And look at that, would you believe our time is up already?" she said, indicating the clock.

"Oh," Wendy said in a low voice, clinging to the cat.

It was tempting to extend the hour and push on, but Laura wanted some time to think about her impressions of Wendy Towne. "When you're having a nice talk the time seems to fly, doesn't it?"

"Yes." Wendy Towne smiled shyly, gently eased the cat off her lap, and stood up.

It was odd, Laura thought, as Wendy put on her yellow windbreaker, but she was the only child who didn't have Jack's eyes. The dark brooding look must be from her mother.

"And please bring your poems next time, I'd love to see them. You bring them, and I'll show you some paintings I did once that I've never shown to anybody but my cats."

"OK." Wendy Towne shrugged.

"Thanks for coming, Wendy. I know it's hard to talk to a stranger." Laura put out her hand. "It's hard for me too, but I feel like I know you a little better now."

"Me too." Wendy's hand was hot and sweaty.

"I'll call you about another appointment."

"OK."

"And Wendy, if you want to talk to me in the meantime, I'll always be here. I mean that. It doesn't have to be important. I don't care if it's the middle of the night. You call me up, all right?" She handed the girl her card.

Wendy stared at the card, and then slowly put it in the breast pocket of her carpenter coveralls. Laura walked her through the office door and out to the lobby.

"Don't forget the poetry," she reminded her.

"I won't." Wendy looked around the reception room. "Goodbye," she said to Barbara awkwardly, and left, leaving the door open and shuffling up the ramp, her head bent forward as she slouched off into the rainy hostile world.

"There goes a very unhappy girl," Laura said, closing the door after her.

"What seems to be the problem?" the gray-haired secretary asked.

"She doesn't think anybody loves her."

"What about her family? Her father who brought her in?"

"I don't know," Laura Jordan said, "that's what I've got to find out. Make a note to remind me to get a hold of Shirley and Jack, will you please?"

Wendy seemed so fragile, like a thin piece of glass ready to crack under the slightest strain.

Barb sighed. "OK, you realize you're booked solid until you leave on your book promotion tour?"

"I'd like to forget the damn tour."

"Well, I'm sure your agent wouldn't. He's expecting you in Los Angeles Sunday. Ten cities are waiting for you to tell them about *The Femme Factor,* according to the schedule."

The matronly secretary poured her another cup of coffee.

"Terrific." Laura tested it by blowing across the rim of the mug and trying a sip. "Have I ever told you, you make great coffee for a woman?" She laughed.

"Yes, you have. Also, I have your tickets for the Waylon Jennings concert Saturday."

"Good."

Barb consulted her appointment book. "Jim called while you were in with Wendy. He said he was lonely and missed you. I tried to cheer him up, but I'm afraid he really wanted to talk to you."

Laura took a long swig, feeling the hot liquid going down her throat, waiting for the lift she knew would come. "Listen, if he missed me so much, he'd stay in Seattle, Washington, instead of commuting to Washington, D.C. Next."

Barbara Adams looked up from her book and fixed Laura with a steady motherly gaze. "Don't be a damn fool," she scolded, "men like Jim don't come along everyday. There's a hundred women out there who would absolutely die for a chance to catch a guy like that. Of course, I'm a little old myself, but I'd still give it a whirl if you weren't my friend." She patted her iron-gray hair playfully and licked her lips.

"Well, I'm not any woman," Laura said, giving her secretary a little show of high strutting. "What are you going to do with a man who'd rather go see John Denver than Waylon Jennings? John Denver, for chrissake?"

"I've always been kinda partial to young John myself. I suppose it's my motherly instinct."

"My God," Laura replied, giving a heavenly roll of her eyes. "What's next on the program?"

"Your father called with an invitation to the weekly family dinner tonight. I told him you'd be charmed to attend as usual. And the Caradeen lecture is this afternoon."

"What time is that?"

"One o'clock."

Laura hadn't even thought about what she was going to say. "Who's left in the barrel this morning?" she asked her secretary.

"The Clairbornes." The Clairbornes married for forty-two years and hating each other for forty-two years.

"Oh, great. What time?"

"In about two minutes. In fact, here they come now."

Mr. and Mrs. Otis Clairborne advanced down the gangplank, Otis graciously assisting his wife with a firm hand on the elbow like the silver-haired gentleman he was.

Laura had been seeing the Clairbornes for over three months, and it was only recently she pinpointed their forty-two-year-old problem. It was sex. Clearly, it was sex. Not only had Otis Clairborne never moved his wife to orgasm, he had the temerity—many years ago—to hire a beautiful secretary at his brokerage firm who Mrs. Clairborne—"Bud"—always suspected, but never confirmed, was something more than a secretary.

This one indiscretion, real or imagined, was the only time Otis strayed off the reservation—if indeed, he had. Laura Jordan strongly suspected he hadn't, that it was an excuse for Bud to take out her sexual frustration on him.

As she ushered them into her office, seating them side by

side on her leather couch overlooking the lake, they were already sniping away at each other with cutting asides and innuendos. How much simpler it would have been, Laura thought, if Bud had told Otis to put his hand on her clitoris and gently rub.

Otis, being a gentleman ready to serve, might have gone along with that, and forty-two years of bitterness could have been avoided. They might even have been happy, Laura thought, watching the tight lines around Bud Clairborne's eyes squeeze together in rage.

"I can't think of one time," she said bitterly, "that you've ever considered anybody's feelings but your own."

"Let's go with that thought," Laura interjected helpfully. "Is it what he says or what he does? Do you feel that way all the time? When he calls you on the phone or when he touches you as well? Do you feel he's being selfish when you have physical contact—a kiss, a hug? And Otis, how do you feel?"

"Oh, I don't know," the stockbroker said wearily, "she's probably right. I'm a very selfish man." The pink skin on his long face hung in sad folds under his eyes.

"Well, you always do things and expect me to go along—and like it," she complained.

Laura sat back and let them talk. It was never simple. Did Otis know what a clitoris was? Did she? And if so, did they know where it was? Could they bring themselves to even use the word? And most important, if Laura took it upon herself to advise them that sexual frustration was at the root of their marital problems, would they believe her? Probably not. She watched them fussing and fuming and squirming around the issue of sex, yet the word had never been mentioned. Laura didn't feel superior to the Clairbornes. She never considered herself superior to clients.

She played the role of a listener because she was convinced it was more effective than other techniques. Occasionally, she made suggestions, but never stepped in and supplied answers. That would defeat her purpose, which was to teach the Clairbornes to communicate with each other. They would arrive at their own conclusions eventually, but it was slow going. Laura looked across the lake. The rain had stopped; it was going to be a nice day. A slash of clear blue sky was widening across the overcast.

They would arrive at their own conclusion if they indeed wanted to solve their problems. She and Jim were like that, always too busy to discover why, after knowing each other intimately for over ten years, they couldn't decide to make it a permanent arrangement.

There were reasons. Maybe I should take him up on the San Juan trip, Laura thought idly. They couldn't go on like this forever.

"I think it started on our wedding night if you want my opinion," Bud Clairborne said loudly. "I'll never forget it. I was scared to death and all you could say was, 'There, that wasn't so bad, was it?' My God." She put her head down and began snuffling.

Startled, Laura turned to Otis. He was tight-lipped with embarrassment and looking away.

"What do you normally do when Bud cries, Otis?" she asked him.

"I try to comfort her," he replied confused.

"Well, why don't you do that now. I think you've both made a remarkable breakthrough this morning."

Tentatively, he put an arm around his wife. "I've never understood why you said that," she sniffed.

"I don't know," he said, "I was as scared as you were. I didn't know what I was doing either, darling."

"What a hell of a forty-five minutes," Laura announced to Barbara Adams once the Clairbornes were safely loaded into a taxi. "Those wonderful people wrote my lecture for me."

She still had to put it together, of course, and time was short. "The weather looks nice. I'm going to walk."

"That's a long way."

"Then I'll jog. I won't be back probably until three-thirty."

"I'll reschedule your afternoon to tomorrow morning and squeeze tomorrow morning into tomorrow afternoon," the secretary joked.

Barbara Adams was used to shuffling people and events with only minutes to spare. She'd discovered Laura liked it that way. If she wasn't busy, she got nervous. Barb sometimes wondered if Laura's tremendous drive to immerse herself in other people's problems might not indicate she was trying to avoid some of her own.

Not that her secretary was ever critical of Laura Jordan. On the contrary, she admired her. But Barb Adams wished Laura would take her advice more seriously and wouldn't treat her relationship with the McClay boy so lightly. Barb knew a lot more about why Jim McClay needed Laura than Laura herself did.

A deep-blue winter sky was spreading over the city as Laura started down the lake shore, the sessions with the Clairbornes had been invigorating, her track shoes felt spring-loaded, and she swung her arms in an exaggerated arc.

The shore was a jumble of boats, new and old, all moored at odd angles. She passed an old stern wheeler that failed to win a second life as a restaurant and was slowly sinking at its mooring. Two half-finished crab boats sat high in their floating drydock and a wooden mine sweeper occupied by something called "The Whole Earth Ecological Commune" was flying a tattered string of laundry from its peak.

She walked along the abandoned railroad tracks, the lake to her right, a road clogged with city-bound traffic on the left. When the sun came out, it was the most gorgeous city in the world.

She thought about Wendy as she went striding along in the bright winter light. A girl who wanted above all else to be loved. And Laura knew those who desperately needed love were at their most vulnerable when the need was the greatest.

Wendy must have been devastated when her mother left and that was enough to cause withdrawal in anyone. But what about the younger sister, Chris, the swimmer? Laura wondered. She seemed to be the head of the family in Wendy's eyes.

It was hard to believe the two girls actually were sisters.

Chris so slim, graceful and hard; Wendy overweight, sloppy and sullen. And yet, they had a similar beauty. It was their skin, Laura decided, the pale, perfect translucent glow they shared. Wendy, despite her best efforts, couldn't hide it. The boy Rob had it too.

She turned onto the Fremont Bridge and crossed over the narrow ship canal running from the lakes to the salt water of Puget Sound. A tug pushing a barge piled high with yellow sawdust whistled sharply for the bridge tender, and Laura jogged the rest of the way across as the horns sounded, and the gates came down to block traffic.

The sharp smell of fresh sawdust hung in the air where the tug had passed as she turned east toward the university. Laura slowed her pace, looking at the sailboats moored in the marinas along the shoreline.

A sailboat was a thing of beauty, and she loved the pure sensation of riding the edge of the wind. Jim McClay, on the other hand, was fascinated with the mechanics of sailing, the physics of speed, the perfect arrangement of every last detail to assure maximum hull thrust under prevailing wind conditions. He didn't feel the wind; he measured it on an expensive array of dials and gauges in the cockpit. It was his constant hauling and pulling and testing of sails that irritated her. He would never try to understand why she didn't care if one rope was a sheet and another a line.

To Jim McClay, it was absolutely vital to know why the wind made the boat sail. He explained the Bernoulli theorem to her. "It's the same reason you get lift on an airplane wing." Laura didn't care about Bernoulli or why he thought airplanes were like sailboats when they obviously weren't.

She walked past the five cement figures standing on the traffic island, waiting for the bus.

"Hi, folks," she said, waving at the sculptures. Someone had put a ski hat on the old lady. It was the best piece of sculpture in town. Early-morning fog or dim twilight, they waited patiently, clutching cement newspapers and shopping bags, a monument to the people who made a city something more than a collection of buildings.

If Jim would really cruise the San Juans instead of racing from anchorage to anchorage, she might go with him, Laura thought, quickening her pace. If he would let the sails go for once and didn't worry about beating some other boat, she might consent to make the trip.

Laura looked at her wristwatch. She had thirty minutes to get her talk together. In a previous lecture, she'd outlined some of her more interesting and successful cases, carefully disguising them, of course. The trouble was, she did all the talking.

By the time she was abreast of the Gas Works Park, Laura had come up with an idea. She would challenge them, force them to become involved by making the flat assertion that all marital difficulties could be traced to money or sex—or both. It was only slightly oversimplified, and at the very least it would start a lively conversation.

The dark towers of the old gas works rose out of the brown rolling grass that went to the edge of the canal. The compressors and engines, converted into children's toys and painted bright reds, purples, and greens, were deserted. On the rise that looked out over the city beyond, a lone figure flew a huge box kite that bounced on the wind.

The jog from the Gas Works Park to the university was mostly uphill, but Laura made it in under thirty minutes and arrived as the students were filing into the second-floor classroom. Fortunately, the introduction by Professor Caradeen was long and flattering, giving her time to catch her breath and collect her scattered thoughts on sex and money. The more she collected, the less she liked her idea.

"I first met Laura Jordan when against my better judgment I was persuaded to attend one of her communications seminars. I went, I must say, in a skeptical frame of mind. I went fully prepared to tear her to pieces, limb from limb—academically speaking, of course."

Caradeen, wiping his dirty-yellow mustache, chuckled heartily at his joke. The students watched him, bored and fidgeting. "I remained skeptical only until Ms. Jordan took the floor herself and took charge—and then I was totally impressed with what I heard and what I saw happening for the next five hours. I realized I was in the presence of a very dynamic lady, an original thinker on the critical subject of human relationships and effective communication.

"Ms. Jordan founded a highly successful family counseling practice at the tender age of twenty-eight. She is the President of InterPerson, a communications institute that has conducted seminars throughout the West for some of the countries largest companies including, I might add, a professional football team. In addition, she is the author of a recently published book, *The Femme Factor,* and the originator of a unique talk-show concept on television which can be seen each Sunday on Channel 9—*Family Line.* I understand that program has been syndicated and will be shown soon in the Bay area down in San Francisco. Is that right, Laura?"

Laura Jordan nodded. She eyed the quiet group, and knew sex and money would only confuse them.

"Well, without further ado," Caradeen concluded, "I give you my good friend, Laura Jordan."

She stood up and made her way to the front of the class. The clock on the back wall lurched forward with a harsh click. It wasn't that she couldn't defend her sex-and-money thesis; she could defend anything. That was one of her father's lessons. Gene Jordan could walk into a meeting without the slightest idea of what was going on and be in charge within five minutes.

"Thank you, Bill." Laura gave Caradeen her best smile.

It took courage to keep inviting her back. She knew the rest of the department considered her a cross between a witch doctor and Ann Landers. After all, she had no academic credentials in her field. She couldn't let Caradeen down by doing some half-ass, shoot-from-the-hip job.

Laura gripped the podium with complete confidence. She had decided what she was going to say, and the outline unreeled in her mind faster than she could talk.

"The most important unanswered question in America

today," she said quietly, projecting her voice to the back of the room and methodically beginning to establish eye contact with each student, "is what will happen to the children, the innocent victims of the breakup of the traditional American family."

Chapter 7

There was always a collie to rush up the Jordans' long curving driveway and greet visitors and a new Oldsmobile or two in the three-car garage. Gene Jordan's first car had been an Oldsmobile and certainly the last one would be too—if the company stayed in business. Laura pulled in her old Volvo behind her father's new black diesel and got out. The current dog's name was Rocky, and he ran around barking happily in the wildly flickering gas lights in front of the California-style bungalow. Before Rocky there had been Sam and before that Dasher, Laura's childhood companion.

The house sat on a little knoll overlooking Lake Washington and had a sweeping view of Seattle directly across the water. Rocky jammed a wet nose into Laura's crotch, the standard collie greeting.

"Take it easy, fella," she said, pushing him back. Her father met her at the door with a martini even though she told him she didn't like martinis anymore. Still, she drank a little to make him happy, and that proved to Gene Jordan she was only being polite. As a result, he continued to mix martinis every family night when his favorite and only child came to dinner.

"How are you, sweetheart?" he asked her, kissing Laura on the cheek.

"Good, Daddy. You know I don't like martinis anymore."

"That French mineral water will rust you out, kid. I made this drink myself, and it's better than any martini you've ever tasted." He was a charmer and his job as political liaison with the biggest bank in Washington and the seventh biggest in the nation was persuasion. Laura took the martini and followed her father into the house.

To her, he had not noticeably aged since his forties. He seemed permanently cast in comfortable middle age, a tall, slightly overweight, slightly bald, well-tanned banker whose face reminded practically everyone who met him of a beefy Paul Newman. Laura thought it was his eyes, not the color, but the penetrating look. Her mother claimed it was his mouth. He held the door for her and shooed the dog outside.

"Laura, I'm in here," her mother called to her from the kitchen.

The house was immaculate as always, not a piece of furniture unpolished, not a *Country Gentleman* magazine out of place in its rack. The white shag rug stood up from its daily vacuuming. The maid usually cooked the meals for the Jordans, but seldom on family night.

"Let me look at you, darling. Oh, oh, you look tired," her mother said, giving her a careful hug to keep her sticky dough-covered hands away from her clothes.

"It's good to see you, Mom. You certainly don't look tired." In fact, with the exception of her silver-gray hair and face leathered somewhat by the sun, her mother looked every bit the homecoming queen she had been thirty-five years ago.

"A little steak and potatoes, instead of all that organic cabbage or whatever it is you eat, will fix you right up."

"They're alfalfa sprouts, Mother, the same thing you eat."

"You and your father sit yourselves down out there because a good old-fashioned American meal is about to be served."

The dining table sat directly in front of the floor-to-ceiling windows running the length of the house and providing a view of Seattle. The two floating bridges crossing the darkened lake were alive with the tangled headlights of evening commuters. A golf-course-size lawn rolled down to the sandy beach of Birch Bay, and the covered boathouse where Gene Jordan kept his fifty-two-foot Chris Craft and a water-ski boat.

The Chris Craft had a flying bridge and an electric barbecue that swung out over the stern, and when Laura was a teenager the family would take long afternoon cruises down the lake in the summer. Laura and her mother would sun themselves in bikinis on the forward deck with Gene high on the flying bridge, his brown pot belly spilling over his white shorts, a drink firmly anchored in the swivel glass at his side, supremely happy and continually adjusting the big twin diesels.

The speedboat was also a Chris Craft, the original mahogany inboard they bought when Laura was only five. Gene Jordan kept it out of the water, hung safely in a cradle all winter, and he painted, polished, and shined it so he could take it over to the opening day of yachting season, the green-and-white Birch Bay Yacht Club pennant flying from the prow.

Laura and her father sat down, side by side, facing the lake.

"So tell me what you've been up to, you famous person you," he said, giving her his Paul Newman smile. "You know I met some joker the other day at the Chamber of Commerce and he said, 'oh, yes, I know you. You're Laura Jordan's father.'"

"That's the price you pay for giving me the best of everything, Daddy."

"You keep it up, Laura. Your mother and I are going to retire and live off your income instead of beating our brains out. Aren't we, baby?"

"No, we are not, baby," Mary Kay Jordan replied, presenting them with steaks Laura knew could be cut with a butter knife, homemade rolls, fresh beans, and a salad that contained at least three avocados. "You're going to keep right on investing her money so she and Jim will have something to start out on when they get married. Now, let's eat before it gets cold."

Laura ignored the remark and cut into the steak. It parted on command with a touch of the knife. It wasn't on the Pritikin diet but then neither was Scotch whiskey.

"This is good."

"Thank you." Her mother took a bow.

"Say, speaking of Jim McClay," her father said, eyes twinkling, "how is your fiancé anyway?"

"Jim's fine. He's going to Washington again, and he's very busy like all of us."

Every family night, it was the first topic of conversation at the Jordan dinner table. It had been for almost ten years.

"I saw Myra McClay down in the Village the other day. I swear that woman doesn't look a day over forty, steady as a big red freckled hunk of rock. I really like that gal," her mother said. "She comes from good solid stock."

"So do I." Laura tried the green beans. They were, as usual, delicious. The martini sat in front of her full to the brim.

"That Jim's got a mind like a steel trap. If they ever catch me with my hand in the cookie jar, he's the one that's going to defend me, I can tell you that." Her father shoveled an overflowing fork full of beans into his mouth.

"Dad, I'll bet you've never even padded an expense voucher, have you?" Laura said, touching his arm.

"If you're smart, you don't need to do anything that stupid," he said, chuckling and chewing.

"Honest to God, you two talk like a couple of embezzlers," her mother said.

"Seriously," her father replied, "you can't be too damn careful these days. The guy who offers you a good deal on a used car is just liable to be with the FBI."

"Well, dishonest people deserve to get caught, Gene," Mary Kay Jordan said emphatically.

"Yeah, true enough, but so far they've only caught Democrats out here. What happens when they nab some nice conservative Republicans? Are you going to be out there clapping then?"

"A real Republican wouldn't get caught doing favors for Arab oil sheiks."

Laura listened, enjoying their traditional non-argument about politics. They were both right-wing Republicans and her father, senior vice president of public affairs for Evergreen First National, knew his way in and out of political tangles blindfolded.

"You remember a guy named Nixon?" her father laughed.

"But, Dad," Laura leaped into the fray, "take a look at the Watergate Committee today. Where are those guys now? Half of those sanctimonious bastards are in jail."

"Thank you, dear," her mother said.

"Not half of them," he argued.

"Well, the ones that aren't should be," Laura insisted.

"I never saw two people talk and eat so fast. Excuse me while I get the coffee and dessert," her mother said getting up.

"She's running away from a good fight again," Gene Jordan said loudly, belching.

"I am not." Mary Kay talked while moving around the spacious kitchen. "Laura, ask him to tell you who got to Warm Springs first on the last run. For years, your father's been telling me women don't have the nerve to be downhill racers. Remember that?"

"Or corporate executives," he added helpfully. "It's the same thing. See, when you have to make split-second decisions on your own and then back them up with nothing but nerve, that's a job for a real man."

Mary Kay set down the coffee and three chilled silver dishes of ice cream.

"Look at your own daughter, Mr. Bank Officer."

"She's not a corporate executive."

"Well, she's certainly successful."

"In her way, yes."

Her father put his arm around her. Laura leaned against him. She had never seen her father in defeat. He could charge into the thorniest problem and come out the other side totally unscathed. Sometimes, Laura wondered, if it wasn't all too easy for him with his glib nerve and total self-confidence. Sometimes she wondered what Gene Jordan could have been if he really put some effort into something. For the fact was, he'd held the same high-paying job all his life, never stumbling but never aspiring to greater things either.

"Ask him who got to Warm Springs first?" her mother insisted.

"Who won, Dad?"

"Well, that's a long story." He sat back and gave his stomach room. It wasn't a big stomach, just a comfortable one.

"I did, and I beat him fair and square."

"Is that right, Dad?"

"I'm afraid so."

"And he was really puffing."

Laura realized her mother was genuinely pleased at the conquest. And a true conquest it was because she knew Gene Jordan never let anybody beat him if he could help it, not even his wife.

"Say," her mother said, deftly changing the subject so she wouldn't rub salt in her husband's wounded ego, "how is that boy, the racer, the son of those people you met over there?"

"Rob Towne? He's all right I guess, nothing serious, a torn ligament apparently. As a matter of fact, I saw one of the daughters this morning as a client."

"No kidding." Her father sat up in his chair and started in on his ice cream. "Her dad's the guy who's got some pipe dream about a ski resort over in Wyoming?"

"Why do you call it a pipe dream?" Laura asked him.

"Listen, my dear, I happen to know that the Vail Corporation had an option on that place for years, and they didn't pick it up. They don't do things for no reason. There were good reasons they didn't buy it. As a matter of fact, I know a few of them."

"You do?"

"Yes, there's very little private land over there. The resort's all on Forest Service land. The little town down there, what's it called, Wilson?"

"Wilson, Idaho. It's over the border."

"Yeah, well, it's right up against the Teton National Park. The airport happens to be operating in a national park, a shaky arrangement. But the main thing is the only private land is way down the mountain, and there isn't much of it."

Gene Jordan finished off his ice cream and sampled the coffee. "And the fact of the matter is you can't make a go of it with a destination resort unless you own enough land to get into the condo business. And that land's got to be close to the ski lift, preferably right on the hill."

"Well, Jack—ah—Mr. Towne seems to have some investors lined up."

"Really? Who?" Gene Jordan was a direct man when it came to money and business deals.

Laura hesitated. She was getting on private ground, and she considered whether it would be giving out privileged information to disclose any of the names. The Townes were her clients. On the other hand, Jack had freely talked about it with her when they first met at Sun Valley long before the subject of counseling came up. "Your bank isn't interested in this deal are they?"

"No. I'm interested personally. I won't say anything. We wouldn't touch a ski resort with a ten-foot pole. We've got a bankrupt one up in the Cascades hanging around our necks already."

"Well, he's got some investors here. A state representative, I think, Howland, and the other one is in politics too. Greenway is the name, I think."

Gene Jordan raised his eyebrows and ran a hand across his partially bald head. "Interesting."

"Why do you say that, Dad?"

"Oh, I didn't know those two were interested in the skiing business. I also doubt financially they could swing something like that."

"Apparently, they think this guy from Boise, T.R. Timberlake, might be interested too."

He blinked rapidly, and Laura could tell she suddenly had her father's undivided attention.

"Well," he said casually as he sipped his coffee, "if your friend Mr. Towne can interest Teddy Timberlake in climbing aboard, he might really have something."

"Do you think so?" Laura asked, trying to keep the

eagerness out of her voice.

She liked the idea of a big resort at Early Winters, the Teton country with its jagged peaks and deep-blue sky held a strong romantic appeal. It was the kind of place you could run free down a treeless mountainside and the lift operators said "yup" and "nope."

"I'll tell you one thing. T.R. Timberlake could swing the whole deal by writing a check if that's what he wanted to do. I still don't see the payoff though. What the hell, maybe that's why he's a multimillionaire, and I work for a salary."

"Now that you've won the modesty award, dear, may I suggest we move into the living room?" her mother asked. "These old straight-back chairs are killing my back."

The Jordan family arranged themselves three abreast on a couch and took in the wide-angle view of Lake Washington and Seattle. Mary Kay sighed. "If I think about moving to Palm Springs to retire, I always get cold feet when I sit right here and look at this view on a winter night."

"You're not really considering moving are you, Mom?"

"Well, we're not getting any younger, dear."

"Mandatory retirement is sixty-seven," her father added.

"Neither of you are ever going to retire," Laura said flatly. They had always lived in the Lake Washington house. "Where could you water ski in Palm Springs?"

"There are lakes in California," her father pointed out.

"But not like this, Daddy."

"No, not like this."

Laura took a drink of coffee. One of her earliest memories was her mother water skiing on Sunday morning, the deep-throated roar of the inboard shattering the quiet stillness of the lake.

"We can go to church on Easter and Christmas," her mother used to say cheerfully, bustling around the kitchen in her terry-cloth robe and slicing up fresh fruit, "otherwise Sundays are for skiing."

In the summer, the Jordans did their water skiing. Jim McClay and her father set up a slalom course of old Purex bottles just off the dock and then took turns driving and skiing and drinking the six pack of beer that was always on ice in back. The mahogany deck got burning hot, but the beer was always cold.

Mary Kay didn't like the slalom course. She preferred long fast runs across the lake where she could swing out in wide graceful arcs and jump the wake. She was the first woman on Birch Bay to wear a string bikini, and her body could still grace one nicely although she'd switched to a leotard suit in her old age.

In the winter, the Jordans went to Sun Valley and later, when Laura became a powder addict, to Jackson Hole and Early Winters. And if they happened to be home on Easter or Christmas, they attended religious services, looking more like an advertisement for sunshine and health than devout worshippers.

"It's not something we have to decide right now anyway," Gene Jordan said. "I've still got a few good years left in me."

"I hope it's more than a few, dear, I need a good man around to take care of my growing sexual needs. It gets better and better for us old gals past the menopause, you know."

He gave a dramatic groan and turned to Laura. "I try to get her on more committees. I even talked her into the Symphony Board to keep her out of the house evenings. She keeps hanging around me. What the hell am I supposed to do?"

"Poor Daddy," she said indulgently, putting on her tolerant daughter face.

Sex had never been hidden behind anything at the Jordan house. When she was fifteen, they had a frank talk with her. It was her body; she could do with it as she wished. However, there were certain precautions that needed to be observed. Also, as a free and independent person, she could abstain from sex as much as she wanted. At the time, Laura and Jim McClay were experimenting with french kissing. It would be four years before they finally, in the euphemism of the time, "went all the way." Gene and Mary Kay Jordan never asked their daughter who she did or did not go to bed with although they knew the relationship with the McClay boy was sexual as well as a long and enduring friendship.

"Well, dear, Laura and I have been considering going to the Bugaboos later this year for a little helicopter skiing, just us athletic girls. That will either take the itch out of my bloomers or give me a chance to pick up something younger. I thought one of those nice Canadian ski guides."

"Like hell. You're not going up there alone. That's dangerous," he growled.

"I thought with you slowing down and all, dear, and with retirement coming up, it might be a little too much for your heart."

"My heart's fine."

The faint ringing of the telephone came from the back of the house. Mary Kay excused herself to answer it.

"Your mother has improved her damn skiing one hundred percent," Gene said to Laura. "The truth be known, I'm going to have to get in shape and take some lessons. I wonder if your good friend Mr. McClay might be interested in taking on a private pupil."

"Jim's too busy even to ski this winter."

"Well, honey, he's got his mom and the two kids to think about. His dad wasn't quite as well off as everybody thought."

"I know, he's done a wonderful job with those kids. They're both honors students. You could ask him about skiing."

"Oh, I don't know," Gene Jordan said, stretching his feet out and kicking off his black loafers. "If he's got any extra time, I'd rather he spent it on you, trying to talk some sense into you about marriage."

"Daddy . . ."

"Well, what's wrong with the poor guy? I like him."

"So do I."

"Well?"

"Well, Dad, I have a thriving business. I've got a TV show. I've got to go out next week and try to sell my book so I can write another one."

"He could help you do that."

"He does. You know, Jim and I are not exactly strangers."

"I know, I know, but what's the matter with marriage? Your mother and I got married. We're supremely happy. We've got a wonderful daughter. We've got everything, everything except . . ."

"Don't say it," she warned him.

"You guys would have kids playing in the Super Bowl."

"It's for you," her mother said, handing her a blue telephone. "You can plug it in over there."

Laura took the call in the corner of the living room, looking out at the twinkling chain of street lights running along the opposite shore. The view reminded her of her childhood. The room had been refurnished, but it still smelled of lemon-scented furniture wax. It was her home. It would always be her home.

"Hello," she said.

"Is this Laura Jordan?"

"Speaking."

"This is Reilley's Answering Service, Miss Jordan, I have a call for you from Wendy Towne. It's long distance. Will you accept the charges?"

"Yes, certainly." There was a series of hissing clicks.

"Hello," the voice said. It sounded far away and lost.

"Wendy? How nice to hear from you. Where are you?"

"I'm going away," Wendy Towne said, her voice trailing off.

"Wendy, what's wrong?"

"I've got to go."

"Don't hang up, Wendy. Where are you?"

"Oh, don't worry, I'll call again. I wanted to see if you were there like you promised. You remember?"

"Certainly. And I'm here. Do you need help, Wendy?"

"Goodbye," the voice grew weaker, and was cut off by the final click of the disconnection.

Laura Jordan stood holding the phone, considering whether she should try to get the call traced. That was probably impossible. And it was unlikely the telephone company would cooperate. Well, Laura thought, Shirley should know.

"What's wrong, dear?" her mother asked.

"Oh, nothing. Dad, could you get me the Seattle directory?"

He nodded and produced it. Laura thumbed through it hurriedly. She went right past the Ts into the Vs and had to back up before she found Jack Towne listed at a Heather Terrace address in West Seattle.

The phone rang six times before Shirley answered. She sounded sleepy. "Did I wake you up, Shirley?"

"Oh, no, Laura, it's good to hear from you. I was resting. It was a long day."

"Shirley," Laura told her, "I just got a call from Wendy and she sounded—lost—it was long distance."

"Long distance?" Shirley asked.

"Yes. Do you know where she is?"

"No, she wasn't home when I got here, but that's not unusual."

Laura considered whether she should downplay her own worry so Shirley wouldn't become alarmed. She decided to be honest.

"I'm worried about her, Shirley. Maybe Jack would know where she might go."

There was a long pause on Shirley's end of the line. "I've been trying to reach Jack since I got home. His room doesn't answer," she said, talking faster. "Nobody's home. Chris is at work; Rob is out with Blue somewhere. I don't know what to do, Laura." Her voice was rising in pitch and as it rose, Laura could sense the desperation rising with it.

"Take it easy. Let's try to think this thing through."

"Oh, yes, thanks. I'm sorry, Laura, I've had a hell of a day, everything went wrong, and I've got an awful headache."

"Well, let's try to think of where she might be."

"That's the problem, Laura," Shirley interrupted, "I have absolutely no idea. I don't know. I feel like I'm falling to pieces." Her voice rose to a plaintive wail. "I don't know who to call."

"Calm down, Shirley. Look, would you like me to get in my car and come over? It's right on my way home. Would that help?"

"Oh, you don't have to do that, Laura," she sniffed. "I'm all right, really I am. I've got to pull myself together. I don't know what's wrong with me."

"I've got the address right here in the telephone book."

"Please, I'll be fine."

"I know you will, but it would be nice to see you again, Shirley, and maybe we can run Wendy down together."

Her father was already on his way to get her raincoat.

"A problem?" her mother inquired, disappointed to be losing her daughter so early in the evening. Later, they usually had popcorn and played Hearts. Gene's favorite game was poker, but the women refused, so Hearts was the family game. Gene played his poker on Thursdays at the Birch Bay Yacht Club.

"Oh, a minor crisis."

"Come again when you can stay a while," her father said, walking her out.

Rocky the collie ran alongside, pleased to have someone to bark at again. The night had turned cold. The stars were gone. "Take care of yourself and get some rest," he said, closing the car door for her.

She kissed him through the open window. "I will, Dad, and thanks. I love you."

"And lock the damn door." He pushed the button down hard. "I swear to God, Laura, you're too damn trusting, especially for a single woman living in the city."

"Yes, Daddy." She started the car.

"I know I sound like an overprotective father, but be careful for chrissake."

"Yes, Daddy." Laura rolled up the window, pointed to the lock still firmly in the down position and went up the driveway, paced by the streaking Rocky. At the top, he came up alongside as she stopped, his tail wagging furiously.

"Goodbye, Rocky," she waved, pulling out into the deserted road.

* * *

The Townes lived only fifteen minutes away from Birch Bay by freeway, and as Laura turned into the Heather Terrace subdivision several fat drops of rain splattered on the windshield. The curving streets were lined with cars parked in front of row after row of tract houses. Using the Volvo's spotlight to search for house numbers, she saw the unmowed lawns matted flat by the winter rains and the discarded Christmas trees still lying in the gutters.

She slowed when she found 10021 and turned in the driveway behind a Ford Pinto with the rear end jacked up. The slamming of her car door triggered a howl from dogs all up and down the street. Laura detoured around a bicycle lying against the front steps and rang the bell.

Shirley Towne was wearing blue jeans that emphasized the weight on her hips. The black circles around her eyes were deep. She looked old.

"Thanks for coming, Laura."

Laura stepped in and gave her a long hug. Shirley coughed and backed away.

"Excuse me, I've got a terrible cold. Come in, sit down."

The house smelled of greasy food and stale smoke. All the curtains were drawn, and the overhead lights left large areas of the square living room in shadows.

"I couldn't get a hold of Chris. The telephone at the store's been busy ever since you called. She works nights until eleven. Excuse me a minute, I've got a TV dinner in the oven."

Laura looked quickly around the room. There was very little furniture and what there was didn't match in style or color. A pile of 45 records was precariously stacked on the stereo in a leaning tower, and there was dust on everything.

"Thanks for coming," Shirley repeated, flopping down in an overstuffed chair with a torn cover. "Excuse me while I eat, I got home late. I'm riding the bus now. That's my car you see out there; the boys are supposed to be fixing it. I had to lie down after work, Laura, otherwise I would have picked things up. It's usually picked up."

"You don't have to apologize. When you work all day, the last thing you want to do is work all night, right?"

That got a weak smile out of Shirley. She peeled off the aluminum top and steam rose off the chicken.

"Wow, that's hot."

"Smells good."

"You want some, Laura?"

"Oh, no thanks."

"Sure?"

"No, really, thanks. I just ate. Did you try Jack again?"

"Yes." Shirley pulled off a limp piece of chicken. "He's still not back in his hotel room. Laura, I don't know what to make of this. Tell me what Wendy said."

"She said she was going away—for a while—I think those were her words. She said not to worry, she would call again. She wanted to see if I was there."

"But why would she call you?" Shirley's black hair was tangled and limp.

"I told her when she left my office that I was always available if she wanted to talk to someone."

"Well, she might have called here earlier. I didn't get home until after seven."

"She probably did. Has she ever done this before?"

Shirley Towne put down her chicken bone. "Once, since Jack and I were married. In fact, it was right after the wedding. She'd been a bridesmaid, you know, and we didn't go on a honeymoon or anything. I mean it wasn't like we were kids." She blushed feebly.

"Wendy took off?"

"Yes. She left a note that time for Jack. She said she went to visit a friend in Yakima. I don't know whether she actually went there or not. She didn't come back for a week though."

"But before that, has she ever wandered off?"

"Yes."

"Where did she go?"

"I don't know, Laura. I don't know. I never talked to Jack about it. He and Wendy don't talk very much. Sometimes I think he ought to pay more attention to her."

"How do you mean?"

"Well, he's always after Chris about something. If she gets home late from work, he gets upset."

"But, of course, Wendy's older."

"That's true, but she needs him too," Shirley said, turning back to her cooling TV dinner. "I feel so sorry for her. I wish I could help her."

A car was pulling into the driveway, the throaty roar of its high-compression engine rattling the windows.

"That must be Rob," Shirley said nervously, standing and putting her half-finished dinner on top of the television set. "I do wish he wouldn't make so much noise."

There was a clatter on the front porch and Rob, limping slightly, came in followed by William Blue.

"Hello, Rob," Laura said.

He blinked into the lights, his long blond hair soaking wet. "Hey, hey, whatdaya say?" he rhymed carelessly.

"Laura Jordan. We met at Sun Valley very briefly."

"Ri-i-ight." William Blue stayed back in the shadows, his overcoat collar turned up.

"We're looking for Wendy, Rob. Have you seen her?" Shirley stepped forward.

Rob Towne turned to his stepmother. His head teetered back and forth.

"No," he said, and turned away. "Come on, Blue Boy, let's go take in some sounds in my room."

"Rob," Shirley intercepted him, "she called Laura long distance from somewhere. We're all very worried. Do you know where she might go?" She reached out to stop him.

He shook her off. "Hey, like I told you, like I don't know, right? OK? I don't."

Laura moved in smoothly from the other side. The two women had him blocked from the hall door.

"How's the leg, Rob?" she asked kindly.

Startled, he looked down at his blue jeans and shuffled his feet. "Oh, it's OK, don't feel a thing. Know what I mean? Not a thing." He looked up at her, his pretty girlish face a stark white. "I remember you, you're the lady with the cat eyes."

Laura smiled. "It looks like you're still having trouble with it. That was a heck of a fall you took."

"Feels good now, real good. Dr. Feelgood fixed me up, right, Blue Boy?" He tried to smile back, but the expression came in pieces that didn't fit together.

"Has Wendy said anything to you in the last couple of days, Rob, about taking a trip or anything?" Laura asked him. She noticed William Blue was moving up behind them silently, trying to find a way through the female wall to get to Rob.

"Naw, she was around, we talked, but nuthin' like that."

"Maybe she flew away like Peter Pan," Blue suggested sharply.

Shirley Towne had been holding her anger inside all day. First, there had been the stupid mistake by one of her people that would delay billing for six hours and cost $22,000 in down time for which Shirley, as the supervisor, was blamed. Then, there was the call from the bank about the payments on Rob's car. As the cosigner, she was responsible. And the long bus ride home, standing, swaying in all those hot sweaty bodies, had only deepened the fury.

She whirled on Blue, grabbing him roughly by the arm. "Now just a minute, young man. You don't talk that way in this house. Do you understand? Not in this house!"

Shirley felt the tears coming, heard her own voice, shrill and unreasonable. Blue yanked his arms back as if she'd contaminated him, a look of angry surprise on his face.

"Hey, what's doing?" Rob wheeled slowly, clumsily in a circle toward her. "It's my house too."

"Rob." Laura stepped in front of him, holding him back.

"I know it's your house, Rob, but you shouldn't allow him to make fun of your sister like that—oh, God," Shirley burst into tears and went over to the couch and sat down.

Blue watched her with hard searching eyes. He held his arms out from his side as if he were going to draw guns.

"Why don't you go home, Mr. Blue, and come back tomorrow," Laura suggested, still holding Rob by the arm.

"Yeah," he said, shooting a murderous look at Rob, who was looking at the floor. "Why don't I do that."

"I'm going upstairs," Rob announced as the door shut behind Blue.

"Sorry," he mumbled as he shuffled past Shirley who sat totally dejected and alone on the couch.

Laura went to her, sat down, and put an arm around her shoulder. "It's all right, they're both high on something. They don't know what they're saying."

Shirley Towne looked up at her, mascara running down her cheeks. "I wish Jack would come home," she said miserably.

"He'll call when he gets in. I can stay until then."

"I don't know how Blue could say something like that—it's despicable."

"He's a lot older than Rob, isn't he?"

"Yes, a couple of years at least."

"How long has Rob been on whatever he's on, Shirley?"

Shirley Towne coughed, covering her mouth. "I don't know, Laura, I don't know anything about drugs. When we were first married, he was smoking marijuana. I know that for sure. I tried to talk to him and tell him what it was going to do to his mind."

"All supplied by Mr. Blue, I'll bet."

"I don't know, Laura."

"Has Jack talked to him?"

Shirley hesitated. "He says he has. I've certainly asked him to, but Jack's funny that way."

"What do you mean?"

"Well, except for Chris, you know, he doesn't tell the kids what to do. I guess he's afraid he'll lose them or something. It makes it hard."

"Sure it does. Is that tea water in the kitchen?" Laura saw the steam boiling out through the half-open door.

"Oh, my gosh, it's been on all this time."

"I'll get it, you relax," Laura told her, and marched into the kitchen. It was a mess. The sink was full of dirty dishes. Three boxes of cereal sat on the formica breakfast table. Laura followed Shirley's directions and found two tea bags and the cups. The steaming tea kettle had covered the kitchen windows with condensation. Pouring the tea, she realized she hadn't paid much attention to Blue at Sun Valley. Now that she'd seen him up close, there was something very sinister about him.

The sugar cubes were in an open package beside a battered coffee maker, its glass pot ringed with stains. On the wall behind it was a sign with a yellow daisy border. "Good Coffee Should be Like a Good Man," it read, "Hot, Sweet, and Strong."

By the time Laura got back to the living room, the plastic cups clattering in their saucers, Shirley had composed herself, wiped the streaked mascara away and recovered at least some of her natural spunk.

"Gosh, Laura, there's nothing as embarrassing as a family fight in front of a guest."

"It's OK, Shirley, my family fights too; it happens to everybody." Actually, Laura could only remember one family fight, and it was not in public. It was over money, and her mother's penchant for writing checks without recording them in the book. "Jesus H. Christ," Gene Jordan had shouted at her, "I'm a bank officer, and you and golden girl here go all over town bouncing checks."

Her mother had cried a little, promised to mend her ways, and the fight was over. She still never recorded checks, however. Neither did Laura.

"I've been imposing on you, Laura, and it's not fair. All this caught me at a bad time."

"Shirley, everyone has to lean on somebody a little. It's nothing to be embarrassed about. You're trying to do a lot of things at once, and I think you're doing a great job."

Shirley sipped her tea. "I wonder if Rob will ever forgive me for yelling at his friend?"

"There's nothing to forgive. Rob should apologize to you, Shirley. You took a firm stand. I was proud of you."

"But I lost my temper."

"That's OK when you're doing the right thing."

Shirley smiled. "Do you really think so?"

"I know so. And I know something else. You're not going

to solve anything by exhausting yourself with worry. As a friend I have a suggestion. Go to bed."

Shirley set her tea down. "But what about Wendy?"

"Wendy's of age; she's a grown woman. She's done this before, and there's nothing either of us can do about it unless we want to call the police."

"Oh, I don't think we should do that, do you?"

"No, I don't."

"But what about Jack?"

"It's not that late, Shirley. We're tired, but it's only nine forty-five. He's probably out dining the famous Mr. Timberlake, making his big deal. Wouldn't that be something?"

"Oh, yes. Do you really think so?" Shirley Towne impulsively took Laura's hands.

"He seemed pretty positive to me."

"Oh, I hope so. Jack needs a success. He works so hard. It was nice of you to come all this way when you hardly know me, Laura. It's meant a lot. You'll never know how much." There were tears in her eyes.

"I'm glad I could help. Actually, I was kind of surprised when Jack called and said you'd decided you weren't coming in to see me."

"Oh, yes, that," Shirley replied quickly, pulling her hands away. "He—we—thought it would be best to send Wendy. And Jack was right, the call tonight proves it." She dabbed her eyes with a blue Kleenex.

"I can't argue with that, Shirley, but don't forget to take care of yourself too."

"Oh, I won't, but the family means more than anything in the world to me, Laura. I'd do anything for those kids. That's why the Early Winters resort project is so important to Jack and to all of us. If it works, I'll be able to quit my job and stay home."

"Is that what you really want to do?" Laura asked, reaching for her raincoat on the couch.

"Oh, yes, it's what I've always wanted. Even though they're older, I think these kids need a full-time mother."

"I do too, Shirley. If you hear from Wendy, get a hold of me,

OK? I don't care what time of night it is. And if I hear from her, I'll call you."

"I will. I'm sorry if this ruined your evening, Laura."

"You didn't ruin anything, Shirley. My folks are used to me eating and running."

Laura put on her raincoat and buttoned it up. She could hear the gutters running on the side of the house. They embraced in the doorway, Laura feeling awkward because she had to bend down. Then Shirley Towne gave her a wet kiss on the cheek.

"That's for being so nice," Shirley half-whispered.

"Why thank you," Laura said, surprised.

The rain was pelting down on Heather Terrace, and the Townes' lawn was deep in standing water. It soaked through her shoes by the time she got in her car. There was a white Corvette parked on the sidewalk that Laura assumed was Rob's car.

As she drove the curving streets to the freeway, Laura kept her hand on the wet spot where Shirley Towne had kissed her. The houses were dark, city commuters resting for the long drive in the morning. The Volvo rattled and squeaked. The freeway was empty. Laura moved into the center lane and headed into the city, the warm saliva turning cold on her cheek.

There were all kinds of kisses, she reflected, all meaning different things. Laura was used to open displays of affection among women, but with Shirley's kiss, the signal was not clear. There was a clinging heavy quality to it; the flat scent of weariness seemed to linger. The kiss made Laura Jordan very uneasy.

The spot was clearly marked. "Private Parking, Tenants Only, Skiff Cove, L. Jordan." The black Lincoln Continental parked in it gleamed under the sweep of the approaching headlights, the falling rain beading up on the long hood like black marbles.

She could see him through the slapping windshield wipers, a monument-sized man in a camel hair overcoat standing in the driving rain beside the car. Mystified, she got out.

"Jack!" she exclaimed, holding her anger in check. He smelled of whiskey.

"You sure keep late hours," he replied cheerfully.

"You're drunk. What are you doing here?"

His massively ugly face folded into a grin of triumph. "Not drunk, celebrating. I'm actually steady as the proverbial rock." He held out his hands, palms up to demonstrate.

"What in the world are you celebrating in my parking space?"

"Victory, Laura. Total and complete victory." He swung one big hand in a wide arc. "T.R. Timberlake was fascinated with my presentation, he listened carefully to our proposal, he hemmed and hawed and asked question after question and, and . . . and . . ."

"And?" Laura asked him, laughing in spite of her anger at finding Jack Towne in Seattle when he was supposed to be in Boise.

"And he agreed to be our financial guardian angel. The Early Winters destination resort is as good as built."

"Terrific! Terrific!"

He beamed at her.

"Say, Jack, it's funny you should drop by. I've been out to your house."

"I know," he said, dropping his grandiose pose, "and you and Shirley have been trying to reach me all evening."

"Well—yes."

"Don't worry, everything's taken care of."

"It is?" She looked at him closely. He seemed to be serious. The rain was staining the camel hair overcoat at the shoulders.

"I called Shirley right after I landed in Seattle—to surprise her about the Early Winters thing, you know. Then I realized I hadn't told her about Wendy."

"What about Wendy?"

"That she decided to visit her grandfather in Kentucky. She left this afternoon on the bus. Wendy called me, and I said 'fine' and like an idiot I completely forgot to let Shirley know. Excitement, I guess." He shrugged.

"She didn't sound well when I talked to her Jack."

"Maybe she was tired. She sounded fine when I talked to her, very excited about seeing her favorite Grandpa. She mentioned that you two had a great talk, Laura. She seemed very pleased."

"Well, I was concerned, naturally."

"Naturally. Listen, don't worry about it. My dad's going to meet her at the station."

"And you have talked to Shirley so she's not sitting at home worried sick?"

"Yes, Laura, Scout's honor," he posted himself carefully and made the scouting sign. "And I stopped by—she wanted me to—to tell you how much we appreciate your help. Shirley was upset that we put you to so much trouble over my little communications foulup. It's really embarrassing. I should have called Shirley to let her know I was coming, but I wanted to surprise her, see? I never dreamed Wendy would leave without telling anyone."

"I'll bet Shirley was surprised." Laura was beginning to see the humor in all of it.

"Mad, surprised, mostly relieved. I don't think the full impact of what this is going to mean to all of us will hit her for a few days. He agreed to do it, Laura. Timberlake agreed to buy in!"

"That's terrific. I'm really happy for you. For both of you. Listen, Jack, I don't know about you, but I'm getting soaking wet. Why don't you come in for a minute and dry out? I'll make you a cup of coffee."

"You twisted my arm, lady, lead on." He gave an abbreviated bow and ushered her down the gangplank.

"You flew through this?" she asked, fumbling for the door key.

"No problem, instruments. You have to trust them, and here I am safe and sound."

All three cats were on the breakfast table when they walked in, and Laura introduced them to Jack. They were fascinated with his camel hair overcoat and circled hungrily as he took it off. Laura explained he'd better hang it up, or it would be graced with three varieties of cat hair.

She was a casual housekeeper, but her kitchen was well stocked, and she provided him with freshly ground coffee and a homemade cookie to go with it, both of which he pronounced marvelous.

"So now tell me about this big deal you put together, Mr. Tycoon."

The hidden blue eyes flashed. "All my life I've waited and worked for something like this," he said sincerely, "and now I've got it right here." He held out a hand and cupped it. Laura remembered how soft it had been to touch. "It's like I told Shirley on the telephone. It won't be long before she can leave that eight-to-five job. You know, she's worked all her life, and this is her ticket out."

"So what happens next?"

"Oh, we make an offer, do an environmental impact statement, renew the permits, and start building. Honest to God, Laura, this thing really feels good."

She watched him as he created the project in the air with his constantly moving hands. Here would be the condominiums; here was the road magically being widened for the yellow buses like they had at Sun Valley. Laura wondered if her father could be wrong about the private property being such a drawback. Jack was right: they used buses at Sun Valley, why not at Early Winters?

Here would be a restaurant, he said, indicating a little hill she knew that provided a sweeping view down to the valley. An open veranda where you could sit in the sun. And over here a bar where they would serve steaks and salad. And moonlight sleigh rides with the bells jingling on the horses; that was important.

And a new lift up Crazy Horse Mountain. He stood up, holding one hand to show the base elevation and swept the other in an upward arc, sketching in transfer points until they were at 11,500 feet and six unobstructed miles of waist-deep powder stretched before them. And a restaurant, like the Round House at Sun Valley, halfway up at the top of the second lift.

Laura watched this performance, fascinated as the vision grew in front of her.

"You could call it The Second Landing," she suggested eagerly.

"Fantastic name, Laura. It will be The Second Landing. In fact, Laura's Second Landing. That has a nice ring to it, don't you think?"

"I think you better ask T.R. Timberlake what he thinks."

Jack Towne threw back his massive head and laughed a deep booming laugh that shook his whole body. "You're right about that, aren't you? Here I am, talking like I'm the big gun of this operation. The fact of the matter is I'm the organizer, not the money man."

"You came up with the idea, the concept. That's more important than money, Jack."

"By golly, I think you're right." He slapped a hand on the table. The cats bolted at the sound. "I'm a bloody genius."

"You're a bloody genius who'd better get on home or your wife is going to wonder what the counselor's up to," she said gently.

"You're right, absolutely right, as usual." Jack Towne stood up and seemed to fill the little room. "I certainly have been talking a blue streak, haven't I? Scared the poor kitties with my big mouth." He squatted down. "Here kitty. Come here."

Cautiously, Christobelle, the young female, advanced toward the outstretched hand. He waited patiently while she sized him up. Slowly, she placed her head within reach. Fat Cat and Puss Puss followed, tails held high.

"The cats like you; they like Wendy too. Fat Cat, particularly, is very, very standoffish."

"Wendy's a sensitive girl."

"Does she like to visit her grandfather? That's your dad isn't it?"

"Oh, yes. Dad loves the kids. I wish he was closer, but he doesn't feel he can move. I'd like to have him out here with us. Maybe when the resort gets going, we can do that. Dad worked hard all his life, but he never understood that it's ideas that make money, not sweat."

The cats gathered around him, rubbing and purring.

"Your mother's dead?" she asked.

He patted each one of the cats on the head and stood up. "Yes. Her big dream in life was to go to Hawaii, but she never got there. My dad couldn't affort it. Poor Mom, I wish she was here to see Early Winters."

"Well, your dad can see it."

"Yes. You know, I'm doing it again, Laura. You have the most uncanny knack of getting people to talk about themselves."

She took his coat out of the closet and held it for him. "I've had some practice."

"Yes," he said, slipping his arms into the sleeves, "you're very good at it, very good."

"Thank you."

He pulled the coat forward, smoothing it carefully, then buttoned it. The cats watched with six unmoving eyes. "I can't tell you how much I appreciate your going out to hold Shirley's hand tonight, Laura. I know it isn't something you'd normally do."

"That's all right."

"I was thinking," he said, pulling the coat collar up, "now that I'm on top of this deal maybe you'd join us for a nice dinner out, the whole clan."

"I'd like that." Bundled up in his camel-hair coat, Jack Towne was an imposing man. Laura didn't consider saying no. She was pleased Jack was finally having some good luck. "It will have to be next month though. I'm going out of town starting Sunday to promote a book I wrote. I'll be gone three weeks."

"You're a writer too?"

"Believe it or not."

If he was drunk when he arrived, he was completely sober now. He stood in the doorway in no hurry to leave, one hand on the doorknob.

"Oh, I believe it, Laura. I'm sure you could do anything you put your mind to. Exactly how are you going to promote this book?"

"Talk on radio, do interviews with newspapers, I guess. I've never really done this before. My agent in Los Angeles set it up. Guaranteed to make me a best seller on the Coast."

"Now you're into my business, Laura. What's the guy's name anyway, your agent, I mean?"

"Terry—Terry Blake."

"Oh, yeah, first-class guy. I'm sure he'll tell you this, but the trick is to decide what you want to say when you go in. Don't pay any attention to their questions, give them your answers, keep hammering away."

"Really?"

"It's the only way. You're there to sell books. They've got a lot of other motives. Some of them are on an ego trip of their own, some of them are out to get you, some of them are plain stupid. They don't know, and they don't care who you are or what you did; they want something to fill dead air or empty space as the case may be." Jack Towne leaned his bulk against her door.

"You make it sound pretty tough," she said.

"Not for somebody like you, Laura. It'll be a piece of cake. I'm only saying you should have your pitch in mind when you walk in and give it come hell or high water. Don't let them control the situation."

"Good advice."

"And you didn't even ask for it. What the hell," he shrugged, "It's free."

"No, I appreciate it, I really do."

"And I appreciate everything you've done. God, Laura, you have no idea how long I've been waiting for my ship to come in. You know in high school, I had a promising athletic career, football scholarship and all that, and then the knee."

He pointed to his knee. "I had to drop out of college later to help my dad, but I kept going. A string of nothing jobs and then, of course, the shock of Ruth walking out like that."

"Your first wife?"

"Yes. Well, that's past, all past. Do you know who the biggest account of Jack Towne and Associates is right now in spite of our impressive office? Take a guess."

"I have no idea."

"The Happy Hot Dog. Can you believe that?"

"That's a big chain, isn't it?"

"Yes, it's a big chain, Laura, lots of billing. But it's not like a ski resort. That's like comparing that Lincoln out there, that crude piece of iron, with a Rolls-Royce. This resort is class; it's a lifetime dream come true."

Laura enjoyed his enthusiasm and shared his pleasure in the triumph. Too many people Jack's age gave up on their dreams and defeated, sank into a life of bitterness and remorse about what might have been.

"By God," he said suddenly, slamming one big hand into the other, "I don't want to wait. What are you doing Saturday?"

"I have a date to go to a Waylon Jennings concert—with a friend."

Laura thought about Jim McClay in his blue pinstripe suit rushing back from Washington to be dragged to what he considered nothing but a country-and western barn dance.

"Chris has a big swim meet that afternoon, the Queen City Invitational. We were planning to have an early dinner. Why don't you join us. Bring your friend, what's his name?"

"Jim. Jim McClay."

"Bring Jim McClay. You can still go to the concert." He opened the door, and one of the cats slipped out.

"Fine. It sounds like fun." Laura wanted to see Chris swim, and she wanted to see the Towne family united and happy over Jack's success.

"Fantastic! Fantastic!" He went out on the porch, and the two remaining cats followed him.

"Laura," he said in a deep penetrating voice for all the neighborhood to hear, "it's the greatest day of my life. We'll go and see my little girl collect all those gold medals, and then we'll go out and toast the best ski resort in the world. It's gonna be the biggest double celebration in history."

Chapter 8

Jack Towne paced back and forth, sweating profusely under his wool checkered suit in the humid swimming pool atmosphere. His face was flushed, he rubbed his hands together nervously.

"Where the hell is she?" he asked Shirley.

"I don't know, Jack, don't worry. Chris is a big girl; she can take care of herself."

"But the sprints are first. She'll miss the sprints."

"The meet hasn't even started yet, Jack."

"I know," he said, sitting down on the narrow wooden bleacher seat, "but it will."

The university pool was packed with spectators. Red, white, and blue plastic pennants hung across the ceiling and an electric scoreboard flashed "Queen City Girls Invitational" over and over in yellow lights.

Lithe young girls in tank suits were everywhere stretching, resting, chattering, giggling. Some gathered in groups, clutching their good luck animals, trying to be sociable while sizing up one another. Others stood alone and looked at the calm surface of the pool, down into the pale-green water where they would succeed or fail. At the far end of the pool, one girl slept on a pile of towels.

White-clad officials consulted clipboards. Stopwatches hung from their necks, and they fiddled with them endlessly as they conferred with each other, glancing occasionally at the flashing scoreboard.

The spectators spilled out of the stands onto the pool deck

and mingled with the swimmers. Cameras clicked. Lunches and sleeping bags lay piled in corners.

"First call for the fifty-meter sprint, age group thirteen and fourteen," the PA system announced.

"What did they say, Shirley?" Jack asked her, "Jesus, what a lousy sound system."

"First call for the sprints, I think."

"Listen, you better go get Chris."

"The senior division won't be up for thirty minutes, Dad," Rob Towne said quietly. He was sitting next to Laura and staring at the empty pool.

"They just called them," Jack insisted, waving his arms in frustration and standing up.

"That's the start of the age groups," the boy said irritably.

"Shirley?" Jack Towne was beside himself, a rivulet of sweat running down each cheek.

"Oh, all right, Jack." She stood up wearily. The early dinner had dictated the women dress for it rather than the swimming meet, and Shirley Towne's green silk dress was already sticking to her backside in the heat. "Laura, would you like to help me find Chris in the locker room before Jack has apoplexy?"

"Sure." Laura gave Jack a pat on the shoulder. "Relax, Daddy, Chris isn't going to miss her event."

"She should be out here," he insisted.

Rob Towne sighed heavily.

They picked their way along the side of the pool, Shirley's high heels clicking as they walked. Laura had opted for a purple pantsuit and comfortable Hush Puppies. The wide flaring bottoms on her pants covered them effectively.

"Honestly, Jack is going to worry himself into a heart attack," Shirley told her.

"It's a big day," Laura remarked. She'd never seen so many beautiful young female bodies gathered in one place. God, she thought, as they entered the locker room, the women of the world would pay billions for the formula that would give them the natural body of a young girl at the peak of her athletic career.

Most of the swimmers were out on the deck now, and Laura and Shirley were confronted with bank after bank of dark-green lockers and a few stragglers still getting ready. Even the more muscular girls were pretty, Laura thought, watching a square-bodied, sandy-haired girl pulling on her tight-fitting suit. She had a big rump and wide shoulders, and from the back she could have been mistaken for a young boy. Her skin was burned to an even golden brown, and as they passed, she turned and smiled at them. It was a superior smile, Laura thought, a smile of complete confidence. She might have been saying to the two women, "Hello, I own this locker room and pool and everything in it."

Chris Towne was sitting on a white wool blanket at the far end of the room, legs tucked under her in the lotus position, eyes closed, back straight against the wall. Laura was going to suggest they not disturb her, but it was too late.

"Chris, Chris," Shirley called.

Chris Towne's eyes slowly opened, and Laura saw the magical blue of Jack in his daughter's eyes. "Oh, hello," she said.

"We didn't mean to disturb you. Your dad's worried you'll miss your event," Laura said quickly.

"Were you sleeping?" Shirley asked.

"No, I was meditating."

Not a muscle in her marble body twitched. Her mustard-yellow nylon tank-suit still showed splotches of wetness from her warmup laps, the damp platinum blonde hair was plastered to her head.

"Yoga?" Laura asked.

"Sort of."

"Where did you learn that, Chris? That's interesting."

"From my mother," the girl said, staring past them into the deserted rows of lockers.

"Well, we don't want to disturb you. Your father wanted to know where you were. He doesn't want you to miss the sprints." Shirley made it sound as if she was delivering a message, and Laura could see the mention of Jack's first wife had upset her.

"The sprints aren't important. I'm thinking about the 200."

"I thought you were swimming in the sprints too," Shirley said. A metal locker door clanged loudly. A low roar went up from the crowd as a starting gun went off.

"I am, but I'm going to set a record in the 200."

"I've taken some yoga classes," Laura said, squatting down beside her. "Do you do the breathing too? I think that's really fascinating."

A flicker of interest crossed Chris Towne's placid face. "Yes, I breathe to calm myself, and I visualize. I was visualizing when you came in. I just started; I wasn't into it very far."

"What do you visualize, Chris?"

"Don't you think we better go, Laura?" Shirley asked nervously.

"Yes, I do. We've bothered Chris enough."

As Laura got up from her squatting position, Chris Towne said quietly, "I visualize winning the 200. I see the start, I see each lap, each turn, I can feel my rhythm, my breathing, my heart beat. I see the finish." As the two women watched, she closed her eyes. Her voice softened to a whisper. "I pull for the finish, I touch. I set a record."

"Really?" Shirley said, astonished at what she was hearing. "Chris are you all right?"

Her stepdaughter didn't answer. Her lips moved, but the voice had gone inward.

"I think she's in a sort of trance," Laura explained.

A roar of approval went up from the crowd. Feet stomped down on wooden bleachers.

"Well, good luck, Chris," Shirley said, still alarmed at her strange behavior.

The girl didn't answer, and Shirley and Laura went back to the pool.

"Is she all right?" Jack asked, his expressive face pulled into long lines of anxiety.

"She's fine," Shirley said. "She's getting ready."

The crack of the starter pistol sounded again, and another

eight lanes of girls raced down the pool in a 50-meter sprint. The speed and the intensity of the competition surprised Laura and she found herself being caught up in the excitement where winning was measured in inches. Some greeted victory with elation, leaping out of the pool to embrace parents and boy friends. Others collapsed in the water, completely spent. Defeat meant intense disappointment and one girl, a loser by a touch, broke down and cried in the tile gutter that ran along the end.

When they called the senior girls' 50-meter sprint, Chris Towne was not at the starting line.

"Where is she?" Jack agonized.

"She's coming," Rob told him, chin resting in the cup of his hand.

She was walking calmly when everyone else was climbing the starting blocks. When they were beginning to crouch down, she stepped up. The rest of the swimmers grabbed the front of the block. Chris Towne pulled her arms up behind her like wings.

"Damn, I wish she wouldn't use that old-fashioned start," Jack complained, but he was cut off by the pop of the starter's gun. They were all even until the turn, but as they came out and headed toward the finish, tiny gaps began to open. Chris Towne swam smoothly. She finished fourth.

Laura's heart was pounding as Chris climbed slowly out of the pool, and said something to a man in a blue-and-gold university blazer. He nodded. He didn't seem to be disappointed.

"That's Jake Tiller, freshman coach at the UW," Jack exclaimed loudly. "He's trying to get Chris a scholarship. Damn, I wish she'd use that rolling start. She would have won."

"It's not a rolling start; it's a grab start," Rob Towne corrected his father, still remaining in his statue-like pose.

"Well, whatever it is I wish she'd use the damn thing. It's a shame; she's faster than all of them."

"I think she did great," Shirley interrupted stubbornly. "You two men are sitting here like she failed. I think fourth is wonderful. She would have done great if she finished last as far as I'm concerned."

Laura noticed there were tears in Shirley Towne's eyes. Good for you, Shirley, she thought. It's not always who comes in first. Besides, Chris seemed to be concentrating on one particular race, not all of them.

"She's faster using that start than the grab start, Dad," Rob said, finally turning to look at Jack Towne.

"Since when have you become the great swimming expert, Rob? I thought skiing was your game."

"It is, but Chris timed herself. That's her best start."

"But Mark Spitz used the grab start, or whatever you call it."

"Not all the time, Dad."

"Kids!" Jack Towne threw up his hands and seemed to relax. "Honest to God, Laura, you're never right with kids. I sometimes wonder why they aren't running the world."

"Maybe they should be."

Jack Towne laughed and gave Shirley a friendly hug. "You're absolutely right, honey. Chris did a great job, and we're all very proud of her."

The 100 meters was the same story. The winner, as in the 50, was a square-shaped little girl from Santa Monica named Cindy Hoffmyer. And when she looked closer, Laura realized it was the same girl with the "I own the world" look in the locker room.

The Hoffmyer girl, Jack confided to the women, was a sure bet to make the next US Olympic team. In fact, he claimed, she was the hottest woman swimmer in the United States at the moment.

With Chris's second fourth-place finish, he seemed to have reconciled himself to Shirley's point of view—his daughter was doing well to even be competing with the likes of Cindy Hoffmyer. He had read articles, he assured them, containing speculation that Cindy Hoffmyer could be a five-gold-medal winner if she kept up her furious training pace.

His face was relaxed now. He took off his suit jacket, rolled it into a ball and leaned forward in his seat as they called the senior 200.

"Isn't this exciting, Laura. Aren't you glad you came?" he asked enthusiastically.

"Yes, I am."

"Are you all right, Rob?" Shirley bent forward to query her stepson who had hardly changed position since coming in.

"I'm fine. Chris said she was going to win this one," he remarked without a trace of emotion in his voice.

"She's going to be in fast company," Jack said, twisting the coat even tighter. "This is Cindy Hoffmyer's best race."

"Jack, you're going to ruin that jacket," Shirley warned him, taking it out of his hands.

He laughed, flushed with excitement. "Thanks, honey. Jesus, I turn into a nervous wreck at these things."

"She's a fantastic swimmer, Jack, like Rob is a great skier. You're very lucky," Laura told him, loud enough for Rob to hear.

She'd noticed that although Rob showed little emotion, he was acutely alert and watched every race, his eyes steadily pacing the leaders as they churned through the green water.

"She's better than I am," he said.

"Hey, listen, sport," Jack told him, clapping a large fatherly hand on his shoulder, "on a good day, there's nobody better than you." He winked at Laura. He had received her message and appreciated the tip.

"They're going to start the race," Shirley announced, and they all watched the eight girls mount the blocks.

Chris and Cindy were matched side by side in the center lanes. Cindy Hoffmyer, big in the shoulder, big in the thighs, big and strong all over, patted Chris Towne on the ass.

Laura watched Chris, her heart pounding violently as the starter called, "Swimmers take your marks." She wondered if the pat on the butt was a genuine sign of affection, a "good luck" gesture, or some devious psychological trick designed to drain confidence.

"Set!" Whatever it was, Chris Towne paid no attention. Her eyes were on the far end of the pool. Again, she was the only one not using the grab start.

The gun fired. Cindy Hoffmyer was gone. Chris was still in the air. "That should have been a false start," she heard Jack complaining, but it was lost in the growing roar of the crowd that rose as the swimmers approached the first turn. In spite of the start, Chris was only one stroke behind Cindy Hoffmyer. When she came out of the turn, she was two strokes down. Back they raced as if linked by a cord, Cindy Hoffmyer plowing through the water, Chris staying with her, stroking smoothly as they approached the second turn.

"Hoffmyer had a false start," Jack yelled in Laura's ear. Hoffmyer also picked up another stroke, Laura noticed, in the second turn. Chris had dropped back to where her head was even with the California girl's feet. The rest of the field trailed behind them. Laura didn't see how they could keep up the pace for eight laps.

She clenched her fists and chanted quietly to herself. "Come on, Chris, come on, come on!"

By the sixth lap, Hoffmyer had stretched her lead to a quarter length of the pool, and Laura felt the sickening lump in her stomach growing as she watched the wide tanned shoulders of Cindy Hoffmyer rolling powerfully, the muscular arms driving through the water.

Still, Chris held her position, never altering the smooth steady style, the redness across her shoulders spreading like a birthmark. Halfway through the seventh lap, Chris Towne went into a sprint. The change in stroke was accomplished as fast as a racing driver shifting gears, and in that instant, Cindy Hoffmyer's lead vanished. The roar of the crowd was deafening as Laura stood on her tiptoes to see the two girls flip into the final turn dead even. When they came out, Chris Towne was pulling ahead almost planing on top of the water in a flat-out sprint.

Laura knew it was victory! "Go, Chris, go, go, go!" she screamed. At mid-pool, Hoffmyer put on a furious kick, but it was too late. Chris matched her surge and won the 200 senior girls freestyle going away.

Shirley hugged Laura and Laura hugged Jack. They pounded each other on the back. "She did it! She did it! She did it!"

they screamed, faces crimson amid the bedlam. "Did you see that! Did you see her? She won! She won! She won!" Cindy Hoffmyer held onto the gutter, stoically dipping her head in and out of the water.

Chris climbed out of the pool, and Jake Tiller gave her a congratulatory kiss on the cheek. The crowd roared its approval, and while hands reached out to touch her, she walked slowly back toward the locker room.

Rob Towne sat amid all this celebration, head down in his seat. Laura, concerned, bent down. "What's wrong?" she shouted.

"Nothing," he said, but he was crying. "I'm glad she won."

"So happy you could cry?" Laura asked, putting her arm around him.

"I guess so," he told her.

After she went in the locker room, the official scorer announced over the public address system that Chris Towne had set a national record and recorded the third fastest time in the world at that distance for the year.

When Jack Towne pulled the black Lincoln Continental into the parking lot at Renie's, three uniformed boys sprang to the doors.

"Hey," Laura said, leaning over the back seat, "this was supposed to be a casual Mexican dinner."

"Surprise! Olympic champions can't live on refried beans. You'll like this place. Mademoiselles?" He motioned to the opened doors each with an eager parking lot attendant attached.

"Well, Jim's going to be surprised. He's meeting us over at Casa Lupita."

Laura, sitting between the Towne children, waited while they slid out and then got out after Rob.

"Thanks a lot," Rob told the attendant uncertainly. The boy was about his age.

Chris looked around the garage dubiously. Her blond hair was still wet, and she was wearing slacks and her warmup jacket. The first-place medal was around her neck, a small gold medallion hung by a red-and-white ribbon. "Are you sure we can get in here dressed like this, Dad?"

"When you're an Olympic champion, they don't care how you dress, honey. You just walk right in." He pressed a folded bill into each attendant's outstretched hand. "Please don't scratch the paint."

"No, sir," they chorused, examining the take and finding Jack Towne more than generous. He waved the party over to a glass elevator that went to the top story dining room overlooking the entrance to the ship canal on Puget Sound.

"Jack, isn't this kind of expensive?" Shirley asked timidly.

"I don't know, never been here," he replied carelessly. "Anyway, don't worry. It's a business expense. I want to check this place out. A French restaurant might be nice at Early Winters."

They all waited while Laura used the pay phone to call the Mexican restaurant where Jack originally said he was going to take them. Jim McClay hadn't arrived.

"Tell him to meet us at Renie's, please," she said loudly. "Yes, he knows where it is."

The elevator rose slowly and quietly. Laura knew Renie's to be the most expensive restaurant in the city by far. Whether it was the best was debatable.

"This makes me dizzy," Shirley said, turning her face to the back. Jack put an arm protectively around her waist. "Don't look down," he joked.

"What kind of food do they have here anyway?" Rob Towne asked nobody in particular.

"French food," Laura said.

"What's it like?"

"Pretty good."

"Oh," Rob grunted.

They stepped off the elevator and onto the thick maroon carpeting of the dining room. The tables, all perfectly aligned in sweeping semi-circles, were covered with crisp white tablecloths and set with silver and crystal. Across the choppy bay, the fading sun still clung to the snowy tops of the Olympic mountains.

"Ah, good afternoon," a mousy little man said, suddenly appearing from behind a partition. "I may be of service?"

"Yes," Jack told him, "We'd like dinner for five, maybe six."

"Excuse. You have a reservation?" the little man asked, folding his hands over his stomach. He wore a dark suit and shiny black shoes.

"Well, no we don't have a reservation," Jack said politely. "This was kind of a spur-of-the-moment thing. Is that a problem?"

"Dinner is by reservation," he said coolly, looking away.

"Well, sure, I understand. And I would have made a reservation, except we were all at a swimming meet where my daughter here set a national record. She beat an Olympic champion. We were so excited I'm afraid I forgot to call ahead."

"I see." The little man glanced at Chris.

"Listen, we don't want to gum up the works or anything, but I'd really appreciate it if you could fit us in. We'll take a corner."

Their host smiled uncomfortably and made a vague motion with his hand that could have been agreement.

"Unfortunately, we don't begin serving until five o'clock as you can see." He shrugged and indicated the empty room.

"We don't mind waiting. Maybe you'll have a cancellation or something. We decided if we were going to celebrate we might as well do it at the best place in town."

The little man searched the deserted dining room. He's looking for help, Laura thought. It's not easy to say no to Jack Towne.

"Perhaps," he suggested, arching a thin eyebrow, "you would care to wait at a table, yes?"

"Certainly, great. Whatever's convenient for you," Jack said as the little man led them across the room. Jack followed, his great lumbering strides threatening to overrun the short mincing steps of their host.

He led them to a window table centrally located. "The best in the house for the best Olympic champion," he announced in his French accent, seating Chris first.

As he moved to seat Jack, the big man grasped his hand and pumped it up and down vigorously.

"I really appreciate this," he said. Laura could see the sparkle of sincerity deep in his electric blue eyes.

The little man was embarrassed, but finally managed to withdraw his hand gracefully. "We will also open the bar. To have a victory celebration one must have a drink, yes?"

"You bet, terrific! Listen, my name's Jack Towne and this is my family. All except for this lady who is Laura Jordan."

Their host bowed formally to the women and gave Rob a stiff military salute. "I am François," he said simply. "Enjoy your dinner and congratulations, Miss Towne."

"How about that?" Jack asked them once he was gone. "Hey, Chrissy, I think you almost got your hand kissed."

They sat around the table and watched a few brave winter sailors heading out into the night, bundled up in yellow slickers, red-and-green running lights bobbing on the incoming swell. They toasted Chris and admired her tiny gold medal. They kidded Rob about being the future ski pro at Early Winters, and he thanked them and said if he wasn't the ski pro, he'd at least be the resident ski bum "or whatever."

By the time the restaurant began to fill with early diners, they were on round three—all except Chris who drank Perrier. The arriving guests, some dressed in formal attire, looked at them curiously and then studiously ignored them.

Finally the menus arrived, huge unwieldy things stamped in gold brocade.

"Hey, I can't read this stuff," Rob complained.

"That's because it's in French," Chris told him.

"What did you want to eat, Rob?" Laura asked.

"Well, I like hamburgers," Rob said stubbornly.

"Ah," Laura consulted the menu, "then you may want to try *Bifstec Hâché à la Lyonnaise.*"

"What's that?"

"Hamburgers, French hamburgers."

They laughed, and decided Laura should order for all of

them. Shirley, as a chicken lover, settled on *Suprêmes de Volaille à la Ecossaise.*

"Are these prices?" she asked Laura in a shocked whisper.

"Yeah, they don't have any dollar signs with them," Rob chimed in. It was as animated as Laura had seen him. Away from the dark influence of William Blue, he seemed to come alive. There was strong color in smooth-skinned cheeks and his eyes sparkled with emotion.

"Maybe there wasn't room with all those big numbers," Laura suggested gaily. She was beginning to have a very good time with the Towne family, pleased to see them having fun together. And then the memory of Wendy's plaintive voice drifted across her mind, restraining her rising spirits like a soft cold glove on the arm.

Wendy was missing, Laura thought suddenly, missing. But missing what? The family celebration, of course, she told herself. For a moment, the melancholy thought held her, and Laura wondered where the girl was on her cross-country bus trip to Kentucky; the girl who above all else said she wanted to be loved. But as quickly as the mood came on Laura, it was gone, and the conversations around her rolled on.

"This is more than I make at the store in a whole day," Chris said seriously, considering the price on the sauté of veal.

"Not more than I'm gonna make, sweetheart," Jack said. "Get what you want and forget it. That's what I'm going to do."

As the dinner courses began arriving, they talked around and around—about swimming and skiing and what they were all going to do on opening day at Early Winters, a resort bigger than Aspen, classier than Sun Valley with the best powder anyplace in the United States.

Jack said he intended to invite every famous person he could get his hands on to the grand opening like they did in 1936 at Sun Valley. He reeled off a list of those names to demonstrate his encyclopedic knowledge and thorough research into the opening at Sun Valley when there had been no snow: Claudette Colbert, David O. Selznik, Errol Flynn,

Julius Fleishchmann, Mrs. Bill Paley, and a host of others.

But the greatest coup, he explained, was how sometime later a clever PR man had lured Ernest Hemingway to Sun Valley where he was given what amounted to free room and board while he wrote *For Whom the Bell Tolls.* Of course, Jack confided, the management denied it, but he knew from reliable sources it was absolutely one hundred percent true. And Hemingway had in turn attracted others, his cronies who liked to drink and hunt with him—people like Gary Cooper and Clark Gable. Tricks of the trade, Jack called these tactics.

Glamour, that was the name of the game, Jack Towne said. As a PR man, he could really appreciate a coup like Hemingway, but it took work—lots of work—and advance planning. That's why he was already considering lists of people for Early Winters. That list included Gerald Ford, Robert Redford, and others, and it was far from complete.

They all listened, Rob watching the boats cruise by the window, Chris sitting quietly, politely turning from person to person as they talked, and Shirley smoking a cigarette, seeming more relaxed with her happy new family than Laura had seen her before.

"I wish Wendy could be here with us," Shirley said.

"She should be close to Louisville by now," Jack said quickly and turned to Laura. "She was really excited about making the trip."

Chris looked at her father sharply. "I don't understand why she wanted to go see Grandpa now. She was looking forward to this meet."

Jack shrugged. "Wendy's got a mind of her own."

"Well, I miss her. There's nobody to talk to when she's gone."

"What about me?" Rob asked her, smiling as he slumped further down in his chair.

"You're about as talkative as a telephone pole," she said, giving him a playful shove.

"Miss High and Mighty Olympic Champion," he said, shoving her back.

"You'd be as famous if you'd learn to pick up your feet,"

Chris responded, getting in the spirit of things.

"Put on your skis, sister dear, and we'll see who's clumsy."

"You can't even ski now, Rob."

"Yes, I can, my leg's better."

"Really?" Laura asked him.

She'd been thinking about Jack's scheme for opening day at Early Winters. It was a very classy idea; it had a 1930s flavor to it that would go over well. In fact, it was an utterly brilliant concept. Jack Towne certainly knew his business.

"Sure I can ski," Rob said, flexing his leg. "You oughtta come with us, Miss Jordan, you, me, and Chris. Mom says you're a rollerball skier."

"That's very nice, Rob, but I have to leave tomorrow on a long boring tour to promote a book I wrote."

Rob looked disappointed. "Well, maybe when you get back."

"I'd love to. I'll look forward to that." It would, Laura thought, be interesting to get the two of them away from their parents.

"You know, I was thinking," Jack Towne cut in, "we've got enough celebrities sitting around this table to make a big splash at Early Winters—Laura Jordan, authoress; my own son Rob the professional skier; and Chris our Olympic champion, a five-gold-medal winner. Hell, we don't need anyone else!" His voice was loud, his face red with pride.

Chris Towne put down her fork. "Daddy, I wish you'd stop that Olympic champion stuff. It's like I said, I'm not even going to swim if I get an academic scholarship."

"Chris, honey, you don't have to worry about scholarships any more. Today changed all that, sweetheart. You'll see. It hasn't hit you yet. Before you were just another swimmer. Now you're a champion. You beat Cindy Hoffmyer."

Chris narrowed her eyes. Across the table, Shirley shifted nervously in her chair and reached for a fresh cigarette.

"I beat Cindy in one race on one day, Dad. Nothing's changed. I'm going to school. It doesn't matter how good I am, I can't train for the Olympics and study to be a doctor at the same time."

"Yes, you can," he said seriously. "You're young. You can go for the Olympics then you can see if you still want to be a doctor."

"It takes ten years to get into practice and make money," she said with cold calculation. "I'll be twenty-eight."

"My God," Jack threw up his hands, "That's young. You don't know what old is. I'm forty-two. That's old."

"I've already decided."

Laura heard the hard determination in Chris Towne's voice. Shirley's lighter made a loud scraping sound as she lit her cigarette.

"Let her have a chance to think about it, Jack," Shirley suggested, exhaling a column of smoke. "It's been a big afternoon for all of us."

Jack sat back in his chair. "You're right, Shirley. Things are happening too fast. First the resort and now this. How much good luck can we have? Heck, Chris has got plenty of time to decide what she wants to do. Right now we're celebrating, and we ought to relax. Right, Laura?"

"Oh, I'm relaxed," she replied, grabbing the opportunity to steer the conversation away from a confrontation. "How about you, Rob, are you relaxed?"

Rob stiffened and let himself slowly slide off the chair, completely rigid, the starched tablecloth creeping over him like a shroud in a crematorium as his body disappeared under the table, eyes bulging in mock panic.

"Rob Towne," Shirley scolded him, aware of the looks they were getting, but also thankful the silly tactic covered up the clash between father and daughter.

Chris smiled at her brother, but maintained her formal debutante posture, back straight and not touching the chair. Her cutting response to Jack had taken Laura by surprise. After all, he was right. Things had changed, Chris was young; it was quite possible to be both an Olympic champion and a doctor.

With dessert, chocolate mousse for the youngsters, pineapple custard for the adults, came brandy. And before Jack could offer an after-dinner toast, Jim McClay arrived in freshly pressed blue jeans and an I. Magnin polo cowboy shirt. He apologized for being late, and kissed Laura on the mouth. She could see he was tired by the paleness of his freckled face and the tiny ridges that formed around his eyes.

Laura introduced him around the table, first to Rob, then Shirley, who flashed Laura a winking signal of approval, and then Chris.

"I understand you beat the pants off some little California girl this afternoon, Chris," he said enthusiastically. "Congratulations."

Chris Towne blushed a bright crimson and looked everywhere but into the square face of Jim McClay.

"I've heard a lot about you," Jack said rather formally, shaking Jim's hand.

"Nothing bad, I hope."

Jim always squeezed a man's hand hard. It was both a habit and a way of testing a new acquaintance. Although Jim McClay knew his grip was stronger, Jack's hand was simply too big to overpower.

"Would you like some dinner, Jim?" Jack Towne offered eagerly.

Jim declined. There wasn't enough time. Jack insisted he was well connected at Renie's. He and the maître d' were old friends.

"You mean that little guy over by the door?" Jim asked him.

Jack nodded confidently. "Really, Jim, I'm sure we could talk François into cooking something up quick so you and Laura won't miss your concert."

Jim McClay fixed him with his steady eyes; the look he gave people who were wrong. "That's not the maître d', Jack. François is the proprietor. He owns Renie's lock, stock, and barrel."

Laura had seen many emotions in Jack Towne—happiness, depression, worry, confusion—but now she saw acute embarrassment as the redness crept up his neck and into his huge face. He blinked rapidly several times, and then broke into a hearty laugh.

"Well, I'll be damned," he said, "I'll be damned. You'd think Renie's would be owned by Renie wouldn't you?" He glanced around the table. "All this time I thought François was the maître d'."

"François was certainly very gracious when Jack explained our problem this evening." Laura said, biting off her words. "As you can see, we have the best table in the house." Jim McClay's insistence on absolute fact irritated her. He didn't understand the concept of poetic license at all.

Jim tried to paper it over with a weary smile. "So he did," he admitted gracefully. "I understand you're involved in a deal to put a resort in at Early Winters?"

"Yes, it looks pretty hopeful. Are you a skier, Jim?"

"I used to be an instructor when I was in college. I had to give it up when my law practice got too big to handle both."

"Where did you teach?"

"Up at Snoqualmie on the weekends. It was a lot of fun. I got some beautiful equipment and made enough to stay in law school."

"Then you must know Webb Brown?" Jack said solicitously.

"Oh, sure I do. Do you know Webb?"

Laura sat back, admiring the way Jack Towne had not only recovered his equilibrium but managed to get Jim McClay talking about himself, not an easy thing to do. Jack, Laura reflected, was a hard man to trip up.

While Jim was telling him a long story about the fight to get a liquor license at Snoqualmie over the opposition of the Parent Teacher Association, Jack quietly slipped his arm around Shirley.

When the story was over, Jack said, "Shirley's taken up skiing recently, Jim, loves it too. I'm real proud of how well she's doing."

Laura knew it was an intentional maneuver calculated to bring the women and children back into the conversation. It wasn't something most men would bother to do.

"I understand Rob is quite a skier," Jim said, getting the cue. "You've really got an athletic family here, Jack."

Laura reached down and gave his hand a squeeze. She was glad to see him. So glad, she wanted to run a hand inside his cowboy shirt and feel the wiry red hair on his chest.

"I tried to encourage them. I had an unfortunate accident when I was young—knee, football, you know—so I couldn't be the athletic one in the family. But I'm so proud of them, heck, both of them are Olympic champions as far as I'm concerned." Jack put a big hand on his daughter's neck.

"I'm sure Rob could give me a couple of ski lessons. Techniques and equipment change so fast. What do you ski on, Rob?"

"Rossi's, Roc Comps."

"Good ski, good if you're good. Not very forgiving. I had a pair once; they dumped me on my ass everytime I wasn't concentrating."

"They'll do that," Rob said with a faint grin.

"I hate to break this up, Jim, but we've got to get going," Laura reminded him.

"Oh, time to make like cowboys, huh? Listen, Rob it's been great talking to you. I like to talk skiing. And Chris, congratulations. Pretty girl like you ought to be on the front of a magazine."

Chris looked down, her face crimson. "Thank you," she said in a muffled voice.

"I'm going to miss you all," Laura said standing. "I've really enjoyed myself today. It's been one of the nicest days I've ever had. I feel very close to all of you, and I'll see you when I get back from California."

"Oh, Laura, you've made it very special." Shirley stood up and hugged her.

"Gee, I wish you could stay longer. I wish we were going to the concert with you," Jack said. "I should have gotten some tickets. I like Waylon Jennings."

"Here, you can have my ticket." Jim made a show of fishing around in his scalloped shirt pocket.

"Jim," Laura said, "wouldn't miss Waylon for the world."

"I'm an old fan of Waylon's," Jack said seriously. "I knew him back when he was a disc jockey in Texas."

"You knew him?" Jim asked.

Laura took his arm. "Time to go," she said.

"Well, met him, you know. I used to be in the PR business in Texas—San Antonio, actually."

"Dad," Chris said standing, "I've got to go too. I'm working tonight."

"Working?"

"We'd be glad to drop you off," Jim offered.

"Work?" Jack Towne looked utterly amazed. "Tonight? You're kidding?"

"No, I've got to be there at eight."

"You mean to tell me that cheap son-of-a-bitch wouldn't let you off for one day—excuse my language—but I'm going to give him a piece of my mind. That's what I'm going to do, honey." Jack stood up, his brown-and-white checked coat open, wash-and-wear shirt wrinkled and coming out of his pants.

"Tonight's his busy night, Dad. I don't mind. I can't let him down."

Laura and Jim waited awkwardly, caught without having said their formal goodbyes.

"I'll call him and explain that we're celebrating. He'll understand. Let me handle it," Jack said.

"Dad, it's my job," she protested.

"You don't need that job now, honey."

"Jack why don't we all go," Shirley suggested, pushing back her chair. "We've had a wonderful time, but I wouldn't mind getting home a little early. I've got to clean that whole mess we call a house from top to bottom tomorrow."

"But, honey, it's early. We're having such a nice time. Come on, Rob, let's talk the ladies into staying."

Rob Towne shrugged. "Let's split," he said.

Jack sighed, a beaten man. "I guess I'm outvoted," he said, picking up the bill off its silver tray. "Let's see what the damage is." He nodded at the total, set the bill back down, and searched his back pockets.

"Jack," Laura said, "I'd be glad to split that with you. After all, I ate half the food."

Rob laughed loudly in his big newly acquired adult voice.

"Rob," Shirley scolded him in a kidding tone, "that's not nice."

"I think I probably can outeat Rob too," Laura joked.

Jack struggled through his pants pockets and started on his suit jacket. "Thanks very much, Laura, but it's my treat. I'll write it off anyway. It's research for Laura's Second Landing at Early Winters."

Shirley opened her white purse and took out a credit card. "Here, Jack, let's use mine." Everything about Renie's made Shirley nervous, from the delicate crystal to the aloof guests, several of whom were watching the Towne family standing around their table discussing the check.

Jack shrugged and reluctantly took the card. "I guess we'll have to, honey. I left my damn wallet in the airplane," he explained to all of them. "I know right where it is. I reminded myself this morning to pick it up after the meet, but I got so excited I completely forgot about it. Isn't that something?"

The concert started late, and the star had yet to appear. "We want Waylon!" somebody behind them yelled angrily, and a beer can flew into the dark. People shuffled their feet and talked while the warmup band struggled through "Wabash Cannonball" and blood-red strobe lights swept through the dingy auditorium. Marijuana smoke hung like ground fog; music howled out of the massive pile of speakers.

"This is going from the sublime to the ridiculous," Jim told Laura, leaning close.

"What?"

"Never mind."

"Jesus Christ," somebody said, "Willie Nelson didn't have any of this shit. He came right out and sang. Nobody knew it was him, a funny little dude in tennis shoes."

A cheer erupted in the back of the auditorium, and a bare-breasted woman went whooping and hollering up the aisle pursued by two overweight policemen.

Jim McClay was tired, and the jet lag made him irritable. A huge man in front of them, his shoulders as wide as a door, white belly spilling over studded belt, clapped time over his head a half beat behind the music. The harder he clapped the further he tilted his chair back until it hit Laura's knees.

"Excuse me," Jim said, tapping his on a blubbery shoulder. He turned and smiled. No teeth. A tiny gold earring in one ear. "You're crowding the lady."

The behemoth grinned stupidly. "Heavens," he said, rolling his glazed eyes and sat the chair down heavily, turning his attention to the band again.

"My, what a big boy," Laura laughed. Jim responded with a grim smile. There were lots of places he wanted to be. The Civic Auditorium on Friday night in a crowd of refugees from a motorcycle gang was not one of them.

"The one, the only, Waylon Jennings!" the announcer boomed. The audience rose, clapping and cheering. Reluctantly, Jim stood up too, his back stiff from sitting five hours in an airplane seat.

Waylon, clad in boot jeans and a leather vest, gave the audience a quick going over and, apparently not pleased with what he saw, turned his back on them and fiddled with the audio equipment.

A chilling electronic screech swept across the room. "Opps," Waylon said, turning to snicker at the front rows. Everyone laughed with him, but Waylon ignored them and returned to his fiddling.

After several more screeches, he worked up an elaborate strum on his guitar. He strolled back and forth, fussing with it, tuning it up and down. Finally, he faced the audience and launched into the first song.

"The only two things in life that make it worth livin' are guitars that are tuned good and firm feelin' women," he sang carelessly. "I don't need my name in the marquee lights. Got my song, got you with me tonight. Maybe it's time we got back to the basics of love."

He paused and faced the band, unconcerned and casual, letting the music drop. They seemed to be ready. Waylon sang: "Let's go to Luckenbach, Texas, with Willy and Waylon and the boys. This successful life we're livin' got us feudin' like the Hatfields and McCoys."

As he sang the beat picked up, became hurried. It seemed to Jim that Waylon Jennings, who kept them waiting for an hour, couldn't wait to get done. No one else seemed to mind.

"So baby, let's sell your diamond ring, buy some boots and faded jeans and fly away."

He didn't wait for the applause. He eyed the audience coolly down the barrel of his guitar and slammed into the next number.

"Are you ready for the country?" he howled. "Are you ready for me?"

They screamed and shouted and stomped. On and on he played, a shadowy hulking figure, faster and faster. The monster with the gold earring in front of Laura threw up noisily, and the stench filled the air.

Waylon was back to fiddling with the sound system, sharing a private joke with one of the band, and then it was over. With a curt nod, Waylon Jennings was gone, and Jim was hurrying her out to the fresh air.

They came up the Cherry Street on-ramp, the Porsche engine wound tight and accelerated onto the freeway. The tires crossed two lane markers with quick thumps.

"I shouldn't drag you to these things when you're tired," she said, massaging his leg. She could feel the big thigh muscle flex as he shifted.

"That's all right. I had a good time."

"I thought success ruined him for a while, but his last album's one of the best he ever did."

"I still like Montevani and John Denver."

"I know you do," she said, snuggling closer. "Speaking of liking, how did you like the Townes?"

"Nice people."

"No, really."

"The kids are sure handsome. They look almost alike. Unisex. Shirley didn't say much."

"She's shy," Laura said, slipping a hand down into his crotch. "Which isn't one on my problems. Damn, it's good to sit next to you."

"Don't bother the driver," he said testily, easing into the center lane, downshifting and moving deftly between two cars with a burst of controlled acceleration.

She ignored him and let her hand rest lightly between his legs. "How about Jack?"

"He has a tendency to exaggerate."

"Mr. Factual Lawyer. You know, most social conversation, even among the best of people, tends to consist of slight exaggerations."

"Yeah, I suppose it doesn't hurt. Jack's OK. He's not my type, but he's a hard guy not to like."

They turned off the freeway and headed down Lake Drive toward the cluster of houseboats. "Are you coming in for a while?" she asked, increasing the pressure on his groin.

"I don't know. I had a hell of a time in Washington; I'm all wrung out. Sometimes it's best to sleep on things. Honestly, Laura, that's the way I feel right now."

"You could sleep on me," she suggested, kissing the big vein in his neck. He laughed, but she could feel the tension in his throat.

"Yeah, I could."

"You don't mind if I try my best to persuade you?" she asked him.

"Of course not."

"I'm hot as a pistol. Old Waylon really got the juices going, and I'm ready to play all night long."

They turned into the parking lot, and he slowed for the bumps. "Maybe you should have hung around the stage door."

"But I don't love Waylon, I love you."

He stopped beside her Volvo. "Yeah, well, I'm not a performer. I'm a very tired lawyer. I'm never any good when I'm this tired."

"I could show you things you never dreamed of. I'll take you anyway I can. I don't care how tired you are," she said, kissing him and running her tongue along his lips.

"Come on, Laura."

She sat back. "Honey, I know you're tired. I know you

worked hard, but for once, I wish you'd forget your seven hours and do something wild. If you'd let yourself go, you'd wake up. I'd wake you up, lover, believe me."

"The trouble is," he replied, "I wouldn't be awake in the morning, and I've got a hundred things to do. I've also got to go see my sister play basketball in the afternoon."

"OK. You'll miss me when I'm gone. Three whole weeks can a horny lawyer make."

"I know, I know. I do want to relax with you, hon, and get away. That's why I want you to come on the San Juan trip with me."

She sat up annoyed. "I might if you'll consider canceling your damn race."

"I might," he said, "I just might."

"Well, good night."

"Good night."

They kissed and Laura felt his mouth, tight and unyielding.

"Say hello to your sister. I hope her team wins."

"So do I. They've lost five so far. And you sell a lot of books. Call me, Laura. I love you."

"I love you too," she said, thinking the phrase was getting to be like some kind of religious chant designed to rouse the faithful.

She heard each squeak in the wooden decking as she went down the gangplank and Jim's Porsche driving away into the night. First gear, second gear, third gear, back to second. She recognized each sound.

The cats waited for her, three little sphinxes in a row on the kitchen table. "Hi, kitties," she greeted them, "The communication counselor is home."

Fat Cat stretched lazily and sat back down. Laura decided she could pack in the morning and worry about where she put her airplane ticket later. She pulled off her Hush Puppies and, in a sudden frenzy of frustration, threw them both violently against the opposite wall. The cats ducked for cover.

"Sorry," she apologized as she went up the stairs. "All is forgiven. Come on, kitties." Still dressed, Laura lay down on the bed and flicked on the portable TV. John Wayne came popping out of the air into her messy bedroom. There were clothes on the chairs and books on the floor.

"Hey, kitties, it's the Duke." She wiggled out of her purple pants and pulled the top over her head. "Come on, you guys," she called them. There was no response. "See if I care," she shouted down the hall. "Just for that, I'm going to put you all in the kennel for three weeks."

That reminded her, she must write a note to Barbara. Laura leaned over the bed, feeling for a piece of paper. When she found it, she wrote the note on the floor. "Barb, by the time you get this, I'll be having a wonderful time, wish you were here. Please put the cats in the kennel and tell them I'm sorry. Call the Clairbornes and tell them I hope their sex life is improving—only kidding. Please tell them I'll see them as soon as I get back. If the TV people call about the program, tell them the producer has three weeks worth of tapes safely in his vault. Have a nice vacation. Love, Laura."

On the way downstairs, she passed the refrigerator, which made her instantly hungry. Laura decided to indulge whatever appetite she could and liberated a big chicken drumstick. Back upstairs, she climbed under the covers, propped herself up on two pillows, and gnawed the chicken leg. After Waylon Jennings, there was nobody better than John Wayne.

When the telephone rang, she lunged for it, hoping Jim was ready to abandon his schedule and ravage her body. But it was only Shirley Towne. "Oh, hi, Shirley."

"I hope I'm not calling too late or bothering you or anything."

"Oh, no, the cats and I are eating a chicken and watching John Wayne kill the bad guys." As if on command, a cat jumped up on the end of the bed. He was after the chicken not her body, she thought, suppressing a snicker.

"Did you laugh?"

"Yes, sort of, it was one of my cats."

"I wanted to wish you the best of luck on your trip and thank you for the wonderful day," Shirley said.

"I had a great time too. Tell Jack it was a fantastic dinner.

And give my best to Wendy when she calls. Incidentally, I think it would be a good idea for her to come in and see me again when she gets back."

"Oh, I do too, I'm sorry she took off like that."

"She missed a great party." Laura ripped the last of the chicken off the bone.

"Yes, she did, but apparently she's very fond of her grandfather."

"Then it's a good place for her to be. With somebody she loves."

Shirley Towne hesitated. "Yes, I guess so. I wish she'd told me she was going though," she finally said. "Laura, do you think she's OK?"

"I don't know. I hope so. From our initial session, I got the impression she has some serious problems. That's why I think it's important to have her come in for regular counseling."

"I'll make sure she comes back, don't worry," Shirley said with forced cheerfulness. "Anyway, I'm keeping you up. I did want to tell you how much I appreciated everything you've done for us."

"But I haven't really done anything, Shirley."

"Well, ever since I met you things seem to be going better—Jack's project, Chris and her swim meet. Even Rob and I seem to get along better. You know, I did take your advice. I asserted myself. I told him our dinner was a family thing and asked him not to bring Blue along."

"Good for you. He seemed very happy."

"He's looking forward to skiing with you. He talks about it all the time. I think he likes you."

"I won't forget. He's a nice boy." She rubbed her eyes recalling her first meeting with Rob Towne along the snowy highway and the feeling he wanted something from her.

"You take care of yourself, Laura, and call me when you get back."

"I will, Shirley. Good night." It had been a long, long day, and it had not ended particularly well. Damn Jim McClay and his seven hours.

She stretched and lay back. The cats were arguing over the chicken bone. I need a man, Laura thought ruefully, and all I get are calls from lonely women.

He was fighting mad, coming down the middle of the dusty street like he meant business. There's what I need, Laura thought, fighting to keep her eyes open and on John Wayne.

"I'm comin' for ya," he said.

As she drifted off to sleep, cats on either side and the sounds of the shootout echoing through the bedroom, she realized that Jack Towne had a walk exactly like John Wayne.

Chapter 9

The sour smell of air-conditioned smog filled the terminal building. No, the brusque young woman at the desk told her, there was no reservation in her name. Laura dumped her shoulder bag on the dirty floor and inquired if she could simply rent a car without one.

Yes, the woman replied, she could arrange that. In fact, she'd be pleased to have it brought around. Laura selected a Mustang. Very soon, she thought, watching the surging crowds of every nationality in the world meshing in the long breezeway, Seattle will be this way too. There's no stopping it. Walking out through the cars lined three deep in front of the Los Angeles International Airport under a hazy Mediterranean sky, a long sailing trip in the San Juan Islands with Jim McClay looked very good.

She drove down the San Diego freeway to the Laguna Canyon exit. They said Los Angeles wasn't growing, but that certainly wasn't true of the suburbs. Acre upon acre of new subdivisions spread across the hills like movie sets. Who could afford these modest tract homes that sold for $100,000 and up? she wondered, heading down the canyon. It had to be people with modest incomes and one hell of a cash-flow problem.

The canyon itself hadn't changed much. Here and there new buildings clustered at the roadside, but the hills were still bare. Laguna's main street was jammed as usual, and brown boys in cutoffs were still playing volleyball on the beach where the Canyon Road intersected the Coast Highway. They looked like the same boys who were playing there fifteen years ago, Laura thought. Maybe they'd found the fountain of youth right there in Laguna Park.

Laura laughed out loud. There had been a time when she wanted to live in Laguna, but that time was past. Still, the air was better here. You could smell the sea. She rolled down the window, loosened her hair with one hand and let it blow in the wind.

Laura fumbled through her purse as she drove slowly down the Coast Highway until she found the crumpled sheet of paper with the directions from Terry Blake, her agent. By then she'd passed the street, and it took three miles to turn around.

Oceanview Drive went straight up the hill in endless switchbacks. Around every corner, cars were parked below houses supported on stilts and jammed tightly up against their neighbors. At the end of Oceanview, she pulled in behind the new blue Mercedes convertible with the vanity license plate TERRY. Laura had arrived.

Terry Blake was not strictly a literary agent. He was also half owner of the New Life Press that published *The Femme Factor* and hundreds of other similar books, vice president of a real estate development company that bought up dry oil fields with a view and turned them into complexes of expensive condominiums, and owner of three health salons for women in Orange County.

He had invited Laura to stay with them before going on her publicity tour for two reasons: to impress her with his material possessions and to seduce her. Terry Blake knew that all women could be seduced by men with power and money, except for his wife who was a lesbian.

Laura was suitably impressed with the house, a rather Roman-feeling villa with tile floors and lots of chrome and open space. A cascading series of jacuzzi baths led down to a triangle-shaped pool that literally hung out over the city of Laguna Beach a thousand feet below and the hazy blue Pacific beyond.

She was less impressed with Terry, whom she'd never seen in anything but a carefully tailored business suit. He stepped out to greet her clad in surfing trunks. His legs were thin, gut thick, breasts pendulous, shoulders rounded. He offered her a drink. It was only one-thirty in the afternoon, and Laura declined, accepting a Perrier as a substitute.

There were two perfect-looking blond children, a boy and a girl of grade-school age, wiry and tan, placidly watching TV in a windowless cool room jammed with electronic gear.

"I do hope you brought your bathing suit, Laura," he said, waddling ahead of her. "Beth and I like to have early drinks in the pool."

"I'm from the north, Terry. We don't swim in the winter," she told him. A Mercedes station wagon pulled in behind Laura's rented Mustang. Its vanity license plate read BETH. A tall, tanned, emaciated woman in a white Roman toga stepped out. The woman of the house was home.

"When in the southland, do as the southlanders do," Terry kidded Laura.

That night they had drinks in the pool. Laura drank very little and kept her eyes on the sharp-faced Beth who continally found excuses to be close and touch her. Terry Blake was a docile farm animal compared to his jungle-raised, hungry-eyed wife.

After steaks and lots of green salad and more drinks, which Laura also declined, she called Jim and told him she was having a wonderful time.

"Great. Listen, Laura, I'm sorry about last night."

"That's all right," she said, looking out her bedroom window onto the twinkling lights of Laguna Beach. "I'm feeling kind of nonsexual myself these days."

"That's a first." He laughed easily.

Laura missed him. He was such a straightforward man. If there were any bends and quirks in Jim, they were hidden so deep nobody would ever find them.

"Yes, it is. Maybe I'm anticipating all this interviewing, I don't know. Anyway, I love you, and I'll call when I get a chance."

"OK, honey. Take care of yourself."

Laura Jordan never gave Terry Blake any reason to believe she was interested in him sexually, and she had tried to give the same message to his wife. Still, she slept badly with her back to the wall and when she woke up in the morning, overheated and sweating in the hot morning sun, she thought she could remember Beth gliding across the room. That Beth had touched her breast. That she had moaned no, no, in her sleep.

She sat up quickly. Nothing like that could have happened. It was like a scene out of the Munsters. In fact, that's where Beth belonged, Laura decided as she showered. In a Charles Addams' cartoon.

The two perfect children left their cantaloupe rinds on the table and were gone by the time Laura came down to the covered patio for breakfast. Beth Blake looked angry and said very little, stalking around silently in a blue silk robe. In contrast, Terry, his flabby body carefully wrapped in a freshly laundered white robe, seemed happy his wife was in such a poor mood.

Maybe it wasn't a dream, Laura thought, as she dug into her cantaloupe. Maybe I turned her down in my sleep. Maybe that's why Terry is so happy. The melon was good. She helped herself to some fresh strawberries. Laura had no idea why that would make Terry happy nor did she care.

"You'll have to come back when you can stay longer, Laura," he remarked. "Our way of life here on the Coast takes some getting used to."

The fruit was good, and Laura was eating most of it. Beth appeared with a platter of scrambled eggs and slammed them down on the glass table, exposing a small dark breast as she did so. Her chest was hard and bony. A chicken breast, thought Laura, sampling the eggs.

"I don't like hot weather, Terry. I never have. I like it cold, the colder the better. My idea of a good kiss is rubbing noses like the Eskimos."

Terry Blake grunted and took out the itinerary. "If you follow this and do a good job, we'll all make some money here, Laura. Just be nice to these people."

"I'm always nice, Terry, except when I'm angry."

Beth grumbled she had an important appointment and, with a cheroot sticking out of her hard red lips, stalked out of the house and roared off in the Mercedes station wagon.

Laura gave Terry what she intended to be a formal kiss on the cheek to acknowledge their southern California business relationship, and he pulled her against him, his hot cantaloupe-laden breath hissing in her ear. She firmly pushed him away, and drove ten miles down the Coast Highway before she stopped and got the cup of coffee Beth Blake had neglected to serve.

That night Laura stayed with an old Birch Bay girl friend in La Jolla who married an importer of Mexican beer and exporter of American dog food. They lived in a house on a hill very similar to the Blakes'.

The next morning a cool breeze was blowing in off the Pacific, the sky was overcast, and Laura appeared at station KEXA San Diego exactly at eight o'clock, the appointed hour on Terry's itinerary, and met the first person she didn't like.

His name was Clarence Hines, but he billed himself as Man Mountain Muldoon, the heaviest country and western disc jockey in the world. He persisted in calling her Linda and scratched his balls nervously while he talked. He wore a huge pink cowboy hat, and there was a banner behind his desk declaring "Sit on a Happy Face."

"Well, tell us, Linda," he said (scratch, scratch, scratch) "what is *The Femme Factor* anyway?"

Laura found herself totally distracted. He was enormously fat and terribly short.

"I mean, it's the title of the book so it must mean something, right?" He laughed in little hiccups, motioning her to talk. Man Mountain Muldoon's show was live.

Things were happening very fast for Laura Jordan. With an effort, she looked away from the Man Mountain and put together an answer, remembering Jack Towne's advice to take control.

"It's the missing factor in the mainstream of American life today. It's what's wrong with politics and business. There aren't enough women in positions of influence." The eyes, hidden behind fold after fold of fat, flicked toward her. "You see, Mr. Muldoon, women are still holding what's left of the American family together. The family is our most basic social unit. It's where we get our values, learn how to cope with the world, and get along with other people. In contrast, men are the first to abandon family responsibilities. They bury themselves in the mainstream of American life, running powerful businesses, making key political decisions. And it's my contention that this is highly dangerous, harmful to our health, you might say, because most of these men have very warped, very skewed views of the world."

He looked at her across the table, the microphone between them, a totally uncomprehending lump of fat, breathing heavily as if he'd just come off a long run.

"In simple terms, they're all screwed up, and they get their jollies, Mr. Muldoon, by taking out their macho perversions on the rest of us. They're the people who send innocent young boys off to war to be killed and maimed and burned beyond recognition. They're the people who fill our delicate beautiful atmosphere full of crap so they can turn out plastic bottles or a better laundry detergent. They're the people who waste the taxpayers' money putting up monuments to an inefficient government when they could be spending it on decent human things that would benefit all of us."

Laura was only getting warmed up. Man Mountain Muldoon was no longer fat, he was putty in her strong hands. She smiled at him. An inviting, calculating smile, welcoming his comment.

"Well," he said, panting, "you sure could have fooled me, Linda. Whatcha gonna do, shoot all the men?" He laughed uncomfortably, his whole body shaking in spasms.

"Heavens no! On the contrary, we need men, Mr. Muldoon. We need them to help rebuild the family. We need them to take an active role in raising the leaders of tomorrow, our children. We need them to love us."

The Man Mountain leaned forward, sweat draining out from under his pink cowboy hat, cascading in fast running streams down his red face. "Now you're talkin', honey."

Laura joined in the laughter. "Most of our male captains of industry and world leaders would benefit by spending a little more time in bed with a good woman, communicating, so to speak," she brashly asserted.

"You know, Linda, I think I'm gonna buy your book. Just

tell me where the good stuff like that is."

"It's on page one twenty-three," she came back, whip quick. She felt the interview flowing under her control. "That's the section on communication. Because communication is the solution. But you see, most men don't communicate very well, Mr. Muldoon, in bed or otherwise."

"Is that so?" he said, beginning to enjoy talking to Laura Jordan. He scratched his groin vigorously. At first he hadn't liked her. She seemed so aloof and superior, so sure of herself. Now he liked her better. She was still all of those things, but also a very sexy woman. He could feel the beginning of an erection. It was the first one he'd had in a long time.

"If we can't get along in a family situation, Mr. Muldoon, there's very little hope for anything else. The world is full of men who can't get along with their wife and kids. They go out and feed their ego by acquiring great power over everybody to our detriment. By the same token, the world is full of liberated women who give speeches on street corners who haven't got the nerve to ask their husbands or boy friends to do the dishes. Both are equally bad."

The world's heaviest disc jockey started to say something, but Laura Jordan politely cut him off. "So you see," she concluded without being asked, "*The Femme Factor* is not a radical book. It advocates going back to the basics, reconstructing the American family. But to do that, men and women are going to have to learn how to communicate better. To do that, women must take the first step because they are the most stable; they are the closest to the family situation. And men have got to stop spending their evening at the office and get back into the home where they belong."

She gave him her most engaging smile. "Instead of working late, getting ulcers and heart attacks, and doing things that will get us all killed for a profit, they should be home learning to talk to their children, communicating with their wives and making love not war.

"And whatever decisions need to be made to run the world, believe me, women can and should take up the slack. And they'll do a better job of it too because they already have their priorities straight."

"Well," he said, cutting back into his radio show, "*The Femme Factor* by Laura Jordan, a counselor, communications specialist, and a very pretty lady. I wish you could see her. That's Viewpoint for this morning. Tune in tomorrow when we'll be talking to somebody else really interesting, Mr. Howard Duff, a man who is suing the government because he was exposed to Agent Orange in Viet Nam. Until tomorrow, this is Man Mountain Muldoon."

As soon as his signature was complete, he captured Laura's hand before she could pull it away. "Hey, maybe we could have a little lunch. I'm off for the day. I work at night (scratch, scratch, scratch), you know, I do it in the day time."

"I'm sorry," she said, "but I have an appointment with the women's editor at the *San Diego Union Bulletin* right away." It took all her will power not to snatch her hand back. His puffy hand stayed over hers like a cold mating toad.

"Maybe later. I'm available. I don't understand a word you said there, Laura, but I respect your mind, and I sure do dig your body."

There it was. Blatant, arrogant, unbelievable. She wanted to tell him exactly what she thought of him, but that would not only be useless, it would be cruel.

"It's nice to be wanted, but I've got a tight schedule," she said mildly, removing her hand from under his.

"Well," he said, standing, a squat little buffalo shape, having used her to fill his air space and seeing he wouldn't be able to fill her full of sperm, "if you ever get back our way, come on in and sit on my face." He thumbed a puggy hand at his slogan.

Laura was sure she betrayed no sign of the seething anger that rushed through her.

"Thanks again for having me on your show," she said, as if she didn't hear him, and left.

It was a bad way to start a long trip, but after she killed some time at the San Diego Zoo, she felt better. The chimpanzees were quite beautiful and civilized compared to Man Mountain Muldoon. No doubt, she thought, heading for her newspaper interview, which was in fact at noon, they would make better lovers too.

From San Diego, she worked her way north, staying for five days in the Los Angeles area, getting up early to jog down unfamiliar streets, trying not to overeat the restaurant food and generally keeping her objective in mind: selling books. Jack Towne had been right. The interviewers had all kinds of motives, and the only way to survive was to promote her book at their expense.

A few she enjoyed talking to, particularly a plain girl at San Fernando Valley State who wrote for both the weekly community paper and the college press. They had a long leisurely talk but unfortunately, it wouldn't sell many books.

Toward the end of her Los Angeles stay, Laura found herself wilting in a hot room with a sallow book editor from the *Los Angeles Times.* There were elbow patches on his corduroy jacket.

"What in the world caused you to write something like this for publication?" he inquired coolly.

"Because in the course of my counseling, I found some patterns that continued to recur. This was one of them. I wrote it because I believe it's true and that it's important."

"Really, Miss Jordan," he said, sighing and leaning back, a yellow pencil held between his hands, "I really don't know how I can review this. It's nothing but a cookbook of the mind and a very mixed up one at that."

Laura had a sore throat and a belly full of half-baked insults picked up in twenty-five interviews from San Diego to L.A. "Where are you from, Mr. Vinters? Originally, I mean?"

"Why, New York," he answered, surprised by the ferocity of her response. "I was with the *New York Times* for several years."

"I thought so. You really don't know anything about the West, do you, Mr. Vinters, or the people who settled it. You came out here for the sunshine. You despise the people. You're a cynical bore who doesn't like anything that doesn't have that Eastern establishment stamp of approval."

"Miss Jordan," he said angrily, coming out of his chair. "I really don't see what all this has to do with the subject which is your book."

"It has everything to do with my book, Mr. Vinters. You don't like it because it was thought up out here, printed out here, and it will sell like hell out here. And you don't even understand—or care—why." Laura paused for breath. She was furious, on the brink of totally losing control. Here she was talking to a man from the biggest newspaper on the Coast and making an ass out of herself.

"I've been reviewing books for thirty years, Miss Jordan, thirty years. My reviews appeared regularly on the front of the *New York Times Book Review,* regularly. I have written books, Miss Jordan." He leaned toward her, his narrow face white with fury. "I am a successful author, and I am telling you quite frankly this is the biggest collection of half-baked retread ideas I have come across in my career."

Laura stood up so suddenly he flinched. "Don't," she replied, careful to keep her voice calm, "get highhanded with me."

He smiled, sensing he was finally reaching her and causing pain. "Nobody's getting highhanded with you, Miss Jordan, but we are a newspaper, a reputable newspaper in the business of reporting events as objectively as possible. Your book, unfortunately, is not much of an event nor is it news. You're simply a saleswoman, Miss Jordan, pushing self-help gimmicks, a promoter, and I categorically refuse to give you any free advertising."

Laura picked up the fluorescent pink copy of *The Femme Factor* intended for Albert Vinters. "Your newspaper, sir, is nothing but free advertising when it comes right down to it."

"Really? You don't say. I surely do wish we had time to discuss that, Miss Jordan, but I'm afraid I'm a little short of that commodity just now."

"So am I," she said and walked out with her book.

It wasn't until she got back to her motel and shut the door that she allowed herself to break down. And once she got started, Laura let herself cry out every frustration of the lonely trip. She clenched her fists, buried her face in the bedspread that smelled of sweet disinfectant, and bawled.

It wasn't fair. In order to sell books, she had been civil to Vinters and Man Mountain Muldoon. In return, they treated her with contempt. It was because she was alone, independent, and a woman. The impotent rage boiling inside stopped her tears. It wasn't healthy; she had to vent it somewhere, to strike out at something.

Wearily, Laura dragged herself up and put on her running clothes, faded silk shorts, halter top, sun shade, battered track shoes, and pushed herself out into the sultry afternoon. In the distance, rising over the smog and sounds of traffic, she saw the faint outlines of the San Gabriel Mountains shimmering like a vision. She headed down the nearest main street, her legs heavy with fatigue, her mind numb, will power sapped. At the cross street with the promising name of Mountain, she turned toward the hills.

It was a long gradual climb, and the mountains were far away, but as she forced herself on, she began to feel better. First came the prickling sweat on her head. She felt it break out and start to run down her forehead. Slowly, the pain in her legs eased. Laura Jordan played a game with herself. Her body was a machine, a steam engine controlled by her mind. With each drive of a piston, her legs turned over three times—one, two, three; one, two, three; one, two, three. When the grade got steeper, she engaged her mental gears to compensate.

On and on she went, past barking dogs penned in back yards, school yards full of children, houses gathered around cul de sacs, until the ruins of what had once been orange groves began to appear. Soon the abandoned groves began to outnumber the houses, dry and quiet in the afternoon heat. A line of huge steel towers, heavy with drooping lines, marched across the road, coming out of the haze on one side and disappearing down the valley on the other. They crackled like rattlesnakes as she passed under them.

Her breath became short. The mountains rose out of the veil of smog clinging to their flanks. Still, Laura kept running. The cars came faster, and the sidewalks were gone. She stumbled uncertainly along the rocky shoulder, shifting her mind for one final push of the machine that was her body. The pain was back and unbearable. She picked a spot ahead on the road where she would turn back.

She ran up and down the dry washes, hanging on the white line painted along the border of the two lane road that was growing steeper and steeper as she mounted the foothills. She was alone, the dry brush all around her, the mysterious buzz of unseen desert insects humming in her ears.

At the spot, a yellow post with a kilometer marker reading 15 km, she turned back for the city, recovering her wind, going down the long grade, and renewing her strength as the breeze cooled the hot sweat against her body.

Back at the motel, she tried to call Jim at his condominium, but nobody answered. She tried his mother's house on the off chance he might be there and had a nice talk with Myra McClay.

"You sound tired, Laura," she said. "Sometimes I wish you and Jim had bought yourself a little business or something right close to me and stayed home. You two are always on the go."

"Sometimes I do too," Laura admitted, pulling off her shorts as she talked and throwing them into the corner.

Standing in nothing but her halter top, she called her mother and then Barb at the office. "I went to see the kitties yesterday, Laura. They send their love," her secretary told her. "How's it going?"

"I'm knocking them dead," Laura assured her. "At least most of them." She was thinking about the *L.A. Times* incident. That would not be good for sales. There was no way Vinters would write something nice after that. Maybe he wouldn't write anything at all.

Laura pulled off her top and looked at herself in the mirror. She was keeping her weight down, and her breasts seemed to be getting smaller. She looked closer. They were getting smaller. It could be all the hard exercise.

As she stepped into the shower, the reality of being alone in the middle of a million people gripped her for an instant with its cold despairing touch. The people who cared about her were far away. And then the feeling was gone, washed away in the spray of scalding water.

That night she ate at a Burger King on the way to a radio talk show where she sat for two hours and answered questions. Laura was tired but calm and felt in control once again.

Most of the calls involved problems. Problems the caller was sure she could fix with a word. It was very much like "Family Line", and she was on familiar ground. And like "Family Line", all but a few were from women.

"It's about my husband," the wavering voice said, "and how he puts people, family members, down. It's my daughter mostly. She's overweight, you see, and every once in a while he says the worst things to her."

"And you're concerned," she coaxed her along. A Wendy Towne, Laura thought, a fat girl looking for love. Of course, this was an entirely different situation.

"Well, yes, and it hurts me as well. But it's mostly my daughter I'm sorry for. I've also noticed my boys are starting to do the same thing. The oldest one is sixteen."

"It sounds like you've got good reason to be concerned. A pattern seems to be forming."

There was a pause. "Yes, but I don't know what to do."

"Tell me a little more about the specific content of these putdowns, who says what, that sort of thing."

"It's like he blows up, you know. Most of the time he's fine. I mean, he doesn't talk much, but he's a very successful man. The people he works with have respect for him. It's at home. He'll call her fatso and things like that. It really hurts her."

"It sounds like it's hurting you too."

"Well, yes."

"And what do you do when these things happen?"

"I try to tell him he shouldn't do that, but he gets worse; he rants and rages. And then when it's over, it's back to normal, you know."

"Back to normal for him, not for you, right?"

"Yes," the woman admitted, "that's right."

"And how do you feel?" Laura asked her, swiveling around in her chair to check the time. The program producer, a tired-looking, middle-aged man, smiled at her from the control booth.

"Angry, hurt, sick. I know it's unreasonable but . . ."

"Now, wait a minute. Let me validate your feelings here," Laura told her. "You have every right to feel that way and more. You're the best judge of how you feel, and if you feel hurt, you are hurt. Don't let him tell you it's nothing or he didn't mean anything by it."

"No, I guess you're right."

"And you've also showed some real insight into your situation. The fact that this sort of thing can become a pattern, and that your older boy is starting to do the same thing."

"But I don't know what to do, you know. I thought maybe you could suggest something."

"I certainly can, but the first thing I want you to feel is that you're a very perceptive person; you're on the right track. Let me ask you something. Does he blow up at people and belittle them like that at work?"

"No, I'm sure he doesn't. He gets along fine."

"What would happen if he did do something like that?"

"I don't know," the woman said. "I'm sure he wouldn't, he'd probably lose his job or something."

"Then why is it so different at home?"

"I don't know what you mean." A train whistle blew in the background. Laura couldn't tell if it was near the studio or at the woman's house.

"I mean, why does he feel he can do this at home?"

"Because he feels he can get away with it probably."

Laura smiled. The producer smiled. He looked supremely happy. "I knew you were a very perceptive woman," Laura assured her. "What you're dealing with is a little power game here, don't you think?"

"Definitely." The weary voice stiffened.

"And I think you need to tell your husband, to communicate with your husband, about that. To let him know he's not going to be get away with it. Why don't you ask him why he does it at home and not at work? Maybe you can help him see what he's doing."

"Well, maybe, but when I try talking to him, he won't listen."

"Then you'll have to figure out something to make him

listen."

"I don't see what you mean." The producer was pointing to the clock. Laura Jordan nodded. She was used to that.

"Let me suggest something. What would happen if the next time he gets one of his downgrading fits, you and your daughter both walk out?"

"I don't know." The woman sounded surprised by the suggestion. "I guess he might ask me what's wrong."

"You're darn right he might. And then you can tell him. I've found there's more than one way to establish communication in a situation like this and the methods aren't always peaceful."

"You know, that might work," the woman said. "Thank you for your help."

Laura glanced at the clock, only minutes remained. "Well, there's no sure formula, but what's important here is that you know that you're doing the right thing, and you feel good about yourself. Then you'll be able to cope with the problem your husband is perpetrating. Remember, it's not your problem. Don't put yourself down. It's his problem."

"Yes, that's right, isn't it?"

"I think so. I also think you've shown a lot of insight into the problem yourself, and I'm sure you can solve it. I also might suggest that your daughter get some counseling because no matter what you do, I'm afraid the accumulation of what's gone on so far may present her with some serious problems she might not be able to handle alone, OK?"

"Yes, and thank you so much."

"Thank you for sharing your situation with us. I'm sure there are a lot of other women out there with similar problems who can really benefit by what we've learned here together."

The sweeping second hand touched the hour as Laura finished. The producer gave her a hug and told her she was fantastic. "Anytime you want a job, lady, look me up. Jesus, you'd have them calling from all over the valley."

"I wish I could. I felt very comfortable here for some reason. I felt very close to the callers. You have no idea how nice this has been."

With her spirits renewed and the *Los Angeles Times* interview behind her, Laura drove over the Grapevine that evening to be ready for an early-morning interview in Bakersfield. At the top of Cajon Pass, she felt the heavy push of wind that slowed the struggling Mustang to a crawl until she stepped hard on the gas. All the way down, the wind buffeted her and as she descended, a pall of dust rose in the headlights until at the bottom of the pass she was stopped by the flashing blue light of the State Highway Patrol.

"You oughtta turn around," the policeman advised her, his voice muffled behind the white scarf he wore bandit style over his mouth. "This is gonna get a lot worse."

"I've got to get to Bakersfield," she insisted.

"It's your paint job," he shouted over the wind, "but you better go now before I get a call to shut it down for good."

"Where's all the dust coming from?" she asked. She could hear it whistling and whispering in the night through the crack in the window.

"It's those old cotton fields back home, blowing away," the patrolman joked. "They pick all the cotton up there and then the wind comes along and picks up the cotton fields."

He was young, and he liked pretty girls.

"Thanks," Laura said, "see you."

Twisters of dust danced across the high beams as Laura pushed on as fast as she could go and still stay on the road. The cross wind grabbed the car, slamming it back and forth.

The further she went, the fewer cars she saw. Grimly, she gave the road all her attention. Laura could not force herself to turn back to Los Angeles. Above all, she wanted to get home to the cool green forests with the constant rain, to the high mountains where you could be alone slipping through the snow. Bakersfield was north, and she was determined to get there. The car paint was the rental company's problem.

She went right by the first turnoff without even seeing it. The wind shrieked across the freeway, sending paper and tumbleweeds ripping along. Finally, she saw the dull gleam of lights on either side and slowly felt her way down the next exit.

It might have been providence or sheer luck, but the first

sign she saw was a Palm West Motor Inn, the motel where Terry Blake had made her reservation.

"I wish I had something to put over your car, but I've got to cover mine up. I just bought it," the owner apologized.

Laura told him it didn't matter. Squinting her eyes, she felt her way up the stairs, the grit and sand stinging her face. The closed door held back the wind, but the noise continued. The palm trees along the back of the motel banged into the side of the building.

Brown dirt, fine as baby powder, filtered through each crack and crevice, making neat piles along each windowsill and in front of the door. Laura sat down in a rattan chair that threatened to collapse under her weight. She was on the verge of crying again.

She closed her eyes and rubbed her hands over her face, the fine dust grinding against her skin. If she wanted to, she could go home, cancel the rest of the tour and fly back tomorrow. Except, she thought miserably, I can't quit.

Terry was a wretched person, but he did know how to sell books, and Laura wanted *The Femme Factor* to be a success. She would not fail. Laura Jordan had never failed. She would, she vowed, push it through.

The television news advised all residents of Bakersfield to stay indoors. School was canceled. Most businesses would remain closed, along with the main highway over Cajon Pass.

"Oh, God," Laura swore out loud to the empty room. "Trapped in Bakersfield without a man. Jesus Christ." She looked at the paintings of Dutch tulip fields adorning the walls. They seemed to be originals. The colors were horrible.

Laura did a circuit of the room, pulled up the blind and stared out into the night. The street lights were blurry fluorescent balls, and she could only see a few of them. A piece of tin roofing banged somewhere close and crashed into the street.

The TV station had gone back to its regular programming, a long noisy car chase, screeching tires, and gunshots. She turned it off and lay on the bed.

Laura was too tired to sleep. The tension of the long drive through the dust storm was still with her. When the phone rang, she grabbed for it.

It was Shirley Towne. "Shirley, what a nice surprise!"

"Oh, Laura, thank God. I had to call Barbara to find you."

"What's wrong, Shirley?" It was a bad connection, and Laura put a finger in her ear to shut out the howling wind.

"Are you there, Laura?"

"Yes, we're having a terrible storm here. What's wrong?"

"It's Wendy, she's—been hurt."

"Hurt? Where? I thought she was in Kentucky."

"She was supposed to be. Oh, Laura, it's horrible. Jack's in Boise. He called his wife—his ex-wife. I don't know why. I don't know what to do."

Laura could hear her sobbing. "Shirley, what happened to Wendy? Just tell me as best you can."

"They found her in New Mexico somewhere. I don't know. She was unconscious. The hospital called."

Laura sat up on the bed, her fatigue gone. She felt alert. "What happened to her, Shirley?"

"She was beaten up and raped. Apparently, she was hitchhiking. I don't know how it happened."

"But she's all right now? I mean somebody's taking care of her?"

"I guess so, yes. I called Jack. He didn't want me to go. He got a hold of Ruth, his ex-wife, and she went to get her. Oh, Laura, what shall I do?"

Laura stood up beside the bed. "The first thing you've got to do, Shirley, is get a grip on yourself. Whatever happened is over. Once you get a hold of yourself, maybe we can figure something out, OK?"

"Thank God I found you, Laura."

"You sound better already. Apparently Wendy didn't take the bus at all. Is that what happened?"

"I guess so. I don't know. Raped, Laura, it's so horrible."

"Shirley, as horrible as it is, we can help. Where is Wendy?"

"It happened almost a week ago. They didn't even know who she was for three days. I guess by now she's home with her mother."

"That's in Oregon—Eugene isn't it?"

"Near there. I've got the address."

"But she's all right?"

"I guess so. Oh, Laura, poor Wendy. She's so sensitive and shy. This is going to kill her. I want to go see her, but I don't feel right intruding on Jack's wife—ex-wife."

"Shirley, listen to me. If you'd like, I could go to Eugene on the way home. I could stop and see her, and I could talk to her and call you right away. There must be a plane up there tomorrow."

"Oh, could you, Laura? That would be wonderful. What would I do without you?"

"Do you want me to call Jack? What's he doing in Boise?"

"No, Jack trusts you, Laura. He's got problems over there, I think. Something to do with the forest service permit or something. I really didn't listen to what he was saying."

"Give me the name and address. I'll catch a flight tomorrow right after my morning interview here."

Her name was now Ruth Curtis, and she lived in a little community outside Eugene, Oregon, called Pleasant Hill. The address was a rural delivery route, and there was no telephone.

Chapter 10

Albert Vinters dismissed *The Femme Factor* in one short paragraph as "another feeble contribution of the me-first movement" in a roundup of minor books entitled "New and Sometimes Interesting" on page 32F of the morning *Times*. Laura read it over twice and then quietly slipped the paper under the airplane seat. The runway had been plowed during the night and dunelike piles of light-colored dirt whipped by the window as the jet, fighting headwinds, struggled into the angry coffee-colored morning sky.

Terry Blake would be upset. He had stressed the importance of the *L.A. Times*. He would be even more disturbed when he found out Laura had canceled the last two stops on her tour—Sacramento and Portland. She swallowed two aspirins and tried to close her eyes, but the constant yawing of the airplane in the rough air made her dizzy. The seat-belt sign stayed on. The cabin lights flickered ominously as they headed north.

Over Pendleton, the pilot advised the quiet passengers that it was snowing and sleeting in Eugene and to be prepared for a bumpy approach. Laura's headache was replaced by a queasy stomach, and she clung to the arm supports as the plane lurched and took sickening drops. The engines backed and whined as they dipped lower and lower into the turbulent black muck.

It was the lack of control that bothered her, not the steepness of the descent. Laura liked to make the turns and drops herself, calculate her chances and take them. She did not like trusting an unseen pilot who might have graduated at the bottom of his class and have an unhappy home life.

If we crash, Laura thought, Albert Vinters will feel guilty for the rest of his life. One of the silent passengers moaned loudly, "Oh, God." Whether it was God, the pilot or both, at that very moment they all heard the welcome rip of rubber wheels against the rough cement runway. For an instant Laura saw the field and the terminal squatting in the distance, and then the engines blew a blind of slush over the windows. As her stomach relaxed, she knew Albert Vinters would never feel guilty about anything. A necessary occupational characteristic for a character assassin.

What she hadn't said to him was what she should have said: "Your trouble, Albert, is you don't like women. You think they're too emotional and shallow. They cry too easily and worst of all, even though they don't have balls, they can destroy you with a look or a word. That's why I'll bet you keep that jacket with the arm patches on in bed, Al."

She joined a forlorn line of passengers gingerly high-stepping their way through the snow to the terminal. Laura was actually glad she hadn't attacked Albert Vinters personally, but it was good therapy to imagine she had.

She rented a car at the airport, got a map and followed it toward Pleasant Hill, driving slowly through the mixed snow and rain that pelted down in great gobs, splattering over the windshield. She went south down the freeway, saw the ghostly outlines of the University of Oregon dormitories looming to her right, and then took the secondary road she'd marked on the map.

There was nothing pleasant about Pleasant Hill on a foul winter day and nothing there but a truck-stop café where she stopped to ask directions. A dozen grizzled heads turned at her entrance. At least half of them gathered around her on the stool, giving conflicting directions on how to reach Forest Service Road 1238, where Ruth Curtis lived. They were rough men who smelled of sweat and wore dirty jeans and high-top boots.

"Well, I'll tell ya one thing, ma'am, when you get there, you'll know for sure. The Curtis place is at the dead-ass end of the line," a younger man with a baseball hat emblazoned

"Four Wheel Drive" told her. "You can't go no further."

His hair stuck out wildly from under the hat. There was an empty gap between his eyeteeth, and two fingers were cut off at the first knuckle. He obligingly drew the route for her in red grease pencil.

Road 1238 started out paved and then changed to gravel, which was slick with melting snow. The smell of male sweat clung to her leather jacket. It was not an unpleasant smell, Laura thought, it had more sex appeal than most after-shaves. A logging truck, its trailer piggybacked up over the cab, roared by her on the narrow road, showering the windshield with a blinding spray of dirt and rocks.

She had to stop and wait for the windshield wipers to laboriously clear a hole. The surrounding country looked ravaged. Stumps dotted rocky pastures that were fenced with barbed wire on tilting posts. Muddy water ran deep in the drainage ditches, overflowing the road and cutting sharp troughs in the gravel.

Laura had no idea what to expect, but she hadn't expected this. Eugene was a nice town. She had attended a summer session there, but the veneer of civilization wore off at the city limits. If Ruth Curtis had a telephone, she would have called ahead. As it was, Laura determined, the best she could do was play the part of the concerned family friend. Poor Wendy, in her desperate search for love and affection, had stumbled into brutality and hate.

When Laura left the end of road 1238 and headed up a rutted driveway cut in the brush marked "Curtis," four big dogs ran out to meet the car, setting up a howling din. As the dogs leaped at the side of the car, she felt it fishtailing in the fresh snow. There were no tire tracks to follow.

Ruth Curtis lived in a house trailer that had once been shiny aluminum and was now streaked a rusty brown. It squatted slightly off center, a fading silver slug with a TV aerial canted to one side. There were four cars parked in front, including an old Buick convertible with the top permanently down, and a pickup truck with no engine. Cautiously, Laura Jordan rolled down the window and eyed the dogs.

They were big rangy hound-dog types. They didn't seem vicious, just happy to see somebody.

"Hi, boys, how you doin'?" she said in her most confident voice, opening the car door.

"Get outta here, you son-of-bitches," a shrill voice screamed and a chunk of firewood struck the closest dog on the back. Yelping, he retreated. The rest scattered in a wide circle.

The voice belonged to a bulky blond woman dressed in blue jeans and an army fatigue shirt. Her hair was tangled, her beautiful translucent skin lined with weariness and age, but Laura knew it was the mother of Chris Towne even from the twenty feet that separated them. "Are you Ruth Curtis?"

"You bet. Whatcha want?"

"My name is Laura Jordan. I'm a friend of the Townes. A friend of Wendy's. Can I come in?"

"Sure, come on. Those dogs are no damn good for anything but barking."

Laura stepped out of the car into six inches of mud and slogged to the wooden steps leading up to the trailer. The air was cold and wet and full of smoke that smelled like burning garbage.

Ruth Curtis ushered her inside. It was uncomfortably hot. A game show played noisily on the big color TV. Ruth turned it down.

"Sit down," she said, motioning Laura to a camp chair occupied by a pregnant cat.

"Oh, I don't want to disturb the little mother," she said, starting for the couch littered with newspapers.

"Beat it, Muffin!" Ruth Curtis made a threatening motion with her hand, and quick as the hand went up, the cat was gone under the couch.

Laura sat down in the chair matted with cat hair. "I was in California when I heard about Wendy, and, as a friend, I naturally thought I ought to stop by and see how she is."

"Naturally," Ruth Curtis said in a gravelly voice, walking over to the kitchen counter. She was light on her feet for a fat woman and held herself erect. "Can I fix you a cup of coffee or something, Miss, ah, Jordan? I'm having a beer myself. Gets my day goin'."

"Please call me Laura. No thanks. I just got off the plane, and I'm coffeed out. Is Wendy around?"

"Yeah, she's asleep, poor kid." The name tag on her wool olive-drab fatigue shirt read "Curtis."

"Let her sleep. I don't want to wake her up."

"She'll wake up soon enough," Ruth Curtis said, popping the top on an aluminum beer can. "You must be a good friend comin' all the way from California," she said, taking a long sip. Her throat was still beautiful arched back, and she took three long swallows. "I never knew Wendy had so many good friends."

"Actually I'm a friend and a counselor, a family counselor. I'm very concerned about Wendy, Mrs. Curtis. I know what a sensitive girl she is." The trailer seemed wide, but the ceiling was low. It pressed down on the squalid room.

"Everybody's concerned about Wendy," she said, sitting on the arm of the couch, her massive bottom slopping over on either side. "Somebody shoulda been concerned enough to keep her at home instead of lettin' her go wanderin' all over the country alone." She took another long thirsty drink. "Ahhh," she said with satisfaction, finishing the can. "You sure I can't get you one, ah, Laura? It makes the darkness light. That's slightly biblical." She chuckled hoarsely.

"No, really, thanks very much. I wanted to drop by and see Wendy for a few minutes. I don't want to intrude on you."

Ruth Curtis got up and went back to the refrigerator. In spite of the fat, her body moved with a slow sensuous roll. "Hell, you're not intruding. It's nice to have somebody come up to see us. My husband, my second husband and I have had a little disagreement, and he decided to live in town for a while," she explained over her shoulder while rummaging in the refrigerator. "Like a permanent arrangement, you know. He's a TV weatherman. Isn't that a kick? I hope he's up to his ass in snow."

"I'm sorry to hear that, about the marriage I mean."

The top of the second can came off with a deep ping, and Ruth Curtis resumed her perch on the couch end. "Nothin' to be sorry about, thanks anyway. I never had much luck with men. You bein' a family counselor and all, I guess you know the type."

"Well, sometimes the men don't hold up their end of things," Laura suggested.

"Yeah, I suppose, I don't know. I could never stay away from them myself. Always have to have one around. It's like these goddamn animals, they just eat your food. You might not believe this, lookin' at me now in this dump, but I'm a college graduate, was gonna be a teacher, a grade school teacher."

Ruth Curtis threw her head back and drank. She licked her thick sensuous lips with pleasure. "But, hell, I never made it. I shoulda made it, but it was my man problem. I met Jack in Chicago in a night club. He was a handsome son-of-a-bitch in those days, Laura," she said, fixing her with a steady gaze. "And he had a line of bullshit that would stretch clear across the United States."

Laura allowed a faint smile to appear on her face and looked directly back at Ruth Curtis. Ruth's dark eyes shifted away.

"I'll tell ya, Laura, for a couple of months there, maybe more, we really had ourselves somethin' goin'. You ever hear that old song 'bout gettin' married in a fever? That was us. We burned it all up like there was no tomorrow, and I'll tell you the truth, Laura, I enjoyed every goddamn minute of it." She finished the second beer. "I guess you hear this kinda stuff all the time, don't you? It's nothin' new," she said, with less brass in her voice, looking down on the dirty carpet. The snow made faint plopping noises on the roof.

"Nobody's life is a total success story, Ruth. Maybe you didn't do as badly as you think. I can tell you one thing; you've got three wonderful children. I like every one of them, and they're the most handsome kids I'ver ever seen."

Ruth smiled for the first time. It was Rob Towne's smile. "No thanks to me. I had them and then I left them." Her voice caught deep in her throat. "I left them, and any mother who leaves her children is no damn good."

There was a scuffle behind her, and Laura turned to see Wendy, her face purple and bruised, holding the pregnant cat. She was wearing a long cotton nightgown with little brown and yellow bears dancing through red flowers.

"Mommy," she said in a little girl's voice, "I have to go to the bathroom."

"Excuse me a minute, Laura, I've got to take Wendy out back. The damn inside toilet doesn't work, and she's scared of the dogs. Come on, honey, put on a coat."

While Ruth and Wendy were outside, Laura looked around the trailer. There were no photographs of any family members, but there was a framed portrait of Jesus in the kitchen with what looked like a prayer underneath.

A broken-down pair of cowboy boots and a checkered cruiser jacket was the only evidence of a second husband, and those clothes could have belonged to Ruth.

When they came back, Wendy stood uncertainly in the middle of the room.

"You remember Miss Jordan, Wendy? It is Miss isn't it?"

"Yes." Wendy looked at her, but Laura knew there was no recognition. Her eyes were glazed and unfocused. She swayed slightly. "I'm tired. I want to go back to bed now," she said.

"Sure, honey, go right ahead. I'll be in to see how you are in a minute."

Wendy left the room, shuffling her muddy overboots, leaving a trail of melting slush on the carpet. The bruised and battered face stayed with Laura after she was gone.

"They caught the men who did it," Ruth said from the kitchen where she was helping herself to another beer.

"Are they in jail?"

"Yeah," she came back, her face frozen in a set mask of hate. Ruth's nostrils flared out. "For whatever good that will do. They said she let them do it, that she didn't care. I told 'em that was bullshit. I also told that son-of-a-bitchin' sheriff down there that I knew how to take care of people like that. I'd shoot the bastards, and it wouldn't bother me a bit. I'd line 'em up and shoot 'em right in the balls." The muscles worked under her sagging face. "But what can you do? You can't do anything." She sat down heavily on the couch.

Laura got up and went over and sat next to her. She could

smell the beer with each heavy breath. Ruth Curtis was crying, but there were no tears visible.

"Ruth, I didn't come here to intrude, but I think something can be done—and has to be done for Wendy—she needs some professional counseling. Usually most counties have services available for rape victims."

"You don't think much of me, do you?" Ruth said sharply. "You don't think I can take care of my own daughter, do you? Listen, I didn't ask for this. Jack called me, you know. He called me. He was too damn busy or something. He called me in the middle of the goddamn night; got my neighbor out of bed. I don't have a phone, see? Jesus!"

"Ruth, how I feel about you doesn't matter. Wendy is the person we're both concerned about. Wendy's the person who matters here."

Ruth sniffed noisily. "Yeah, I'm sorry; it's the booze. I am takin' her into Eugene. I've done it already. I don't know if it's goin' to do any good. She's seein' a psychiatrist at Lane County; he seems sincere."

"Good. You know, Ruth, a little bit of that counseling might help you too. Everybody has to tell their troubles to someone. A lot of us simply don't have friends to turn to when things get really serious. It's a fact of life."

"You can say that again." The big woman shifted away from her so she could hoist the rest of her beer up to a drinking angle. She swallowed it and banged the can down on the scarred coffee table. "But I've got me a counselor, Laura, and a good friend. In good times, it's old Dr. Jack Daniels. When things get tough like now, it's that old reliable William Randolph Coors or whatever the hell his name is."

"They can let you down pretty bad, Ruth."

"Oh, hell," Ruth said, standing up, "I been let down so many times, lady, I feel like a yo-yo. I appreciate your concern. I really do, but the fact is, I got nobody but myself to blame."

She swung around and faced Laura, a cruel parody of a smile on her sad face. "I didn't have to marry Jack Towne, but I was a smart-ass kid with hot pants and I did. I didn't have to stay with him when he left a perfectly good job in Chicago to make his fortune in real estate out in Colorado, but shit, I wanted to be rich. Who doesn't? So I went along with the gag, dragging the kids over half the country. I waited tables while he put every last dime we had in that goddamn company in Denver."

She went back to the refrigerator, and Laura saw she was drawing from a case on the bottom shelf. Ruth Curtis ripped the top off another can. "That's right. He's flyin' around in a Lear Jet, Vice President of Public Relations for the Golden West Development Corporation, and I'm hustlin' tips and car hoppin' at the Arctic Circle Drive-in."

She burped and squinted at Laura. "Hey, Laura, I was pretty cute in my little short dress, red like a ballerina, right?" She twirled around in a tight circle, lost her balance and lurched into the wall. "I was a little younger," she said sarcastically, panting from her pirouette, "and I had a nice little top that barely covered up the end of my little titties that weren't so damn little then. I got more fuckin' tips and propositions than any other waitress they ever had."

"What about Jack's job? Wasn't he getting a salary?" She watched Ruth Curtis sympathetically, sensing the intense anger and guilt that was destroying her, terminal cancer spreading into her soul.

"Listen, Jack had a nice job in Chicago. They paid him every two weeks like a clock. He did publicity for heating oil companies and stuff like that. I always thought he should have stayed," she claimed loudly, contradicting her earlier statement, "but he wanted the big time, more glamour, more interesting and challenging work. What a bunch of shit! These guys in Denver were sharpies, I coulda told him that. The whole thing went belly up. He worked for almost a year without a paycheck. He never got a fuckin' dime."

She pushed herself off the wall, worn alcoholic face red with effort. "Well, I can tell you when I got home at night he sure didn't get much sympathy from me. So then he starts coming in late, been working, he said. In a pig's ass. He found somebody else's shoulder to cry on, workin' on his secretary's fat little behind, that's what he was doin'. I know all about that stuff. I had a little sexy behind once myself."

Neither of them noticed Wendy standing in the doorway again, a lost figure in her child's nightgown. "I'm afraid, Mommy. Come and sing to me, sing to me," she begged in a frightened voice. Laura's eyes clouded with tears, the ordeal had taken most of Wendy's weight, and she looked frail. It was almost as if what was left of her delicate spirit was about to take leave of her abused body.

"OK, honey, I'll be right there. Is the kitty with you?"

"Yes," Wendy said, "kitty's there." Her eyes were swollen shut to purple slits, her mouth was scabbed over on both the lower and upper lip.

Laura went to her and took the girl in her arms. "Oh, Wendy, I want you to love your kitty and get better. Everybody in Seattle sends their love. You've got a lot of people in your corner who love you, Wendy. Don't forget that."

The girl didn't move in her embrace. She stood as if Laura wasn't there. Laura kissed her battered cheek. It was cold.

"I'll be right in, honey. You get back to bed," Ruth told her.

Laura's leather jacket was still wet from the snow. The mud had partially dried on her boots and broke off in chunks on the carpet. "Sorry," she said awkwardly, "I'm making a mess."

"This whole place is a mess," Ruth replied, opening the door for her. It screeched on its hinges. "We all end up down in the mud. That's where we come from anyway. Some of us go back sooner than others, I guess." She sounded hopeful.

"If I can be of any help, please give me a call," Laura told her. "Let me give you my card."

"Why would I need your help?" Ruth Curtis slouched in the doorway, letting the snow fall on Laura's bare head. The dogs gathered around the foot of the steps, silently wagging their tails, hot breaths puffing into the freezing air.

Laura gave her the card. "I don't know. It's like I said, everybody needs a friend sometimes, and sometimes women need other women."

Ruth snorted. "You don't even like me. You don't have to pretend. You think I'm no good because I walked out on everybody. Well, I'll tell you something, Miss Fancy Lady

Counselor," she said angrily, "I lived with Jack Towne for fourteen years, and I got to know him pretty well. And that's exactly what I did. One day, I fuckin' well left. And I don't give a goddamn what you think about that," she shouted, staggering forward.

Laura grabbed her arm instinctively to steady her. One of the dogs barked, finally seeing the possibility of some action. Ruth jerked her arm away. "I'm all right."

"I never make judgments about what people do because that's a very personal thing. If you felt you had to, your reasons were good. That's the way I feel about it. And I can accept that."

Ruth stared down at the card. She was out in front of the overhang, and the snow was falling on her too. "You do, huh?"

"Yes. And the offer stands. If you need my help, give me a call. I mean that." Laura stepped down to the ground, the dogs surrounded her, whining and competing for attention.

Ruth faced her from the top of the steps, arms on big hips, her blond hair blowing up in the wind. "Well, being as how we're such good friends, Miss Jordan, let me give you a little advice. Don't you look too all fired long in those sparkly blue eyes Jack has. They can ruin you for good." Ruth Curtis leaned forward from the waist. "And don't tell me you haven't been lookin' some 'cause I can tell, honey. It's as plain as the nose on your goddamn pretty little face."

Ruth Curtis turned on her heel and slammed the door, sending a sheet of wet snow cascading off the fiberglass porch roof onto the ground at Laura's feet.

Chapter 11

Laura arrived home at two-thirty in the morning after a twenty-dollar cab ride in the rain from the airport. The driver, a black man who didn't speak the entire trip, said "thank you" when she gave him a two-dollar tip. The rain came straight down from the black windless sky and hissed across the glassed lake surface. The tap, tap, tap of leaking gutters was the only sound coming from the darkened houseboat.

It was damp and lonely inside. She left her bags in the entryway and slowly climbed the stairs. There was nobody to greet her; the cats were still at the kennel.

When she turned on the light, Laura saw the roses on the night stand. They were long stemmed American Beauties so fresh beads of moisture still clung to the velvet petals. Laura sat down on the bed and read Jim McClay's note.

Dear Laura,

Barb tells me you're coming home early. What a wonderful surprise for me! I'm very sorry to hear about the Towne girl; I hope she'll be all right. Anyway, you get some sleep so you can come out to dinner and tell me all about it. Pick you up at eight. The place is a secret but dress casually. Unfortunately, I'll be in Portland all day, but should be back in plenty of time. Also, please have your best excuse ready for not coming to the San Juans with me so I can destroy it with my legal logic.

Love as always,
Jim

Underneath, he had drawn a lopsided heart with a crooked arrow through it, the same lopsided heart and crooked arrow he'd been drawing for fifteen years. Jim had come over in the middle of the night to deliver his flowers. Laura put her head in her hands and cried. She cried over battered Wendy Towne and her ordeal, she cried over the plight of ambitious independent women alone who had to be so hard and tough, she cried from exhaustion and the deep affection she had for Jim McClay, a loyal and true friend.

Oh, God, she thought, her nose clogged and hot tears of relief running down her cheeks. I'm acting like a high school girl. He sent me roses!

And then she laughed. Jim McClay was not going to get his seven hours of sleep tonight. Either he had an easy day tomorrow in Portland or he was getting desperate. Laura went on laughing and crying quietly to herself until she felt the hysteria subside. Then she set the alarm for nine and, still fully clothed, turned over and tried to sleep. It was a restless, turbulent effort. The plane went falling and spinning through the black stormy sky. She sat up straight, a sickening feeling in her stomach. It was three A.M. Laura pulled a pillow over her head and dozed off again.

The cab driver, or somebody who looked like the cab driver, was raping Wendy Towne as she tried to crawl along the burning hot pavement of a New Mexico highway.

Over and over he forced her down, his huge black penis driving into her and sending up spurts of blood. Terry Blake and his wife watched in dark glasses, drinking Cokes. "Stop it," Laura screamed, but they only smiled. A car was coming. "A car's coming," she cried in triumph, but it was a long convertible with Man Mountain Muldoon at the wheel. He was naked, an ugly pink pile of quivering flesh. His penis was shriveled to the size of a peanut. "Leave some for me," he politely asked the black man who had pushed his way so far into Wendy Towne she was skewered to the road. Her eyes rolled. "Mommy!" she cried. Laura twisted and fell off the bed. She was sweating.

"Shit!" she said and stood up uncertainly. In the bathroom, she swallowed two vitamin Cs and an aspirin, took off her clothes, left them on the bathroom floor, and went back to bed. Laura closed her eyes and tried to think of something pleasant: the murmur of the waves against the side of Jim's racing sloop as it cut through the water, the faint creak of the rigging, the smell of fiberglass and teak oil.

She was sleeping in the forward cabin, wrapped in the blue wool blankets stamped with the white naval insignia; she was safe. She could hear his breathing beside her. Somebody was shaking her. "Who did it?" Ruth Curtis demanded angrily.

"I don't know," she said. This must be a dream, Laura thought, it must be a dream. Ruth was carrying a 30.06 rifle, the kind her father used to hunt deer with. "It was the nigger cab driver wasn't it?" Ruth demanded, chambering a shell. "I'm gonna kill him." She couldn't be sure. She tried to tell Ruth, but the words didn't come. Ruth was going up the companionway. "I'll kill them all and then I'll kill myself, don't worry." Ruth rang the bronze bell at the mast head. Clang, clang, clang. "Stop that, I'm trying to sleep," Laura shouted. The bell had been on Jim's father's boat. He would be furious, it was very old.

Laura opened her eyes and saw the familiar checkerboard pattern on the ceiling of her houseboat and felt the sweat running down her face. The telephone was ringing on the night stand beside her.

"Hello," she croaked, clearing her throat. "Hello?"

"Laura, this is Shirley."

"Shirley, what's wrong? What time is it?"

"Oh, I know it's late, and I'm really sorry, Laura, I really am. But I've got to talk to you, I've got to." She spoke rapidly, clipping her words off.

"Has something happened to Wendy?"

"No, I mean not that I know of. It's me, Laura. Something's happened to me. I've got to talk to you."

Laura glanced at the clock: 4:15. "OK, fine, look, let me splash a little water on my face. I'm kinda groggy. I got in a couple of hours ago."

"I know, I know. I called your secretary, Laura. I've been

trying to get a hold of you all day. I don't know what to do. I don't want to bother you. I know it's awful to call, but I had to."

"Sure, that's OK, Shirley. Take it easy. Let me wake up here, and you can tell me what the problem is. I'll be glad to help."

"I—I can't talk about it on the phone. I'm at home."

"What do you mean?"

"Well, I'd rather not," she said evasively. Her panic seemed to be subsiding.

Christ, Laura thought irritably. Why call me in the middle of the damn night? She checked her anger. I'm tired, I must be fair, I must be calm, she told herself. "Well, where then? Would you like to come in first thing in the morning?"

"I've got to work. I know I'm bothering you, Laura, but I don't know who else to go to."

Laura took a deep breath and metered it out in short little bursts. "You're not bothering me, Shirley. Now where can I meet you and when? How about coffee or something before you go to work?"

"Oh, that would be great." It was as if Shirley Towne had been leading her to that very suggestion. Laura had lifted the burden of decision from her. "It would have to be early. I'm sorry, but I can't help it."

"What time?"

"Around seven. Is that too early?"

God, Laura thought, anytime's too early when you get in at two in the morning. "No, that's fine. Where? How about the coffee shop in that hotel right across from your building there. What's the name of that place?"

"The Winston."

"Yeah, the Winston. I'll meet you there at seven. Don't worry, Shirley. Whatever it is, we'll work it out together."

"Oh, Laura, I love you. I don't know what I'd do without you. You're the only real friend I have. Thanks, thanks so much."

"It's OK. Everything will look better in the morning. Try to get some sleep and hang in there. I'll see you soon."

"All right. Thanks for being there, Laura."

"You bet, see you soon."

She hung up and reset her clock in time for her appointment with Shirley. It was the clinging that repelled her. Laura tried to hide under the covers, but it was too hot. She threw them off and lay naked on the cold sheets, but soon she was shivering. She pulled the top sheet over her, but the bottom had pulled out and made her feel unbalanced. She got up, remade the bed and climbed back inside.

Laura believed that with practice the mind could be controlled like any other part of the body, and by concentrating, she could transport herself back to the *Laura J.* This time, she determined, they would be at anchor in some peaceful cove, gently swinging on a buoy in the early morning.

A light mist would cover the calm water; far away came the mournful call of a foghorn. She was at peace. She felt him pushing against her. "No," she protested irritably, "I want to sleep." But in spite of her protest, the surge of desire tingled in her legs. She reached for his penis. It wasn't there. Nothing but hair and the slippery hot feel of a woman's vagina. She pulled back horrified.

Shirley Towne pressed against her. "I'm sorry," she whined, "I know I'm bothering you, but I'm so cold. Thank God you're here, Laura." She reached out for her, pressing her soft belly into Laura's hand.

Laura's back was to the side of the boat. I'll sleep like this all night long if I have to, she vowed. "It's OK, Shirley, I understand, but don't crowd me." Laura didn't want to tell Shirley she was afraid of her advances. She didn't want to hurt her feelings.

"I won't bother you. I'll just stay here a while. If I could get close to you, I'd feel better. I won't do anything, I promise."

"It will all be better in the morning," Laura told her, feeling like a hypocrite. The air in the cabin was close. She tried to call out to Jim, but there was no sound.

"Oh, thanks, Laura," Shirley murmured.

I'll stay awake, Laura thought. It's the only solution. Damn Jim and his stupid seven hours.

The hand was between her legs. With a surge of panic

mixed with overwhelming sexual desire, Laura pushed her away. Panicked, she vaulted out of the bunk and ran naked onto the upper deck, slippery with dew.

Jim was standing in the bow, his back to her, staring off into the mist. "Jim!" she cried, stumbling toward him. He would save her. She needed a man to make love to; it was wrong to love other women. "Save me," she cried out to him.

When he turned, it was Jack Towne. He looked handsome in his heavy Norwegian sweater and yellow southwestern boots. "I know the problem," he said quietly. "She wants to get too close to you. Shirley's a great little gal, but she hangs on."

"I am not a homosexual," Laura cried indignantly, forgetting she was naked.

"Of course you're not," he said reassuringly. "Nobody would ever think that, Laura. My God, you're the most beautiful woman I've ever seen." His electric blue eyes flashed.

Laura awoke with a blinding headache, her hand between her legs, and the alarm buzzing angrily. She sleepwalked into the bathroom, went straight into the shower, and stood under the hot water. She missed her cats. It was so lonely to wake up alone.

Laura could remember the edges of her dream, still feel the tingle of desire. It was symbolic, of course. She had gotten angry at Shirley for calling her and in the dream Shirley had become mixed up with that horrible Beth Blake who wanted to commit the ultimate imposition on Laura—to use her body.

She leaned her head against the wall and listened to the roar of the shower water. The details of the Wendy Towne dream were much clearer and so was the explanation. The sight of Wendy had profoundly affected her, and the black taxi driver was the first handy villain. What a nightmare, Laura thought, rubbing herself pink with the washcloth until her skin hurt. And the greatest shock of all was finding Jack Towne standing in the bow of *Laura J.* where only Jim McClay should be.

The dream followed her around the room, and as she

dressed, bits and pieces came to her at strange moments. Reaching in the closet for her coat, she remembered Ruth with her father's deer rifle. It was 5:45, and Laura was not looking forward to meeting Shirley.

On the way out, she went through her messages and found one from the producer of "Family Line", asking her to call "ASAP—Urgent." He was worried about having no tape in the can for next Sunday. She scribbled a quick note to Barb and went out into the darkness.

It was still raining, and Laura knew that when dawn came it would be sullen and gray. Nothing moved; everything dripped. The Volvo was freezing inside, and the seat was wet where the window leaked. The battery was dead from sitting for three weeks, so Laura hiked to the main road and caught a bus.

She felt tired but calm. The body scrub had cleared her mind as well. She had to get busy, she had to get moving, she had to make progress.

Usually when she rode the bus at mid-morning, the passengers were businessmen and early shoppers. At six A.M., it was an entirely different group. These were the people that unlocked the doors, made the coffee, swept the sidewalk, fired the boilers, turned on the lights, warmed up the engines.

A woman in a white polyester pantsuit climbed aboard, patting the driver on the shoulder as she passed down the aisle. "Hello, Al, how's the dog?"

"Had puppies," the driver said. "Want three?" He followed her in the rearview mirror. She sat down opposite Laura.

"Lord no. Three? Quite a litter. How's your arthritis?"

"Good as can be expected. Doctor gave me some new medicine to try," he said over the roar of the diesel engine. "That always helps for a while."

The woman had a sixty-year-old face. She pulled off her raincoat. Her body was about thirty-five. Laura Jordan vowed to run faster and harder.

At 6th and Main, the sidewalks were already filling with people: men carrying briefcases and black umbrellas, women with plastic rain hats, purses held firmly under their arms. The bus doors hissed closed behind her as she stepped off.

A slender white boy in a tattered leather flight jacket, his hair in corn braids, stopped in front of her. He was soaking wet, his nose was running, and he was crying. The tears dripped down his day-old beard. "Oh, God," he lisped, "they're so mean to me. They love me and leave me, and now I don't know where to go."

"You must be freezing," Laura said, uncertain about what he wanted. His cheeks had been rouged, but only flecks remained. When he talked his hands fluttered like delicate wings not strong enough to lift him out of his sordid condition.

"Nice lady, where to sleep? Where to go?" His black pants clung to his pipe stem legs.

"There's a youth hostel at First and Senecca," she told him. "Here, buy yourself some breakfast." She gave him two dollars and started walking.

"Oh, thank you, lady," he enthused, lisping until the spittle flew as he minced along beside her.

She picked up her pace, heading for the red fluorescent Winston Hotel sign hung out over the sidewalk and left him behind. At the entrance, a man in a heavy mackinaw and pile cap with a hand-lettered sign reading "Be Saved Sinner" bellowed at her. "Have you listened to the words of Je-sus-Christ, sister? Je-s-us will save you."

"Not this morning," she said, smiling. He had a voice like a foghorn.

"Then it's not too late," he said slyly, smiling back and handing her a leaflet.

"Thank you." Laura stuffed it into her raincoat pocket.

The Winston was an old brick hotel catering to senior citizen bus tours, salesmen on the way up or down, minor league athletic teams, and oriental businessmen. There was a pile of brown duffel bags in the lobby with crossed hockey sticks and "New Westminster Eskimos" stenciled on the side.

She stepped down into the coffee shop, down into a room lit dimly with hanging lamps, their bulbs shaped like candles.

The central feature of the coffee shop, a low self-recycling waterfall illuminated by dayglo colors in a fake rock grotto, filled the room with vague patterns of multicolored lights and a constant gurgling. The palm trees in each corner were plastic, and there were miniature Canadian and American flags mounted on the tables.

The New Westminster Eskimos sat at the far end of the room next to the juke box. Shirley Towne waited at a small table along the wall across from the waterfall, smoking nervously.

Laura waved and picked her way over through the empty tables, feeling slightly unsteady when the heavy carpet sank under each step. Rod Stewart ground out of the jukebox.

"Hey, missy," an ice hockey player yelled at the waitress, "how do you turn this thing up?"

Shirley looked physically sick and seemed to have aged in the three weeks Laura had been gone. She put down her cigarette in an ashtray overflowing with butts and rose to greet her. Laura hugged her, recalling for an instant the strange dream, but quickly put it out of her mind.

"It's good to see you, Shirley," she said sincerely.

They sat down, and Shirley picked up her cigarette. "I'm awful, calling you like that. I shouldn't have done it," she said quickly.

"Let's forget it. I'm here; you're here. Things will get better."

"Oh, Laura, I hope so," Shirley said in a defeated voice, grinding out the cigarette.

"They will. Say, I didn't get a chance to tell you. I saw Wendy and, of course, met Ruth."

"Oh, yes." Shirley wasn't looking at her. She seemed to be thinking about something else.

Laura went on to describe the meeting, leaving out the worst aspects of Wendy's appearance and stressing she was getting professional counseling from the county. Laura took a little less care with Ruth. "She's an alcoholic and like all alcoholics, you really can't put too much stock in what she says."

"I knew she was a drinker, but I didn't know how bad,"

Shirley commented without interest.

"I do think Jack ought to go down there as soon as possible to visit her. I think that's very important."

"Jack won't be home until this afternoon."

"He's in Boise again?"

"Yes."

The waitress came by, and Laura ordered a grapefruit and coffee. She urged Shirley to eat, but she wanted more coffee. Shirley Towne had a bad case of the shakes. Her cup rattled against the saucer when she picked it up.

Rod Stewart repeated "Do ya think I'm sexy?" A boy, with a neck bigger than his head and ears that stuck out like doorknobs, was feeding quarters into the jukebox and pounding out the time with his fist on top of the machine.

"I—I wanted to talk to you before he came home," Shirley said timidly, fumbling with another cigarette.

"Tell me about it."

"I don't know where to start," Shirley replied.

"At the beginning or wherever you feel comfortable."

Shirley pulled out a cigarette and rolled it along the tablecloth.

"Well, I sometimes feel like I'm doing it all. That's not fair, I suppose, but that's the way I feel," she said quietly.

"Doing what? The housework and taking care of the kids?"

"That," she said lighting a cigarette, "and more."

"Why don't you tell me about the 'more'?"

"Mostly it's that Jack's never there. I mean I know he has to work too, but I end up trying to do it all alone. I pay the bills, I do the housework, mostly alone."

"The children don't help?"

"Chris takes care of herself pretty much, and, you know, she kept house before Jack and I got married. But it's like she resents me doing it, and she won't help me."

"Have you asked her about it?"

"Yes." Shirley exhaled a cloud of smoke with a quick nervous puff toward the dark ceiling.

"What did she say?"

"That she took care of herself, and she didn't have time to

do other things."

"Has Jack talked to her?"

"That's just it. I've asked him, but so far, he hasn't, or at least he hasn't told me. I don't think so because Chris isn't acting any different. And that's another thing. Jack's always asking me what time she comes in. Is she out with a boy? All sorts of things that he never asks Chris. It's like he expects me to find out for him."

"Well, that's something you need to get straight with Jack. You've got a very tough situation here, particularly with kids that age plus the way their mother walked out. They've had to cope with a lot, and then you come along. You're younger, and you're not their mother."

"I know."

"What about Rob?"

"He won't do a darn thing unless I get angry, and then he does it, but he won't talk to me afterward—sometimes for days."

"He's trying to punish you."

"For what?" she said, a flash of anger showing in her dark eyes. "Being me?"

"That and taking his mother's place. I think Rob misses his mother very much. She left him at a critical time in his development."

"Oh, I know it's not his fault. Honestly, Laura, I love Rob like my own, I do. I'd do anything for that boy. It's not from lack of trying on my part."

"I know it isn't, Shirley, but sometimes all the love and good intentions in the world won't get things straightened out. You and Jack need to have a clear understanding of what you're dealing with here, and I think you're going to need some help doing it."

"You mean counseling?"

"That's exactly what I mean, particularly in light of the incident with Wendy. If not with me, then with somebody else. I'd be glad to recommend several good people."

A shadow crossed Shirley's face. "Oh, if it was anybody, Laura, it would be you, but there's something I've got to talk to you about right away. Something personal."

"Let's talk about it then."

Laura wasn't counting but estimated Rod Stewart must be on his twelfth rendition of "Do ya Think I'm Sexy?" for the New Westminster Eskimos. The dayglo falls roared in the background. Her coffee had gone cold.

"I—I get calls from people," Shirley stammered uncertainly. "Like I got one the other day about the bill for Jack's flying lessons. The man, whoever he was, got really abusive. I tried to tell him he'd have to talk to Jack because I've never seen the bill."

"What does Jack say?"

"He says he'll take care of it." Shirley paused, fumbling with her cigarette package. Laura looked closely at her. "Is there something else bothering you?"

Shirley Towne found no cigarettes in her empty pack. She crushed it and rolled it in her hand. "Yes." She was blushing heavily. "I'm sorry, I'm not used to talking about personal things, you know?"

"Like sex?"

"Yes."

"It's a tough subject for most people, Shirley. I know it's hard for me too. But sometimes it's necessary. You have to trust the person you're talking to." Laura was saying one thing and thinking another. She was thinking about finding her hand on Shirley's soft belly in her dreams.

Shirley Towne squeezed the cigarette pack tightly. "The thing is, Laura," she said, looking at her, "I'm pregnant."

Laura Jordan quickly reviewed all the things she had imagined Shirley might say, and then she laughed. "Why, Shirley, that's wonderful, isn't it?"

She smiled shyly, her face still red. "I think so, yes."

"What's the problem?"

"I haven't told Jack."

Laura allowed herself to relax and stretched her legs under the table. She was finally getting hungry. The New Westminster Eskimos were paying their bill. Rod Stewart had finally quit. A bus started outside the hotel.

"Shirley, I think you'd better tell him," she said easily.

"I'm afraid to."

Laura brought her hand up quickly to her face and ran a finger along her lower lip. "Why?"

"Because Jack doesn't want any more children."

"Did he say that?"

"Yes, even before we were married. He thinks he's got enough."

"What do you think?"

"I love Jack's children, but they're not like children of my own."

"You want children of your own?"

"Oh, yes, I guess I've always wanted that. I was willing to wait until his were grown."

"It looks like things got away from you, Shirley."

"Jack's going to be upset."

"You'll have to work that out. Really, it's not the end of the world. He can hardly be all that surprised. Are you still a good Catholic?"

Shirley Towne blushed again. "Do you mean do I use birth control?"

"Yes."

"I would if he wanted to, but he doesn't." She stopped and looked at the tablecloth where the twisted cigarette pack lay. "He says it doesn't feel good."

"What doesn't feel good?"

"You know," she stumbled, mortally embarrassed now, "for him. The condom spoils it, he says."

"But Shirley, there're pills and creams and shields and vasectomies and all kinds of things."

"I'm afraid to take pills. I've heard so many bad things about them," she said miserably. "And I guess as far as the rest of that stuff goes, I'm still a Catholic. I was raised a Catholic."

"There's nothing wrong with that, Shirley, nothing at all. It's just that you and Jack have gotten yourselves into a little bit of a jam here. I'm afraid it's a classic case of failure to communicate."

"I know," she said sadly.

"You've got to tell him."

"I know."

"The way to do that is say, 'Jack, I've got some good news

for you!'" Laura looked for the waitress, but she seemed to have disappeared along with the hockey players.

"But what if he doesn't think it's good news, Laura? What if he doesn't want me to have the baby?"

Laura pinched her nose between her thumb and forefinger. The long tour was catching up with her, and she needed another cup of coffee in the worst way. "That would upset you terribly, wouldn't it?"

"Oh, yes. I don't think I could stand that."

Laura sighed. "I'll tell you what. Would you like me to come out to the house tonight when you tell him, sit down with you both and talk it through?" She felt compelled to make the offer while at the same time she knew it was the wrong thing to do.

"Oh, would you, Laura? That would be wonderful."

I would, Laura thought, angry at herself for making the suggestion, but I don't know why. She had just canceled Jim McClay's surprise dinner.

"Oh, gosh," Shirley said, jumping to her feet, "I'm going to be late for work. I am late. Where's the bill?"

"Don't worry. I'll take care of it."

"Oh, thanks, Laura. I'll never be able to thank you enough."

As they embraced, Laura felt the line between reality and her dreams wavering, the Shirley Towne who wanted to be close to her in the dream becoming the Shirley Towne who was pressing against her now.

Outside, the bus revved its engine. "In your spare time today," Laura told her, "you'd better start thinking of names. Is it going to be a boy or a girl?"

"A girl," Shirley said firmly, her face glowing pink, "it's going to be a girl."

After paying the bill, Laura went into a phone booth in the lobby and closed the hinged doors. The pile of duffel bags was gone and so were the New Westminster Eskimos. She was not looking forward to telling Jim their dinner was off.

From his Seattle office, she got the number where he could be reached in Portland. It was an odd sensation, she thought as she dialed, feeling her dreams intruding on reality. The telephone rang. It's the tour and lack of sleep, she told herself.

Mr. McClay was there but not available a crisp female voice in Portland advised her. He was in conference.

"Please tell him Laura Jordan is calling."

"I don't know if I can do that."

"Sure you can," Laura said warmly. "Just walk in the conference and tell him."

"I'll try," she replied reluctantly.

It was a revelation that came suddenly and with great force. The hand on the belly was to show her Shirley was pregnant. It was not a homosexual advance at all. It was a sign of what was growing inside. Of course, she thought with relief as she waited for Jim to come on the line, that's why the touch was so warm and life-giving.

And it had to be part of the reason she'd so readily suggested going out to their house tonight against her better judgment. Jack had been standing in the bow alone while Shirley was clinging to Laura below deck. That wasn't right. Jack and Shirley had to be together at a time like this. It was Laura's role to effect that joining.

If he was angry at being interrupted, he didn't let it show. On the contrary, he sounded overjoyed to hear from her.

"The roses were beautiful," she told him. "It was a very thoughtful thing to do."

"I'm glad you liked them. Hey, listen to this. My sister's basketball team won. They snapped a five-game losing streak. She scored twenty points. Twenty points, can you believe that?"

"That's great!"

"God, Laura, I was so proud of her. I wish Dad was here to see it. He always said she'd outshine us all."

"Tell her congratulations for me. We ladies need a lot more like her."

"Oh, I will. You know, Laura, seeing her out there reminded me of him, Dad, I mean. I never noticed it before. She's got that same determination he had, you know, the way he used to stick out his chin and dare somebody to tell him he was wrong. Her chin's a little smaller, but she puts it right out there the same way."

"You're starting to sound like a regular feminist," she laughed uneasily, knowing she was going to dampen his enthusiasm when she told him about dinner.

"Honey, I've always been a feminist, maybe a little more now that my sister's grown up. Say, are you all right? You sound a little funny?"

"Fine, fine. It was a hard trip."

"How's the Towne girl?"

"As good as can be expected." The cab driver's face passed through her mind. That's not real, she reminded herself sternly, the cab driver didn't do anything. "Not good, actually. She's in bad shape mentally."

"I'm sorry to hear that."

"Yes. I feel awful about it. Jim?"

"Yes?"

"I'm going to have to cancel our dinner tonight. I've got to go see the Townes—it's important."

He paused. "OK," he finally said, "how about Thursday or Friday?"

"That would be nice. I'll let you know. You're not disappointed?" She knew he was; she could tell by his voice.

"Not as long as I get to see you soon."

"We'll make it soon, I promise. You better get back to your conference."

"Yeah, I will in a minute. Laura, I don't want to give you advice about your work, but are you sure you're not getting too involved with these folks? I mean you can only carry so much of a load for other people."

She considered telling him about the dream, how powerful it was and the odd sense of reality that clung to it. She thought about telling him how she'd reached out for him and found it was Jack Towne instead. But she didn't.

Jim McClay was not a dreamer. "No, I think I'm doing the right thing," she said.

"You're the best judge of that, honey. Just be careful. I love you. See you tomorrow maybe."

"Tomorrow," she said.

Chapter 12

Rob Towne was under Shirley's Pinto, pulling the transmission while the tape deck in his Corvette, parked just outside the garage, blared hard rock into the rainy night. It was freezing on the dirty cement floor, and his fingers were so numb he couldn't feel the cuts that oozed blood through the black grease.

"Hold it steady," he told Blue Boy who squatted by the side of the car with the trouble light.

"I'm doing the best I can," he said. "I'm freezing my ass off."

"Tough shit. It's no fun down here either," Rob growled, fumbling for a ratchet wrench.

"Oh, I know; poor Robby is covered with ugly dirt."

"Shut up and hold the light."

Rob Towne attacked the bolts with an adolescent fury, twisting on his side for leverage, powering them out with his strong arms. He was furious at Shirley for insinuating he hadn't done what his father asked him to do—fix Shirley's junky car. "I'd get me a new car," he'd told her.

The quickness of his stepmother's anger shocked him. "I can't afford a new car, Rob. I'm too busy paying for yours. Didn't that ever occur to you?" And with that, she'd burst into tears and rushed into the house.

"Tich, tich," Blue Boy had said, following her with his hard eyes. "I think your stepmommy has the rag on."

Rob Towne grabbed him by the front of his torso-hugging shirt and told him to shut his filthy mouth. At first, he was bewildered at her outburst, and then it occurred to him perhaps there was a chance Shirley actually liked him so he was now under the car that wasn't worth fixing.

He was also angry with his father for being gone when Wendy needed him. He got physically sick if he thought about what had happened to his sister, so he tried to blank it out. But to do that he needed Blue and his assortment of magic pills and his stash of weed. And Rob hated himself for what he did to get the dope, but William Blue loved it. He loved it right in the ass and the harder the better.

The ratchet stripped off a worn bolt, and Rob's hand smashed into the sharp undercarriage. "Goddamn son-of-a-goddamn-bitch." He threw the wrench as hard as he could, barely missing Blue's narrow face poking under the car. It careened off the metal workbench at the far end of the garage.

Blood gushed from his hand. "You almost hit me with that thing," Blue scolded him.

Rob Towne slammed his hand into the undercarriage with all his strength. He slammed it again, each blow making a dull, flat splatting sound. Then he stopped, feeling the excruciating, welcome pain.

Breathing hard, he stared at the dirt-and-grease-encrusted frame. Most of all, he was furious for hurting himself in a stupid asshole ski race to show his father he was a man. He didn't give a shit if he was a man. Rob Towne wanted only one thing out of life. He wanted his mother back. "Give me the wrench," he ordered Blue.

"Will you throw it at me again, Robby?"

"Just give me that goddamn wrench and shut up."

"Touchy, touchy. Dr. Blue's got a little white pill for that."

Rob's hand was beginning to throb. He examined it in the low wavering light. It might be broken, he thought. That would help keep his mind off Wendy for a while.

"Hello, under there." It was a woman's voice. He turned and saw a pair of soft leather boots, stained around the bottoms by the rain.

"I need the wrench," he said stubbornly. He knew the

voice. It was Laura Jordan, and the tall blond made Rob Towne squirm everytime she looked at him.

"Here," she said, kneeling down on the cement and handling the silver ratchet to him.

"You'll get your clothes dirty." He didn't look at her. Her eyes probed: soft cat eyes that knew everything. He got breathless when she looked at him.

"What did you do to your hand? There's blood all over."

"Nothing," he replied, happy she'd noticed. He pulled hard on the bolt again. "Ahhh," he groaned. Pain shot through the hand.

"Rob," she said, sounding even more concerned this time. "That looks pretty bad."

He kept right on cranking. The bolt was coming loose. He pumped the handle as fast as he could.

"He did it himself. It's his own fault," Blue said contemptuously.

"I don't care how it happened," Laura told the boy with authority, "it's got to be looked at."

Rob had the bolt out; the whole transmission was loose now. Maybe it would fall on him, he hoped, right on his chest. That happened to a boy in his class last summer except, he thought sadly, it was a differential not a transmission. Differentials were a lot more dangerous. "You get out of there," she was saying, "or I'll come in and get you, young man."

He came slowly, reluctantly. His blue jeans were slippery with grease, T-shirt torn and plastered to his back with sweat. Two garden hose-size blue veins pulsed in his biceps. The hand was dripping dark red blood.

"You come in the house with me," she said firmly. "Where's Shirley?"

"Inside. I'm all right."

"We'll see about that."

This close, he could smell her. Laura smelled like fresh flowers. Her light-colored slacks were stained at the knees. "You got dirty," he pointed out, wanting to stay close.

"So I did," she laughed. "You don't look like you've been

on a picnic yourself."

He turned, and before he could stop himself, he was looking directly at her. How long had she been standing by the car? he wondered. Behind her, Blue gave him a wink and wiggled his ass. Rob ignored him.

"Shirley told me you went to see Wendy in Eugene," he said, trying hard to find something to look at beside her eyes. He found it difficult to meet her steady gaze. He tried her mouth. The full lips were moist, her tongue was bright pink.

"Yes, I did visit her."

"Is she OK?" Rob could see there was nothing between Laura Jordan's white ruffled blouse and her bare breasts. His mother had breasts like that.

"No, she's not. She's been through quite an ordeal."

"Yeah," he said. The fury boiled in him. He wanted to slam into the wall, to run at it head down, but they were already in the kitchen.

"Laura," Shirley said, surprised to see her. She was holding a stack of empty aluminum TV dinner trays.

"I meant to come in the front, but this mechanic here needs some attention." She pointed to his hand.

"My God, Rob!" Shirley Towne dropped the trays with a clatter. "What have you done?" Blue stood in the kitchen door, watching the two women.

"Nothing," Rob grunted.

"Let's get you cleaned up. Oh, Rob, it looks terrible," Shirley said, her voice full of motherly concern.

"Do you need my help?" Laura asked.

"No, why don't you go in the living room and keep Jack company. We've been expecting you. This will take a minute."

As Laura turned, she noticed Blue swinging the kitchen door shut and disappearing into the garage. The boy moved, she observed, like the little sneaky weasel he was.

It was the same living room, but there were no longer newspapers on the couch. It had been picked up and vacuumed. Laura could still see the marks where the wheels pressed down the shag. Jack looked tan and fit. He bounced up, took her hand in his, and gave her a light kiss on the cheek.

"It's wonderful to see you, Laura."

"Likewise," she said startled. "I brought your son in for a little first aid. He smashed his hand under the car."

"Nothing serious I hope?" Jack smelled of whiskey. He motioned her to a chair and resumed his seat on the couch.

"I don't think so," she said, sitting.

"Good. I asked Rob to look at Shirley's car. We could take it to the Ford dealer, but you know how those guys are. Besides, Rob's darn handy with tools. It doesn't hurt to have a second occupation in this day and age."

"No, I guess not."

"Would you like an after-dinner drink? Have you had dinner?"

"No, thanks, and yes, I've had dinner. How are you, Jack? You're looking great."

"Thanks." He smiled modestly, his heavy face crinkling. "It's unavoidable in the ski business to get in the sunshine. T.R. and I—Timberlake that is—made a little on-site inspection at Early Winters."

"How did it go?"

"We're in first-class shape. Absolutely first-class shape. I was a little worried there for a while. It seems when you change ownership like this you have to get renewals on the permits from the Forest Service, and T.R. isn't putting up any money until we've got those permits. You can hardly blame him; he didn't get rich by being careless."

"But you've worked that out?"

"Yes, we had a great meeting with the regional director in Boise. They'll have to hold a public hearing over in Wilson, but he assured us that's just a formality and then we're on our way."

"Terrific." His resonant voice, so full of confidence, seemed to roll out of him. And draped on the couch, relaxed and tan, he looked like a man who knew his dreams were about to come true.

"I'll tell you, Laura, the day we flew over to Early Winters I flew T.R. in one of his planes. Anyway, God it was a gorgeous day. You know that blue sky over there? Of course, you do. Well, it was bluer than blue." He rubbed his face, making a scraping noise as he ran his hand down one cheek and up the other. "Just like the French Riviera. And dry? You could see the plumes off the skiers for a mile. It was magnificent."

"I'll bet it was." There was absolutely no sensation Laura Jordan had ever experienced like flying through deep powder, and the picture Jack described started her imagination going. Powder was a thrill of the first order, a clear, cold pure lift that drove you right out of your skin into ecstasy.

Jack sipped his drink. "And incidentally," he leaned forward, lowering his voice, "before Shirley gets in here, I want to thank you for going by to see Wendy. It really meant a lot to Shirley. Honestly, Laura, she was beside herself. I've never seen her that way."

"I was pretty upset myself."

"Sure you were. We all are, but your going down there meant a lot to us, all of us."

"Hello, Miss Jordan." Chris Towne announced herself formally. She was dressed for the weather in a belted raincoat and peaked yellow rubberized hat. "How is Wendy?"

"She's had a severe trauma, Chris. She's doing her best, but she's extremely withdrawn."

Chris's face was a picture of serenity and control. "I'm going to go down and see her as soon as I can get a couple of days off."

"I think that would do her a lot of good, Chris. The sooner the better. She's getting professional help. The county down there has a very fine program, but having people that love her around is always good."

"I would have gone sooner, but I couldn't get off." Chris stood very straight. She didn't look at her father.

"We all have commitments, Chris," Laura said kindly, "as long as you go, that's what's important. Wendy needs all the love you can give her. She doesn't have much else to hang onto."

"Well," Chris said, "I've got to go."

When the door shut behind her, Jack turned to Laura. "Do you realize that girl's out of high school already?" he asked her, his voice quiet and low. "She graduated this week in mid-term. She's going to college. She's only seventeen." He ran a hand over his fleshy face. "Where does the time go, Laura? It seems like she was in grade school only yesterday." Jack stared at the closed door. "I worry about her," he said very slowly. "She's so serious about college and this doctor thing, she's neglecting her swimming. And after what happened to Wendy, I don't like to think of her going clear over there to work on the bus all alone at night. She doesn't need that darn job anyway."

"Tell your son," Shirley interrupted them coming down the stairs with Rob, his hand heavily bandaged, "that he should stay out from under my car tonight. He says he's going back out there. I told him he should do no such thing."

"Sure. What the heck, Rob, hang it up for the night," Jack suggested. Rob shrugged.

"Say, can you ski with that hand, or are we going to have to put our trip off?" Laura asked him.

"I guess I can. You still want to go?"

"Sure I do, Rob. When's a good time for you?"

"Blue and me was thinkin' of goin' tomorrow night," he said, looking around the room at the objects, not the people, and holding his bandaged hand in front of him like an exhibit.

"I thought it was going to be Chris and you and me?"

"Chris has to work."

"And you want to go with Blue?"

"Blue's OK."

"All right, your car or mine?"

"I sold my snow tires," Rob said, looking at his feet. "I don't have any snow tires."

Shirley Towne walked over to the coffee table and picked up a cigarette.

"Well, I do," Laura said, "I'll pick you up at five."

Rob nodded and backed toward the hall. "You better stay on your toes, Laura," Jack kidded her, sipping his drink, "Rob is known for being quite the ladies' man up on the mountain, aren't you?"

Rob Towne turned, stumbling against the doorjamb as he went into the kitchen.

"I think you embarrassed him," Shirley said, settling herself on the couch with her cigarette.

"I was kidding. Rob gets embarrassed too easy. Heck, a big handsome boy like him attracts a certain amount of attention; that's only natural. Isn't that right, Laura?"

"Sure." Was it possible, she wondered, that Shirley and Jack didn't see how close Blue stayed to Rob. She sat down in the overstuffed chair opposite the Townes, who were side by side on the couch. It was possible, but the purpose of her visit tonight was to discuss Shirley's pregnancy, not Rob's problems. Those would have to wait.

"Well, here we are," Laura said. "Did you give him the good news, Shirley?"

"Oh, yes," she laughed uncomfortably and glanced at Jack.

He smoothly fielded the pitch. "Isn't that something? I guess I'm not as old as I thought I was."

"You should have seen Rob's hand," Shirley said loudly, changing the subject abruptly. "It had strips of skin torn off it, literally torn off. It was like he'd done it intentionally."

"Oh, Rob wouldn't do that," Jack scoffed, going back to his drink. "Still, I am worried about him. He seems a little morose. Have you noticed that, Laura?"

"I don't know if morose is the right word. Say, you two, I don't want to be the band leader here, but I was under the impression we were going to talk about you—the two of you together. And if I might suggest it, the most interesting thing going on right now is the little event occurring in Shirley's tummy.

Jack laughed. "Funny you should mention that, Laura. As a matter of fact, that's all we've been talking about since I got back from Boise this afternoon. Isn't it, Shirley?"

She smiled and nodded. "Oh, yes."

"I got in early and for once Shirley got home on time, and we've been having a great talk, Laura. Maybe the best talk we've ever had." Seeing she was about to say something, he held up his hands to stop her. "I know it's been a long time coming. You're absolutely right. What you told Shirley is one hundred percent correct. We need to get things out on the table, and that's exactly what we've been doing this afternoon."

"That's good," Laura said, careful not to commit herself any further.

"You know, I came to realize this afternoon for the first time that I've been less than honest with Shirley."

"Oh, that's not true, Jack," she protested.

"No, now wait a minute. It is true. It wasn't intentional, but that doesn't matter. I'd never explained to her why I have to stay away from home so much right now. That all my work on Early Winters has to come first because my family comes first. In the end, that's what it means."

"I can see that now," Shirley said beaming. "I guess I never quite understood it before."

"What I'm working for is a situation where we can get the family together in one place and lead a normal life," Jack added quickly. "A life where Shirley won't have to feel she's carrying the whole load. I realize that I've been asking too much of her without an explanation."

"But I haven't understood what kind of a strain he's under either, Laura," Shirley said, lighting another cigarette and drawing deeply. "And that includes his reason for asking Ruth to get Wendy while he was in Boise."

"It was a do-or-die thing, Laura," Jack said. "I mean I know that sounds callous, but the whole thing literally was going to fall through if I didn't convince T.R. Timberlake right at that very moment that the permit thing was all straightened out. If he'd backed out, no resort. No resort and I'll be back to picking up small change, and I wouldn't be able to take care of Wendy or anybody else the way they deserve to be taken care of."

"I didn't see that before, Laura," Shirley said, letting the smoke flow out her nose.

"And that's understandable because I didn't tell her," Jack

said, patting her knee. "And unless two people talk to each other, they can't communicate."

"I couldn't have said it better myself," Laura told them, pleased to be a spectator.

"Are you sure you won't have a drink, Laura?" Jack asked her.

"No thanks, I'm watching my diet this week for a change."

Jack put his arm around Shirley. "So we've also talked over the family situation. I understand Shirley's feelings about a family a lot better than I ever did before. Right, hon?" He pulled her against him. "And I think Shirley understands my feeling about trying to work out this ski resort thing and keep the family we've got together at the same time. Particularly after what happened to Wendy. I'm in full agreement with Shirley. Wendy ought to come up here to her real home. The arrangement with her mother was never meant to be a permanent thing."

"I don't know if that would be a good idea," Laura said. "My suggestion would be that you visit her down there first."

"But, Laura, Wendy belongs here with us," Shirley put in a little too quickly. She leaned forward as if hinged at the waist and tamped out her cigarette in a glass ashtray.

"Shirley's right," Jack said, "this is Wendy's home."

"I think you ought to consider Wendy's condition before you make that decision," Laura warned them. "I don't want to be pessimistic, but I have to be honest. Wendy seems to have reverted to a childlike state. She needs someone to take care of her all the time, and she needs professional counseling—psychiatric counseling."

"What do you mean, can't take care of herself?" Jack Towne asked, alarmed.

"I mean she needs someone with her, Jack. She needs constant reassurance everything's going to be all right. I realize the situation may not be ideal from your point of view as far as Ruth is concerned, but I've given it a great deal of thought. Ruth does love Wendy, and, the fact of the matter is, she can be with her twenty-four hours a day if necessary."

"We all love Wendy, that's not the point," he protested.

"Ruth, well, Ruth has a problem and—"

"A drinking problem." Laura glanced at Shirley who sat pale and strained beside her husband.

"Yes, a drinking problem. That and the way I understand she's living down there," he added sourly.

"We have to do what's best for Wendy," Shirley suddenly blurted.

"Sure we do, honey, but we can take care of her here too."

"I suppose so, but who can do that?" Shirley asked him.

"Well, you."

"I have to work, Jack."

"Yeah, but between you and Chris. She could quit her job."

"That's a possibility," Laura said. "I'm not telling you what to do. I do want to make sure you take all the facts into account before you make a decision."

"We'd have to ask Chris first," Shirley said to herself.

"Sure we would," Jack told her. "Laura's right though. We've got to look at the situation and do what's right for Wendy."

"And for you," Laura added, "what's right for both of you. Don't forget yourselves here. You have feelings and needs too. And that's particularly true in light of Shirley's pregnancy."

"Wendy has to come first," Shirley insisted, holding her hands together in a praying position.

"You bet," Jack agreed. "Whatever's best for Wendy."

"That's a starting place for your decision-making process. Sometimes it even helps to write it down," Laura told them, "so you don't get confused about what you're trying to do."

"That's a good point," Jack said. "I've never thought about it that way. That's a good way of looking at it."

"And around this starting place, you might draw a circle." Laura held her hands to form an enclosure in the air. "That circle represents the boundaries of your decision-making process. Those boundaries are made up of the feelings and needs of the other people involved—you two, Chris, Rob, and, of course, Wendy."

"What do you mean our feelings?" Shirley asked, lighting

another cigarette. Her dark face was somber and attentive.

"I mean, Shirley, you must understand Jack's need to succeed with this Early Winters thing, how important it is to him as a person. And you, Jack, you've got to consider the depth of Shirley's feelings about the baby and having a family of her own. And both of you should consider Chris's plans to become a doctor and what kind of commitment she has to make. And you must consider Rob's situation too. I have a feeling that Rob may feel left out of things. He seems to be down about his accident, down on himself, and he needs both of you to love him very much."

"Oh, Laura, you're right about Rob. He seems to be hurt deep inside, and he won't let it out." Shirley's eyes glistened with concern.

"Yeah, he seems morose," Jack added reflectively. "You know, there for a while he really had a competitive edge."

"You see," Laura explained, "all these things are interconnected. You have to work them through one at a time, but everybody's got to participate. That's why I suggested to Shirley that you—the two of you—ought to consider formal counseling so you can deal with these things and work out a good foundation for the communication process."

Shirley and Jack looked at each other. "Sure, I guess we could," Jack Towne said, standing and pacing across the living room. "It's the time thing that always gets in our way. Shirley and I have really come a long way this afternoon. Haven't we, honey?"

Shirley nodded.

"Personally, now that everything seems to be working out at Early Winters, I can spend more time with Shirley. Quite frankly, I feel you've given us the basic tools we need to get this whole thing on the right track, Laura."

Shirley nodded again.

"It's a lot cheaper to work things out on your own."

"Oh, it's not that, not that at all. Believe me, no price is too high if that's what it takes. It seems this whole thing with Wendy has pulled us together. Hasn't it, Shirley?"

"Yes, it has. But you know, Jack, it might not hurt to sit

down with Laura once or twice," she suggested.

Jack turned at the end of the room and came back. "Well, sure. That's a good idea. Let's try to set something up later next week."

"You've got a couple of important decisions to make here," Laura pointed out. "How about the first of the week?"

"Fine," Jack agreed, putting his hands on his hips. "By then you'll have a chance to talk to Rob and maybe we could discuss that too. A kid with that much talent shouldn't be sitting around feeling sorry for himself."

"The topics are up to you," Laura told them.

"Laura," Jack said, extending his hand and drawing her up, "I want you to know that you've changed my life—our lives. You came along when we needed you the most, and I want you to know how much we appreciate it."

Shirley stood with them, and Jack put his arm around her.

"You're the only ones who can change your lives," Laura said, giving Shirley a hug and allowing herself to be drawn into an embrace with Jack.

"I hope this is all right," he said, "hugging your counselor, I mean." He felt hot against her. Shirley pressed in from the other side.

"It probably does more good than all the counseling and therapy put together," she said, laughing. "At least that's what the research says."

"Who cares about the research?" Jack said in a stage whisper. "It's a damn good excuse to get next to the two prettiest girls in the world."

Chapter 13

There were long pauses in their telephone conversation. Jim McClay was not happy to be canceled out for the second straight night so Laura could go skiing with Rob Towne. He even offered to come along and go night skiing, something he hadn't done with her all year, but Laura explained the trip was business and his presence might be inhibiting. She told him Rob was already shy enough around women without having a competing male along. She did not tell him about the third member of the party, William Blue.

"How much are you charging these people, Laura?"

"Why?" she asked him.

"Because if it's business, you ought to be charging them."

She told him she hadn't thought about it, all the while trying to keep the growing anger out of her voice. When he had clients to entertain at dinner or a sporting event, it was business for him. Now when she went skiing, he refused to accept it as her business.

What upset her even more was that she didn't know if it was business or not. Laura certainly hadn't considered charging the Townes for anything. It didn't feel right. At the moment they were halfway between friends and clients.

"Jim, I do believe you're jealous, aren't you?" she asked him, trying to find a way to avoid the uncertainty.

"I don't know," he replied seriously, "maybe I am. I do know I haven't seen you for almost a month."

That was undeniably true. "I've missed you too," she said.

"Have you?" he asked her, still serious. "Why don't you

cancel a couple of appointments then? What are you doing this afternoon?"

Laura told him she had to tape "Family Line," which was the truth. And she added, not bothering to hide her growing irritation, if he missed her so much, why didn't he cancel a few appointments of his own? Why wasn't he waiting for her when she got home instead of being in Portland, Oregon? Laura knew it was unfair, but wanted Jim to understand that her work was as important as his. Perhaps more important, she thought stubbornly.

When he finally replied to that blast, Laura knew she had succeeded in hurting him, and she felt bad about it.

"I don't know, honey, it seems like we go around and around and never get any closer to an answer," he said sadly.

"Yes, it does, doesn't it?" she answered coldly, while fighting back the tears.

"It's not just tonight," he explained, "I understand that. It's that we never get a chance to really talk to each other."

Again, he was right. "Jim, I'm already late. I've really got to run. I'll call you in the morning, OK?"

"Yes, fine. Goodbye, Laura."

She was down very low when she walked into the television studio. The producer, noting her mood, asked her if she'd like to wait until later. She told him she was ready, the guests were there, and she wouldn't cancel on them. She had no respect for people who didn't keep appointments.

Once the show got going, Laura felt much better as she always did. Under the hot lights and in front of the cameras with their winking red eyes, Laura Jordan came into her own. It was ironic, she thought, while conversing with a middle-aged, dowdy-looking woman with a teenage daughter on the rampage, I become a warm lovable caring Laura Jordan before an audience that isn't even here, an audience that exists only in my mind. It was a disturbing insight, but she let it pass. There was no time. The recording tape was rolling.

"She and this girl hitchhiked most of the way to California before they got picked up, and now she's seeing this same girl again," the woman said, twisting her hands in her lap.

"And you, quite naturally, are concerned about it happening again?"

"Yes, and I don't know what to do. You see if I tell her not to go, well, she'll probably go anyway. And by the same token if I tell her not to see this friend, she's stubborn enough to go right ahead and do it."

Laura smiled at the floor director. He smiled back from his position between cameras one and two. She turned in her swivel chair. The set looked exactly like a bright living room with two comfortable chairs, a vase of fresh flowers on a teak table between the chairs, a pot of coffee and two china cups.

"You've certainly got an excellent insight into what you're facing. The teenage years are particularly difficult, and the thing you have to remember is things will get better if you hang in there."

"That's what I'm told. Somehow facing all of this alone as a single parent, it gets very frustrating. I don't know what to do."

"Don't sell yourself short because you're a single parent. There are a lot of other single parents out there, and it may not be as easy, but you can cope. Now, tell me how you see this situation. Do you have any ideas?"

"I've tried to tell her about the dangers of hitchhiking. I told her I can't permit it to happen again even if I have to lock her up."

"That's certainly sound advice. In fact, I have some very dear friends whose daughter was attacked while hitchhiking. I can tell you from the personal experience of seeing this girl, your fears are well founded."

"It's with this other girl where I have the trouble. I have certain standards of behavior, but this girl is such a bad influence . . . I don't know."

Laura swung back in her chair. The cameras obediently followed. The show was going smoothly. The whole crew was working well together. These taped portions were used during live Sunday night broadcasts in between the segments where she took telephone calls.

"First, you've got to stick to your standards; that's very important. And you're doing the right thing by letting your daughter know what those standards are and that you expect them followed."

"Yes," the woman nodded, "but what about the other girl?"

"I don't think it does any good to try to cut your daughter off from the people she sees as her friends. That's one of the hardest things for parents to realize, but it's true. You cannot choose the child's friend."

She turned back and felt the cameras with her. She saw the floor director talking into his mike, saw the ghostly faces of the producer and the rest of the crew in the glassed-in control booth. "But what you can do is stick to your standards. And you say to your daughter, 'Here are the standards. I expect you in at such and such a time. I expect your school work done by eight o'clock and so forth. If you comply with these rules, you may see this girl. I trust you'."

"Yes, that's a good idea."

Laura reached over and took the woman's hand. "God only knows, this doesn't always go as smoothly as I've described it, but it's the general idea you need to keep in mind. I think you're halfway there. You see what to do. You need to be consistent in doing it."

"It's nice to know I'm on the right track, you know?"

"Sure it is, and that's the whole purpose of this program, to let you know that you, personally, can make a difference. And I can tell you there are hundreds of other people out there, men and women, thousands, with the same problem. And you've given them some excellent insight and the courage to come to grips with it."

"Oh, I'm not very brave. Sometimes it takes all the strength I have to confront it. Sometimes I feel like letting it go, you know. But I can't. I don't have much choice. Somebody's got to take care of her so I try to do my best."

"I think you're doing fine. I think anybody who has survived the teenage years—children or parents—deserves a medal. And certainly for a single parent like you, it ought to be the medal of honor."

The floor director clenched his fist, pumping it up and down. It was their private signal for a good strong closing line to end the tape. Laura Jordan faced the cameras squarely. "I'm very serious. I think this single parent deserves the medal of honor for doing her level best to preserve a life, to guide her child with all the experience and knowledge she has so that child can go on to guide her children. It takes courage to raise a family in this troubled world we live in today whether you're a single parent or a couple or a group banded together for that purpose. I think you are the real heroes and the hope of tomorrow."

The director was counting down the last seconds. They were right on the mark. "But it doesn't really matter what I think because 'Family Line' is your program. A place for you to share your thoughts with all of us. So let's go to the telephones. Here are the toll-free numbers."

Even though the actual program wouldn't be aired until that Sunday when the live telephone calls came in, Laura knew as she left the studio they had everything required for an outstanding three hours. The director agreed and told her she was a media genius. She told him it was all due to his skill and daring in producing a program the experts said nobody would watch.

She was still feeling exhilarated by the recording session when she pulled up in front of the Townes' house and honked the horn. In deference to her younger companions and the threatening weather, she had forgone her bell bottoms and opted for a cinnamon ski suit. Naturally, she would still use her White Stag hat with the bow and ear flaps. It was a family heirloom.

Rob piled in the front seat, wearing dirty off-white stretch pants, a sweater and down vest, with a pair of Scott goggles hung around his neck.

"It's snowing like crazy up there, according to the radio," Laura said, wondering if teenage boys like Rob ever got cold.

"I know," he said, "that's good."

William Blue got in back. He was in his shiny royal-blue

neoprene racing suit, and he was in a bad mood.

"How old is this car anyway?" he asked her as they headed out the freeway and across the Lake Washington floating bridge with the evening traffic. The other cars kicked up a haze of water off their tires that smeared across the windshield.

"About as old as you are—Bill. May I call you Bill? How old are you anyway?"

He snickered. "The girls call me Blue Boy," he retorted in a singsong feminine voice, "but you may call me plain Blue. Let's put it this way, I dropped out of high school several years ago in my senior year."

"Bored?" she asked, finally getting into the outside lane on the floating bridge. On one side the lake was stormy, and waves broke under the orange bridge lights. On the other, in the lee, it was calm.

"No, it wasn't much of a high. I had better things to do."

"Like skiing?" she asked him. Rob sat silently beside her, chin resting in his hand, watching the commuter traffic starting to bunch over for the Bellevue and Eastgate exists.

"Certainly," he replied, sounding pleased with himself. "And other things that concerned me more than spelling pussy cat."

"Comes in handy sometimes, being able to spell pussy cat." There were eight lanes now, and she floored the gas pedal to get around the thinning traffic. The windshield wipers slapped at the pouring rain. The skis on the car-top rack howled in the wind.

"That," William Blue retorted from the darkness of the back seat, "is a word I will never, never have to use."

Laura decided to let it go at that. Once they got beyond the suburbs, the street lights disappeared, and they were alone on the four-lane road, occasionally passing other skiers or long lines of semi-trucks heading for Eastern Washington on the evening run. Their red running lights showed up suddenly through the rain squalls and then were gone.

On the North Bend hill, it started snowing big wet, sloppy flakes that dissolved on impact. Laura listened to the welcome whine of the metal snow-tire studs on the pavement.

"Hey, anybody want to do a little number with me?" Blue asked them, extending a pack of cigarette papers.

This is a test, Laura thought, he wants to see how I'll react.

"Not in my car," she answered politely. "Smoke bothers me, all kinds of smoke."

She felt Rob looking at her in the darkness from his window seat.

"Oh, really, you don't say," Blue replied, trying to make a joke out of it. She detected the faint quavering in his voice, and knew she had scored very high.

In North Bend, they pulled off the freeway and got some chicken at a restaurant called The Nifty. Blue excused himself as soon as the waitress took their order.

"Oh, Rob, care to join me?" he giggled, nodding toward the restroom and holding up his cigarette papers.

"Naw." Rob fumbled with his goggles and looked out the window. Blue stalked off, his skin-tight uniform drawing rave reviews from some of the loggers along the counter.

"My God, look at that," one of them said loudly.

"I've only smoked grass once," Laura said, looking around the cafe. "I didn't particularly like it."

"It's OK," Rob replied, still staring out the window. The street light standards shuddered in the strong wind.

"I've always liked to feel I was in control of myself. It's a phobia I have."

The Nifty had been there ever since Laura could remember with the same dusty pull-tab prizes over the soda fountain. There was a .22 rifle wrapped in yellow cellophane and three bowie knives. The fountain was closed permanently. The pull tabs were outlawed ten years ago.

"It slows you down some," Rob said quietly. "I don't like it when I ski."

"Me neither. Skiing's enough for me." It was a small connection she had established, Laura thought, but she could build on it.

When Blue came back from the restroom, he strolled

easily, his eyes fixed on some faraway point.

"We almost ate your chicken," Laura told him.

"Oh, too bad, I hope you saved a breast for me," he said sarcastically.

"Of course," she replied graciously, biting into a crisp wing. Right across the street was a Happy Hot Dog stand. Ever since Jack had mentioned it was one of his accounts, Laura had been anxious to try one. Maybe on the way back, she thought.

As they cleared the truck stop on the outskirts of town, the snow started to stick on the highway. At first, it splattered and banged under the car, and then, as they went higher and the snow became deeper and more compact, the noise quieted to a faint hiss. They were entering a quiet alpine world where heavy stands of firs, dark and dripping below, were transformed into a wall of dazzling white that sparkled as the headlights swept across them.

There were five resorts at the pass, but only Snowcrest looked like a traditional ski area. The others were skiing supermarkets with wide flat terrain lined with perfectly spaced vertical lifts. Skiers dotted these hills like ants under the spotlights.

Snowcrest, in contrast, was hidden at the end of a narrow canyon where its Bavarian-style buildings hung on the edge of a steep ravine. It had fewer lifts than the other resorts, but they went higher, much higher, almost to the top of the peak that dominated the resort—10,000-foot Silver Star Mountain.

By the time they turned off the highway, the snow had become light and powdery. Its tiny flakes clogged the headlights and danced toward them, seeming to bounce off the hood and windshield. Condominium lights twinkled across the fresh coat of white powder snow.

"All right!" Rob said, sitting up. "All right!"

Blue didn't say anything. Since his trip to the restroom in North Bend, he had been silent.

"Looks good," Laura said, as she pulled into the parking lot and stopped.

They put their boots on in the car and climbed to the

lodge where they bought tickets from a young girl who had a tiny rose tattoo on her thumb.

"How perfectly gory," Blue remarked as they went outside.

On the first wide slope, two orange snow cats, yellow dome lights flashing and safety bells clanging, moved side-by-side up the hill, packing the newly fallen snow.

They took the first few runs on the lower lift under spotlights that gave the snow a faint pink tinge. Then they headed up the second lift to ski the top of the mountain. It was practically deserted; most of the skiers stayed on the lower slopes with the snow cats. Rob Towne skied hard and recklessly, but with a flawless assurance he would not fall. Blue was more of a stylist, but he was still faster than Laura, or at least faster than she cared to ski.

On the first run from the top, however, she noticed Blue's style was begining to disintegrate in the untracked snow. If she was ever going to get Rob Towne alone, Laura knew she was going to have to break them up. Blue's skiing, which became more tentative the deeper the snow got, offered a way.

On their second run, Laura slipped aboard the chair with William Blue. "This is terrific," she said as the hill dropped away beneath their feet, and they went gliding silently over the tall snow-coated alpine firs that clung to the steep mountainside.

"Yeah, it's good stuff," he answered reluctantly, unable to hide the fact he was panting. In spite of the cold, sweat ran down his narrow face, his scraggly long mustache drooped.

"What are you smiling at?" he asked her.

They were over a steep gorge. Long black shadows hung under the cliff where the bright tower lights couldn't reach.

"I was thinking you must be awfully hot in that suit. Don't you ever take it off?"

"Sweetheart," he said in a hard tough voice, "I never expose my precious body to strangers."

At the top, Laura Jordan made her move. They were alone on a narrow knob in knee-deep snow so dry it shifted around them in the wind.

"You guys ever skied the backside on Nationale?" she asked them.

"Yeah," Rob said.

"It's also closed," William Blue pointed out with irrefutable logic, waving a ski pole at the rope barrier held up by bamboo poles.

"Shit, it's always closed, Blue. That doesn't make any difference." Rob Towne ran his skis back and forth nervously. He seemed ready to go.

Blue did not. "Well, I'm not going down there, man. They'll kick you off the hill if they catch you." Blue was watching Laura now. She pulled her White Stag hat low over her goggles.

"There's nobody to catch you, Blue Boy." Rob checked his bindings.

"Well, you do what you want. I'm going where there's some light."

"See that, it's the moon." Rob pointed at the pale blob hidden in the thin clouds scudding low over the steep mountain.

"You'll get avalanched over there," Blue snapped angrily, his voice rising. "It's dangerous; that's why they close it. The hell with you. I'm not going." He executed a quick kick turn and skied off the ridge toward the tower lights.

"Chicken shit!" Rob called after him, but Blue had disappeared in the falling snow.

"That leaves only two of us chicken shits," Laura pointed out, careful to keep the clear note of triumph she felt out of her voice.

"Yeah, you up to this?" he asked her. "It's a total vertical."

"Rob, I like to ski out of bounds now and then. I've skied Nationale. Don't worry about me."

"I'm not worried about you. I never saw a woman ski it before that's all."

"I'm a woman, and I have. Lead on."

"Far out! All right! Let's make it!" Rob Towne said enthusiastically and ducked under the rope. "This area is closed," the orange sign, partially buried in the snow, read. "Crossing barrier may result in serious injury or death. USFS"

She caught Rob halfway down the first gentle slope, their skis hissing through the untracked snow. He was doing long lazy S's, and Laura crossed them into figure eights. He had incredible balance and control, never faltering or doubting his ability even when the pale moonlight all but disappeared.

They stopped at the top of Nationale, reputed to be one of steepest ski runs in North America. The ground broke away under their feet so sharply it was difficult to follow the slope. On a clear day under ideal conditions, it was enough to make the best skier stop and take a deep breath. At night, it was awesome.

Laura had climbed the hill once in the springtime with Jim McClay. She remembered the pounding heart, the pungent smell of pine and fir in the hot sun as she pressed her face to the ground, clinging to each bush and branch and not looking down until they made the top.

When Nationale was icy, it was unskiable. When the snow was deep, it tended to avalanche.

"It could be a little grabby in the middle," Rob panted, sighting down the long drop.

"Could be," Laura replied. Getting started, making that initial commitment was the hard part.

"Gonna go for it?" he asked, turning his yellow-lensed goggles on her. The moonlight was coming up. It was a good time.

"Sure. Why not?"

"See ya." He went up and over, driving himself into a long curving turn. Laura took a more conservative angle, but on Nationale, there were no conservative angles.

She was totally committed. There was no time to think about anything but survival, each turn became the ultimate effort, muscles pulling, the push to unweight, the feel of the lift and then down into the deep snow until it blew up into her nostrils in a choking screen of white. Toward the bottom, Laura tried to find Rob ahead of her and in looking up lost a ski tip in the deep snow.

She felt it catch and let herself go into a rolling fall, tumbling over and landing on her feet, firmly edging into the hill. It was a perfect execution of the "slam and roll" technique she learned at Jackson Hole, Wyoming, from an odd little man named Barrow.

As Nationale flattened into an ordinary ski run, Laura tried to close up on Rob, but he went on down the hill, seemingly lost in himself, cutting graceful arcs in the virgin snow, a lone figure in a rolling field of white. When he reached the trees that screened the lodge, he finally stopped.

Laura went straight after him, concentrating only on staying upright for the last hundred yards.

"God, that was really something," she said when she finally caught him.

"The best," he replied, his beautiful face dripping with sweat.

"Speaking of the best, I don't think I've ever seen it skied better, Rob." She leaned forward on her poles, taking deep breaths.

"It's my thing. It's all mine."

"You like that better than racing?"

He pulled off his goggles and wiped his face with his sweater sleeve. "Racing's for assholes," he said shortly.

"You don't like to race?"

"Never did." He looked around them at the long waves of smooth, fresh snow.

"They why do you do it?"

"My dad. He thinks it's a good idea." He cleared his throat noisily and spit.

"Did you ever try to tell your dad how you feel? That you don't like racing, that you like to ski like this?"

"He doesn't know anything about skiing or what I like to do."

"But did you ever try to tell him?" she persisted.

The air felt cold now and steam rose off them in the moonlight. Down on the highway and far away, a heavy truck shifted gears coming up the pass.

"Are you a doctor?" he asked her, brushing off his sweater.

They were both plastered with snow from the chest down. "I mean a headshrinker? Do you think I'm crazy or something? Is that why you're here?"

She laughed quietly. "I'm not a doctor, Rob, or a head-shrinker. I'm here because I like you. I'm a counselor, a communications specialist. That's a fancy word for talking. I'm here because I want to help all of you—your dad, Shirley, and your sisters get in touch with each other so you can have a better family life."

"You're a little late for that," he said bitterly, looking toward the trees. "Our family life went to hell a long time ago."

"You mean when your mom left? How old were you then, Rob?"

"I don't know. Ten, around there. I really don't remember much about it."

"But you miss your mother, don't you?"

"I guess so." The reply was muffled.

"Do you understand why she left?"

"No."

"Did you ever ask your father to explain it to you?"

"No." This time the reply was angry. He swung around. He was crying. "It's none of your business anyway. Leave me alone." He was a child in a man's body, the deep hurt showing in his reddened eyes. She stepped over toward him, lifting her skis high in the soft snow.

"Don't touch me."

"I won't touch you if you don't want me to, Rob," she said, standing beside him. "But I want you to know there's nothing wrong with a man crying when he feels hurt."

"I can't help it."

"Then why hide it? You tried to hide it at Sun Valley too. I don't think any less of you for crying, Rob."

"That was different."

"At Sun Valley? You were disappointed about losing, weren't you? Disappointed that you fell?"

"Hell, no. I was pissed off at myself for being such a jerk, for trying to be a goddamn rocket, for letting those people see me. I hated myself. I hate myself now."

"Rob," she put a hand gently on his arm.

"Don't." He pulled it away. "Why do women always want to touch me?"

"Because they care about you."

"Like hell. Look, can we go? I'm freezing my ass off."

"Lead on."

"You go first," he insisted.

Laura went down through the trees, picking her path carefully, thinking about Rob Towne as she skied. She could hear him tracking her turn for turn as they came out onto the main hill. She stopped at the top of the lower lift, and let him pull up beside her.

"It was a good run," he said awkwardly, licking his lips and looking down the hill to the lodge. Laura couldn't see his eyes behind the goggles.

"Yes. Maybe we can do it again sometime."

"Maybe."

Blue was waiting for them impatiently in the lodge, a drink on the table.

"Well, well," he said sarcastically, "how are the macho explorers?"

"Where you been, Blue, showing them how it's done on the bunny hill?" Rob shot back, kicking the snow off his boots.

"As a matter of fact, I met some very nice boys on the bunny hill, Robbie."

"Good, maybe that's where you belong."

"Oh?" William Blue arched an eyebrow and gave Laura a withering look. "And where do you belong, Rob?"

"Alone, man. All alone up there." He gestured toward the mountain. "Where I can breathe and stay away from assholes and shitheads."

"My, my, it sounds like we've had a religious conversion, Robbie."

Rob Towne slapped Blue across the face with a leather glove. The blow cracked like a pistol across the lodge.

"When I want your opinion, cocksucker, I'll ask for it."

"Rob, stop that!" Laura held his arm, but he pulled away easily.

Blue stayed on his bar stool, but she could see the thin body coiling to strike back.

"Try me, man, and I'll punch out your fuckin' lights," Rob warned him, dropping his gloves and doubling his bandaged fist.

The only sign of the blow on William Blue's face was a faint red splotch. "Well," he said evenly, "this looks like the end of a beautiful friendship."

"I don't have any friends, Blue. I never did." He turned to Laura. "Let's go," he said. His eyes were steady and unblinking. They showed no emotion at all.

Nobody spoke on the return trip until Laura finally turned on the tape deck. "Whoever is that creature?" Blue inquired sullenly from the back seat. She knew he hated her for what she'd done.

"Willie Nelson. Do you like him?" she asked politely.

"No, he can't carry a tune. I detest disharmony."

"But he has other things to recommend him, Blue."

"Such as? The lyrics are silly; they're so common. All that cowboy gibberish."

"I think there's a little cowboy in all of us, Blue. You know, the lone stranger riding off into the sunset. It's our heritage."

"I like it so shut up, Blue," Rob said moodily, not moving his head from its resting place against the window.

Blue sighed. "Oh, tragedy," he emoted, "outvoted two to one. Democracy rules. How dull."

It was the last word from William Blue. When they dropped him at his apartment, he pulled his skis off the top of the car with a clatter and stalked off into the rain.

It hadn't been her intention to drive such a large wedge between Rob and Blue, but Laura wasn't at all unhappy it turned out that way. What worried her, however, was the deep-seated anger and self-hate Rob had revealed. Clearly, Rob Towne had been seriously wounded when his mother walked out, and the only way to resolve that hurt was to have his father explain to him what had happened and why.

"I enjoyed it," Laura told him when she pulled up in front of the house. "I'm sorry you and Blue got into an argument."

"It was a bummer anyway," he said vaguely. "Thanks for skiing Nationale with me."

"It was a big thrill wasn't it?"

"Yeah," he said, opening the door and getting out into the rain. "I love it up there. It's so clean, and there's nobody to hassle you."

"You've got to learn to live down here too," she said, leaning across the seat.

Suddenly he ducked his head back into the car. "Wendy's hurt pretty bad, isn't she?" he asked her, his smooth face delicate as glass in the faint yellow glow of the interior light.

"Yes, she's been through an awful experience. She's hurt very badly, mentally and physically."

"What did they do to her, whoever it was?"

"They raped her. They repeatedly raped her and beat her up. I'm sorry, Rob, but that's the truth."

He was bracing himself on the car seat, leaning on his hands. There was fresh blood showing on the soiled bandage.

"I don't want to learn to live down here, Miss Jordan. I don't like it here."

When she got home, Laura fed the cats and looked up Jack Towne's office number. There was something she wanted to discuss with him alone before the regular session involving all three of them. She wanted to ask him why Ruth left.

"Hello," Jack's recorded voice said happily. "This is Jack Towne. We're not in the office right now, but if you'll leave your name and number at the tone, I'll call you back right away."

At the beep, Laura spoke loudly into the telephone. "Jack, this is Laura, Laura Jordan. I need to talk to you as soon as possible about Rob."

Chapter 14

The storm that swept across the Cascade Mountains left only a damp chill in the clear morning air. From her second-story bedroom window in the houseboat, Laura could see the dark silhouettes of downtown Seattle office buildings outlined by the rising sun behind them, the pale white of fresh snow on the foothills where they had skied the night before. The cats nodded sleepily on the end of the bed.

"You guys are nothing but lazy bums," she said, whipping the covers back and sitting naked on the edge of her bed.

"Hello, down there," she called into the intercom.

Barbara Adams answered promptly. "Let's have our coffee on the roof," Laura suggested.

There was a pause from the downstairs office. "Maybe you should look at the calendar," her secretary suggested, "it's still March." Fat Cat stretched lazily, turned around three times and lay back down in the pile of warm cats.

"That's the sun out there, Barb, it looks like spring. See you topside, over and out," she called back, standing and stretching in front of the window. Laura felt good. She was convinced this was going to be one of those days when everything would break her way. She splashed some cold water on her face, slipped into a vanilla-and-maroon jogging outfit and dashed up the narrow stairs to the roof.

"This is really pushing the season," Barb remarked. She was bundled up in a down jacket, her cheeks flushed with cold. A light breeze rippled through the pile of telephone messages firmly grounded to the redwood table by a rock.

Laura poured herself a cup of coffee and walked along the rail. Dead leaves still clogged the corners, and the dry stalks of last years perennials were festooned with spider webs. The smell of coffee in the fresh air was exhilarating. "Spiders," she pointed out to Barb, "that means spring is coming."

"I thought it was the opposite."

The coffee was strong, and Laura sipped it carefully as she walked, feeling the cold of the rough decking against her bare feet. The clatter of the shipyard at the far end of the lake was muffled by the light mist that hung over the surface of the water. A single scull was gliding by off the mooring, the ripples from the sleek wooden shell moving steadily outward in a perfect V. Laura waved at the rower, and he nodded to her. His long dark hair was tied back with a red bandana; his bare arms glistened.

Laura was surprised to find her legs were stiff from the run down Nationale, and she stopped to stretch her calves. She had not kept up with her regular running and weight-lifting program since she got back from Sun Valley. And it wasn't only the running program that was disorganized, she thought, it was also her whole business.

A gray-and-white sea gull came winging by, floating over the mist. He turned his head to look at her and then resumed his tour of the houseboats, looking for something to eat. The book tour had seriously disrupted her schedule, and her relationship with the Townes was the most disorganized counseling she had ever become involved in. As much as she liked them, Laura vowed that today was the day she got the Townes scheduled on a regular basis and started being a professional counselor instead of just a friend. This was particularly important, she thought, scanning the lake as she walked, because of what happened to Wendy and what she had found out about Rob Towne last night.

Back at the redwood table, Laura sat down, helped herself to another cup of steaming coffee and several English muffins with strawberry jam. She savored each bite, crunching down with gusto and tasting the rich butter and sweet jam.

"Good," she nodded to Barb and, licking a glob of jam off her thumb, began going through the mail, glancing up occasionally to watch the sailboats dodging in and out of the mist.

A sloop with a candy-striped jib tacked close in, its sails flapping and cracking in the breeze. They were Saturday morning sailors, and Saturday was Laura's favorite time on the houseboat. The steady drone of commuter traffic along the shore was missing, and in the afternoon, the lake would be crowded with all kinds of boats: long, graceful Whitebear rowing skiffs; little sailboats; and ponderous luxury cabin cruisers that came slowly along the shore, heavy diesel engines idling, pennants flying, sightseers sitting on the fantail with drinks in hand, waving to the peasants along the shore.

There was nothing interesting in the morning mail. "How's your love life?" Laura asked her secretary, ignoring the last English muffin with effort. Laura was starving. I am not starving, Laura told herself; I am thin. I will always remain at 130 pounds and be beautiful even after I turn thirty-three.

"Fine. You know, Laura, I think I'm finally entering the golden years. For a long time, all I met were losers, but now that I'm older, suddenly the world is full of nice white-haired old men with lots of money. And they seem to like a full-figured woman like me. Maybe they're through chasing and want to be comfortable for a change, you think?" She laughed and patted her graying hair.

"They can't be the ones who like to chase tall blonds because I still meet them everywhere I go."

Barb laughed, her motherly face rosy with cold. "Well, there must be a shortage of willing tall blonds then because I'm sure enjoying myself. Speaking of a hot love life, how's yours, Laura?"

"I don't know. Did Jim call?" She still felt badly about putting him off because of Rob Towne.

Barb consulted the message slips. "No, why? Did you expect one?"

"Oh, I don't know. Are you sure he didn't call?"

"If he did, he didn't leave a message. I keep telling you, dear, not to let that gorgeous handsome red-haired man out of your sight. Have you been neglecting him again?"

"Sort of."

"Laura Jordan! Life's been too easy on you. You don't know the difference between a real gold mine and one that's been salted. You don't know good luck when you see it."

"That's what you keep telling me. You're probably right. You are right. I'll call Jim myself."

"That's the spirit."

"Anything else?"

"Well, there's a call from a Mrs. Goldsborough. She says it's important."

"She's an interesting lady. Let me have that one."

"And a call from Jack Towne. He called at seven this morning. Can you believe that?"

Laured tried to hide her surprise. "Jack, at seven?"

"That's what it says."

"I'd better call him back. I'll see you downstairs in a minute."

"You mean we can go inside where it's warm?" Barb kidded her. "I thought you'd never ask."

Laura went down to her apartment, grateful for the cozy feel of the deep shag on her numb feet. The cats were gone off the bed. She consulted the slip of paper and dialed the number.

"Jack Towne and Associates," a formal male voice announced. It sounded like Jack, but it wasn't.

"Jack?"

"Just a moment, I'll connect you." She was put on hold and canned music popped on the line. It was an annoying sound, but Laura waited patiently, her feet on the unmade bed.

"This is Jack Towne," he answered in an eager voice.

"This is Laura. I got your message. As a matter of fact, I slept in, or I would have called sooner. You sure keep some Spartan office hours."

"Laura! Good to hear from you. I've been working since

the sun came up, before that actually. I was a little concerned by your message. Is something wrong?"

"No, nothing's wrong. I wanted to get together with you and talk about Rob for a little bit—before you and Shirley come in."

"Secret stuff?"

"No, Jack, it's not secret stuff. I think it would be productive for you and me to talk about Rob. I had a very nice time with him last night, but there are several things that came up that you ought to be aware of."

"Great. Fine. When's a good time? How about ten minutes, Laura? I've got something you'll want to see. It's a layout of Early Winters."

"Already? That sounds interesting. Do you want me to come over to your office?" It occurred to Laura as she talked she didn't know where Jack's office was.

"No, no. That's too much trouble. You're always running around for us. I'll bring it over there. Are you decent?"

"Yes, sort of. I will be."

"Good. See you in five minutes."

"You said ten, Jack."

"So I exaggerated. See you soon." He hung up.

Laura smiled at herself and shook her head. Her resolve to get organized with the Townes was dissolving. Already she had offered to go to his office, and now he was coming over with a layout. What was it about Jack Towne that continually kept her off balance? she wondered.

She thought about changing out of her jogging suit, but then decided not to. It was a good-looking outfit, and it was comfortable. She went into the bathroom and combed out her long blond hair, taking her time, examining her face in the mirror.

It was an interesting face, high cheek bones with only a hint of wrinkles around the corner of each eye. She stopped combing and massaged some cream into the wrinkles. The never-ending battle against the inevitable, she thought, smoothing the twenty-dollar-a-jar potion in vigorously.

Jack's enthusiasm about the model caught her by surprise,

but it would have been impolite to turn him down. Besides, she admitted, staring into her own hazel-flecked eyes, you do want to see the model, don't you?

"Yes, I do," she said aloud, going back to the bedroom where the unmade bed was occupied by Puss Puss. "Where are your buddies?" Laura asked the cat. She stared back at Laura. "Independent little bitch aren't you?" Laura groped for a pair of shoes in a closet piled high with ski boots, tennis racquets, and other sporting paraphernalia. "It's all right, kitty," she said, emerging with a pair of battered jogging shoes, "it runs in the family."

Jack Towne came down the gangplank in exactly five minutes, looking casually elegant in his designer field pants and white polo shirt. His golden brown hair was combed back, and even with a day's growth of beard, he looked like a visiting nobleman bearing a building model in front of him like a jeweled crown. Laura went out to meet him.

"My God," she said, "what is that?" She had expected plans or drawings, but this was an exact replica down to the last detail.

"It's the lodge," he said happily. "Hold the door there."

He set it proudly on Barb's desk, and they all admired the magnificent structure of steel and wood and glass that rose like a living thing from a narrow base and shot out at bold angles under the steep shake roofs and culminated in a smoked-glass solarium to catch the winter sun.

"This is beautiful," Barb told him. "I don't believe we've met. I'm the hired help around here."

Laura introduced them. Jack took Barb's hand and held it.

"I wondered how Laura got all her work done while she's out running around. I never dreamed she had such a lovely helper," he blushed without a trace of sarcasm.

"Goodness," Barb said, blushing herself, "flattery will get you everywhere, young man."

"Young man?" Jack threw back his head and laughed. "I'm going to like you, Barb."

Carefully, he picked up the model and moved it into Laura's office. "No wonder you wanted us to come down here," he said, putting the Early Winters lodge on her desk and looking out at the lake. "What a view!"

"I thought you were bringing drawings," Laura said.

"Well, this is just the first piece. There's a lot more to come including, I might add, Laura's Famous Second Landing."

"Jack, you're not serious about that are you?"

"I've never been more serious in my life. I think it's a marvelous name, marvelous. Kind of romantic, don't you think?"

"I don't know."

"I'm concerned about the food though. Renie's food was interesting, but it's all wrong for Early Winters. I don't know. Have you got any ideas, Laura?"

"Yes," she said, walking around the lodge model. "Keep it simple—salads, steaks, drinks, maybe fish, a fish of the day, and hamburgers for the kids. You've got to have something for the kids. Oh, yes, and homemade bread, hot homemade bread and spiced wine. That ought to do it."

"That sounds terrific."

"I made it up, Jack, just now. I don't know anything about the restaurant business."

"But you know what you like to eat. That's what's important."

"I suppose. Still, don't you have to figure out prices and what you can afford and what people will buy for how much? That sort of thing?"

"Laura, you've gone right to the heart of the matter. Good food, that's the key. People will buy good food, and there's darn little of it around."

She smiled at his enthusiasm. He looked young this morning, his craggy face alive with expression—surprise, excitement, intense interest, contemplation. "People will come in and eat and like it and tell their friends."

"You could barbecue the steaks and vent the smoke onto the slope. Also bake the break up there. Blast the smell out onto the hill. You'd catch ever hungry skier on the lift."

"Fantastic!" He slapped his knee. "Absolutely fantastic!

Laura Jordan, have you ever thought about going into marketing?"

"Not really. My father says my tastes are too expensive for the mass market, and I think he's right."

"He's wrong," Jack said emphatically, unable to stand still. He paced the room, hands behind him, a great bear foraging for ideas. "Besides this is not the mass market. I'm not kidding, Laura, you'd make a great marketing director for Early Winters, beautiful, vibrant, full of ideas."

For a moment, Laura Jordan actually allowed herself to think about it even though she knew Jack Towne was only making conversation. She could ski all day, live any way she wanted to live; there would be tennis in the summer. Laura knew she could make the resort a success. She could do anything she put her mind to. "You don't want a woman marketing director, Jack. You want a nice steady man," she kidded him.

"Listen, Laura, Teddy—T.R.—likes women! He adores women! And whatever Teddy says goes at Early Winters." He swung around at the end of the room and bore down on her, waving his arms wide, striding with enthusiasm. "We're going to have an absolutely first-class operation, and you, Laura, are an absolutely first-class woman."

"I'm also a woman with a half dozen irons in the fire right now, Jack."

"Oh, I realize that. I was only throwing something out. I tend to get ahead of myself sometimes, you know. It's one of my great faults. I've got it all planned in my head, and it isn't even built yet. Isn't that something?"

"I tend to do that myself."

"You do?" He sat down opposite her. "That's great. I mean I'm glad to meet somebody else that puts the cart before the horse. God, Laura, I've dreamed this thing so many ways. I can see it all. I can even see you as the marketing director. How about that for wishful thinking?"

"Yes, especially considering I have a full schedule of appointments today and into next year."

"Oh, I'm sorry," he said. "Here I am running off at the

mouth about a ski resort, and you asked me over here to talk about Rob. So let's get down to business."

"Jack, I'm as worked up over that resort as you are. There's no need to apologize. As a matter of fact, I think the design is magnificent," she said, leaning back in her chair and admiring the model.

"I'm glad you approve, Laura, but let's talk about Rob. I'm concerned about that boy."

"Well, so am I. As I told you, we had a nice time last night. But after being around him, I'm convinced Rob has a great deal of anguish stored up inside. Anguish that's hurting him. Anguish that needs to be let out."

"How do we do that?" he asked quietly, folding his big hands together.

"Well, we've got to find the cause, and we find the cause by looking at the symptoms first."

"OK, what are the symptoms?" he asked.

"I'm going to be very direct, Jack. I don't know any other way to get at it."

"Please do."

"It's been my observation that Rob has great difficulty relating to women. Have you noticed that?"

"No, no, I haven't."

"Well, I have. He's very shy with women, extremely shy. It's as if he doesn't trust them. It may even be a hatred; I'm not sure."

"Oh, not a hatred. Not a big good-looking boy like that." Jack was protesting, looking down at his hands.

"Whatever it is, I find it disturbing. Something else I find disturbing is his relationship with William Blue."

"Blue? What relationship?" He hunched his shoulders to ward off the blow. "Blue's a guy he skis with, a guy on the team." He paused. "He's not even a very good skier. They're friends; that's all."

"More than friends I think, Jack, more than friends. Blue's probably a homosexual. I know he uses drugs. I wouldn't be surprised if he was a dealer. I don't think Rob's involvement with him is a healthy thing."

He jerked his head toward her in alarm. "Now, wait a minute, hold on. Blue's a little odd. I know what you mean, but that doesn't mean he's—a queer. And the drugs—well—a little marijuana doesn't mean he's a dealer. Kids are different today, Laura." Jack's blue eyes were squinted so she couldn't see them.

"You really don't know him very well, do you, Jack?"

"No, I guess not. I'm not around that much, but my God, I never thought Rob would be involved in anything like that." He turned uncomfortably in the chair and twisted his hands.

"It's nothing to be embarrassed about, Jack. Did you know that approximately thirty-five percent of the young men Rob's age have, at some time in their lives, been involved in what might be called a homosexual experience?"

"No," his voice gurgled deep inside him, "no, I didn't."

"And besides, remember it's a symptom not the disease, so to speak. I find Rob to be a charming, talented, good-looking young man. All those things you think about him are true. But he's also a young man with a serious problem I think we better try to get at."

"Oh, I do too," he said quickly, obviously relieved to be off the subject, "you sort of caught me unprepared."

"I think it's important to get these things out in the open. Also, Jack, I could be dead wrong, don't forget that. Don't take my word for everything."

"I trust you, Laura, and it is important. I was surprised, that's all. What else? I'm tougher than I look."

Laura steepled her hands and leaned on the desk. "One other thing I'd like to mention is that I don't see the boy as the competitor you want him to be, Jack, as the competitor you imagine he is."

"I don't follow you," he said sharply, showing resentment at her probing for the first time. "First you tell me he's a queer, and now you say he's no competitor. What the hell was he doing at Sun Valley then, hanging in there with those blue-chip racers? He did darn well."

"He was trying to please you. And in trying to please you, he was hating himself for what he was doing."

"I don't follow that at all," he said abruptly, turning to face her, his eyes burning and flashing anger.

Laura felt the hostility growing, and she moved to check it. "Jack, this is not an attack. I know it's difficult. We've got to go through this to get at what's really bothering Rob. I think he's a great boy, but I think he's going to have a serious problem growing up if we don't give him a hand."

He rubbed his hands back and forth, and the dry scraping sound took on a rhythm. "I know it's not an attack. I know that. It's very hard for me to understand. I thought he liked to race."

"He loves to ski, Jack, and he's very talented. Last night we skied Nationale up on Silver Star Mountain. That's as tough as they come, and he was absolutely magnificent. I've never seen him looking so vibrant and alive, so pleased with himself—not ever."

"Maybe you're right. I haven't spent as much time with Rob as I should."

"You have other responsibilities. You also have two other children, and you raised them all under very difficult circumstances. Don't blame yourself. There's not time for that anyway. What we want to do is get at the cause and help Rob."

"Yes," he said, forcing a smile. "I can see that."

"In his case, I think the cause is rather obvious."

"It is?"

"Yes, it centers on his mother, the way she left. I don't know what you told him about that, but it seems to have hit him very hard. That's an age when a little boy is still very dependent on his mother. I don't think he understands what happened or why."

"No, that's probably true." Jack Towne held his hands quietly in front of him. "And it's entirely my fault. I couldn't bring myself to do it, to explain to a ten-year-old boy why his mother simply walked out. I know I should have tried, Laura, but it was beyond me. I didn't even understand it myself."

"What did you tell the children?" She picked up an unsharpened yellow pencil and held it between her fingers, rolling it slowly, feeling each beveled edge as it passed, acutely aware of the pain she was causing Jack Towne.

"Oh, I told them that she was going away for a while. That she was sick with a disease which she was, of course, in a way—booze. Anyway, I kind of let it go and hoped that time would take care of it. I can see now I was wrong."

"You did your best. There's no sense in second guessing what you might have done," Laura said kindly. "The important thing is that you understand it better now, and you can explain it. Rob needs that."

"Well, you're right. Over the years, I came to see it more clearly." He pulled one knee up and held it with his hands. "There was a certain element of my own pride involved too," he said, reflectively looking out at the lake where the fog was thinning to long streamers running above the water.

"Of course there was. You were hurt and abandoned yourself."

"Yes, that's right." Jack Towne cleared his throat. "It was a hell of a shock, Laura. I don't mind telling you. There I was, I thought I had a pretty good marriage, you know, not perfect but pretty good. Three wonderful kids and wham, she walks out."

"You must have had some indication it was coming."

"Now I see it. Sure. Now I do. At the time, I honestly didn't. Maybe I was blind. I must have been."

"I think it would help if we put that story together. It will be painful, Jack. I know it will be, but it's something you ought to tell Rob and Chris and Wendy. And probably Shirley too."

Jack rubbed his face with both hands, massaging the skin. "God bless Shirley, she never asked. She took me the way I was, and she never asked. You're right, Laura, they all deserve to know."

"Not so much deserve, Jack, it's a need. And I'm glad you brought Shirley up because I think that would be a good place to start when we have our first meeting—the three of us."

"And sort of use this as a time to get the story straight,

right? Before I try it out on other people?" he smiled. "I don't mean make something up, but get it down right. I've never told anyone before."

"I think it would help you too, Jack. It would be good to have it out in the open where you can deal with it."

"Sounds like a good idea. I don't know where to start."

"Anywhere you want to."

"Someplace after my birth. I was born . . ." He cleared his throat.

"We could start a little later I think." Laura laid the pencil down carefully. A seaplane went by, kicking up a cloud of spray.

"I was born poor in Kentucky, Laura. It wasn't that we didn't have a good home life, gosh, my mom was a saint, a real saint. And my dad, well, he did the best he could. But there's nothing like poor white in Kentucky, Laura. Nothing you've seen in the slums of New York or L.A. or anywhere else compares to it."

He paused and turned the heavy gold ring on his left hand. "It was so long ago, but it's still so real. My life has been a struggle to escape all that. My father worked hard, but it wasn't steady. And it wasn't until I went to high school that he got on with the warehouse there in Louisville and things were a little better. Anyway, I always had a lot of ambition, not all for myself really, more for my mom. You know, it's funny, Mom's dream was to take a vacation in Hawaii. I hadn't thought about that for a long time."

Laura watched the white clouds boil up over the hill across the lake. They were constantly changing, assuming fantastic amorphous shapes as they drifted from west to east. A small white cotton fluff would suddenly expand itself into a billowing mountain of white, dwarfing the tiny houses perched on the rim of the city.

"Anyway, I always had this dream about getting her that vacation in Hawaii. At first, I figured I'd do it playing football. Of course, the professional leagues were nothing like they are today, but still, it looked pretty good to this barefoot boy. And I worked like hell. I had talent too," he smiled shyly. His teeth were even and white. "But then I got hurt. I was going for a touchdown in the Frankfort game—or was it the Clay game? It doesn't matter. Anyway, a guy blindsided me, and that was it, out for the season. As it turned out, I was out for good."

He twisted the ring around as he talked, looking closely at it. "I guess I told you all this before didn't I?"

"Part of it."

"Well, no sense crying over spilt milk. It happened, and I still live with it." He patted his leg. "So then, I got my sights set on college. Figured I'd get a good job that way. Maybe that doesn't sound all that important to a gal like you, but it was a fantastic thing to even think about where I came from. I'm afraid my dad thought I was crazy. But I was serious, and I actually went—at least for a while—but it was hard seeing Mom getting by on practically nothing and Dad, well, he wasn't getting anywhere."

"You worked while you went to college?"

"Oh, yeah, I did everything, pumped gas, parked cars, I even was a process server for a while. Now there's an interesting job, Laura."

"I can imagine."

"Anyway, Mom got sick. It wasn't anybody's fault, but she got sick; and I had to drop out of school to help with the bills. I wasn't bitter. That was the way it was."

"She died when you were young then?"

"Yes. Cancer. There was nothing I could do. She never got to see Hawaii." His face hardened, the lines stiffened into sharp ridges. "I was pretty shook up. My dad and I had a little misunderstanding at that point, you could say. He was a good man, Laura, but sort of a plodder. He accepted everything the way it was. If he had a crummy job, well, he had a crummy job. If there was never enough money, then that was it. If Mom had cancer, well, she was going to die. He didn't cry at the funeral. That was the kind of man he was. Not a bad man, but a little short of caring sometimes. Over the years, we've buried the hatchet. I've helped him out whenever I could, financially, you know."

Now the white clouds were formed into a massive U-shaped canyon. Laura could see the crests on each side breaking away in what must have been hurricane force winds, miles in the air. A whole magnificent landscape was being sculpted by wind and changing temperatures, a sculpture to be enjoyed only for an instant before it became something else.

Jack was rubbing his hands again. Laura noticed they were never still and remembered how soft they felt in spite of their size. "That's really a long-winded way of explaining why I've always been a pusher, a driver, a dreamer, I suppose you could say. Always after something better. The best for the people I love. I let my mother down. I was only a kid, but I should have done better. I still feel that way. I left right after she died and got a job in Chicago with an ad agency there. That's where I met Ruth, and we got married.

"For a while, things went fine, but it really wasn't much of a job. It was the best I ever had, but it wasn't much. There was no future in it. It was one of those things where they used you until there's nothing left. Like my dad's job in the warehouse. But I was doing very well. I got to know some people, and I got some very good offers.

"Ruth was kind of a homebody. She didn't want to leave the security and all which was understandable. On the other hand, she sure liked to spend the money, you know? I tried to explain to her how you had to take chances, make moves if you wanted to get ahead. That the rewards went to the people who saw the future, not the people who were always stuck in the present, working away eight to five."

"Ruth didn't see it that way?"

"No, she went along, of course, but she wasn't happy about it. Mostly she was unhappy because she had to work. Heck, you can't move halfway across the country without spending money, a lot more than I made. But we were young; we could take it. But Ruth never did like it. Frankly, she missed the nightlife in Chicago. We moved quite a bit for a while, some pretty crummy little places, down to Arizona and finally on to Colorado.

"By then, she'd started to drink. I never did realize how much. I guess I was naive. But now I can see she was into it pretty heavily. I didn't have any excuse except that I was working like hell, trying to make ends meet, you know? I didn't have a lot of time to notice things like that. On the surface, everything seemed fine. The kids were happy, we were both working, we could pay the bills.

"Golly," he said, looking straight at her, the blue eyes revealing themselves. "I'd forgotten what a happy bunch of kids they were. I'd come home all beat, and they'd be out in the yard. That was when we were living in Tucson. I was partners with a guy in a little agency there, and God we were struggling. Anyway, I'd come home all beat, and the kids would be out running around in the sprinkler, stark naked, having a hell of a time. Darn, you know, we were living well then. They didn't care about money; they were having fun. It was Ruth that was getting sour on everything. She was working too, of course, as a cocktail waitress.

"Poor Ruth. Poor Ruth." Jack Towne stood up and walked over to the window. The boat traffic on the lake was heavy now that the fog was gone. Sailboats tacked back and forth in a fresh breeze. "You know, Laura," he said, his back to her, "Ruth always thought she was too good for that kind of work. She always had this idea that somebody was going to hand it all to her, that you didn't have to work for it. 'I'm a college graduate.' She used to throw that in my face."

Laura recalled her conversation with Ruth in Eugene with the snow falling on the overheated trailer. Ruth had used those exact words—"I'm a college graduate."

Jack turned back and faced Laura, his hands in his pants pockets. He shrugged his big shoulders. "But, you know, I didn't understand that. Maybe I should have, but I didn't. I didn't see any kind of work as demeaning, not where I came from. Where I came from you were damn lucky to have work at all. I don't know. Maybe that was what put her on the bottle. I do remember I wasn't as sensitive to that issue as maybe I should have been."

The sun was warming the room, the lake had turned a

deep blue. "Then I got the break I was looking for, at least that's what I thought at the time. I've gone over and over this in my head and even knowing what I know now, I still would have taken the job. It was with a big land development outfit in Colorado during the building boom down there in the Sixties. I mean everything was up for sale and being sold. I got on as vice president of public relations and advertising. Hell, we got a house in one of the best subdivisions. The company was the subdeveloper, right? It was beautiful. All of a sudden, we were on easy street. We bought a new car. The kids were getting bigger, and they got new bikes. Ruth didn't have to work. She was happy at the time. I know she was happy. It was what we always wanted." Jack put the gold ring to his lips and then lowered his hand. "And I was happy. You bet I was. Finally, I was there. And I worked my ass off I'll tell you. I was down in that fancy office day and night."

He shrugged again. "But all the hard work in the world couldn't turn the slump around. Heck, we hung on longer than a lot of them. I mean people were going bankrupt like crazy. We figured if we could hang on things had to get better. The thing was Ruth had to go back to work.

"I knew she wasn't happy," he said quietly, "but I didn't see what kind of pressure was on her. I mean we were still OK. We had the house and three wonderful kids. It wasn't the end of the world. But I guess she thought it was." He paced slowly to the other end of the room. "This is hard," he confessed.

"Do you want to take a break? Have a cup of coffee?" she asked him still sitting behind the desk.

"No, actually it feels good to get it out. It only hurts when I laugh." He padded back, hunched over, thinking as he walked. "You were right, Laura. I should have seen it coming, but at the time I didn't, and that's the honest-to-God truth. I admit it, I was wrapped up in the business. I couldn't walk out, don't you see? I couldn't."

"You thought you owed it to the company to stay on?"

"Yes. They trusted me. They gave me the job in the first place. I couldn't leave them. And nobody knew how long the depression in the housing market would go on. As it turned out," he said sadly, sitting back down in the chair, "we were dead long before the company folded. We just didn't know it."

"And Ruth didn't agree with your stand?"

"Oh, no, she thought I was a fool. She told me so on many occasions. She also resented working. I knew that, of course, but there was very little I could do about it. If she'd stuck it out a little while longer, I would have quit anyway. I had to. The company was totally bankrupt."

"Suddenly, she just left?"

"Actually, there was a little more to it than that." The clouds had drifted to the far horizon. They looked like little cotton balls at the bottom of a deep-blue bowl. The wake from a passing cruiser splashed up against the side of the houseboat. "Why don't you tell me about it?" she said.

He bit the end of his thumbnail and examined it carefully. "We were sitting at home one night, the kids were in bed, Ruth was in a bad mood. She'd been drinking and crying about work, and all of a sudden she says, 'I'm getting out of here.' Just like that.

"'Well,' I said, 'what did you say?' or something like that. I didn't take it seriously. I was tired, and I thought she was kidding. I didn't know what she was talking about. But she pointed to this guy on TV, the weatherman, a guy named Bill Curtis. And she said, 'I've been having an affair with Bill Curtis. I'm leaving you, and I'm not coming back.'"

"I sort of laughed, you know. But I mean to tell you, it was awful. I thought she was joking. She didn't even look at me, just kept watching this—this clown—draw these funny little pictures and talk about air inversions. So I said. 'Well, good luck' or something to make conversation. And she said as cool as you please, 'Bill and I are moving to Eugene, Oregon. In case you need to get a hold of me, he's got a better job up there.'"

Jack considered the end of his thumbnail and then examined all this fingernails. They were neatly trimmed, the cuticles pushed back. "I simply went to bed. I had a million other things on my mind. Things I thought at the time were more important. I hadn't received a paycheck in two months. I knew it couldn't go on forever. In the morning, Ruth was gone. Gone. No note, no nothing. Gone. Fourteen years of marriage was over. It was unbelievable. I still can't believe it."

He put his hands down deliberately, willing them to stay still. "It was the most humiliating, devastating experience of my life. I mean, Jesus, there I was the vice president of a big company or what had been a big company, and she was running off with a—a picture drawer that reads the weather. 'The cartooning weatherman.'"

Laura waited and then nudged him along with a question. "So you took the kids and came up here?"

"After a while, yeah, that's essentially what happened. I had to send them to live with my dad. I couldn't go around looking for a job with three kids trailing after me. Hell, the truth was I couldn't even pay the rent in Denver."

Jack Towne stood up again and walked over to the window. "There was a time when I thought I'd never make it, that I was washed up, you know. But when I got to Seattle, I found a place I wanted to stay. My God, Laura, do you realize how much most of the people in this country would pay for a view like this—boats, mountains covered with snow, a beautiful city?"

"I've always been fond of it. It's my favorite place."

"You've traveled quite a lot, haven't you?" he asked her, coming back to the desk. "You've seen your share of the world?"

"I suppose so. I've been to Europe, Scandinavia, Mexico. There isn't a place I'd trade for the Pacific Northwest though, not one."

"I'm glad to hear you say that, Laura, because you know when I got here I knew, I had this feeling, that finally I was where I belonged. I never did like Kentucky. What they call a mountain down there is nothing but a hill."

"How long did the kids live with your dad?"

"Oh, six, maybe eight months until I got up here and

started Jack Towne and Associates from scratch. I'll tell you, Laura, the first month I made fifty dollars. It wasn't even enough to pay my phone bill. But I stuck with it. It's what I do best, and the next month it was five hundred dollars."

"It's not easy running a small business. Most people have no idea what it's like."

"You can say that again. It's not like working for a salary. Anyway, once I got things going, the kids came out, and we set up housekeeping. It was rough, but we got along. The girls did the cooking and so forth. Of course, they had to take care of Rob too. He was only a little guy."

Jack Towne sat down heavily in the chair. "And then I met Shirley, and it was like a dream come true. Everything seemed to be going my way again until this horrible thing with Wendy. And now Rob. I can't understand that, Laura. It's beyond me. I don't know what to do."

"Jack, you've got to learn to communicate better with people, starting with your own kids. For instance, they probably resent Shirley. Have you ever thought about that? Shirley's fairly young and you bring her into the house that they've been running. It must have come as quite a shock."

"Well, sure, I knew that, but she's such a great gal; everybody likes Shirley."

"That's the point. She is a great gal. She takes some of your attention and affection, and kids that are starved for affection and attention don't like that. Don't you see?"

"Yes, I guess I do."

"That's something both you and Shirley ought to work out when we get together next week. Right now our concern is Rob, and you can do something. You can talk to him. Tell him what you've told me. Explain it to him. Don't be afraid to tell him how hurt you were."

"I guess I should have done that a long time ago."

"Maybe. But now is a good time too. Something else. Has Rob ever been to visit Ruth in Oregon?"

"No. The girls have been down. He never asked about it and honestly, Laura, I never brought it up."

"I think it might be very helpful to him once you've talked

to him. He's a big boy, and Ruth may have her faults, but I think she does love Rob in her way. He ought to see that; I think he needs that assurance."

Laura glanced at her watch. "That's about it, Jack. It's been a very productive hour. It doesn't seem like we've been talking that long, does it?"

"No, no, it doesn't. That's a good idea, Laura. I will get with Rob, sort of a man-to-man thing. I really appreciate your taking the time for me this morning, I really do. You're an easy lady to talk to, Laura Jordan."

"Thank you," she said, pleased with the compliment. "And Jack, talk to Shirley too. Tell her what we've discussed this morning. It might really help when you two come in next week."

"Oh, sure. You bet. Say, listen. Now that we're no longer talking business, could I ask you something?"

"Sure."

"It's sort of personal, but I'm interested."

"Fire away."

"Why aren't you married? I mean, Jim what's his name? McClay? He seems like a nice guy, very bright and all. I take it you two have known each other for quite a while?"

"Quite a while. Since high school, as a matter of fact."

"You two sort of go together? I'm sorry, I don't mean to pry, but I am curious."

"That's all right. Yes, we go together. We're also very good friends, but we have separate careers, and we're pretty busy people. That's an uncomfortable question, Jack. The answer is I don't know why we never got married. I guess we haven't gotten around to it."

"I didn't mean to make you uncomfortable."

"I was only kidding. It's a question that comes up frequently. An unmarried family counselor. Maybe I need some counseling myself."

"Well, I'm a good listener if you ever need somebody to listen," Jack said, standing. "That's what you said makes a good counselor isn't it, a good listener?"

"That's a big part of it."

"Incidentally, I saw a very nice review of your book in Boise in the paper there. Did I tell you?"

"No. In Boise?"

"Yes, they said it was a welcome plea for reconstituting the family as the primary value giver, something like that. It was very complimentary."

"Good for them."

"I thought it was a good book too."

"You read it?"

"Of course. I bought it and took it with me on my last trip. I thought it was excellent. Why are you so surprised?"

"Oh, because it's what you call a woman's book. It has a decidedly feminist outlook."

"Well, can't a man have a decidedly feminist outlook?" he said easily, coming over to the desk.

"Sure, why not? Say, Jack, may I ask you one more thing before you go?"

"How can I refuse?"

"Have you ever worn a beard?"

"No, do you think I'd look good in one?"

"Yes," Laura told him. "I think you'd look overpowering."

Barb Adams agreed, and the two women forced Jack to present a profile for their inspection.

"Most definitely," Barb told him, "a beard would be the finishing touch."

Jack was clearly embarrassed, but flattered to be receiving so much attention. "I'll think about it," he mumbled.

"The president of Early Winters ought to have a beard," Laura told him, taking his hand. He placed his other hand on top of hers. "Give my love to Shirley," she said.

"I will, I will," he said, pressing her hand between his.

"Well," Laura said, as they watched Jack go up the gangplank, "what do you think of the fabulous Mr. Towne?"

"I don't trust a man who tells me I'm lovely, not even as a joke. I'm a lot of things, but I'm not lovely."

"Oh, come on, Barb, he was being nice. Don't you think he's handsome in a sort of ruined way?"

"No. No, not handsome, something else."

"Sexy?"

"On a scale of one to ten, not sexy. Probably not better than a five between the sheets."

"Really, for a grandma, you certainly check a man out, don't you?"

"It's a hobby of mine," Barb said, sitting down at her desk. "Ever since you saved me from my husband, I've made a serious study of men, and I'm damn careful who I let get next to me in bed, I'll tell you that. Towne, there, is a five."

"But there is something about him, something terribly attractive, alluring, don't you feel it?" Christabelle, the young female cat, stepped lightly across the desk, ignoring both of them, her fluffy tail held high, quivering.

"Oh, yes, he's romantic, very romantic looking. That's what it is. He has that faraway look like he's done a lot of things he shouldn't have. Mr. Towne has seen his ups and downs I'll bet. Somewhere, there's somebody that calls him old blue eyes."

Laura Jordan laughed. Barbara had certainly come a long way from the shy, self-doubting woman who sat staring out the window of her office for days and cried every time she mentioned her husband.

"His wife Ruth, the one I stopped to see in Oregon, called him that. Or at least she referred to his eyes. She told me to watch out for his blue eyes."

"Good idea." Barb gave a quick nod of her head. "Very good idea. Mr. Jack Towne is right out a fairy tale."

"Oh, Barb, you're something else."

"You never met my husband, did you, Laura? Good old Bert is the reason I wear a plate instead of front teeth. Pious old Bert, a pillar of the Baptist Church on Sunday morning who beat me black and blue every Sunday night."

"No, I never did meet Bert. But after our sessions, I felt I knew him pretty well."

"Yes, there's something missing in that picture though. What he looked like. He was a romantic-looking character too. You know, the Squire Somebody out of an English fairy tale, kindly Squire Bumbleberry with a flowing yellow beard.

I don't trust them. They're dangerous."

"Well, Ms. Adams, I shall watch myself in the future. Now if you will excuse me, I think I'll take some advice you gave me previously and call Jim and beg him to come over here tonight. I feel romantic after the session with Mr. Towne."

"Don't be so smug, Laura Jordan. Someday Jim might not come."

She called Jim McClay's number, impatiently waiting for him to answer. Romantic and dangerous, she thought, what a delicious combination. "This is Laura Jordan," she mimicked in her best Mae West voice. "I got a couple hours free tonight, big boy, so why don't you drop over about eight for a yummy pizza and anything else you can get your hands on?"

Chapter 15

Jim McClay was up at six that morning, and Laura watched him through the open bathroom door as he tried to plaster down a stubborn cowlick of stiff red hair. Stale pizza and sex hung in the bedroom air. The cats sat on the windowsill, waiting for dawn.

No matter how much water he splashed on his head, the cowlick came springing back to life. Finally he gave up.

"Wait a while," she murmured as he came back into the bedroom, buttoning his shirt. But she knew he wouldn't. She knew he had things to do.

"That would be nice, wouldn't it?" he said without really meaning it. Jim sat on the edge of the bed, smelling of toothpaste and shaving cream. She reached up and ran her hand down his face; it felt unnaturally smooth. She pulled his head down to her bare breast and as he kissed it impatiently, Laura felt the surge of excitement starting again and saw her pink nipple harden under the brush of his lips.

She shifted in the bed, pulling him closer, and ran a hand inside his open necked shirt to the stiff wiry hair on his chest.

"I'll definitely make it worth your while to be just a teensy bit late," she said in a throaty whisper, pressing her lips to his ear.

"You never get enough do you?" He was half-kidding her, and his hand went down her bare body and came to rest between her legs. She moved her hips up, tempting him, forcing her pelvis against his fingers. "Give you a sample, and you want the whole package," he said, laughing uneasily.

Sunday was family day for Jim. First, he would accompany his mother to church and then take his mother, brother, and sister to the Cedar Tree for brunch, the restaurant where his father took them every Sunday before he died. In the afternoon, they would all go to Myra McClay's house and work on household projects. In the summer Jim liked to mow the huge lawn and in the winter he cleaned out the garage or the basement. These were jobs he could afford to hire out, but he felt should be done by a member of the family.

It wasn't that Laura was excluded from these activities. Myra would have been more than pleased to see Laura sitting beside them in the First Presbyterian Church and have her join them for brunch. It was Laura who made the choice not to spend Sundays with the McClays.

This was partly because she liked to sleep late on Sundays and then had to prepare herself for the live telecast of *Family Line* that night. But mostly, Laura felt that by going to church with Myra McClay and enjoying a family brunch at the Cedar Tree, she put herself in the position of a prospective daughter-in-law in the eyes of the McClays and their friends. And the McClays' friends were the Jordans' friends at Birch Bay.

Laura felt the slippery secretion between her legs transferring to his fingers. She put her arms around his neck and pulled him down on her, kissed him, pushing her tongue between his lips. He kissed her back, allowing her to get as far as his hard white teeth. Thus far and no farther, she thought, damn!

"Somehow there's something very exciting about trying to seduce you on Sunday morning, love. Maybe it's because you act like such a puritan when you're ready to go to church."

He laughed quietly, still holding her, and Laura felt the beginning of excitement in his groin. She moved a hand over his penis, hoping to promote the real thing. "This puritan can't get it up more than three or four times, and I'm over my limit."

"I could do something about that," she murmured, deftly

unzipping his pants. "I could give you a kiss like the magic princess that would wake you up."

"Jesus, Laura!" He sat up quickly, rezipping his pants. "I'll miss the Reverend Haldaine Guff." The pastor of the First Presbyterian was actually named Ruff, not Guff. It was another one of Jim's little jokes.

"The pussies and I will miss you," she said, sliding her hot body out of bed and kissing him at the belt buckle.

"I've got to go cleanse my soul and then get a bite to eat." He pulled her up firmly and gave her a kiss that was a final goodbye. "Really, honey, I've got to run. I'll give you a call."

"OK, Mr. Dull Puritan," she said, messing up his hair.

"Hey, I just spent fifteen minutes fixing my face."

"Tough," Laura said and rolled over, wrapping herself up like a mummy in the blankets. "I'll throw you a kiss on TV tonight."

"I'll be watching," he said. "Goodbye, Laura; goodbye, kitties."

When he left, she always felt lonely. It was unfair, she supposed, to expect him to change his Sunday for her. It wasn't that Jim was a mother's boy. He was the head of a household, and he took those responsibilities seriously. It was that for once Laura wanted him to do something totally reckless, to stay simply to please her, ignore his responsibilities, and cater to her every passion, to make love to her until she didn't want to make love anymore. Laura groaned and buried her head under the pillow. A totally selfish idea, of course, but it was what she wanted. The stillness was penetrating when he left. She felt one of the cats making its way stealthily along the bed, searching for a warm place to lie down. He or she thumped against Laura's back.

The calmness of Sunday morning was on the lake, not a wave lapped, not a rope creaked. She let herself slip back into a drifting semi-consciousness where she could keep the sexual warmth on a low simmer and relive their passionate Saturday night. She felt his hands on her, stroking her clitoris, slipping into her. She could taste his semen.

Laura bit down hard on her finger. She felt another touch

on the edge of her imagination, a cold hand on her breast. It was calloused and thin. "Go away, you bitch," she told Terry Blake's bony wife, haunting her in the dark. "Go back in your cartoon and vamp somebody else." Poor Terry, he had been so upset by the *Los Angeles Times* interview. Surely, he pleaded with her, there must have been some sort of misunderstanding. Laura assured him there was not. She was in no mood to take any crap from Terry, a man who invited her into his house so he could take a shot at her, and when that didn't work, left her to the mercies of his lesbian wife.

Laura thrashed across the bed. I should really get up, she thought, but then allowed herself to drift away again, wrapped in sheets that smelled of last night's passion. They were like a map, she thought to herself. Here we have the telltale stiffness of dried semen, and over here the musky odor of two sweating bodies enjoying each other. And finally, anchovies-and-crab pizza.

She would sleep until noon. She would get up when she pleased and sit up on the roof and drink coffee and look at things. She would do absolutely nothing until she had to. And then the telephone rang. She let it go, but it wouldn't stop. "Goddamn it to hell!" Laura Jordan reached across the bed and knocked the receiver off the hook. It landed on the floor with a bang. A tiny Donald Duck voice protested. Serves you right, she thought, feeling for the receiver with her hand.

"Oh, Laura," Shirley said, "are you there?"

"Barely."

"I'm sorry, I didn't mean to wake you up."

"That's OK, Shirley, I should be up anyway." Like hell you're sorry, Laura thought, her anger suddenly igniting. It was Shirley's favorite word, "sorry."

"I had to talk to somebody, Laura, and I didn't know who else to call." There was a desperate little-girl tone in her voice.

"It's OK, I'm here. I may have to stand on my head for a minute to get myself organized, but I'm here." To get my feelings out of my ass and back into my head, she thought.

"Stand on your head?" Shirley was confused. Laura

realized it was no time to crack a bad obscure joke.

"Never mind. What's wrong, Shirley?"

"Oh, I had a terrible scene with Chris. She's leaving. She announced it at the breakfast table, just like that. She's getting her own apartment and moving out this afternoon. I told her she was doing no such thing, not until we discussed it. She said she had made up her mind. She was out of high school, she was going to college, and she was going to live in an apartment. She got her academic scholarship, and it pays her tuition and living expenses."

Laura sat up in bed and pulled the blankets under her chin. A sunbeam poked through the window and tiny particles of dust danced across the shaft. "That's good, about the scholarship, I mean."

"But that doesn't mean she has the right to move out, does it? She's only seventeen," Shirley protested shrilly. "My God, Laura, you should have heard what she said. I said, 'Well now, Chris, there are other people to think about.' And she said she had always done everything on her own anyway, and she didn't owe anybody anything. Can you imagine that? She was very hard about it. She sat there and didn't eat her breakfast that I'd fixed, and said she could make her own decisions about her life and that was it. I tried to reason with her, but she wouldn't listen. She said she already put a deposit on the apartment, and she was going upstairs to pack her things. She walked out of the room. She walked out on me, Laura, right when I was trying to explain to her how I felt. She is upstairs packing. She left me standing there all alone."

"What does Jack have to say about all this?" Laura had been waiting for an opening, and when she found it, she forced the question in.

"Nothing. He came in late last night and left early this morning without a bite of breakfast. I don't know why I bother to fix it anymore. He doesn't even know about Chris. I tried to call his office, but all I get is that darn answering machine. I hate that thing. I hate it! He's gone all the time. He's obsessed with that ski resort. I tried to tell him yesterday that he needed to spend some time with the kids, particularly Rob. I don't know what's going on with Rob. He hardly says a word to me and ever since you went skiing with him, Laura, that's all he thinks about—skiing. He stays down in the basement late at night, waxing his skis and listening to rock and roll; and he's gone all the rest of the time. He's up on the mountain this morning all alone. Blue keeps calling, asking for him, but Rob won't talk to him. I got a grade notice from school; he's going to flunk out. Flunk out of high school, Laura."

Laura rubbed her eyes. "Wait a minute, just a minute. Didn't Jack tell you about Rob? Didn't he tell you that he and I had a long talk about Rob yesterday morning?"

"You and Jack? You mean this Saturday? I never heard anything about that. I thought we were both supposed to meet with you?"

Shirley's voice had a cutting edge to it. She's upset, Laura reminded herself. She's upset, and I'm her best friend. But sitting there feeling the growing warmth of the sun against her bare skin, Laura realized it had never been a real friendship. She was playing the familiar role of the stronger woman, the counselor, the dominant woman with all the answers. Something had shifted as it always did. It saddened Laura. The emptiness of the Sunday morning pressed in on her.

"You were both supposed to meet me. You still are," she replied with professional firmness. "I suggested the first of this week, but you and Jack have to decide on the date and time. That's up to you." She paused, making sure her impatience wasn't getting the best of her and then went on. "I called Jack because there were some things I wanted to get straightened out about Rob before we had that meeting, Shirley. We had a very productive discussion, and I was under the impression Jack would talk to both you and Rob about it."

"He hasn't said a thing to me. My gosh, Laura, I'm feeling left out of everything. I'd at least like to know what you're talking to my husband about."

"Shirley," Laura said with quick authority, "there was

never any intention of cutting you out or anything like that. I certainly didn't mean to hurt you by doing it. It was just that I thought Jack needed to talk about Rob."

"Oh, I know that, Laura, I'm sorry. I'm very upset. This thing with Chris did me in. I'm sure Jack forgot to mention it. He's probably discussed it with Rob. What a mess."

"Look, Shirley, why don't you try talking to Chris again right now without laying down the law to her? Show her you love her and that you care. I think you're going to have to face the fact she has pretty much taken care of herself for the last several years, and that she can move out if she wants to; and there's very little either you or Jack can do about it. I wouldn't make that the issue. She's a serious girl. She'll be all right."

"Oh, I know. Chris is very responsible. But Jack will be furious if I let her go like this."

"Let Jack talk to her. But you might try to get the thing in perspective for him first before he tries to strong-arm her. I don't think that will work."

"That's a good idea, Laura," Shirley said quietly. "I'm really sorry I got so upset. I don't seem to be myself lately. I've got so many things on my mind."

"Don't worry about it. It's perfectly understandable. How are you feeling? You sound a little washed out."

"Yes, I guess I do. I get sick in the morning."

"That's a pleasure I've never had. How's Jack adjusting to the idea of being a father again?"

"Oh," she said, as if surprised by the question, "we talked about that. It's going to be all right."

"You don't sound so sure."

"Did Jack say something to you?" There was a sudden sharpness in the question. "He told me it was between us. Did you talk about that too?"

Laura ignored the implications. "No," she said honestly, "that was something I understood you were going to work out with Jack. We discussed Rob's mother. I told Jack he should explain to Rob why she left. He never has, you know. I also told him he ought to try and explain it to you."

"Well," Shirley Towne said in a small voice. "I see. I guess I'll have to ask him about that."

"Shirley, let's get something straight here. If you think I'm interfering, you ought to tell me so. I feel I'm upsetting you, that I'm making you angry, and that's the last thing in the world I want to do, believe me."

"Oh, no, not at all." Shirley sounded shocked by the suggestion. "I'm sorry. It's just that, like I said, I've got a lot on my mind, and this thing with Chris upset me. It came at a bad time. I know you're only trying to help, Laura. You're a good friend." There was a muffled cough on Shirley's end of the telephone. "The only really good friend I have," she added.

"I'll tell you what I'd like you to do, Shirley. First, go upstairs right now and have that talk with Chris woman-to-woman. Don't let it go. And second, get a hold of that husband of yours and set a date and time to come down here. I want to help, I really do. I am concerned about all of you, but you and Jack are the only ones who can come to grips with these things. I can't do it for you."

"Oh, I know you are, and I will." She stopped and laughed at her own confusion. "And, thanks, Laura, thanks for being there. I feel better already."

"Good."

"I got up for early mass, but I didn't go."

"Well, take two aspirins, drink plenty of fluids and go and talk to your stepdaughter then."

"I will. And thanks so much. I don't know how I can ever thank you."

"Don't worry, I'll think of something," Laura said.

You could start by not getting me out of bed on Sunday morning, she thought, as she pulled on a wrinkled sweatshirt and got her weights out of the closet. You could start by not suspecting me of playing around with your husband. Although Shirley hadn't said anything directly, and it wasn't an intentional accusation, Laura sensed what was bothering her. She hefted the light dumbbells, consulting the glossy countenance of the male weight-lifter gazing at her from the pages of his women's weight-lifting book, male biceps pumped to enormous proportions.

"If I work very hard, will I look like the ladies in your book?" she asked him, feeling the prickly sweat break out on her scalp. The stick-thin young ladies stared back with hard confident eyes. Doggedly, Laura pushed on through the exercises until the sweat ran hot under her shirt. God, she thought, I smell like a French whore.

As she worked through the exercises, Laura let herself wonder if she had arranged the meeting with Jack Towne for something other than professional reasons. The answer came bounding back as the weights went up and down. Of course, she had. There were always other reasons. There was something about Jack she found attractive. Maybe it was the mysterious undefined element of danger Barb felt. Maybe there wasn't enough excitement in her life. The five-pound dumbbells felt like fifty, and her arms burned with the strain. But that was ridiculous, Laura thought. Jack Towne was a teddy bear of a man and every day of her life was exciting. The harder she lifted, the faster the vestiges of last night's passion receded, all the blood was rushing into her shoulders and arms.

Up went the iron for another ten repetitions. Still, Jack was an unusual man. He admired her and was genuinely interested in what she was doing for one thing, and she liked that. But there was more, much more if she would only admit it. Laura growled with strain, and the cats jumped at the noise like flighty sheep, scattering to the corners of the room where they crouched with wary eyes. Laura knew, she sensed the possibility of being dominant when she was with Jack. He needed her help, and he would be appreciative. Goddamn you, Muscle Man, she swore at the book, straining to finish the set, pushing, panting, giving it everything she had.

The thought of being dominant—sexually dominant—sent a warm glow spreading deep into her pelvis. The weights went feather-light in her hands. "Nine, ten," she counted out loud, finishing strongly. Panting for breath, she wondered what it would be like to go to bed with a man where she was in control.

Laura had always been attracted to such strong men, the muscle men and Jim McClays of the world where making love became a contest of equals, thrilling but somewhat akin to a sexual arm-wrestling contest in bed. What would it be like to love a softer, more gentle man who was willing to let her lead, who would submit to her?

She slammed the glossy book cover over on the man's conceited face. She didn't have to finish his torturous exercises if she didn't want to. But there was no escape, he was also on the back cover. The best part about being independent was that you could choose: choose how you wanted to make a living; choose what you did for fun; and choose the man you wanted to make love to—or the woman. You were free.

And being free, Laura chose not to finish his daily dozen. She would be damned if she would. She wrapped a towel around her neck, filled a plastic bread bag with a collection of leftover rolls and muffins and went for a long leisurely jog along the lake shore. When she got tired, she stopped and fed the ducks.

Soon, they were following her, quacking and honking, darting in each cove to see if the nice lady in the shapeless gray suit was going to feed them again. They were such brave little birds, and the plain brown females pushed their gaily colored mates out of the way to get first choice on bread crumbs.

"That's the way, girls. Show them who's boss," she encouraged them.

As she walked and ran, she felt her shoulder and arm muscles loosening from the tension of weight lifting. Her breath came easily now, and her body moved as she wanted it to, light and relaxed under the cool sun filtering through the high overcast. It looked like yesterday's spring was a false one. Winter was pushing back.

On the way home, Laura picked up a Sunday paper and a quart of chocolate milk at the Chinese grocery on the corner. She drank the milk in a hot shower and took the paper to bed, reading until she fell asleep.

At five o'clock the alarm went off, and Laura sat up in the darkness, momentarily disoriented. The rain was running in steady streams off the roof. The wind rattled against the windows, and she felt the pang of loneliness stab deep. She got up quickly, fed the cats, and dressed in her pale blue pantsuit and added a lemon-yellow silk scarf. She drove to the television studio where she usually ate with the producer before her show.

He was an expert at his job. It was his consuming interest, and she liked him because in the two years they'd worked together he had never mentioned a personal problem. Presumably the producer had a family and financial worries like everybody else, but those were never discussed over the spaghetti dinners he had ordered into his cluttered office over the main studio. He talked camera angles, lighting, hand gestures, the way to zero in on what he called "the velvet magic quality" of her voice. The first time he'd used the phrase Laura thought he was joking, but the producer never joked. She knew that now, but hadn't then.

"Listen," he'd told her, "that's ninety percent of your appeal, Laura. I know you're beautiful and smart and all that, but it's in your voice. You sound like you care. You sound so caring and confident. It's magic; that's what it is. It makes people believe. It makes them believe you never had a personal problem yourself, and that all your attention is focused on them. With a voice like that, you could convert them to Christianity, start a world war, or make me the best PBS producer in the country."

Laura had laughed, and then went out to try to give him what he was talking about, adding a little dash of Marlene Dietrich to the velvet.

"Don't do that," he admonished her. "Don't ever ham it up with your talent because that's what it is; it's a talent. Relax and use it. We'll accentuate it by shooting you from a variety of angles. If they don't see your face all the time so much the better. We want to make you a presence in the lives of the people watching, not simply a personality."

"Oh, Christ," she had said, "let's drop the hocus-pocus."

He took her hand, the only time he ever touched her except in directing her where to stand and sit. "It isn't hocus-pocus," he told her. "This is a magic medium, television. People believe it. It's like the Bible, and you're one of the prophets, Laura."

Tonight it was small talk over the spaghetti, however. The show was going well. And when things went well, the producer was superstitious about discussing even minor faults. He believed they would work themselves out "under the lights."

He asked how *The Femme Factor* was selling. She told him well even though her agent was still angry with her for telling a reviewer from the *Los Angeles Times* where to get off.

"Don't worry about it," he assured her, "you're an electronic media creature, Laura, you don't need newspapers."

"Family Line" was done in front of a live audience, and before the show, she liked to go out and get acquainted with them and then watch while the prerecorded portion of the show aired. That way, when the lights came up, Laura was already on the set, ready to take calls.

"This isn't very serious," the woman said, anguish hanging on every word and went on to relate how her daughter had altered a report card. The daughter was a bright sixteen year old who was lazy: the type of girl, the mother said, who when told to clean up her room would push the mess under the bed.

Her parents expected her to get As or there would be trouble. She got Cs, tried to change them to Bs and got caught. For this, her driving privileges had been revoked. The girl's response was to withdraw from family life, become sullen, and let her grades drop to Ds.

"Sometimes I find it helpful to try and put yourself in the other person's shoes," Laura suggested smoothly, and listened while the woman tried.

When the first program aired, there was a great deal of concern over "dead air," but now it was recognized that was part of the appeal—anxious people groping, struggling with real problems. The woman finally said she might feel that by getting a C she would lose her parents' love. She also might feel embarrassed because they had such a stupid daughter. She admitted she might be so desperate that changing a grade would seem like a small risk to take under the circumstances.

"You've got the knowledge and insight to solve this problem yourself," Laura reassured her. "Tell your daughter your love doesn't depend on grades."

"Well, thank you so much," the woman said. "I knew I was on the right track, but I needed to talk to somebody, to get some reassurance."

Laura thanked her for the call and swung around in the chair, prepared for the next one. Across the studio she could see the raised fist that signaled a hostile caller was on the line. She had the option of waving it off or accepting the call. Tonight she nodded, the signal to let the call come through. Laura Jordan felt ready for anything. His voice was pompous, and she let him talk. He identified himself as a psychiatrist and accused her of practicing without a license. Her anger flared white hot, but she held it back, waiting to use it at the right moment.

Laura had no idea what she was going to say to this man who went on to accuse her of meddling with things she didn't understand, giving sugar-coated advice to people who needed board certified medical help, and making a media circus out of conversations that ought to be private.

"Cheerleading is all very well for football games," he said condescendingly, "but I object to your elevating it to a mind-healing science."

She waited, watching for her opening, still not having formulated a reply. But Laura knew exactly what she was going to do. She was going to attack and then attack again. It was her father's most valuable lesson for getting along in the world. Attack them at the weakest spot, and before they could recover, hit them again and keep on hitting until they were finished.

"I wasn't aware I needed a license to listen to people's problems," she said suddenly, "to try and help them get in touch with their feelings, to encourage them to feel better about themselves so they can get through life a little easier. Are you in favor of licensing priests and clergymen, Doctor? Do you think bartenders or hairdressers ought to take a test? Because the truth is those people probably offer better help than you and I put together."

Of course, he didn't believe that, he sputtered. She was twisting his words, taking them out of context.

"Or friends?" she cut him off sharply. "Do you think everybody's best friend who picks them up when they're down ought to go to medical school first, Doctor?"

"I'm afraid that's typical of your thoroughly confused mushy reasoning, Miss Jordan," he said from on high.

Now that he was attacking her, it was time to withdraw and become the considerate host. "I'll leave that judgment to the audience," she said easily. "I'm really sorry you feel I'm performing some sort of criminal act by simply conducting a dialogue with people, people likc you and me, Doctor, who need to talk to somebody. Don't you ever have a time when you need to talk to somebody about a problem? When you don't know where to turn?"

"Of course. But you're still avoiding the point, Miss Jordan."

"Who do you talk to, Doctor? Who do you talk to when you feel down, when you're confronting something you absolutely can't handle alone? Or do you ever have problems like that?" She allowed herself a faint madonnalike smile.

"Of course, I do. I talk to my wife. Or if it's a serious problem, a really serious problem, I consult one of my colleagues," he replied stiffly.

"Not everyone can afford one of your colleagues, Doctor," she reminded him gently.

"Oh come, Miss Jordan, your fees are as high as mine, maybe higher."

"Not on this program, Doctor." She had allowed him to feel he was getting the upper hand. She sensed the triumph creeping into his voice. "I'll tell you what, though. Let me hereby extend you a formal invitation to appear with me next Sunday in person and among other things we can compare notes on our success rate; the number of people helped, Doctor; the bottom line in any business including yours."

"I certainly will not appear with you or anybody else that makes a mockery out of legitimate counselors, Miss Jordan."

"I'm sorry to hear that, Doctor," she replied mildly, and then went for his jugular. "I'm sorry to hear that you're not willing to consider anything outside the narrow realm of your specialty. It's too bad ordinary people don't fit into specialties, Doctor."

"Now that's not what I said," he came back angrily, "I don't claim to know it all, Miss Jordan. I'm perfectly willing to let a priest take care of spiritual needs, and I'm perfectly willing to let competently trained para-professionals take care of family problems. But I know my limitations, Miss Jordan, I know them very well. What I'm not willing to accept is a show business personality like you without any formal training whatsoever who doesn't know her limitations. Who mixes a little bit of this and that, some Norman Vincent Peale and Freud, with a pretty smile and a charming personality and sallies forth like Don Quixote to take on windmills in people's minds, Miss Jordan."

Laura felt the flush spreading across her face. She had been nice to this ass long enough, she thought, gathering herself up in the chair.

"I have no doubt you've helped people, Miss Jordan, and as you point out, the same function is performed by bartenders without any specialized training. However, bartenders don't have their own television shows. They don't write books that are read by thousands of people. My point is simply that you've wandered very far afield from your original expertise —communications—I might add, supposed expertise in communications."

"Doctor, why do you feel compelled to call me up? What drives you to want to humiliate me in front of all these people? Could it be that you're very insecure in your male-dominated profession? Could it be that you're afraid that underneath all your degrees and starched white coat, you really don't know any more than I do? Why are you afraid to come down here and talk to me face-to-face? Come down out of your ivory tower, Doctor, and join the common people."

The caller paused. Laura was glad for the pause. There was something else she wanted to say, some other point that should be made, but she couldn't find it. Laura felt badly about attacking him, but he'd asked for it.

"No, I must gratefully decline your invitation, Miss Jordan," he said with resignation. "And although my motives may not be one hundred percent pure, I called primarily to warn you—and your audience—that one of those windmills you're charging out there is going to blow up in your face some day with tragic consequences for both you and whoever you're trying to help, that's all. I think you ought to go back to conducting communication seminars, where you belong."

"Back to the kitchen," she said quickly, but not quick enough. The doctor had hung up.

Laura was not satisfied with the exchange, not at all. It wasn't over. What had started out as an easy target had subtly shifted somewhere, and she hadn't landed the telling blows. There was a dead silence on "Family Line." Should she make further comments, she wondered, or would that only make things worse?

"I think the good doctor and I both have some problems," she finally remarked, "some anger deep inside us that we ought to get out and examine. I must apologize to you for displaying that anger on a show where you are the guests and I'm the host. There's no excuse for it. Maybe I got up on the wrong side of the bed. What do you think, Doctor? Or is it something more profound?" She paused. "Well, now that I've got that out of my system, let's see if we can get back to communicating in the family. Hello, you're on the 'Family Line' with Laura Jordan."

The rest of the show had gone smoothly and every caller supported her. It was a vote of confidence Laura knew she didn't deserve.

"The guy was a ringer," the producer said afterward. "I never should have even asked you. We don't need that kind of stuff. The audience isn't interested. I'll bet we lost viewers."

"I don't think it hurts," Laura told him. "I didn't handle it very well, that's all."

On the way home, driving in the rain through the deserted Sunday night streets, Laura turned the conversation over and over in her mind. She had not handled it well. That was clear, but why? As her father always reminded her, you had to keep your eye on what mattered and what did not matter. In this case, what did not matter was her uneasy feeling that something had gone wrong, Laura reminded herself. What mattered was the final vote, the overwhelming support she received from her viewers. By all accounts, she had emerged the clear winner. She had made a fool out of her opponent. Still, as she pulled into the parking lot seeing the rain slanting down over the lake like a heavy curtain, she knew the doctor had struck a heavy blow. It was his remark about not knowing her limitations.

Laura fumbled for her key, feeling the cold rain soaking through her coat at the shoulders. She put the key in upside down and swore at it. "Get in there, you little bastard."

She knew her limitations. It was simply that she had marked them out on the far boundaries for a woman and that was what men like the psychiatrist resented. They always tried to question her ability, and she knew as much as any of them. "Damn right," she reassured herself, twisting the key.

The telephone was ringing as the door swung open. Oh, God, Laura thought, I'll bet that's Shirley.

Shirley Towne didn't even say hello. "Have you heard from Jack?" she demanded.

Laura, dripping wet, let that abrupt greeting sink in. "I just got back from the TV studio. I'm standing here soaking wet," she replied evenly.

"I can't find him. He hasn't come home."

Laura opened her coat, propped the telephone under her chin and started to ease the raincoat off. "What time is it, ten?"

"He hasn't been home all day, Laura. I'm worried about him. He's—well, he's under a lot of pressure. I got a call from one of his accounts, The Happy Hot Dog, long distance from Chicago. He's supposed to have sent a bunch of stuff to them, and it's not there. I don't understand it. They said he's not answering his telephone at the office."

"Have you tried to call him?" Laura asked her, getting the wet coat off and hanging it over Barb's desk to dry.

"Nobody answers. Where can he be? Oh, Laura, I feel so awful. Something's happened, I know it!"

"Shirley, I think you're reading a lot of your own feelings into this. You seem to be under a terrific strain too. Jack's not the first man who stayed out late. Besides, he's probably working. Maybe he's ignoring the phone. I do that sometimes."

"Do you think so? I can't help worrying, Laura. He said he would be home for dinner."

Laura was getting tired of Shirley's constant telephoning. She was being used as a sounding board for each problem in Shirley's life as it came up, regardless of the time of day. "Shirley, there's very little we can do right now. You're going to have to wait it out." Laura shifted her feet, her shoes were wet and pinching. "I know," she said, trying some humor, "stand behind the door and let him have it with the frying pan when he comes in."

Shirley responded by becoming even more demanding. "But what if he doesn't come back? I don't know what I'll do then."

"Shirley, are sure there isn't something else bothering you?"

"I'm scared. He said he would be here, and he isn't. Isn't that enough?"

Laura sighed heavily to herself. "Yes, I suppose it is." She kicked off her shoes and wiggled her feet on the cold floor.

She was tired. She felt uncomfortable. Something was out of place or about to go wrong with her life. The conversation with the psychiatrist had upset her. "I really don't see what else you can do, Shirley, except call the police if you think it's that serious."

"The police? You're talking like he's dead or something."

"Shirley, I don't think any such thing. I think he's late, that he's working, and maybe stopped off for a drink. I really don't know. I don't. I'm sorry, but that's the best I can do."

"You're probably right," she replied sullenly. Shirley Towne gave another muffled cough. "I'll have to wait."

"Call me in the morning, Shirley. If he's not back, we'll figure something out. I'll be glad to help anyway I can. I'm not trying to put you off, really I'm not, but I don't know what else to do right now. Do you understand what I'm trying to say? I don't know how I can be of help to you right now."

"I guess so. I'm sorry I called," Shirley replied and hung up.

Laura held the phone in her hand for a few moments and then carefully replaced the receiver. Once again, she felt something going wrong, an almost imperceptible but steady slippage taking place somewhere beneath the surface in her life. She sat quietly on the edge of the receptionist's desk, trying to discover what it was, but Laura was too tired to think. It will all be clear tomorrow, she reassured herself. And she turned off the lights and went to bed.

Chapter 16

Ghosts of the present and doubts of the past haunted Laura through the night and into early morning. Miss Jordan didn't know her limitations, the psychiatrist said. In a sense, that was true. She didn't know where the limits were. She wasn't even sure limits existed.

The room was stuffy and overheated, and Laura got up to open a window. Back in bed, she lined up the Towne family in her mind: Jack struggling to carry them all alone; Shirley sick, exhausted, and pregnant, hanging on him, asking what she was supposed to do; Chris, a marble statue of a girl; Rob hugging and kissing William Blue.

Laura felt a weight pressing on her. "Get away from me." The cat jumped onto the floor. It was still too hot in the room. The rain came harder and harder.

She got up again and went to the window and opened it wide. The lake was black, slapping and splashing against the side of the houseboat. Laura felt a slight sway as it rocked in its moorings. She could visualize all of the Townes except Wendy, the girl would come only as a ghostly figure, trailing gossamer robes, something out of *Green Mansions*. Laura padded back to the bed and threw herself down.

Shirley was accusing her of not knowing what she was doing. "You haven't helped us, and I thought you were my friend."

"That's not true. I've helped a lot of people. I helped the Clairbornes. They're happy. I have lists and lists. You won't listen. You won't try, Shirley."

"I've read your book. It makes sense," Jack said.

Rob was gone. In his place was Blue Boy, smiling like a rabid wolf. "Where's Rob?" Laura cried, rushing at him. He fended her off. "I got rid of him," he said. "If I can't have him, nobody can have him." She attacked him, but he was stronger, much stronger. She had made a terrible, terrible mistake. He was pushing her down. "Help me, help me!" she screamed. Blue smelled like the Austrian ski instructor who had made love to her expertly twice a day for an entire summer. It was the smell of leather worn close to the skin.

She awoke with a start, sweating. Why hadn't Jack come to help her? Why didn't Jack get rid of William Blue? Didn't he know what he was? Laura looked at the clock. It was three A.M. At any moment, the telephone might ring, and it would be Shirley Towne again. Laura closed her eyes, dreading the sound but anxious for it to come. If Shirley didn't call, Laura would have to call her.

Half asleep, she tried to concentrate her thoughts on relaxing, working up her body, willing each separate member to drop off into a mindless suspension. But she got no further than her knees, and Shirley Towne came marching back into her consciousness, demanding explanations. "What am I doing wrong?" Shirley cried out, tears in her eyes.

How dare you treat me like this after all I've done for you, Laura wanted to scold her but couldn't, not even in her dreams. "You have to be loyal. You have to forgive small faults in a family, Shirley. So Jack's a little late, so he pushes a little hard, he's only trying to make things easier for all of you. Give him a chance," she pleaded.

"You hate me," Shirley said stubbornly.

"I don't, I don't. I'm only trying to help."

When the telephone finally did ring, it was after seven, and it was her agent Terry Blake calling from La Jolla. He wanted her to contact the radio station in Pomona where she'd made such a hit on the talk show for a second appearance. She promised him she would, but didn't even write down the telephone number.

The dawn never came. A dull golden light passed over the office buildings across the lake and then was gone. Morning twilight was an extension of the night. The rain kept falling, and Laura took her temperature because she felt overheated and sick. It was normal.

She considered going for a run, but it was too wet. She considered lifting weights, but she was tired. Already, Barb was calling on the intercom to remind her she had a full schedule, plus an evening Effective Communications seminar with the local chapter of the American Management Association.

"Damn," Laura said, "I forgot all about that."

"You've also got a call from Shirley Towne holding."

Shirley was at work. Laura could hear the machines clicking in the background, processing thousands upon thousands of telephone bills. "He didn't come home," she said dully. "I'm going to call the police."

"Not at all?" It registered on Laura with a physical, jolting shock. Where could Jack Towne be?

"You're sure he didn't go to Boise or something?"

"I don't know. He didn't tell me. This is the busiest day of the month, and I can't leave. I'm going to have to call the police."

"Do you want me to help?"

"I've already asked too much of you, Laura."

"Let me help. I can make some calls. I'm worried about him too."

"What do you think it's been like for me?" Shirley asked her, the shrillness hardening into anger. "Chris is gone, moved out. Rob went skiing again this morning. I don't know what I'm *supposed* to do."

"Shirley, I'm sorry about last night. I was a bit rough on you. I was in a bad mood, and I'm sorry."

"It's OK, Laura, I understand." Laura could hear her cover the mouth piece and say something to somebody in the office. "Excuse me. Bills are like taxes; they can't wait. I would really appreciate it if you could do some calling. I'm worried sick."

Together they compiled a list of possible sources of information: Jack's father in Kentucky; T.R. Timberlake in Boise; his Seattle partners in Early Winters, Jack Howland the

State Representative, and State Senator Frank Greenway; and Ruth in Oregon.

"Have you tried calling Chris?" Laura asked her. "Does she have a phone yet?"

"No. I mean, yes, she has a phone, but I wouldn't know what to say to her. I'd be embarrassed. Laura, nothing like this ever happened to me before. I feel like I'm going crazy. He's got to come back."

"I know it's hard, Shirley, but let's not assume the worst until we know what's happened."

Laura gave the list to Barb and asked her to find the numbers and make the calls while she took her first clients into the office, hoping she could fake the attention and concern required to deal with their problems. She was doing a credible job of at least listening to a story involving lifelong bitterness over a family debt that was never repaid when Barb interrupted her via the intercom with a call, something Barb would do only if it was important. Laura excused herself and went to the outer office to take the call.

Barb told her it was T.R. Timberlake. He hadn't seen Jack, but he wanted to talk to her. "Mr. Timberlake, this is Laura Jordan."

"Listen, honey, I don't know how you fit into this operation, but if you're on Jack's payroll, you better tell him to get his ass over to Wilson, Idaho, *max schnell,* or he can kiss the Early Winters project goodbye."

"I'm just a friend, Mr. Timberlake. I'm looking for Jack too. You haven't seen him?"

"Hell no, that's what I'm telling you, darlin'. If I knew where he was, I'd put his hide on my office door. You can call me Teddy, all the girls do." He had a raw gravelly voice, and his harsh words were tempered by what sounded like a touch of rough but genuine humor.

Laura decided to take a chance on her judgment. After all, what could the Potato King do to her? "Thanks—Teddy—what went on in Wilson anyway?"

"A hearing, dear. A hearing that was supposed to be a formality. Turned into a goddamn three-ring circus. Bunch of environmentalists and broken-down cowboys over there decided they didn't like our idea so they grabbed some headlines and, near as I can figure out, stalled the whole thing. You tell Jack I got other places for my money that can't wait so he better fix this thing. He's supposed to be the fixer here."

"I'm sure Jack would have been there if he'd known about it," Laura said diplomatically.

"He sure as hell shoulda been there. He shoulda been there three weeks ago sniffin' around, findin' out who these donkeys were and greasin' the skids. You tell him I'm mighty pissed, young lady, mighty pissed. I had my damn heart set on that place. Goddamn!"

"Don't give up the ship yet, Teddy. The permit hasn't actually been denied yet, has it?"

"Good as, darlin', good as. These Sierra Club types get on their high horse, you're in trouble. I used to be a member of that organization. 'Course that was before it got taken over by them radicals in California."

"Two can play that game, Mr. Timberlake. Give Jack a chance." Laura didn't want to see Jack's dream shattered because of one missed cue.

"You don't say, you don't say. Just a friend, eh? Good friend, I'd say. Listen, Laura, if this whole thing falls through and you're lookin' for a new place to settle down, give me a call. I could use a gal with a voice like yours. You could sell an icebox to an Eskimo."

"Thanks but no thanks, Teddy. I have my own business."

"No kiddin'. A fellow capitalist, huh? Well, if you're ever in Boise look me up. Just ask anybody where I hang out. They all know me. I run the biggest potato outfit in the world. You can't buy a french fry without my permission." He chuckled deep in his throat.

"I'll keep that in mind."

"Nice talkin' to you. You tell Jack to get on over here and get this mess straightened out. I want to ski at my own place next winter. You tell him that, goddamn it!"

Laura smiled and gave the telephone to Barb. "Put Mr. Timberlake's number in our directory, will you?" she asked her and went back to the tangled financial problems that plagued her clients.

"The worst thing you can do is handle financial affairs in a family with a handshake," she told them smoothly. "They need to be handled strictly as a business with a clear understanding of who is obligated for what. You've allowed it to create misunderstandings because nobody was clear on the terms." It was good sound advice. She didn't care what the psychiatrist said.

At noon, Barb got her a pastrami sandwich, and she learned that the two Seattle partners in Early Winters, the politicians, were both out of town and that Jack's father hadn't heard from him since he'd called to say he was sending Wendy to Kentucky.

"He was sending her? I was under the impression Wendy wanted to go, it was her idea."

"Not according to Jack's dad, but then he wasn't very talkative."

"How so?"

"I explained who I was and all and why I was calling, and he got angry. 'What makes you think he tells me anything, lady?' I almost said because, my dear sir, it's reported he is your son and you are his father."

"I don't think they got along very well," Laura said, talking with her mouth full of pastrami. "Jack doesn't think his father provided a good home, and maybe the old man knows it."

"Whatever it was, he sure was snappy with me."

After lunch, Laura saw one more client before she cut off all telephone calls and sat down to review her notes for the Effective Communications seminar. It was one of her original presentations, but she liked to change it each time and update the examples so they were current. At four o'clock, feeling washed out from the lack of sleep and fat because she hadn't done any exercising, Laura decided to make a couple of calls on her own.

First, she called Jack's office and got a recording. Jack sounded positively jubilant as his taped voice advised callers he was not in now but would be back shortly. At the tone, Laura left a message: "For God's sake, Jack, call me."

The uncertainty had been eating away at her all day, and as

she sat at her desk, looking out across the lake, a dirty brown under a dark drizzling sky, she had to admit she was extremely worried about Jack Towne.

Tapping her finger impatiently, she ran down the possibilities. He had left Shirley for some reason. Tap, tap, tap went her fingers. It was interesting, she mused, that such a possibility was in first place. But she knew from experience how it could happen. Ordinary people did strange and bizarre things in the name of love and hate, and they did them every day of the week, rich or poor, Catholic or Jew, white, black, yellow, or brown. Faithful husbands ran off with the babysitter. PTA presidents had affairs with the kid's high school math teacher. Suburban housewives flew off to Tahiti.

The fact that Shirley deliberately avoided mentioning her pregnancy to Laura during their recent conversations only made the possibility even stronger. Fathers deserted pregnant wives and girl friends in droves. With three children almost grown and serious problems with Wendy and Rob, the unpleasant possibility of desertion belonged in first place, Laura decided.

She increased the tempo of finger tapping, changing it to a drumming roll. Possibility two: he was so busy working he'd lost all track of time and didn't know if it was day or night. Laura thought that was improbable at best.

Which brought up the worst case. Jack Towne had been in a serious accident. He was unconscious, suffering from amnesia, or he was dead and either he didn't know who he was or where he was, or the people who found him couldn't identify the body. Grisly. Not pleasant to think about, but that would explain why he hadn't shown up in Wilson to attend the Early Winters permit hearing.

Laura slapped her hand flat on the table. That had to be it. He was hurt somewhere, and the thought revitalized her. She called information and got Chris Towne's new number, but nobody answered. Then she tried Shirley at work, but found out she'd gone home. Nobody answered at the house.

Laura was out of time. "Why don't you come up while I get dressed and tell me what you found out about Jack," she suggested to Barb, dashing by her desk on the way upstairs.

The Effective Communications course involved attending the dinner prior to the session. This was usually a gathering where the executives of the various companies involved who were paying her fee made an appearance and then left the learning to their middle-management subordinates. It was an unproductive but necessary affair. Laura picked out a conservative navy-blue suit with black shoes while she talked to Barb.

The secretary had spoken at length to Ruth Curtis in Oregon and had received absolutely no information on Jack's whereabouts, but had been treated to a long recitation about his faults, real or imagined.

"To hear her tell it, Jack Towne is quite an operator when it comes to screwing things up," Barb remarked, sitting on the edge of the unmade bed while Laura struggled into a slip.

"I'd take anything Ruth Curtis said with a grain of salt. She's addicted to booze, and she's a very bitter woman. That's fairly typical, you know, blaming your own problems on somebody else who happens to be less than perfect."

"Still, there's two sides to every story," Barb remarked mildly.

"So true. Listen, thanks for your help today. I'll try to get a hold of Shirley while I'm at this dinner," Laura said. "How do I look?"

"Like the model of the female executive, Laura."

The impression was important at corporate dinners. Any hint of careless, fickle, emotional, unstable feminity would result in cancellation of future contracts, and Laura Jordan knew it. What she did, as she poked politely at the overcooked chicken and canned peas, was to give a performance. The first goal of the performance was to convince her fellow diners at the head table that Laura Jordan was an enthusiastic, totally committed supporter of the free enterprise system in general and their private corner of it in particular. The second goal was to exude complete confidence in effective communications as a cure-all for whatever ailed their companies, a cure that would reach right down to the profit-and-loss statement, thereby proving to them that her $5,000 fee for the course was a wise investment.

Laura listened politely while the assistant vice president of finance on her left related a long story about salmon fishing at Campbell River, British Columbia, and then turned deftly to her other side to listen to an equally fascinating tale regarding a senior vice president's brilliant son who could not only throw the shotput a country mile, but had his eye set on being a Rhodes Scholar as well.

"Sounds like a regular Pete Dawkins," Laura remarked pleasantly, showing her male companions she was one of them in casual conversation. They already knew about her on-the-job performance from a slick brochure furnished in advance, which was careful to point out her success as a businesswoman as well as a counselor.

After an hour and fifteen minutes of mostly listening and just before the pie and coffee, Laura gracefully excused herself to call her office and went to a closed booth at the far end of the banquet room.

The brown waiters rushed by carrying trays of pie Laura knew, from previous catered dinners in this same hotel, had the consistency of glue. The phone at the Townes' rang eight times before somebody answered, and then it was Chris, not Shirley.

"Chris," Laura said, surprised, "how are you?"

"I'm fine, Miss Jordan. I'm not so sure about Shirley."

"Is she there?"

"Yes, she's very upset about Dad." Chris, Laura thought, was being very matter-of-fact under the circumstances. Her voice was even and unemotional.

"You haven't heard from him?"

"No. Miss Jordan, I think Shirley's going to have some kind of a breakdown. She was almost hysterical when I got here."

"It was nice of you to go over, Chris."

"I had to pick up some things anyway. I like Shirley, Miss Jordan. I really do. I'm concerned about her."

"What about your dad, Chris? Do you know where he might be?"

"Daddy can take care of himself," she said coolly. "He always has."

"But not like this, for heaven's sake," Laura said, angered by the girl's nonchalance. "Have the police called?"

"Only to say they don't know anything. Dad will be back, Miss Jordan. I told Shirley that. She doesn't know him like I do."

"I don't follow you, Chris."

"When Daddy gets in trouble or he has a problem, sometimes he stays away. He always comes back." If it was a facade to cover her real feelings, Laura thought, it was certainly a strong one.

"I hope you're right, Chris. Could I talk to Shirley?"

"She's asleep. She was exhausted, shaking all over. I had her lie down."

"Don't wake her up. Give her my love, and please let me know if you hear anything, Chris. Thanks for helping Shirley out. You have no idea how much that will mean to her. I know you two have had your differences, but in her way, she loves you very much. You might not believe this, but she'd go to the ends of the earth for you, Chris."

"I'm beginning to realize that, Miss Jordan. I really am. I told her I was sorry for arguing with her about moving out. She said it was all right. She wanted to do the best thing for me."

"Well, good. I'm glad you two had a nice talk," Laura said, feeling tears coming into her own eyes. "And call me if you hear from your dad."

Laura went back to the dinner, feeling much better even though Jack Towne was still missing. Knowing that Chris and Shirley had at least discussed their differences and worked them out was a small but important success. And carrying that feeling, she went into the seminar, burning with enough missionary zeal to get even the slouchers in the back row to sit up. In a deliberately quiet voice, she told the assembled participants there was nothing in this life or on their job they could not achieve if they would only work for it by using effective communications. Because they were mostly men, she went on to tell them a good football story about a coach who was failing.

"And why was he failing?" she asked, perching on the edge

of a table, feeling them all watching her, hanging on every quiet well-modulated word. "Because he didn't know how to talk to his team."

This, she assured them, was a true story about a Montana high school coach who had taken his tiny school on to win the state championship over schools five times their size. Fortunately, as her father Gene was fond of remarking, the coach hadn't cashed in on his discovery and left the field to Laura.

"One day, standing on the sidelines, watching his quarterback make one mistake after another, he realized there was something drastically wrong. Not with the quarterback, but with himself. Instead of telling the quarterback what he was doing right and reinforcing it, all he was doing was telling him what he was doing wrong, and the boy was out there doing it—wrong.

"So, because he had nothing to lose, he decided to try something new. He stopped communicating negative things and decided to try communicating positive things. He showed the quarterback how to hold the ball and how to cock his arm like a gun, and then fire it."

At this point, Laura always went through a little pantomime, which impressed men. Her father and Jim McClay taught her the proper throwing stance.

"When the boy did it right, he congratulated him. When he did it wrong, he did not go running out on the field and say, 'You stupid jerk, I told you not to throw the ball that way.' That wouldn't do any good. Naturally, the boy didn't want to throw the ball wrong.

"He wanted to throw it right, and so the coach showed him how. 'Like this, and this. Now try it!' Slowly but surely, this approach began to take. And so he did it with everybody: linemen, ends, runners. Soon this tiny high school was winning a few games. The next year they won some more, until finally Chief Joseph High with only five hundred students beat Grover Cleveland of Missulou 12 to 6 for the state championship in 1975. An impossible dream? Anybody would have said so. But it happened. It's a fact. And all because of effective communication."

Laura's eyes glittered with the intensity of the true believer and, unlike her dramatic act at dinner, this was the real thing. This was the reason she put on the act, to get the message across, to change people's lives, to help them improve, to make their dreams come true. Laura Jordan was no fake. She was the genuine article, and when the self-improvement spirit moved her, she could send an audience rushing out to take a fresh look at life and all its possibilities.

She was still riding this high when she arrived home around ten that evening and found Jack Towne swaying uncertainly up the gangplank to meet her. He was drunk, and there was blood splattered down the front of his ruffled white-on-white shirt.

"Sorry to disturb you at this late hour, Laura, but I was in the neighborhood," he said, holding his arms wide.

"My God, Jack, what happened to you?"

He laughed a deep belly laugh. "I had a little setback."

"Well, come inside and sit down. You've got to call Shirley right away. She's been looking for you all day."

He allowed himself to be led. Jack Towne was not staggering drunk. He was light on her arm, maneuvering his bulk through the door without assistance. She sat him down in the receptionist's chair and went to get a wash rag for his nose that was still dripping blood.

"Did you run into a door?" she called over the running water from the office bathroom.

"No, actually I ran into a very large black man, baseball player or something. Called me poor white trash. I haven't heard that phrase since I left Kentucky. People used to call my father that. I hit him. I'm not a very good fighter."

He sat fairly straight in the chair, his heavy camel hair overcoat hanging open. His tie, if he'd been wearing one, was gone. The well cut blue suit showed tiny flecks of dried blood. "Here, put this on your nose. It ought to stop the bleeding. And as soon as it stops, you've got to call Shirley."

He shook his head. Whether to clear it or indicate he was not going to call Shirley, she couldn't tell.

"Hey," she said, "for chrissake, hold still and put your head back."

A curious cat hopped up on the desk and looked at him. Jack reached out and scratched its ears. "I can't call Shirley, not yet," he said in a nasal voice, nose pinched shut.

"Be quiet," she ordered, holding the wash rag firmly against his nostrils. There was an abrasion on his cheek like a burn. He reeked of whiskey and cigarette smoke.

The cat maneuvered in closer, and he continued to stroke it while he blinked into the overhead lights. "I'm all done, finished," he said without a trace of self-pity, "as a businessman, as a man, all done."

"I could put this rag in your mouth, Jack."

"Right." He nodded and licked his lips. "I sure could use a drink of water."

"In a minute." She cautiously removed the wash rag to examine the nose. It was already swollen, but the bleeding was stopped.

"How am I, doctor?" he asked her, his head still obediently tilted.

"I think you're going to live. Now what's all this about being done?"

"I blew it," he said, bringing his head down slowly and fingering his swollen nose. "The hearing got out of control. I wasn't even there."

She smiled and sat on the edge of the desk. "Yeah, I know a little bit about that. Shirley and I were trying to hunt you down and I called Timberlake today."

"Well," he said steadily, "then you know the whole sad story. T.R. Timberlake is not a forgiving man." His face, flushed with drink, had taken on the texture of old leather. He shrugged his big shoulders. "There was no excuse for it. They used the oldest trick in the book. Switched the dates at the last minute. Claimed they couldn't get a hold of me and went ahead without me. I wasn't even there. I should have seen it coming. I don't know, maybe I wasn't concentrating. I was worried about Wendy, about Shirley, and so forth. But there's no excuse. I blew the whole goddamn thing."

"Have you talked to Timberlake?"

"No, what's there to talk about? Sure I felt bad, but what could I do? Those things happen. It's no big deal to him. He's got a lot of irons in the fire. I went out and got good and drunk."

"Terrific, Jack. That's just terrific." She stood up and surveyed him. Jack Towne made a very distinguished drunk. He looked like a character right out of a movie. His black shoes were even shined. Deep behind the multiple squinting folds around his eyes, the electric blue still flashed.

"No," he said slowly, "it's pitiful, and it's cowardly."

"Bullshit," she said. "There's nothing wrong with you that a good cup of coffee and a shower won't cure. Now get on the telephone and call Shirley."

"I can't, Laura. Not after what I've done to her. She'll never understand."

"Jack, you're not the first man that went out and tied one on, you know."

"It's not that. It's not that. I need some time to think. I just can't talk to her right now."

Laura put her hands on her hips, still watching Jack carefully. He was a man who looked good in clothes, a monument to good tailoring. "I'll tell you what," she said, "I'll make us some coffee, I'll even loan you a shirt. I've got a sweatshirt that ought to fit. We'll get you cleaned up, have a cup of coffee, and then you can call Shirley. Is that a deal?"

"Sure." He followed her up the narrow stairs to her apartment, supporting himself with his hands on either side as he climbed.

"When I talked to Timberlake," she said, watching him with an amused smile on her face from the top of the stairs, "he really didn't seem that upset. He was mad, but he's not as hard as you think he is, Jack. He wants that ski resort so bad he can taste it. It's his dream too."

"Well, he can afford to dream. I'm a little overextended myself," he said, achieving the top step, huffing like a switch engine.

Laura helped him off with his overcoat and suit jacket, and led him into the bathroom. The ruffled shirt was bloody and torn.

"Jesus, that's my best shirt." He fumbled with the buttons.

"Here," Laura said, "let me do that. What did he hit you

with, a baseball bat?"

"No, with a fist I think. It happened so fast I don't know what it was. One minute I was standing there," he demonstrated, backing up and assuming a fighter's pose, shirt half unbuttoned, "and the next minute I was on my ass. It was sort of like that damn hearing in Wilson," he chuckled.

"Come here and let me get that horrible shirt off," she said, finishing her unbuttoning job and helping him slide out of it.

His torso was covered with fine, silky hair, soft as a baby's to her touch. The rolling expanse of his chest and stomach under this fine meadow of hair fascinated her. It was so unlike Jim McClay who was all hard angles and muscles, or her Austrian lover who had a stomach like a washboard. Laura threw the bloody shirt in the bathtub.

"Try this," she said, giving him one of her oversize gray sweatshirts. But Jack Towne couldn't even get his huge head through the neck. "No go," he said.

She came up with a pink wool blanket to drape around his shoulders that sloped away from the massive head like the sides of a crumbling mountain. He looked older undressed, the flesh hanging on long soft muscles. Laura Jordan was seeing a male body totally different than she had ever seen before. He perched uneasily on the edge of the sofa and examined the room while she made coffee in the kitchen. It was a pleasure seeker's body, she mused, an easy comfortable expanse to accommodate its owner, a man who liked nice clothes and good whiskey and taking chances. Once, she imagined, when he was young, before he was hurt playing football, it housed crushing strength.

"So tell me," she said, flipping the switch on the electric coffeemaker, "what worries you so much about calling Shirley?"

"What do I say?" he asked, folding his hands together and looking down at them. "What do I say to her?"

"You tell her you had some bad luck and went out and got schnockered, please forgive me, I'll be right home." The coffeepot went *ca-chug,ca-chug* in the kitchen.

"There's more to it than that."

"There is?"

"Yes, there is," he said slowly. "I haven't been doing too well—in business, I mean. Shirley's been sort of carrying the ball as far as the bills and so forth. Hell," he said, bringing the folded hands up to his mouth, "she's been carrying it all and with the kids and so forth she's—well—have you noticed she's sort of unstable lately? I don't mean crazy or anything but jumpy, you know?"

The coffeepot was steaming into the home stretch, gurgling furiously. "She seems to be under a strain. Yes, I have noticed that."

"Finding out about this could really do it. God, I feel awful. I put all my money and time into this, Laura, and now it's down the drain. I aimed high, maybe too high, but goddamnit, I thought I could do it. I really did."

Laura poured two cups of coffee. "I'm going to have a little Scotch with mine," she said casually. "That doesn't interest you does it?"

"I'd better not," he replied mournfully, standing up and wandering around the room, a roaming blanket-covered beast.

"Come over here and sit down, Jack. You drive me crazy always moving around. You're a hard man to keep track of."

He came, she noticed, without argument and sat on the bar stool across from her while she metered a generous portion of Scotch into her coffee. Laura Jordon felt very good about herself tonight, and she was not going to let Jack Towne fall on his face. She took a sip.

"Hot," she warned him.

He nodded and blew across the cup, his thick lips flaring out until she could see there was a bad cut on his mouth. "I think that baseball player hit you more than once."

"Oh, hell, maybe he did." He winced as the hot liquid hit the open wound. "Anyway," he went on, "I don't want to make it worse for her."

"Oh come off it, Jack, you're scared to face her, that's all." Laura took a long hot drink.

"Maybe. Yeah, you're probably right." He smiled sheepishly, his blue eyes flickering. "She's not the easiest woman to explain failure to, Laura. You know how much she makes a year?"

Laura admitted she had no idea. "Thirty-two thousand dollars a year. Can you believe that? That's more than I ever made in my life except, of course, when I was vice president of the Golden Triangle Land Company down there in Denver. She's in charge of something like twenty people."

"That's a lot of people."

"It gives her a different view of things. The phone company, I mean. They're never going broke. It's nice steady work. Shirley's done her best to help me, but it isn't the kind of help I need." He ran a hand along his jaw. "Say, I might take a touch of that stuff to clear my head."

She looked at him dubiously. "Please?" he said. She poured a jigger into the outstretched mug.

"The truth is Shirley and I haven't been getting along too well, Laura. It seems like she's so tense about everything lately. And this is just gonna tear it with us; that's what I'm afraid of. She's getting unstable as hell. She never did really understand what I was trying to do over there at Early Winters. She tried, I don't mean to make it sound like she didn't try, but she doesn't understand you have to spend money to make money. You know all about that." He sipped noisily at the coffee. "Say, this is darn good."

"Jack, I didn't realize you were having problems with Shirley, but I don't think you've blown the Early Winters deal as badly as you think. That's not my impression at all. My impression is that if you want to go back over there and pick up the pieces, T.R. Timberlake is ready to go along with you."

Jack sighed and pulled the blanket tighter around him. "Yeah, maybe, but that takes money. See, Teddy isn't putting one dime into this thing until we've got the permit. Can you see me going home and talking Shirley into financing me for another three or four months? Hell, I can't even get her into bed with me lately."

Laura glanced up sharply. Jack was draining his coffee cup. "So there is a little more to it, isn't there?" she asked him.

"The plot thickens. Listen, can I have another one of these?"

"That's what you don't need. I need one, you don't." But

she moved the bottle out onto the bar in full view and went to refill the coffee cups. When she came back, she put the cup in front of him and poured herself a generous portion of Scotch. "Help yourself," she said, "I guess you're of age."

"Over age and feeling older all the time," he replied, pouring himself a shot.

They touched coffee cups with a hollow clank. A jet plane circled low over the lake on its final approach to the airport forty miles away.

"Shirley seems to be pregnant, Jack," Laura reminded him, feeling the Scotch numbing the tip of her nose. A fantastic, reckless scheme was forming in her head to save Jack Towne.

"Oh, that," he said.

"Yeah, that. How did that happen?" She heard her own voice, echoing loudly in the dimly lit room. Could that really be me? Laura wondered.

"For children, it's fine with her, but for anything else—well, she's not very keen on that sort of thing if you know what I mean," he said obscurely, stirring his coffee with a spoon that clanked against the sides of the cup. "She's Catholic, you know, at least sort of. Enough so she pretty much likes to stick to a missionary approach to things."

A tense expectation gripped Laura, tightening her throat, sending a rush of blood to her pelvis, making her hands tingle with excitement. She could hear herself breathing.

"She doesn't like to make love to you?" Laura looked directly into his blue eyes.

Jack Towne glanced away with what seemed to Laura to be almost a coy shyness. It was an odd reaction for a man, she thought. He fumbled awkwardly with the cup. "That's not her fault. She works hard. She's tired. She's, like I said, under this strain that makes her sort of odd. And I let her down, you know. If I'd been a little luckier, if things had gone my way right after we got married, if we didn't have these problems with money and the kids, maybe it would be easier for both of us."

"It could always be a little easier, Jack, but you're avoiding my question, aren't you? It could also simply be that things aren't going well in bed. That can make a difference." Laura thought about the Clairbornes—'this is the clitoris.' She was breathless with excitement. She took another drink of Scotch-laced coffee.

"I've tried to get her to loosen up. I even bought her a book, *The Gourmet's Guide of Exotic Lovemaking,* or something like that. She got pretty uptight about the whole thing," he said, talking down to the floor. "I don't know, Laura, I don't seem to have the magic touch with anything anymore."

He sat, his shoulders slumped and loose, fumbling with his hands again. "Magic doesn't have anything to do with it, Jack. You can't let other people drag you down. You're a bright, capable, dynamic man, and I'll be damned if I'm going to sit here and let you run yourself into the ground. I'm not going to let you quit on yourself when you're so close to your goal."

He looked at her and smiled. "I've been working at this thing all my life in one form or another, Laura. I've been at it so long sometimes I wonder if it's possible anymore, or if it's just a childhood dream, the foolish dream of a poor boy without shoes in Kentucky who looked at one too many big-city magazines. Maybe I ought to admit it's never going to happen."

"You're the one who can make it happen, Jack," she challenged him, coming around the bar.

"It's so damn complicated," he complained.

"No, it's not if you go about it in the right way. It can be very, very simple." Laura knew she should not put her hands on his neck. She knew it would ruin everything.

"It's one thing after another," he said bitterly, "I don't mind a little bit of bad luck, but I've had a lifetime of it. Maybe Dad was right. He always said people like us were playing against a stacked deck. I never wanted to believe it. I always thought there could be something better, but maybe he was right."

She put her hands on his neck; they burned against flesh. "A man can't live on dreams," he said.

"What if I could show you how to make those dreams come true," she said calmly, running her hand under the blanket.

"Not my dreams," he said, holding perfectly still.

"Yes, your dreams." She pushed her breasts against his shoulders. Laura Jordan was going to do exactly what she wanted to do. "I can make you a success, Jack," she whispered fiercely, close to his ear.

"That would be something, wouldn't it?" he replied quietly, turning to her.

"Tell me what your wildest most improbable dream is right at this very moment," she asked, moving her fingers lightly across his rough cheek. Up close his face was a dented and scarred battlefield. "Something you really want in the worst way. Some impossible, secret fantasy."

"Laura," he said softly, stopping the progress of her hand with his own. "You don't have to do this." But his grip was steady and held her hand against his cheek. The heavy gold ring on his third finger caught the light and flashed.

"And you're not answering my question."

"I'd like to have, for once, something purely beautiful happen to me. To touch it, to actually feel it happening, to smell it close so I could be sure it was real and warm, not a dream."

The wild, wild blue of his unblinking eyes flared, and he moved his face against her breasts. Laura held the top of his head, still wet from the rain, against her and unbuttoned her blouse until his lips touched her bra.

"You do exactly what I say, and I'll show you how to touch and feel and taste things you never even dreamed about," she said huskily. Laura took his hand and placed it on her leg.

"I have a little trouble sometimes when I drink," he confessed.

Laura guided his hand up and over her pelvis to the top of her silk panties, thrilling to the touch of the unfamiliar.

"Not with me, you won't," she said.

Chapter 17

Barbara Adams always left home before first light so she could arrive at work in time to see the sun coming up over the hillside across the lake. The sunrise was never the same, and now that she was over fifty, it seemed to have a special significance in her life, reminding her to live each day to its fullest. This morning it was a thin angry band of blood red that hovered above the rooftops and then faded into the boiling thunderheads sweeping across the darkening sky.

She locked her car and walked down the gangplank, pausing to say hello to the family of ducks that seemed to have settled permanently around the houseboat. With alimony from her husband and the family house that had appreciated considerably over the past thirty years, Barb didn't have to work for Laura Jordan or anybody else. Barb worked because she liked it. A job represented freedom after almost twenty-five years of being a prisoner in her own home. And she continued to work for Laura because the two women had developed a satisfying relationship over the years that, if it wasn't quite friendship, was certainly much more than an employee-employer acquaintance.

She opened the door and found the cats waiting all in a row, licking their chops and following her every move as she took off her coat, propped her umbrella against the wall and deposited her purse in the bottom desk drawer. They waited loyally, she knew, for one reason only. Because she fed them.

"You ungrateful kitties," she scolded them, pulling the sack of dry meal out of the closet. "What have you done to earn your keep today?"

They clustered around her ankles, purring and rubbing. Laura loved them for their independence, and Barb Adams was attracted to Laura for the same reason. There was nobody else in the world like Laura Jordan, and Barb often thought that if she'd had a daughter she would have been proud to have one like her employer.

Now the cats were happy, each with a separate bowl. Barb turned on all the lower level lights and went into Laura's office to brew a fresh pot of coffee. She hummed quietly as she measured out the teaspoons a tune from *Man of La Mancha,* one of her favorite shows. Barb Adams was content to work for Laura although they both knew she was capable of doing other more lucrative things. Laura regularly threatened to throw her out into the bigger world where she could be a success.

Still, Barb thought, heading back for her desk and the pile of mail and instructions that were always there, it was a quiet port after a lifetime storm, and she might be content to enjoy the calm ebb and flow of Laura Jordan's daily routine forever. Also, Barb felt a certain motherly concern for Laura who was, after all, a young woman who had come a long way in a very short time. Barb was quite sure that there were times when Laura needed outside advice and the restraining hand of an older person. This very morning was a sterling example, she thought, spotting the note written in Laura's distinctive block letters.

She did not like what she read. With a full day of appointments ahead of her, urgent calls taken by the answering service from Jim McClay, her agent, and Shirley Towne all scattered across the desk, Laura had left Barb Adams holding the bag.

> *"Dear Barb,*
> *Please cancel everything today, regrets and all that etc. etc. I've done a very stupid thing, and I have to get the old head put back on before I can face the world. Sorry. Do the best you can. I shall return.*
> *Laura."*

"Well," Barb said to the cats, who had already cleaned up

the crunchies, "no liver today for you guys." Laura, who usually got up with Barb's call on the intercom, always kept her refrigerator stocked with beef liver and fed it to the cats when they came up to see her in the morning. Barb thought it was a wasteful practice and told her so.

She sat down in her chair and read the note again. This time she found it more disturbing than annoying. It was a strange note to get from Laura, Barb thought. It could signal real trouble. Laura frequently did things on the spur of the moment, but she was never cagey about it. She would leave a note saying she felt like going skiing so she went; she forgot her father's birthday and she knew it was a lot of trouble, but reschedule the morning. This note, however, was quite explicit—Laura had done a stupid thing. Well, Barb thought, arranging the papers across the desk, there was no use worrying about it now. When Laura got ready to tell her, she would tell her.

First, she placed a call to Terry Blake in Laguna, California, who was hot under the collar about Laura's failure to meet a commitment with a radio station in Pomona. Barb knew nothing about it. She calmly told Mr. Blake that Laura had been unavailable at the appointed time. Would he care to schedule another date? He would. This was important, he emphasized. "I'll give it to her first thing, Mr. Blake. Thanks for your call," she said and hung up.

She called Shirley Towne, and there was no answer. Jim McClay's secretary answered his phone and, although Jim was not available, she and Barb had a nice talk. Her name was SueEllen Winters, and she was back at work after having a baby. Barb chatted enough to learn Sean Winters, Jr., weighed a massive ten and a half pounds at birth before finishing her calls to cancel the day's appointments. Finally, she started on the pile of mail.

Through the window that faced the dock, Barb saw two of the cats huddling under the gangplank out of the wind, watching the ducks paddling up and down in the bouncy water. Although they were not chummy, the cats and the ducks had a mutual non-belligerence policy, and they both kept a silent watch over the lake this morning.

Barb opened the first letter. It was from the Society of Professional Engineers and Architects asking Laura to speak on June 14 at a symposium on communication. Barb consulted the appointment book. It was absolutely impossible. Laura Jordan had a commitment in San Francisco the day before. "Gentlemen:" Barb wrote, her fingers flying over the IBM Selectric, "Thank you for the kind invitation to speak at your meeting in June. It sounds like an exciting and productive topic, unfortunately . . ."

Laura Jordan felt awful. She had been walking since four A.M., right after Jack Towne left the houseboat with her promise: "I'll always be here, Jack, when you need me." She had walked clear across town trying to focus her mind on the enormity of what had happened. It wasn't the whiskey, she decided, it was something else. She had been drunk on power, intoxicated by the will to dominate, and driven by the sheer lust of wanting to know what it would be like.

She had walked through the deserted streets of downtown Seattle, past windows advertising tours of the Orient, and a health food store with a life-size replica of Buster Crabbe behind its glass door. She had seen cruising police cars who slowed when they saw her and went by when she waved them off—a tall woman in blue jeans, track shoes, and a wet leather jacket, her blond hair tangled and blowing in the wind.

She walked down the hill, past the urban renewal projects with their neat piles of bricks and silent machines, waved to a group of winos huddled under a viaduct. She walked along the waterfront, smelling the deep brine of salt water in the murky tide flats. Cars rushed by, shaking the street built over a landfill some fifty years ago.

Laura had never noticed how gray everything was: the silent pier buildings, most of them deserted and falling down; the sky; the water clogged with Styrofoam cups and broken slimy timbers. It was the dreariest day of her life. Overhead, clouds that set the dark color scheme for the city boiled and threatened, kicking up harsh bursts of wind that drove sand and papers into the air and then let them silently fall. She turned her jacket collar up and pulled her chin down, shivering in spite of her brisk pace.

She had betrayed Shirley Towne. There was no avoiding that single, horrible, undeniable fact—betrayed her trust and loyalty and all those noble things. And there was no excuse, no place to hide. She would have to face her friend with this terrible thing she'd done—sooner or later.

A ferryboat whistled in the distance. A man was slouched against the cement bulkhead railing ahead of her. Instinctively, Laura moved away from him to the far edge of the sidewalk. As she drew abreast, he came toward her. A youngish man with a dirty blank face, the hollow cheeks, and stick-size wrist bones of an alcoholic.

"Hey, lady, could I ask you one thing? Wait a minute. Could you help a guy get some food? Could you help a guy out?"

He moved alongside her aggressively. She could smell him, sour, unwashed.

"How much do you need?" she said, not looking at him.

"A dollar?"

She pulled out two and put them in his outstretched hands. "Jesus, thanks."

Laura nodded and kept walking, and the bum dropped back, fingering his good fortune. He was so grateful. Like Jack Towne, she thought. Grateful.

The two-tier cement overhead viaduct running along the waterfront was roaring to life. Blue exhaust hung heavy in the air. Was it her dream or his, she wondered, that they pursued so wantonly?

It had not been a night of wild passion. Barb was right: Jack was not even a five, maybe only a three and a half. He had difficulty achieving full erection. She turned up a narrow steep street, heading toward the financial district. The ominous thunderheads towered over the office buildings, making them seem short and insignificant. A humid stillness hung in the air, her clothes stuck to her, the jeans were rubbing her crotch raw.

Punishment for a bad girl, she thought with grim humor, self-flagellation for the sinner. She had to admit it. She had wanted Jack Towne very badly and, in a way, she still wanted him. His body had its own particular fascination, and she had achieved pleasure with it although nothing close to orgasm. Still, it had excited her tremendously, the feel of his huge limp penis, the size of his balls.

Oh, God, she thought, what am I going to do? A biblical phrase emerged from some long-buried subconsciousness as she walked the wet streets. "Let this cup pass from me, let this cup pass from me." It was sacrilegious, she thought, even to use the phrase in connection with something like this, and yet it was a perfect expression of her desperate feeling.

She had only intended to be kind, to help, to restore his self-confidence. But that motive had been overcome by a senseless passion on her part to explore, to experiment, to see what would happen. That was the truth.

And now she knew. Laura swung from despair to silly hysterical highs, and her pace mirrored her mood. She was walking slowly by the Federal Court House, a huge, cold white block. She felt very low. Were those lawyers or criminals going in the front door? Was one of them Jim McClay?

The betrayal was complete: a woman who trusted her as a friend and counselor; and Jim who said he loved her. But did she love him? Laura didn't know. Her pace got faster. A whole new career was opening up if she could brazen it through. Her mood rose with the ridiculous thought. She was just the girl to brazen it through.

Laura Jordan, sex therapist, surrogate wife and lover, impotence-cured-or-your-money-back. Laura was as sure she could bring Jack Towne to a full erection as she was that she could get T.R. Timberlake to finance Early Winters. Look what your arrogance has done, she thought, lowering her head into the cold wind rushing down the canyonlike streets.

Laura pushed against it, out onto the freeway overpass where eight concrete arteries came together and cloverleafed into exits, new freeways, and parking garages. She looked down, hypnotized by the steady penetrating drone of the cars and the whoosh of air as they passed. She stepped back, dizzy. There was no way she could slip and fall into the traffic. It wasn't in her. She would go on in spite of everything. She would never give up.

Mary Kay Jordan was enjoying a quiet restful moment in her sitting room that was actually a glassed-in porch overlooking Lake Washington. The brooding overcast that had been hanging over the lake all day looked even more threatening. Inside, however, everything was cheerful and warm the way she liked it.

Mary Kay had spent the morning playing a hard-fought game of racquetball at the Birch Bay Club with one of her neighbors, a younger woman she had no trouble trouncing. Then she attended a luncheon meeting of the Orthopedic Guild where she allowed herself to drink coffee, but nothing more because at one o'clock she was due at the swimming pool.

Every other day, Mary Kay swam a mile of brisk crawl stroke, and, sick or hung over, she seldom altered the schedule. Now with everything taken care of, she finished a hearty lunch of homemade vegetable soup, cottage cheese, sprouts, and pineapple yogurt. She felt as good as she had ever felt in her life, and everybody said she looked as good too, even though she would turn fifty-four in a month.

Later, she would go down to the greenhouse and water the plants, which took an hour or so, and then it would be time to start dinner for Gene and Laura. Tonight's family night menu was Mexican food, and she'd asked Carmelita to stay over for the occasion. Already the maid, who spoke very little English, was busy in the kitchen.

Mary Kay was flipping through a *Sunset* magazine when she heard the dog bark and the doorbell ring and heard Carmelita's electric mixer stop as she went to answer it. She was surprised to hear Laura's voice. A visit from her daughter in the middle of the day was unusual.

"Laura," she said, pleased to have the company on such a dreary afternoon, "what a nice surprise!"

She was pale and looked exhausted. "Hi, Mom, if I'm breaking anything up please ignore me."

"Why, of course not. What's the matter, dear, are you sick?"

"No, I've been walking."

"Walking from where?"

"From my office, all around town. I was feeling a little down so I thought I'd come and see my favorite Mother."

"Oh, honey, it's good to see you." Mary Kay hugged her daughter close to her and felt the wet coldness of her clothes. "I wish you'd come out more often. I miss you sometimes still. Hell, Laura, I miss you all the time."

"I miss you too, Mom." She stood in the center of the room, looking bedraggled and forlorn. Her feet hurt, and she was very cold.

"Would you think I was being an interfering old mother if I ran you a bath and got you out of those clothes?"

Laura shook her head and allowed herself to be led into her old bedroom. The picture of Jim McClay in his high school football uniform, charging the camera, still hung on the wall. Her favorite tiger, a huge, battered stuffed animal half as big as the bed, was in the corner. "Hello, tiger," she said.

"You take a bath and put on a robe, and I'll make us some tea. Your dear sweet daddy won't be home for hours. We can chatter all we want to."

Laura stood in the steamy bathroom and pulled off her blouse. "Barb called earlier and said she was sure you were coming to dinner," her mother called to her over the roar of the water.

"Good. I knew she would. She knows what I'm going to do better than I do."

"She's a terrific gal, so full of life and vitality. I like that in older women," her mother kidded her.

"Vim and vigor, the family religion."

"It's as good as any," her mother said. "Get a move on, girl, we've got a lot to talk about."

Laura let herself sink into the bubble bath, feeling the rich soap lubricating her buttocks so, if she didn't brace with her feet on the end, she might slide into a billowing pile of bubbles. She laid in the water, only her face out, listening to the funny sounds of her feet squeaking against the sides of the tub.

She didn't think about anything. Every so often, she sat up to run more hot water, feeling dizzier each time as the temperature in the bathroom went higher. She used to sit in this same tub and think about Jim McClay and school, her life and who she would marry, her friends and dogs and how someday she wanted to jump out an airplane. Those things crossed her mind, but didn't stay. Mostly, she felt the healing, soothing hot water restoring her confidence, burning out the dull and sickening ache she'd been carrying around all morning. Finally, flushed with heat, the skin on her toes and fingers wrinkled from immersion, she got out and put on the robe her mother left on the bed.

It felt cold in the house after the heat of the bath, and Mary Kay Jordan got out a down comforter and wrapped it around her daughter's legs in the sitting room. The tea was peppermint and strong, and it came with homemade chocolate chip cookies, the same recipe Laura remembered her mother making when Laura was a little girl.

The dull afternoon light was fading. The far shore seemed to be sinking beneath the slow rollers the wind was pushing down the lake.

"Feel better?" her mother asked.

"Yes, thanks. There's nothing a warm bath won't cure."

"Well, practically nothing. You want to tell me about it?"

"It's something I've got to handle alone, Mom. It's sort of business, but I feel better about it already."

"Good, I'm dying to know, but I won't ask. Those cookies are healthy, you know, whole wheat flour, no sugar, pure honey."

Laura nibbled on one, finished it, and then another. They talked about her father and his scheme to get a newer and bigger boat. They talked about helicopter skiing, a favorite idea of Mary Kay's that Laura was trying to put off until next year.

"Next year," her mother said, radiant with perfect health, "I might be dead. I wasn't born yesterday, Laura Jordan. Your father and I will celebrate our thirty-second wedding anniversary this year."

"To coincide with my thirty-second birthday. Very suspicious," Laura said with her mouth full of cookies.

"You brought us together, so to speak," her mother said, matter-of-factly, "a decision I certainly never regretted."

Laura sipped her tea. It was a story she'd heard before, and it was true. The so-called shotgun wedding had scandalized both the Jordans and her mother's parents. But Mary Kay had always treated it like an astounding piece of good luck.

"Mother, have you ever thought about what's kept you and Dad together and so happy all this time? I mean really sat down and figured it out?"

Her mother laughed and sat up a little straighter in her chair. "No, I haven't," she said. "Does that surprise you?"

"No, I just wondered."

"You've got man trouble, Laura, I can tell. Well, I won't pry. I've already given you my prescription for that problem. With all due respect to your lucrative profession of better communication and all that sort of thing, the answer is Jim McClay."

"I know, Mother."

"I said I wouldn't go into it, and I won't. But it's my opinion you've become somewhat obsessed with your specialty in regards to marriage. You and Jim fit together, that's all. Even if you never said a word to each other except good morning and good evening."

"Pretty sure of yourself, aren't you? That also runs in this darn family."

"Sure about that. I guess that's really the way I feel about your father. We fit together. I enjoy his company; I like to do things with him; I miss him when he isn't here. We're comfortable with each other. We get along."

"But is that enough for thirty-two years?"

"It doesn't seem like thirty-two years."

"But haven't you ever been interested in another man?"

Her mother put down her tea cup. "I'm pleased to say that plenty of other men have been interested in me and, as a matter of fact, they still are, which makes me feel ever so good." She picked up a chocolate chip cookie and examined it. "But to answer your question directly, dear, the answer is no, never, not ever. I wouldn't consider it. Other men are so dull compared to your father, and, besides, I'm no husband swapper. I get my extra kicks from skiing or a good game of racquetball."

"But haven't you ever been tempted to try?"

"Is this a quiz?" her mother asked. "Are you searching for some sort of fault in my moral character? I may not go to church with any seriousness whatsoever, my dear, and you may find this hard to believe in this age of free sex, but I have never ever ravished anybody but your father."

"But why?" Laura persisted, feeling her head begin to throb. "Is it love or what?"

"I suppose so. Call it what you want. Maybe I'm a coward."

"That's not true, Mom, you're the original daredevil," Laura laughed.

"Coming down a ski hill and going to bed with other men would require two different kinds of courage, I think."

"Maybe you're right."

"I don't know, honey," she said reflectively, staring out the window. "I know I feel a great deal of loyalty toward your father. We share a trust between us that's very important. I've also, over the years, compromised with him, given quite a bit of myself over to him I suppose. But he's done the same thing. He could hurt me terribly if he wanted to, and I could hurt him the same way."

Mary Kay paused and poured herself another cup of tea. "But why would we hurt each other? That would ruin a very good thing."

They talked about the divorces of friends and neighbors and the tragic results. The Townes were never far from Laura's mind. They talked movie stars and diets, and finally her mother asked her if she was feeling well.

"I guess not," Laura confessed, "I'm beat."

"Why don't you lie down on the couch before dinner? Remember how you used to do that in junior high? You'd come home so exhausted you could hardly keep your eyes open."

Laura did remember. The warm security of the down

comforter, listening to the sounds of dinner cooking in the kitchen. She heard a collie barking in the driveway again and knew her father was home. His greeting, always the same. "Where is everybody? The lord and master's home; all women and children front and center."

Laura wondered sleepily whether he was putting that on for her benefit, or he actually still did it when she wasn't there? He must do it all the time, she thought, because he couldn't possibly know I'm here tonight.

When Gene Jordan found out his daughter was sleeping on the couch, he lowered his voice. She could hear them talking in whispers like they used to, and it made Laura feel young and strong again.

"Sometimes I think you pushed her too hard, Gene," her mother whispered. "She's trying to carry too much all alone."

"All alone is her choice," he whispered back. "She's a smart girl, she can take it. Let's let her sleep it off. I'm starving."

At midnight, Laura woke and saw the moon glinting off the smooth water. Groggy and hungry, she found the freezer by habit and on the middle shelf, prominently displayed, was a pint of banana nut ice cream, her staple through high school. There was a note under it in her father's hand, "DON'T GET FAT."

Pulling it out and scooping out a big spoon full, she realized her father must have driven clear into the city after dinner. The brand was sold only in a downtown gourmet shop.

She intended to have a few bites, but stayed to eat it all. Tomorrow she would have to face Shirley and Jack and Jim McClay. Face them with the truth. It was only midnight. For now she was safe and full. Laura rolled back up in the comforter, lay down on her parents' couch and fell back into a deep dreamless sleep.

There were now three unanswered calls from Shirley Towne sitting on Barb Adams' desk. Laura's secretary had faithfully tried to return them yesterday, but the one this morning was labeled "Urgent." She was surprised to find that when she started dialing the number it was neither the familiar home number nor Shirley's office phone. "The Fletcher Clinic," a woman answered.

"Extension 545," Barb told her, examining the message as she waited.

"Recovery Room." A voice answered.

"Yes, I'm calling for Mrs. Shirley Towne. I was told she could be reached at this number."

"Just a moment."

She ran down the list of canceled appointments as she waited. Gene Jordan had called early that morning to tell her Laura was sick and stayed overnight at their house. Although her father indicated she might be in later, Barb had prudently decided to cancel all appointments.

"This is Shirley Towne," a weak voice finally responded.

"Shirley, this is Barbara Adams, returning your call to Laura. We've been trying to reach you at home for some time."

"Is she there?" Shirley interrupted her explanation.

"No, I'm afraid she's not."

"Can you get a hold of her?" The more Shirley talked, the stronger her voice became.

She sounded very determined to Barb Adams. "Yes, I think so."

"Would you tell her, ask her, to please come and get me. Please do that for me?"

"What's wrong, Mrs. Towne?"

"I've had an abortion." Her voice broke. She spat the words out. "I need her help to get home. I wouldn't ask, but I don't have anyone else to call."

"Let me see if I can get a hold of her, Mrs. Towne. And if I can't, I'll come myself."

"Oh, thanks, I appreciate that," her voice softened. "Tell her to come soon—please."

Laura was up drinking coffee, wearing a pair of her old corduroy slacks and tank top from days when she was younger and lighter. Both were tight. She smelled the familiar steak and eggs her father liked in the morning, felt the brush of his lips on her cheek.

She had reached up and grabbed him around the neck. "Thanks for the ice cream, Daddy."

He still wore the same aftershave. "You're welcome." His Paul Newman face smiled at her. "Say, are you OK?"

"I think so."

"If there's anything I can do you call, hear? I've got to run down to Olympia and bribe a few politicians."

The coffee tasted good. She felt calm and analytical. It was just a matter of setting the record straight, and this was a good morning to do it. Laura was firming up her resolve with a second cup of coffee when her mother called her to the telephone.

It was Barb Adams, and she got straight to the point. Shirley Towne was at the Fletcher Clinic and needed her help. Laura's horizon closed to a smudge on the wall directly in front of her. Desperately switching the telephone receiver from hand to hand, she tried to think of a way out. There was none. She was caught in a trap of her own making. She could not deny her friend. In a voice choking with dryness, she told Barb to let Shirley know she would be there as quickly as possible.

She borrowed the Olds station wagon and in five minutes found herself in the late-morning traffic going to the city, her stomach queasy with fear and apprehension. The diesel fumes from the big hinged buses came in the vents; the car felt gigantic compared to her Volvo. The speeding tires picked up the wetness off the pavement, scattering blinding dots of mud across her windshield.

Why in God's name did Shirley have an abortion? Laura wondered, clenching her teeth together as she went speeding across the bridge. It was the last thing Laura expected her to do. There had been no mention of anything like that at all. Never!

And where was Jack? What had he told her when he came in at four A.M. drunk and reeking of another woman? What did he tell Shirley? Did Shirley know?

Laura Jordan had no answers. The drivers of the cars around her stared grimly ahead, seemingly intent on nothing beyond getting themselves safely into the city. What waited for them there? She wondered. Were some facing momentous decisions that twisted and writhed in their stomachs? Operations for deadly diseases? Jail sentences? Did any of them feel like she did?

Shirley waited for her, sitting on the edge of a turned-down bed in a pale-blue gown, her packed suitcase at her feet.

"Oh God, Laura," she cried, her strained white face wet with tears.

Laura went to her, stiffly tried to comfort her, reminding herself that she must tell Shirley Towne the truth. But that would have to come later. For now, she held Shirley in her arms as best she could. An orderly popped in and out like a jack-in-the-box.

"I'm sorry," he kept saying, "but we have to make up this bed."

"Go away," Laura told him.

Finally, her sobs under control, and with Laura's assistance, Shirley stood up slowly and painfully.

"Are you sure you ought to be doing this?" Laura asked her, feeling her own womb contracting in a sympathetic reaction.

"I want to get out of here," Shirley said firmly. "Please."

Laura held her under the arm. Shirley groaned with the first few steps, and then gathering strength, she forced herself into a slow shuffle.

"Where's Jack?" Laura asked, making the question sound natural.

"I don't know."

"Didn't he come with you?"

"Yes. He brought me down. He promised to stay. He left. I couldn't stand it alone, Laura. I just couldn't."

"It's going to be all right," she reassured the smaller woman, feeling the pain with her, the sorrow, the humiliation.

People passed them in the corridor—crisp young doctors, efficient nurses. Laura took her to the elevator and then down to the parking garage and helped her into the Olds. Shirley's face was chalk white without makeup; she looked ten years older. Her hands shook with the pain as she eased slowly and carefully back in the seat.

"How's that?" Laura asked her with that tone reserved for the very sick.

"It's OK," she breathed out a long sigh and sucked in another breath.

Shirley sat straight, unmoving in the front seat, one hand braced on the dashboard in front of her to ward off any sudden jolt. Laura was sweating from the strain; a ticklish drip ran down her cheek. Nervously, she adjusted the heater and tried to concentrate on driving. Shirley Towne smelled sick. It was the hospital, the smell of dying.

They were pulling up onto the freeway when Laura finally spoke. "I didn't know anything about this, Shirley. When did you decide to have an abortion?"

The question hung uneasily between them. "There's a lot you don't know about, Laura," Shirley finally replied, her voice so strong and firm Laura risked a quick glance at her.

Laura concentrated on getting out into the traffic, grateful for the need to give all her attention to four lanes of cars trying to squeeze together.

"The other thing," Shirley said loudly over the noise of the onrushing traffic, "is that I'm leaving Jack."

"Leaving?" Oh God, thought Laura, here it comes.

They were in the outside lane, and Laura realized she was going faster and faster. Carefully, she eased off the gas and watched the red needle drop from 70 to 55.

"I can put up with everything but this," Shirley said with dogged determination. "I don't mind paying all the bills or being treated like a servant or being ignored and insulted by his children, but this—this crime—this thing—this thing that I've done to myself—is—more—than—I—can—stand."

"Oh, no," Laura said, aware her words made no sense, that they were halfway between a denial and an exclamation of hopelessness.

"God will never forgive me for this, Laura, never. It's wrong, wrong, wrong!" Her fists were clenched and trembling.

"Don't say that, Shirley." The Episcopalian God of Laura's

childhood had faded, and in its place was a vague feeling that in all living things there was a common spirit that didn't deal in such things as forgiveness or blessing.

"But it's true. I knew it was wrong. I felt it. I only did it for Wendy so Jack could bring her home. Jack said a new baby would be too much. He begged me to do this. He said he would make it up to me and, like a fool, I believed him." Her voice broke. "He didn't stay with me. He left me a note. He said it was urgent business. Oh, God, what have I done?" She was still sitting straight in the seat, tears running down her face.

The traffic thinned as they left the central city. Delivery trucks, station wagons full of kids, salesmen thumbing through sample books while they drove, all moved with them.

"It must have been important," Laura said feeling the inadequacy of her explanation. She reached out to touch her.

Shirley pushed her hand away. "It was not," she said angrily. "Not as important as what was going on in that hospital room. It was a person. There were little fingers and toes. I saw them! They put it in a bucket! I deserve to die, Laura, to die for what I've done."

They went on into the suburbs, shopping centers on either side. Laura drove, and Shirley Towne sobbed quietly. Finally, Shirley took out a Kleenex and blew her nose.

"Are you going to be all right at home?" Laura asked her. She felt the immediate crushing weight of confession easing temporarily. Apparently, Jack had said nothing about their affair. Laura still intended to tell Shirley, but they had miles to go.

Shirley stopped crying. She took a deep breath and exhaled slowly. "I'm fine. I need to lie down for a while. The doctor said I was fine. A big strong girl. Oh, Laura, I wanted that baby more than anything in the world, and now I've destroyed it. All for someone who doesn't care."

"Shirley, Jack cares. I'm sure he does." But before she finished the sentence, Laura knew she was wrong.

Shirley Towne didn't reply. She looked straight ahead. "It doesn't matter," she said calmly. "I've made up my mind,

Laura. This is the end of it. I can't take anymore; I'm leaving. I'm going to save myself."

The house looked even more depressing in the daylight than Laura remembered it. The front curtains didn't match. Shirley's Pinto was still in the open garage propped up on blocks, the driver's door standing open. Rob's white Corvette, with two pairs of skis on top, was sitting crossways on the front lawn.

Laura parked in the street along the curb and got out. A mangey spaniel, his long hair wet and muddy, came rushing at her, barking furiously. "Go away," she said, but the dog kept nipping at her. As she went to open Shirley's door, his front teeth closed on her pants.

"Goddamn it!" she whirled and kicked at him, and he slunk away, whining. A woman across the street in a housecoat and hair curlers shouted at her. "If you'd be nice to him, he'd be nice to you!"

"Do you want me to stay with you, Shirley?" Laura asked her as she helped her walk to the house. More than anything else, Laura wanted to leave, to get away from Shirley as fast as possible.

"No, Rob's here. He can drive me. I'm going to move in with a friend at work for a while."

"Shirley, are you sure about this?"

Shirley's hand quivered on her arm, shaking with the strain of holding up her torn body. "I'm sure," she said.

Rob Towne was eating a peanut-butter-and-jelly sandwich when Shirley and Laura came in. Shirtless, he stood in the kitchen, stretch pants turned up at the knee.

"Oh, hello," he said to them, his mouth full of peanut butter and jelly. He glanced at them both, seeing Shirley's gown, and turned away. He seemed to know something was very wrong.

"What's the matter with you?" he asked Shirley, slapping a glob of peanut butter on a spongy piece of white bread. The stuff went clear through, smearing on his hands. Rob licked it off.

"She's been in the hospital, Rob," Laura said.

"Oh," he said, folding the bread double.

"Rob," Shirley asked him, "I wonder if you could do me a favor?"

"Sure." He downed the sandwich in two big bites.

"I need you to drive me some place. Could you do that?"

"I'm going skiing," he said, "but I'll drop you. Where are you going?"

"I'm leaving," she told him, her dark eyes wide with emotion. "I'm leaving your father. I'm leaving all of you."

Laura knew the words cut deep into Rob. She saw the involuntary shudder, the spasmodic quivering of his lower lip. She wanted to reach out, to fold him in her arms and rock him like a baby, to tell him everything would be all right. But instead, she stood paralyzed in the Townes' kitchen and watched him turn to Shirley, a mask of contrived nonchalance over his beautiful face.

"Well," he said, turning away, "have a nice trip."

For the next two days, Laura Jordan tried to conduct her business normally. She didn't hear from either Shirley or Jack, and she made no attempt to contact them. Friday afternoon, she held a ghastly TV recording session on child abuse with two women who had been sexually molested as children.

What amazed Laura was that these two women were fairly normal in spite of their experiences. While one related how an endless series of stepfathers had climbed into her bed, followed by foster parents who committed their sexual abuses together, including burning her twelve-year-old buttocks with cigarettes, Laura wondered when and how she should approach Shirley and tell her the truth.

"It wasn't until I was about sixteen that I realized what I was doing was wrong, that it wasn't the way things were. I was used to it. I didn't know anything else."

"You've certainly demonstrated that you're made of superior stuff," Laura told her with frank admiration. "What kind of problems have you had as a result of these experiences?"

"For years, even after I was happily married, I was continually overweight because I didn't want to be attractive. At least that's what I figure. I associated being attractive with what my parents did to me."

"I can only hope that your experiences will alert others," Laura heard herself saying piously. "So that people can become more aware of what can be going on in what seems to be perfectly normal situations."

The producer, fidgeting with his unlit pipe after the taping, allowed as how the guests were dynamite, but he felt she didn't have her mind on the program.

Laura agreed with him and then reached a decision. This Sunday would be the last "Family Line," she said, for at least two weeks. He had that much film in the can. She would ask a friend and colleague of hers to fill in.

The producer sat her down and, pointing with his gnawed pipe stem, asked what was the matter.

"I'm tired," Laura told him, "I'm sick of the whole thing."

That same day, she broke the news to Barb that she was locking up the office for a while. Together, they mapped out the necessary arrangements to refer clients and take care of the publisher and her agent. That night, she called Jim McClay, whose calls she'd neglected for three days.

"Are you all right?" he asked her. He sounded cautious and far away.

She assured him she was still among the living. "Jim," she asked, "can I talk you into taking me to the San Juans like you asked me?"

"That was an open invitation."

"I know, but I mean now."

"Like when?"

"Like Monday morning."

He paused. "Sure, if that's when you want to go."

"That's when I want to go. Are you sure it's OK? You don't have some important court dates or anything?"

"All my court dates are important. We'll go on Monday."

"I need to talk to you about some things. I'm sorry to have to push you like this."

"You're not pushing me. It's nice to hear your voice."

"Me too."

"Bring a raincoat."

"I will."

On Monday morning, Laura Jordan walked into the telephone building with the rest of the workers. Her sail bag and yellow slicker attracted some attention in the elevator, but when she stepped out on the sub-basement where Shirley Towne worked, nobody even looked up.

It was quiet and cold in the computer room, and Shirley was smoking a cigarette in her glassed-in office. Laura walked like a condemned criminal, imagining eyes watching her from behind each partition. If Shirley supervised twenty people, none of them were in evidence today. The door was open, and she walked in. Shirley stood up quickly leaving her cigarette burning in the ashtray. The smoke was sucked away in a steady stream by an overhead ventilator.

"I'm sorry I have to bother you," Laura said, hearing herself use the same words she'd condemned Shirley for using so often.

"That's all right. When something's bothering you, it's best to talk about it." Shirley sat down and picked up her cigarette. Our roles have been completely reversed, Laura thought. Shirley sat back in her chair, a powerful supervisor secure in her glass world of machines.

"I'm afraid this is going to hurt—both of us."

"Sometimes that can't be avoided," Shirley said, exhaling strongly, sending the smoke up and away toward the ceiling.

"I went to bed with your husband. I want you to know that."

"It doesn't surprise me," Shirley said, tapping off a long ash. "Nothing surprises me anymore."

Laura sat on the edge of her chair, feeling the ground fall away under her. "I don't know really how it happened, but it did, and I wanted you to know."

"So I know," Shirley said, glancing past her toward the door, "and I really don't want to talk about it." One of the buttons on her telephone was flashing.

Laura Jordan stood up. "Well, goodbye."

"Goodbye, Laura." She stabbed the button and cradled the phone under her chin. "Operations," she snapped, shaking out another cigarette. "Shirley Harter speaking."

In front of the building, Laura slipped the envelope addressed to Jack Towne into the mailbox.

> *"Dear Jack,*
>
> *I think it's best if we don't see each other for a while. I realize that this is a bad time for you, but I think it's better if I stay out of it. I need some time to sort things out. I hope you can respect my wishes. I do care about all of you.*
>
> *With affection,*
>
> *Laura"*

She had agonized over the signature block, rewriting the note late into the night, crossing out love, sincerely, with love, and your friend, all of which seemed to be abominations. "With affection" was as close as she could come to the truth.

The white card on the mailbox showed a scheduled pickup time of 9:45 that morning. By then, she would be on her way to the San Juan Islands with Jim McClay.

Chapter 18

They left Seattle in the morning under full sail and headed north up Puget Sound, the forty-two-foot *Laura J.* slicing cleanly through the light chop. Less than a mile offshore, the city faded into the turbulent overcast. They were alone on the dark-green water with only the slap of the waves along the waterline and an occasional gull for company.

To the west, the low profile of the Sound islands crouched under scudding storm clouds. Laura stood at the chromed navy wheel, her bright yellow slicker buttoned under her chin, listening to the delicate quivering of the luff in the sails. She ignored the array of gauges under the weather hood in front of her that provided digital readings from keel to masthead, and steered by feel.

Laura concentrated all her attention on keeping the boat pointing at exactly the right angle and the sails trimmed while Jim McClay rummaged below, storing gear and arranging his sails in the forward locker. Down the narrow companionway leading to the main cabin, she could hear the radio talk going back and forth between unseen ships somewhere ahead. She was content to let Jim do his own on-board housekeeping. She knew he was uncomfortable until everything was properly stowed, and when it was, he would come up on deck and begin sailing the sloop in earnest.

Laura wasn't ready for that yet, she thought, feeling the big boat heeling under a strong gust. She had intended to talk to him before they sailed, but his younger brother had been there, helping him load groceries for the last-minute trip.

Now she wanted to put it off again, to concentrate on the

sensation of gliding, to enjoy the smooth lifting sensuous feeling of flying across the water like a great slow-moving bird.

Jim had not been talkative, and his face seemed pale in contrast to his usual ruddiness.

"Top of the morning," he said to her.

"Hello," she replied, standing on the dock watching them transfer bags of groceries from the dock cart.

"I had to work late last night so I sent my little brother out shopping for me this morning. I'm not very well organized," he apologized.

His brother smiled, a big, square powerful boy. Jim had looked like that during his football playing days, prime beef on the hoof.

"I hope you like Chet's Chicken Pot Pies," the brother kidded her.

"I guess I'll have to learn," she told him.

Laura had kissed Jim lightly on the cheek and climbed aboard. He'd lost the football player look. The Army and Viet Nam had altered his face and body forever. He was thinner, much thinner, and harder. Definite bold lines sliced down his once boyish face. The truth was he got better looking every year, she thought, as she stowed her bag in the teak-paneled stateroom where the wide double berth was covered with his father's blue Annapolis blanket with white navy crest.

A freighter, three stories high with not a porthole showing, was coming at them down the sea lane, its bow thruster poking out of the water like an enormous ram designed to sink everything in its path. Laura held her course aggressively. There was room to spare, and she didn't like the idea of giving way to such an ugly piece of technology. It was a Japanese car carrier, a floating boxcar with a tiny pointed bow and a bridge so high its bristling antennas were running in the clouds. The slanted blue-tinted windows stared blindly down on them as it arrogantly sounded a whistle. The ship plowed up the sea before it, sending out a bow wave so steep it curled toward them like surf.

Forgetting Jack Towne who would soon be getting his

letter and Shirley hiding among her computers, Laura watched as the massive white-sided carrier slipped by to port and brought the *Laura J.* smartly across its stern. The sharp sleek bow of the sailboat cut through the hissing waves and the boat held steady on its course.

They didn't care, Laura thought angrily. They'd run anything down to keep on their precious timetable, which was no doubt entrusted to a computer that ran the giant engines. A box within a box. All that was left was the square stern with black lettering and a boiling, foaming wake of bubbles and whirlpools.

"Playing chicken again?" he asked her, emerging from the open companionway.

"Just hanging tough."

"Good idea except when you're up against insurmountable odds. Want me to take the wheel for a while? There's hot coffee below."

"OK, you want some?"

He nodded and put a hand over hers that still gripped the chrome wheel. "I'm glad you decided to come," he said.

"So am I."

As she went down the narrow ladder, she heard the winches going and knew Jim McClay had his eyes glued not on the horizon but on the instruments he put so much faith in. The familiar smell of teak oil and fiberglass in the cabin made her nostalgic, and she sat at the galley table for a minute, looking around the cabin.

The piles of baggage and sacks of groceries were gone, all stored in nooks and crannies and closets and compartments that were labeled as to content. "Dish Washing Stuff" was one sign under the sink. "Rain Gear" was another, neatly stenciled inside the closet.

The stove quivered slightly on its gimbels. Nothing would break, slide, turn over or spill no matter how rough the weather became. Jim had raced the boat since it was new, and although it was furnished to cruise, it had a certain spartan air inside that indicated speed took precedence over luxury.

It had been over a cabin table like this one, but on another boat, that Jim's father had taken her hand and told Laura that he wanted her to marry his son. "You marry that boy, Laura. He needs somebody to slow him down once in a while and show him the good things in life."

Red-faced, hard-driving Angus McClay, who contested everything in life and wore kilts and played the bagpipes in the Birch Bay Fourth of July parade, had never been able to take his own advice, and died from a massive coronary at age forty-eight, sailing in the same Race Light Classic Jim would miss this year because of her.

Laura felt tears coming and stood up quickly, banging her ear against the overhead. "Damn," she swore. She couldn't afford to get sentimental. Those were simpler days when she was a girl. She was a woman now and had to face the fact she betrayed people she cared about. There was no avoiding it.

Although she hadn't told Barbara Adams what happened, her perceptive secretary seemed to understand why she was going.

"Go and stay as long as it takes," she told Laura. "Things will look different when you get back."

Laura hoped so. She hoped she could find the courage to face what she had done, and the intelligence to deal with it. It really wasn't that complicated, she thought, gathering up the steaming coffee mugs. The first thing she had to do was get up on deck and tell Jim McClay the truth.

She handed him the coffee, and he grunted his thanks. "Wind's shifting," he muttered. She nodded, waiting for his attention, some signal that he was ready to listen, a sign that he knew what was coming. "Get up there and see if you can kick that telltale loose on the port side, will you?"

Obediently, she made her way forward, feeling the quivering of the boat under her feet as she went. The wind tugged at her hair. The bow hissed through the water.

Back in the cockpit, she settled down in the corner, pulling her rainhood up against the wind, sipping at the coffee which was going cold. She waited. How could she say it? she wondered, her stomach rebelling against the harsh sour bite of the caffeine. She took another sip. She had to do it, but he was asking her to take the wheel while he tried another genoa.

She watched him hanking the new sail. He was so sure, so efficient on the slippery deck that was beginning to roll hard. The waves were darker and showed some white at the tips; briny foam was collecting in the troughs. A drop of rain hit Laura on the face.

"Hey there, helmsman, look smart," he shouted at her. Both sails were luffing badly, slapping and cracking in the wind. Embarrassed, she spun the wheel and brought it around to a sailing angle.

All morning long they beat north with the wind rising. They saw very few other boats, practically no pleasure craft at all. It was too early in the season. April weather was always blustery and unpredictable. Jim's second genoa was no better than the first so he tried a third.

In the early afternoon, Laura fixed them some thick tomato soup and crackers, and they ate it in the open cockpit, crouching behind the canvas storm canopy.

"You cold?" he asked her, putting a wet yellow-slickered arm around her. The rain came and went in light squalls.

"No, I'm fine." He wasn't talking much. He must know, she thought miserably; he knows and he's angry. He knows and he feels beaten. To him, it's a contest of male egos. "Don't touch my girl." She pulled her hands up inside the oversize raincoat sleeves and clenched her fists.

But it had nothing to do with male egos. So why should she feel guilty? Laura wondered. She hadn't seduced Jack Towne to satisfy some curiosity and unrequited lust, although that was part of it. She'd also gone with him because he needed her; she could help him recover his drive to succeed. She could renew his faith in himself.

The *Laura J.* heeled sharply under a blast of wind that set Jim trimming sails again. She handled the wheel while he manned the winches. Of course, in the process, she made a mess of other peoples' lives. And now she was about to drop the bomb on Jim McClay.

"Goddamn, Laura, you're wandering all over the bay. Hold her into the wind," he shouted roughly. A cloud of spray burst over the side, drenching both of them. The wind seemed to be coming from all directions; she'd lost her feel for it.

"Here," he said, taking the wheel, "let's see what I can do."

Head down, he watched his gauges then leaned outboard and looked up into the sails then back to the gauges again. "I cut my goddamn hand," he said, not looking at her.

Blood was oozing between the fingers on his left hand. Laura went into the forward cabin and got the first aid kit. It was almost three in the afternoon. She couldn't wait much longer.

Back on deck, the sway had increased, and the wind was clearly shifting to the southwest and blowing hard. She bandaged his hand while he stood at the wheel. They were off the high cape at the end of Whidbey Island. He glanced at his gold wristwatch and back at the sky.

"Jim," she said, standing next to him, feet braced against the roll, "I've got to tell you something."

"Shoot."

"I went to bed with Jack Towne. I had sex with him. I don't know how or why I did it, but I did it."

A small fishing boat was plowing toward them, sheets of white spray crashing off the bows.

"I thought it was something like that," he said eyeing the boat.

"I'm not confessing," she said over the wind, "even though I feel like it. It was just something I wanted you to know."

Keeping one hand on the wheel, he reached out with his bandaged hand and touched her on the arm. "It's all right," he said. The freckles stood out in black dots across his face; his lips were thinned down and pressing hard against each other.

"Is that all you've got to say?" she cried into the wind.

"What do you want me to say?" he shouted back, and removed his hand from her arm.

He hunched into the wind, pointing the *Laura J.* as high as she would go, daring the weather to blow him off course. The fishing boat was abeam of them, and Laura could see the heavy wipers on the cabin window sweeping back and forth. The bow rose high out of the water on the crest of each oncoming wave, exposing the dull-red bottom paint and then slammed down into the trough.

"Get the glasses," he ordered her. "I want to talk to that Norwegian."

She found the heavy binoculars and tried to hold them on the boat. It's name was *Dauntless.* She could see two men in the cabin.

"Can you hold her up?" he asked, indicating the wheel.

"Yes."

Jim McClay slipped quickly down into the cabin while she took the helm. At first she was afraid. The boat felt so much different in the high wind, but then she realized the *Laura J.* was steady in the water; she was the one who was shaking.

He came back, grim-faced. "Goddamn squareheads, you can hardly understand the bastards. Why can't they speak English? 'Nasty veder, captain,'" he mimicked, taking the wheel.

She waited for him to say something. She'd told him the truth. Finally he turned to her. "What's your pleasure?" he asked calmly. "We can turn back here and find a hole and wait till morning, or we can go for it and run the Straits. That could get rough. They've got gale warnings up all the way."

She saw the hard glint of determination in his eyes. He wanted to cross. He was not a man to hide in a hole until morning. The sky darkened over them. In front lay over twenty miles of open sea, the wide cold Strait of Juan deFuca cutting in from the North Pacific.

He was giving her a choice. "If you want to sleep, we'd better turn around," he advised her. Already, she could feel the heavy action of the ocean swells amid the tossing waves. "Let's go for it," she said.

He slapped her hard on the back. "That's my girl," he told her. "That's my girl."

By the time they cleared the last landfall, the sky was black, and fat raindrops were bursting across the teak decks like beebees. The waves were comers, building upward until the shrieking wind tore their foaming tops off and sent them flying into the air. Their running lights glowed in the dark, and Laura could hear the calm precise voice of the U.S.

Weather Bureau broadcaster on the radio, advising all small craft from Restoration Head to northern Vancouver Island to clear the water.

Jim went forward, ran up a storm jib and reefed the main down while she found herself gasping for breath at the feel of being in the teeth of a gale.

"I want you to go down and get a polar suit on," he told her when he got back. "Get one out for me too."

"I'll be all right," she protested.

"Like hell. I can't afford to lose you, babe. I can't sail this thing alone."

Laura made her way down into the cabin, crouching low against the constant bucking roll that made everything seem out of kilter. She pulled two polar suits out of the locker, and braced against a bulkhead to get out of her clothes.

She was sweating, pulling and hauling against the tight neoprene rubber that stuck against her bare skin. She tore a nail; the nail tore the suit. "Shit," she swore to herself. Suddenly the boat lurched violently, and she fell forward on her face, hitting her nose. For a minute, Laura didn't know if she was upside down or right side up. Panicked, she struggled to her feet. Panting, braced against the walls, she fought to regain her composure. She was angry. Angry at Jack Towne for showing up on her doorstep drunk and feeling sorry for himself. Angry at Shirley for being such a perfect victim, and furious at Jim McClay. "What do you want me to say?" she shouted in the empty cabin. The water crashed and slammed against the sides of the boat only inches away.

Having succeeded in pulling on the top of the bright orange suit, she zipped it up, almost catching the tip of her breast in the heavy duty zipper. "Goddamn," she said out loud, "I've got to save that for the kids."

Feeling like a spaceman, Laura staggered back through the stateroom with its bed still neatly made, the galley with its stove forever level on its gimbels and through the main saloon. The distress light slapped against her hooded head. The safety harness clanked as she walked.

Son-of-a-bitch, she thought, I'm ready for anything. While she held the wheel, Jim McClay dressed in the open companionway where he could get back on deck in a hurry. Laura was feeling better. She felt confident in the big boat as it bashed through the seas. Waves the size of small houses marched by them on all sides. He was undressed when a big comer hit, turning the bow sharply. Furious at its challenge, she brought the helm back.

"You need some help?" he asked her anxiously.

"You better get some pants on, buster," she told him with spirit. His penis was shriveled in the cold, nothing but a cute string bean, she thought. The heavy river of red hair she knew ran from crotch to navel was blowing in the wind.

They were committed by now, trying to steer a course that would bring them into the shelter of the first of the San Juans by midnight. The *Laura J.* shuddered under the relentless attack; the wind howled through the rigging.

At ten o'clock, the jib broke loose with a resounding crack and sail and sheets went tangling up into the dark night, flogging around the mast. Jim swung the boat around quickly so they were running with the wind.

"Whatever you do, keep your ass to those waves," he shouted at her, putting her behind the wheel and climbing out onto the pitching deck.

"Be careful!" she called after him, but he was gone.

The sail streamed out in front of the bow, cracking like a long, white flag. She glanced back at the enormous wave bearing down on them. It rose, tall as a building, an evil black presence that lifted them up like a climbing airplane. Laura's stomach tightened in fear, and down they went, surfing the front of the wave and the bow slipping away no matter how hard she held the wheel.

"Jim!" she screamed, with the sickening fear tearing at her.

They were going to broach! Forty-two feet and 25,000 pounds of sailboat was going to broach on her. They plunged down, but then she felt some response in the rudder. The bow dug in, buried itself and pulled up, shedding tons of white water that poured over her and down the scuppers with a terrible sucking noise.

Desperately, she braced against the wheel, glancing

behind her for the next wave and couldn't find it. The following sea was mild by comparison. She looked forward. It was all darkness and clanging rigging. We pushed the odds too far, she thought. She couldn't see Jim at all.

She fumbled for the searchlight, found the switch, and sent the powerful beam sweeping through the driving rain. He was still on the bow, held firmly by his lifeline, methodically cutting the tattered sail loose and rigging a replacement. Laura Jordan hung on the wheel, crying with relief in long sobs.

He cam back, crawling along the heaving deck, breathless with excitement. "Son-of-a-bitch! Did you see how she pulled out of that?" he shouted at her.

Laura cried on. He wasn't afraid at all. He was ecstactic over the performance of his boat.

"I thought you were gone," she sobbed, "I thought I lost you."

"Nice try," he said, "but I'm tougher than that. So is your old namesake here." He slapped the side of the boat. He didn't seem to notice she was crying.

Jim swung the *Laura J.* back around into the wind. "It'll take more weather than that to chase us off!" he shouted. "Hang on, we're going to ride this one all the way in!"

Laura, relieved and silent, hung on. Hung on until long after midnight, long after she had given up thinking about anything. At about the time she was realizing a human being could sleep anywhere, Laura felt the boat settling down in the water. Groggy and stiff, she sat up thinking they were sinking, but then realized it was the calm water.

"Where are we?" she murmured, untangling her arm from the lifeline that held her tethered in the cockpit.

"Sunday Cove." His face was hard and alert in the dull light from the binnacle. The rain had stopped, and she saw the high looming side of an island. The spotlight flashed on the surf breaking along the narrow curved beach and black rock. The diesel coughed, sputtered, then caught its deep throbbing rhythm. Laura tried to stand, but was so dizzy she had to sit back down.

"Take it easy. Go on down below. We're here, babe."

Bleary-eyed, she went into the main saloon, shivering in the slimy polar suit, tasting the salt on her lips. She heard the welcome rattle of the anchor chain, the engine backing and then idling.

Laura pulled off the suit and climbed into a down sleeping bag, shaking in the cold. The dull yellow lights in the cabin made everything seem fuzzy. Jim McClay's footsteps were going down the deck, directly over her head. The chain rattled again, the diesel engine turned over and over and over.

The boat rolled gently at its anchor. High overhead in the bare rigging, two pieces of metal scraped gently against each other making a squeak with each movement of the *Laura J.* as it swung on the ebb tide of Sunday Cove. She listened until she went to sleep.

Jim McClay was an early riser by habit, and he quietly dressed in the dark cabin, listening to the reassuring sighs and groans of the boat at anchor. Going out through the main saloon, he stopped by Laura. She stretched full length, the down bag up to her chin, a bare arm thrown across her beautiful face like a child, lips parted slightly. He leaned close until he could hear her breathing, feel the warmth of her against his cheek, and then he tiptoed up the companionway ladder out onto the deck slick with dew.

A low mist blanketed the lake-calm water of Sunday Cove and broke up like drifting smoke as it encountered the faint breezes dancing across the open sound beyond. The steep rugged sides of Teachers Island rose in front of him, tall as a mountaintop coming out of the sea. Stretching across the horizon were other similar islands.

Quietly, he unlashed the dinghy from the cabin top and slipped it into the water. The wooden seat was wet and soaked through his denim pants as he rowed toward the beach. Jim McClay had recovered from hearing about Jack Towne. He had put the anger and jealous rage in the back of his mind, far enough back so he could control it.

But the thought of Laura touching Jack Towne, being with him, set Jim's body unconsciously in motion. The wooden oar blades drove deeper into the pale-green water. Harder and harder he rowed, the oarlocks squeaking with the strain, the fiberglass skiff bending under the force of each pull.

He could tear Jack Towne apart. He wanted to close with that fat man, to stand over him and feel the hot blood of revenge clogging his nostrils. Abruptly, he leaned back on the oars, letting them trail in the water, watching the tiny wavelets spread out and disappear into the mist. It was a low tide; the primeval ooze of life was in the air.

He knew it would be an uneven contest and that would not please Laura Jordan nor would it win her love. And above all else in life, Jim McClay wanted her love, wanted it beyond reason or logic. Thick brown weeds surrounded the drifting dingy as it reached the shallows. A Great Blue Heron gave a startled *awk,* and launched itself into the air with a flap of its gigantic wings. Black crows huddled in the mist, picking along the rocks. They moved back cautiously in their strange sinister hop as the bow scraped against the beach.

Jim found a staff-length stick, a branch stripped of its bark by the water and whitened by sun and salt. He poked it into the sand as he walked, stopping occasionally to probe the tide pools and turn over rocks where tiny green crabs, surprised by the morning light, scuttled for cover.

Laura had changed so much from the girl he knew in high school that sometimes Jim felt he didn't know her at all. She was his peaches-and-cream girl. He looked back and saw the crows had boldly recaptured their territory and were examining the dingy for signs of food. Nervy little bastards, he thought. His footprints stretched behind him, filling with tidal water.

She was so wild and enthusiastic then, so willing to give herself to him or go water skiing at midnight in the middle of winter. And then she had changed somehow. Far across the strait, an oil tanker, its black hull barely visible above the horizon, was coming in from the open sea, black smoke trailing. It looked like a toy in a bathtub. The islands rose around it, dwarfing the ship, dozens of Valhallas coming up out of the sea.

Of course, Jim McClay thought, climbing up onto the

black rocks that ran along the steep bank, he had changed as well. Everything seemed different when he came back from Viet Nam. Laura was still as enthusiastic as ever, but she was harder, more sure of herself as a person, more independent and determined to be a success in her own right.

Which was fine Jim McClay. He wanted her to be all those things. But he also wanted her to be the mother of his children and live in that dream world he carried into the jungles of Southeast Asia, the vision of a kitchen overlooking the lake with golden sunshine streaming through the windows and children, lots of children, half naked, blond like Laura, running around in the cool fresh air. And he imagined evenings on a wide veranda where they could sit and look at the city lights and smell the flowers and each child would have a room with special wallpaper, each room different, to suit the child's personality—stars, moons, clowns. . . .

He climbed over the slippery rocks until he could see the open water along the south side of the island. Teachers Island had once been inhabited. First by an old man with a herd of sheep in the late thirties and later in the mid-sixties by a group of wealthy young Californians who wanted to retreat from the world of war and find a peaceful communal farm and live out their lives.

But there was no water on Teachers Island, and as the old man had discovered in the thirties, there was practically no rain in the summer. The green grass that looked so inviting in the spring was gone by June, burned off by the rentless sun. The Californians had run out of money and patience. Now the island was owned by a Florida investment group, waiting for better days to develop it or a more favorable market to sell.

The death grin of a dogfish stared up at Jim McClay. The miniature shark, its lethal body stripped and chewed, lay on the rocks where it had been deposited by the tide below his feet.

At first, he had been scared in Viet Nam, nothing seemed to make sense or be organized for any purpose. Then fear turned to anger when he realized what the purpose was. By the time he flew back into Travis Air Force Base twenty-five pounds lighter and tanned almost black, First Lieutenant James Angus McClay had learned some fundamental truths and made some lifetime resolutions.

He picked up a rock and hurled it into the water. It disappeared with a dull plop into the deep, the concentric rings of impact fading rapidly on the surface. He understood now that human life was very fragile and very short, that some men's motives were beyond reason and sanity, that there were very real evils loose in the world that could easily get out of control.

And he had resolved to protect those he loved and cherished with every means available from those evils and the men who perpetrated them. He would use any means at his disposal—physical force, political power, or money. He would take this responsibility for a small group of people, his nearest and dearest and keep them close. And Laura Jordan was one of the nearest and dearest, whether she wanted to be or not.

He sat, chin in his hand, and watched the *Laura J.* swinging at anchor. There were faster boats now, lighter ones with taller masts that could cut minutes off his winning time from last year in the Race Light Classic. He would have to sell the boat or retire from serious racing. In a way, he had already made that decision by coming up here with Laura. It represented a definite break in his life. He had left his work and responsibilities to please her. He flexed the hand she bandaged. It throbbed under the dirty, torn gauze dressing. But was that going to be enough?

He stood up and clambered down the rocks, and then strolled along the beach, watching the thin film of water running in and out with each gentle wave. Jim was beginning to feel a sense of urgency about his relationship with Laura. As surely as the tide moved, he felt he was losing her, the gulf between them was growing as she became more involved in her work that was evolving into something almost like a religion.

And now this thing with Jack Towne. The crows moved back to the rocks as he approached. The dinghy was high and dry. Jim picked it up by the stern and dragged it to the water, leaving a narrow groove in the sand behind him.

He knew about men like Jack Towne. He had seen them in Viet Nam, and now he saw them in Washington, D.C. Big jovial men full of self-confidence and an easy-going charm that allowed them to evade the tough spots in life, time after time without a scratch. They were always patting you on the back, touching you, thanking you for your help they appreciated so much.

He pushed the dinghy off in the shallow water and eased into the seat. Already, the crows were venturing back onto the beach. The problem with those people, Jim knew, was that in evading their responsibilities they usually hurt people who tried to help them. Or worse.

He fitted the oars into the metal locks. Jim McClay spit on his hands to get better purchase on the smooth varnish, grasped the oars, and pulled hard for the sailboat.

She heard him come into the cabin, picking things up and the sizzle of frying bacon. The smell of bacon and fresh coffee filled the cabin. John Denver sang "Rocky Mountain High" softly on the stereo. Laura scrunched further down inside her sleeping bag and waited, not ready to face the day. She knew what he was trying to do.

"Come on." He poked her in the rear. "Time to get up. Let's eat on deck. It's a beautiful day."

She stuck her head out, blinking in the light. "You're worse than my mother," she said. "Always up early, pulling the covers off people."

John Denver sang on. He knew it was the only John Denver song she would tolerate. "It's my old firehorse blood. Come on before this stuff gets cold." He disappeared up the companionway, balancing two steaming plates and carrying a vacuum jug under his arm.

Reluctantly, she pulled herself out of the warm bag. The pants she'd left carelessly thrown on the cabin floor the night before were neatly folded on the galley table. She pulled them on.

John Denver was singing about a farm that was just like a

long-lost friend. Laura found one of Jim's old sweaters, pulled it over her head and ran a comb through her tangled hair. Even little John didn't sound so bad this morning, but she turned him off before she went on deck.

The morning sun came blazing across the water at them, a burnt-orange ball that chased the last wisps of fog into the coves of Teachers Island where they hung like delicate bridal veils, vanishing under the passionate assault of the heat.

"Your good friend Mr. Denver said he wasn't hungry so I put him in the sail locker," she said cheerfully and kissed him hard on the cheek. The bristles of his beard scraped against her lips and tasted of salt.

"All the more for us."

Laura sat on a red kapok life cushion and ate her breakfast: burnt bacon—Jim's specialty; scrambled eggs laced with onions and melted gooey American cheese, her favorite; and whole-wheat toast limp with real butter and plastered down with Canadian strawberry jam. It tasted marvelous; she was ravenous. I feel one hell of a lot better than I have any right to feel, she thought, watching a ferryboat moving across the horizon. It shimmered through the heat waves rising off the water.

"This is good," she said.

"Anything tastes good in this kind of weather. I was going to break out the champagne, but I didn't want you to lose your head. That comes later."

"I don't think I ever tasted bacon so burnt that tasted so good."

"Cowboy bacon. You want some more coffee?"

"Please." He got up and poured her a mug from the stainless steel jug.

Jim McClay, she observed, looked much better in his torn rugby shirt, faded dungarees and deck shoes than he did in a suit and tie. She wanted to go to him and muss up the tangled red hair that curled over his head like coils of wire.

"Well," he said, handing her the coffee, "what do you want to do today?"

"Nothing, absolutely nothing. Go up and cook my bottom brown on the foredeck."

"Oh, good. I can keep an eye out for airplanes."

"Or you could come up there and cook with me," she said, feeling a ripple of excitement run through her.

"That sounds like fun. My God, Laura, this is like old times," he said, kicking off his loafers and stretching his feet out.

"Yes, it is, isn't it?" She blew across the top of the mug and tried a sip of coffee.

She followed the delicate crescent curve of Sunday Cove, let her eyes wander through the deep stands of trees on the side of Teachers Island up to the tall waving grass on the crest. From up there, she knew, you could see clear into Canada.

"Incidentally," he said, snatching the last piece of toast away from her and mopping up the remains of scrambled eggs on his plate, "You did a hell of a job last night keeping us afloat. I've got to admit I was worried there for a minute."

She smiled, watching him stuff the toast into his mouth and lick his fingers. "Worried? Hell, I wasn't worried."

"You weren't? You looked like a damn ghost when I crawled back there. Your hands were welded to the wheel."

She put down the coffee mug. "Oh God, Jim, I was scared stiff. I was so afraid that I'd lost you."

He came over and sat down beside her. "You'll never lose me, Laura." The salt made tiny rough whorls on her smooth tanned skin.

"I'm sorry I hurt you by what I did," she said. "I mean by what I said last night."

"Don't worry about it."

"But I do, I mean I should. I can't forget it."

"Look," he said, taking her by the shoulders, "I didn't go over the side. You came through like a veteran. We're alive and well, and we've got open water from here to Alaska and a fantastic day. That's what counts."

"True," she said. The ferry was gone. The horizon was clear. They could sail north, Laura thought, for days, weeks even months. They could summer in the Canadian Gulf Islands where the currents were as warm as the tropics. They could travel the Inside Passage to Alaska. "But I've made one hell of a mess."

He stood up. "Let it go," he said.

"I can't. What I didn't tell you was the rest of the story."

Jim got up and moved restlessly to the rail and looked down into the water. "You can see clear to the bottom here," he said. "If we get ourselves in gear, we could get the diving stuff out and do a little snorkeling."

"Jim will you listen to me—please?"

He turned back to her, leaning against the rail. "Yes, of course, I will." She could see his jaw muscles flexing.

"Right after Jack and I had our—affair—Shirley Towne had an abortion. It wasn't something she wanted to do. In fact, she has a very Catholic attitude about it, but she went ahead because that was what Jack wanted. She did it for him." Laura cleared her throat; the emotion tightened her chest. "He took her to the hospital, but he left her. He got called away on business or something so she called me. She wanted me to come get her. She didn't know what had happened." Laura put her head in her hands, reliving the agony of seeing Shirley holding her stomach as if she'd just been stabbed.

She felt his arm around her, and she leaned against him. "I'm sorry," he said.

"I had to go. I felt I had to go, but I couldn't tell her about Jack—and me. She was very strange, Jim. She seemed to have turned into a block of ice. You know, she always seemed so, well, vulnerable. You met her."

"She seemed like a nice lady," he said, holding Laura close.

"She said she was going to divorce Jack. That he had broken his promise to wait for her at the hospital. I tried to tell her that wasn't reasonable, but she shut me off, and under the circumstances, what could I say anyway? Oh God, Jim, I'm such a traitor. I sold them both out. She was my friend. She wanted to be my friend, and I betrayed her." Laura let the tears come. She was beyond caring. She pressed her face against his chest and cried until she was done.

The *Laura J.* was swinging on her anchor with the change of the tide; the stern was facing the beach. The crows had moved back out of the sun and sat in neat rows in a big fir just above the rocks.

Laura wiped her eyes and sat up. "I didn't mean to get into all this again, but I don't know what to do."

"Are you asking for my advice?"

"Yes."

"I'm not an unbiased observer, Laura. If I followed my best instincts, I'd go back to Seattle and break Jack Towne in about three pieces." He doubled a hard fist.

Laura forced a smile and blinked her red-rimmed eyes. "That's not exactly what I had in mind."

Jim McClay stood up and began pacing the deck. "OK," he said, "this is going to cost you, lady. My advice is even more expensive than yours."

"We'll just see how damn good it is first," she told him, getting in the spirit of things.

"Oh, no. I'm the expert. You have to trust me. Cash in advance." He hooked his thumbs in the belt loops of his dungarees.

"All right, you can put it on my VISA card."

"Those, we do accept. Listen, Laura. Forget the Townes. So you made a mess of it for whatever reasons. OK. Everybody does that once in a while. My advice is to cut your losses. Stay out of their life. Let them work things out. In the meantime, you and I are going to take a vacation and enjoy ourselves."

"I guess I never understood them. I thought I did. I wanted to. I really wanted to help."

"Of course, you did. Laura, don't be so damn hard on yourself, honey."

"A psychiatrist called in the other night on the show. He was a nasty little man, and he told me I didn't know what my limits were. He told me to go back to teaching seminars on communications before something blew up in my face. Did you see that?"

"Yes," he said, still leaning against the rail. "I did." A single-engine plane went over so high its engine was only a faint drone.

"Do you think that's true?"

He paused and rubbed his chin. "No," he said finally, "I

don't. I think you got into a situation you didn't fully understand. I think you got emotionally involved first and then tried to back into an objective analysis. At least, that's the way it seems to me. You liked them, and they're likeable people—even old what's-his-name." He gave her a wry grin. "He appeals to your romantic sense," he went on, choosing his words carefully. "He has something of the swashbuckler about him. He seems to be a little bigger than life."

"I'm considering closing the office and getting out of the whole thing," she said abruptly, ignoring his analysis of Jack Towne.

"Goddamn it, Laura," he said sharply, stopping at the railing again, "self pity doesn't become you. I didn't say anything about closing your business. Why should you do that? You're a highly successful woman with an excellent reputation."

"I made promises to those people, Jim," she said, standing up to face him. "Promises I didn't keep."

"I'll say it again, Laura. You let things get out of hand. You let your emotions get in the way, and you got all tangled up in them. But that's no crime, honey. That's no reason to throw everything away. Hell, you didn't create the Townes' problems, whatever they are."

"But I feel like I made them worse. I did make them worse. My God, I ended up being the other woman. It's like a grade-B movie, for chrissake."

"Well, you're not the other woman now, are you?" he demanded angrily.

"No."

"Good. You can be my woman. Also, you haven't heard the second part of my biased analysis." He went to her, took her hands and held them. "Let it go, Laura, let it all go. Champagne will be served on the foredeck. It's not every day you can get a suntan on April first."

"Don't you hate me a little bit?" she asked him.

"No. I love you. I've been telling you that for over fifteen years. For better or worse."

"It can't get much worse," she said, putting her arms around his hard body.

"No, it's bound to get better. Especially if you stop brooding about it and get your bottom up there. We already missed the tide, let's not miss the sun."

"You seemed obsessed with my bottom," she said, remembering the sensuous lazy pleasure of lying naked on a teak deck.

"It's always been my favorite one," he said.

They lay on the foredeck in the sunshine, the ice bucket of champagne beading up under the dry heat while the *Laura J.* rode the incoming tide. An occasional outboard motor or jet engine far away was the only sound in the hot stillness. Laura felt the sweat forming, felt it trickle and pool under her belly, and stayed motionless.

Every once in a while, she roused herself to turn on her side. Now on her back, the heat soaked into her. He was close. If she moved her hand slightly, not even an inch, she could touch him. It was seduction by osmosis, she thought, and it was a delicious sensation.

Laura felt shy about making the first move since telling him about Jack Towne. She knew that underneath the surface calm, Jim McClay was suffering, and she felt bad about being the cause. Maybe, she thought, letting her worries drift in the sun, she was a fool for not marrying him and getting on with life.

She dozed and remembered her promises to Jack Towne. "If you need me, I'll always be there." What had driven her to say those foolish things? She groaned aloud.

"Are you all right?" he asked her, not moving.

"Fine." She moved her hand slightly. One infinitesimal fraction of an inch, and she would touch him. The deck burned her hand.

Finally, she moved, and his fingers caught hers in a tight hook as if he'd been waiting. Eyes closed, she extended her other fingers and felt them being pulled into his hand. The muscles in his wrist felt tight as violin strings. Laura moved his hand over her pelvis, feeling her own pubic hair burning in the sun.

She touched his leg, ran her hand over the long, hard muscles.

"That feels nice," he murmured.

"Let me try to make it feel better, love," she said rolling over to face him.

When they were done, they lay in the sun side by side until the sweat dried, and the noontime heat cooled. Suddenly, Laura sat up.

"I'll race you to the beach," she said, kneeling over him.

"Oh God," he groaned, getting up on one elbow. "It's not summer, you know. It only feels like it."

But she was at the rail, standing naked, her back to him. "Oh, Mr. Super Competitor," she jeered, "I'll bet I can whip your sunburned ass for fifty yards."

"Bullshit." He was on his feet running.

"Hey," she said, but he was by her and in the air, diving into the water.

Laura went after him. The water was beyond cold. It drove sharp pains into her head as she thrashed to the beach, arms numb and heavy. He was already lying face down on the narrow strip of sand in front of the rocks when she got out of the water. Laura poked him with her big toe in the bare ass.

"Jesus," she said, "that was cold!"

He rolled over, sand all over his body red from the sun. "I beat you. Now do I get my prize?" He reached for her.

"Oh, I'm sorry," Laura told him, "you didn't read the rules? It's to the beach and back." She took off running down the sand and hit the freezing water at a full gallop. She pulled for the boat, braving the cold water on her head for the sake of speed. At the boarding ladder, she heard him thrashing behind her and felt his hand reaching for her leg just as she pulled herself up and over the rail.

They drank the rest of the warm champagne standing in the cockpit, chattering with cold and made love again on the saloon floor before packing the dinghy with kindling and steaks, and rowing to Teachers Island. On the rocks above the high-water mark, Jim built a massive bonfire, and they broiled their steaks and ate the dinner on paper plates that collapsed and knives that wouldn't cut the rare meat.

Red meat juice running down their hands, they gnawed on the steaks and drank brandy while the sun went down, and the sparks from the fire rose into the night, spiraling on light currents of invisible air.

"Somebody will think we're in distress," Laura told him as he put another piece of beachwood on the fire that was already so hot they had to sit back against the rock to keep from being burned.

"I like a big fire," he told her. "It makes me feel good. It's like a beacon in the night. Look out there. You can't see a light. This says we're here."

"No doubt about that."

They lay back and watched the stars until the fire died to a glow of coals. And even back on the deck of the *Laura J.* they could see it, a bright marker left on Teachers Island.

In the morning after breakfast, they climbed to the top of the hill and looked over the strait. A fresh breeze was blowing.

"This would be a good place for pirates," she told him. "They could come here to spot their victims and then run down the hill, and jump on their boat to zap them."

"Pirates didn't zap people. Besides, there were never any pirates up this far. Just the Spanish, but they were looking for something else, a passage to the Orient, and that wasn't here."

"They weren't very smart," Laura said, turning around on the hilltop, feeling the wind lift her, "they should have stayed."

Later that morning, heading into the San Juan chain with a steady wind behind them, Jim McClay popped the tartan spinnaker that had belonged to his father, and it ballooned out over the bow of the *Laura J.*, a gaudy blaze of colors that drew friendly waves from the ferry dock on Shaw Island as they came gliding down the narrow passage. At noon, they ate tuna-fish sandwiches Laura fixed in the galley while they sailed.

"Thanks," Jim said, stuffing half the sandwich into his mouth, one hand on the wheel. "We work well together. Where the hell is my coffee?"

"That's easy for you to say, white man. I work and you sail." She ducked back into the cabin and emerged with a cup of coffee.

"Thanks," he told her, kissing her on the cheek. "But you can't say we aren't having a good time. It's a good arrangement."

"Naturally," she kidded him. Laura had pulled her hair back with a blue bandanna, her face was already deeply tanned.

"Here, you want to sail? Fine. I'll eat. I'll make the sacrifice." He bowed and ushered her to the wheel. "See that buoy up there? Don't go inside that or we'll spend the rest of our life on a rock. It's about four inches under the water."

She pretended to sight over the wheel, her mouth still full of tuna fish. Carefully, she turned the boat in. "Did you say inside?" she kidded him.

"Dammit, Laura. Don't kid about something like that," he forced the wheel back. "Outside." He spelled outside for her.

"I wanted to make sure, Captain. I like to kid you. It forces you to talk. You don't talk much anymore, Jim. In fact, you talk less every year. Someday you're going to be writing me letters."

He stood at the wheel with her. "I don't feel a need to talk all the time when I'm around you. I feel good just being next to you like this." He pressed against her.

"Not while I'm driving the boat," she protested, forcing her hip into his groin.

"Another first in the San Juans," he said and laughed. "And you're at the helm, you're steering not driving. Are you serious? Do you think I'm going silent on you?"

"Sometimes. Sometimes I'd like to know what you're thinking." She rounded the buoy and headed up the open channel. A tug and barge were coming toward them. "I mean here I am supposedly a communications expert, and I feel the need for better communications with a man I've known intimately—" she stressed the word by rolling her hips—"for a hell of a long time."

"You're also a family counselor without a family. Did you ever think of that?"

"Is that what's on your mind?"

"Sometimes," he said. "The preferred method of passing is port to port, Laura." He pointed to the tugboat that was looming large over the bow, a thick white wave being pushed up by its blunt nose. The wooden barge secured alongside was empty and rode high in the water.

"What difference does it make?" she asked, swinging the *Laura J.* back slightly so she would pass to the tug's left.

"Rules of the road, custom, it seems to work."

"You'd like children, wouldn't you?" she asked him. The tug had the wheel house windows lowered to take in the warm air. The helmsman waved; she waved back. Laura could see a cook in a white hat working in the open galley.

"Yes. I always have."

"We ought to talk about that sometime," she replied, "but right now I want another one of those sandwiches."

They stopped at a marina just before dusk and got some diesel and fresh ice before anchoring out in the harbor among a half dozen other pleasure boats that night.

During the next two days while they cruised the islands, the weather gradually deteriorated until on the morning of the fourth day Laura wore her down jacket on deck. Thin clouds rolled across the sky, moving quickly, allowing only glimpses of filtered sun. The choppy water spanked against the smooth sides of the *Laura J.*

"I've got a great idea," he said, when she brought him his mid-morning coffee. "Let's put into Rosario and have a fancy dinner and sleep in real beds."

Laura hugged him. "You're reading my mind. And take a real shower."

"What do you mean?" he said. "I've got a real shower."

"I don't like taking showers where you can't turn around," she said. "I also like tons of hot water."

All afternoon, they beat against a strong westerly wind that kept them both busy. Laura enjoyed going forward to handle the sails. She liked the feel of working hard, the satisfaction of seeing a bundle of white shooting aloft, filling with wind, becoming an object of curving beauty, lifting them forward. Braced against the rail, enjoying the heave of the deck, she looked back at Jim bundled up in his dirty sweater, leaning over the rail to look up and examine the sail pattern sixty feet above him.

They did work well together, she thought. They liked doing the same things, even eating the same food. Then what was keeping her from making the simple commitment to marry him? she wondered.

"Look lively," he shouted up to her, "the wind's coming up. We've got to get that monster down."

"You mean the one I just put up?"

"That's the one, babe."

Rosario sat at the end of a long fjord-like bay, a glittering white Victorian mansion perched on the rocks above the sea, its towers and gables flashed in the fading afternoon sun. The clouds parted briefly as they made the turn for their final run to the long docks off the beach, and a burst of rain stretched a rainbow over them. They tied up between an old wooden schooner full of dogs and children all secured behind a mesh of stiff safety net, four feet high, and a massive steel yacht with a needle nose and a flying bridge that dwarfed the *Laura J.*

The owner of the yacht, a tall pale man with a pot belly, wearing a navy-blue yachting jacket, helped them tie up. "You folks local?" he asked them.

"If you call the Northwest local," Jim said, giving the huge boat a going over. The name *Esperanza* was emblazoned across the bow in gilt.

"They told us the weather would be beautiful up here. We just flew in from San Diego, had the boat brought up last week. This isn't beautiful."

"No, and it's going to get a lot worse according to the weather report."

The San Diego man turned to Laura and gave her an appraisal. "This place isn't what we expected at all. Have you stayed here before?"

"Yes," she said. "What did you expect?"

"Well, it's pretty old."

"We call that quaint," she laughed. "My name is Laura Jordan; this is Jim McClay."

He introduced himself as Lawrence Tailor, said he was a land developer, and invited them to have a drink, all the while not taking his eyes off Laura. She felt Jim bristle.

"Maybe later, thanks," Jim said. "Right now we've got to wash some salt off."

"You weren't very nice to him," she said as they walked up the dock.

"He's an asshole. Sometimes I get tired of being nice to assholes," he snapped.

Laura let him go in the shower first so she could take her time, and when he got out, she let the hot water cascade over her until she felt weak. Her hands were calloused from just four days of handling lines, and the salt had rubbed her skin raw along her legs where the jeans were tight. Thick billowing steam filled the bathroom, and she turned on more hot water.

"Hello!" he shouted, throwing the shower door open, "I've come to rescue you."

She grabbed his arm and tried to pull him into the shower. He pulled back.

"Let's go eat," he urged her.

She shut the door behind him. Laura didn't want to eat; she wanted to stay in the shower. "Go ahead, I'll meet you over there," she called over the partition.

There was no answer, but after a while, she thought she heard the door close. Laura didn't like being hurried, especially when she was enjoying herself. After a suitable time, she emerged beet red and seeing there was nobody there, she walked dripping and naked into the main room, pulled down the covers on the queen-size double bed, and threw her hot body on the cold sheets and lay there until she had cooled.

The main dining room faced out toward the bay, and the seating was in raised tiers so that each half circle of tables had a view. The dinner was served buffet-styled on a long table manned by waiters in crisp whites. An ice sculpture of a leaping salmon dripped quietly over the salad bar.

A convention of weekly newspaper publishers in the

lobby was noisy, but the only occupants of the dining room were Jim and the land developer Tailor, having a drink at a table by the window. The land developer turned his pale lined face on her as she stepped down the carpeted tiers, the flowing purple pantsuit clinging to her stately body. Her entrance, Laura thought, was awkward. It was like stepping down, instead of up, to an altar.

"I'll say one thing for you, Jim," Tailor exclaimed loud enough for her to hear, "you've sure got good taste in women."

"Good evening," she said coolly, seating herself before Jim could get up. He had changed into khakis. The shirt had epaulets and looked military. Laura didn't like it. She didn't like to think of Jim as a soldier.

Spotlights on each corner of the mansion lit up the water fifty feet below them. The steep waves banging into the cliff rebounded out to meet others, creating a confused zigzagging of water. A heavy rain battered the surface into a mottled angry foam.

"A good night to stay inside," the land developer observed. "You will have to excuse me."

"I'm sorry you can't stay for dinner," Jim gave Laura a surreptitious wink.

"My wife doesn't like to dine early. It gives her a headache," he said wearily.

"Maybe tomorrow. It was nice talking to you, sir," Jim said politely.

Laura ordered a double Scotch. "I've got to go out and run in the morning," she said.

"Sounds like fun. I'll come with you."

"Great. I haven't heard you 'sir' someone in a long time, Jim."

"Good for business, honey. Mr. Tailor—Larry—thinks the San Juans are ripe for development. He's up here to look around. He mentioned he might need a good lawyer. He's not an asshole after all."

She sipped her drink. "I'd just as soon he went back and developed something else in California."

"Oh, he is. He's also interested in ski resorts. He already

owns one at Big Bear, complete with a couple millions' worth of snowmaking equipment."

"You should have asked him about Early Winters."

"I did, as a matter of fact. He said nobody would ever get financing over there." Jim gave her a steady look over his drink.

"Jack seems to have found a way around that," she said quickly. "I'm sorry, I didn't mean to get into that."

"That's OK, we both brought it up. Let's eat."

The buffet was a magnificent affair. The cold dishes pressed into exotic shapes, the roast beef razor thin, and an array of desserts that Laura did not resist. After an agonizing moment of going from pies of mousse to glazed cakes, she finally settled on her first choice—mocha cheesecake.

The convention was moving in behind them, hacking into the delicately displayed food. Settled in their window seat, Laura and Jim watched them as they ate.

"I hate conventions," he said. "You see that guy going around slapping everybody on the back. He's a type. Every convention has one. He's the guy who will take up the collection to give the help a present."

Laura smiled. "Somebody has to do it," she said.

The slanted windows in front of them were running wet, the raindrops forced flat by the wind, gathered in puddles that hung until they became too heavy and then cascaded down the pane.

"I've always liked this place," she said, slicing up her roast beef. "Especially the food."

"Yeah, it's good," Jim said. "It reminds me of something out of Disneyland. It's a little too cute, if you know what I mean."

"It was built for a woman. Baron Von Something built it for his wife. He had to, otherwise, she would have stayed in merry old England."

"It's too ornate. It would be a hell of a place to paint. Jesus, all that scroll work."

"Jim," she said, putting down her knife and fork, "would you build a place like this for me?"

He laughed. "Hell, Laura, I couldn't afford to build the

south wing."

"No, I mean, assuming you had the money. Would you build a place like this for me, a dream house, to please me?" She thought of Jack's plan for Laura's Second Landing.

"That's a hypothetical question," he said uncomfortably.

She smiled wickedly and leaned over the table toward him. "Give me a hypothetical answer. Would you build this to flatter me? To win my love?"

"Come on, be serious, Laura." He turned back to his dinner. "This baby shrimp is pretty good, even if it is frozen."

"I am serious." She wet her lips. "Would you?"

He put the shrimp down. Somebody in the convention was hitting a water glass with a spoon. "May I have your attention, may I have your attention?" the somebody called.

"Would you marry me if I built you a place like this?" he asked her. Their eyes locked for a moment, and then she looked away.

"I don't know," Laura admitted.

"You tell me if you'll marry me, and I'll tell you about the house."

"OK," she said. "You made your point."

The convention was silent, listening to a white-haired man who talked in spurts with long silences in between when he shuffled his feet.

"Well, what do you say, Laura? You said you wanted to talk, let's talk. Let's talk about getting married."

"Do we have to, Jim?"

"I'd like to."

"All right, you've got the floor."

"I asked the question," he protested. The waiter interrupted them to ask if they'd like coffee with dessert. Yes, he told him. Two. Very black.

"I don't know," she said.

"What's so damn complicated about it?" he said loudly and then, realizing he was broadcasting to the convention, lowered his voice. "We like each other. We're sexually compatible. We have mutual interests. We love each other, or at least I love you."

"It's not that," she said, cutting into the cheesecake.

"Well, what is it then? I'd like to have kids before I'm sixty, Laura. I like kids. I'd like to have kids with you, goddammit. I'd like to go right up to that room and have kids. You could get off those pills, and we could go at it."

Several convention goers, mostly women, turned their heads in the direction of Jim and Laura like birds suddenly alerted to a new and possibly dangerous sound.

Laura took a bite of cheesecake. "Some of those ladies might take you up on that if I can't make it."

"Dammit, you're not answering me," he said fiercely, reaching across and arresting bite number two of mocha cheesecake in midair.

"Did you say with or without cream, sir?" the waiter asked politely, pretending not to see the tussle over the cheesecake.

Reluctantly, Jim released her hand. Laura jammed the cheesecake into her mouth.

"No cream," Jim said.

"I'm sorry, sir, I thought you said cream, and I brought cream."

"Leave it, that's all right. This lady could use a little fattening up."

The waiter arched his eyebrows and withdrew.

"Speak for yourself, piggy boy," Laura said, finishing the cheesecake. "That was delicious. I may have another piece. If I'm going to be pregnant, I have to pork up."

"Laura, sometimes you act like a spoiled child. You've had it too easy, you know that? You've always had everything your way. Exactly the way you want it. Sometimes I think I should have been a little less careful that first time in the boathouse, and then we would have settled this years ago."

She dropped her fork with a clatter. "Oh, you do, do you? Listen, buster, we may have been born in the same neighborhood, but I had to fight like hell for everything I ever got, at least as far as my career goes. If you'd listen to what I say once in a while, maybe you'd know why I don't marry you." She felt her voice raising to a penetrating level, but she went on. Several male members of the convention elbowed each other and snickered. "I don't know if I'll ever marry you because I don't know if I'm willing to give up what I have, which is self-worth, independence, and a life of my own."

Jim McClay's face was getting red. He glanced quickly at two men who were openly discussing the strange couple at the front table. He steadied a murderous glance at one of them.

"Oh, stop it," she said. "Who cares about them anyway? Typical nosey men. For two cents I'd go up there and tell them to stick it in their ear."

He laughed. "You would, wouldn't you?"

"Damn right."

"Oh hell, Laura, how did I ever get hooked up with you?"

"You were after my body, smart boy. Unfortunately my mind came with it."

"Oh Jesus," he said, shaking his head and rubbing his eyes. "I withdraw the question."

The waiter was back to refill their cups. He had a wary look in his eyes. "Bring this lady another piece of cheesecake," Jim ordered him, "and make it a big one."

"I'm not going to eat it," she said stubbornly.

"You can take it back to the room. You'll want it later."

The cheesecake sat in front of her while the wind howled out on the bay. Jim McClay folded his hands on the table and looked out the window.

"I know we could make it," he said. "I don't want you to give up your career, Laura. We could work it out. We could hire babysitters. Both our folks live near us; they'd be glad to lend a hand."

"Thrilled, you mean," she added glumly.

"All right, thrilled. What's wrong with that?"

"Nothing. Nothing except for one little thing. I don't know if it would work."

"Why not, Laura? Why not for God's sake?" he asked her, earnest concern on his solid freckled face.

"You say we could work it out, but I have a feeling I'd be the one who would be doing the adjusting. That's the woman's role, you know."

"I don't expect you to do it all."

"How much of your law practice are you going to give up,

Jim, half, a third, or none at all? Are you willing to give up trips so you can be home with the kids when I'm gone? Babies require feeding two or three times a night, you know. I don't want my kids raised by a babysitter."

"I'd be willing to stay home—sometimes."

"Honey, I know you too well. I know us—both of us. We're committed to other things. Think about what you're saying. Remember when I wanted you to stay all night with me, but you had a court case? You remember that?"

"Laura, be fair."

"I am being fair. That was silly, I know, hardly necessary, a lusty little whim of yours truly. But children are like that too. They make unreasonable demands, just like working wives. You'd never get your seven hours, hon." She reached across the table and took his hands.

"Please, Laura, please." She was alarmed to see tears in his eyes.

"Jim, I love you. I always have, and I always will. But I have other responsibilities, people who depend on me, people who need me to help them. Those things are important to me. Every bit as important as your law practice is to you."

The gathering behind them burst into a spontaneous laughter over some unheard joke. One high-pitched woman hawed long after everybody else was ready for the next act.

"I'm not that committed to the law, Laura. I enjoy it. It's a good way to make money, to take care of my responsibilities, but it's not a religion to me. It's simply a complex system for keeping order in a society. It's not something I worship."

"What would happen," she asked him, still holding his hands, "if you got a call right now, an emergency call from your best and biggest clients, saying they needed you back in Washington, D.C.? What would you do?"

"Laura, that's not a reasonable question. That would depend on the situation."

"But what would you do? Would you say, 'Look, Mr. Big Important Client, I can't come right now because my girl friend or my wife or my kids need me? Little Billy's got a fever, I'm not coming?'"

"I don't know," he replied sullenly, pulling his hands away.

"What would you do? I could make up the same kind of situation for you, you know that, don't you?"

"I'd probably go," she said sadly. "That's what I've been trying to tell you. We've both got things that are more important to us, and we might as well admit it."

He watched the storm lashing against the rocks. "I'd better go down and see if the boat's OK," he said absently, fiddling with his cup and saucer.

"I'll come with you," she said.

"No, I'd rather go alone," he replied without looking at her.

The *Laura J.* was secure, but Jim helped the skipper of the *Esperanza* put some extra spring lines on the big yacht whose high superstructure took the full brunt of the wind that was driving a stinging rain almost vertically at them. The floating dock heaved and groaned under the waves. In the distance, the dining room at Rosario was a haze of bright light and vague shapes through the storm. Reluctantly, he joined the insistent land developer for a drink on the big yacht.

"I'll tell you, McClay," he said, "I'm not at all impressed by the weather."

"It's not always like this," Jim replied half-heartedly, wishing that the Larsons of the world would go home and stay there.

By the time he got back to the room, it was late, and he was soaking wet. He undressed by the door, leaving his clothes in a pile and went into the bathroom to dry off. He felt tired and very, very sad. He supposed she was right about him not being willing to give up as much as she would have to, but dammit all, he thought, I'm not the one having the babies.

Jim McClay didn't know what to do, so he toweled himself off and climbed into bed beside Laura, trying not to wake her. Her body heat radiated out to him even though he wasn't touching her. There was a smell that went with her that was unique. Something close to a lily, he thought, staring at the ceiling. It must be perfume. He'd known her all these years and never thought about it before.

He was willing to consider the sort of commitment she seemed to be asking if she, in turn, would consider a similar commitment. He had given up the sailboat race. He would give up other things. But what did he want Laura to give up? He glanced at the luminous dial on his wristwatch. It was 11:30. He listened to the rain of the roof. The fir trees at the end of the building lashed their branches back and forth in the wind. Her light breathing was smooth and effortless.

Jim McClay wanted her to realize she couldn't save the world and shouldn't try. He wanted her to make a commitment and save her deepest feelings, her best qualities for him, for the family they would have together. He didn't want to see her giving herself wholesale to people like Jack Towne.

He clenched his fist underneath the blanket. When you strip it all away, he thought, it's nothing but ordinary jealousy. If he closed his eyes and thought about Jack Towne or any man close to her, the rage would build until he wanted to strike out like an animal and protect what was rightfully his.

He rolled over on his side, putting his back to her. He wanted to fight for her, hut he didn't know who to fight. Sadly, he thought, they would end up fighting each other. The wind buffeted the old mansion, sending the walls creaking. A door slammed shut downstairs with a crash.

She had isolated the major problem, however. They were both too independent and ambitious for their own good. On one hand, Jim McClay wanted to remain in charge of his own destiny. On the other, he wanted Laura Jordan so badly he would do practically anything to get her. It was an unsolvable problem, and he fell asleep, tossing and turning it over in his mind while she slept on beside him oblivious to the storm or his torment.

At twelve-thirty the incessant ringing of the telephone awakened him. Automatically, he sat up and swung his feet around, ready to force himself into a suit and tie, and then realized it was not a wake-up call. He went around the bed and picked up the telephone.

"I have a long-distance call, person to person, for Miss

Laura Jordan," a male operator with a Southern accent told him.

Laura turned over and opened her eyes. Jim flipped on the bedside light.

"It's for you," he said, feeling a tenseness in his stomach.

Still lying down, she put the phone to her ear. "Jack?" she said, coming up out of the bed. "What is it? What's wrong? Calm down. I can't understand you."

Jim McClay went over and leaned heavily on the dresser, listening to the conversation going on behind him. With some time alone, they might have worked it out. It appeared their time was up.

"Yes, I will. No, I'll be there as quickly as I can. You sit tight."

She hung up the phone. "What is it?" he said.

"It's Rob. He's missing up on Silver Star Mountain. He went skiing this morning, and he didn't come back."

Chapter 19

The small terminal building was deserted at six-thirty A.M. and the San Juan commuter plane was late. When they saw it coming in low over the trees to the south, Jim McClay carried Laura's sail bag outside, and they waited under the awning out of the rain while the Beechcraft pulled around in front of them. Its twin engines surged and backed off as it turned, kicking up circular clouds of water from the puddles spotting the blacktop runway.

"Call me on the VHF when you know something," he said, kissing her. "I'll start back this afternoon."

Laura nodded and touched his unshaven cheek. As soon as the engines idled and the ramp came down, she followed the white overalled attendant out into the rain and climbed through the narrow hatch. There were three other passengers already on the plane from its previous stops in the island chain. They were all men, and they looked sleepy.

Laura eased into a seat over the wing and waved at Jim. She could see his unsmiling face as he waved back. Poor Jim, she thought, I'm making his life hell for him. The door slammed shut and almost instantly the engines revved, and the plane was bumping down the runway. They roared past the main terminal and into the air. She looked back. He was standing motionless where she'd left him, alone in front of the stucco terminal that had "Orcas Island" printed across its black roof in white letters.

Nausea churned in her stomach as they climbed steeply into the clouds. The single piece of toast she had tried to eat was coming up with the endless cups of coffee. Laura swallowed hard. The island was gone, buried in the overcast.

They had talked most of the night, sitting uncomfortably in their stuffy room while the rain rumbled on the roof of the Rosario mansion high over them. Jim insisted she was going far beyond her role as a counselor or even a friend, and Jack Towne had no right to ask her to come. She saw the deep agony in his eyes and knew he was trying to reason with her when he was on the edge of irrationality. She, in turn, quietly told him that as painful as it was she felt obliged to see it through. True, she'd made some bad mistakes. But she had promised to come if Jack needed her, and he did need her.

Jim had put his head down on the table, squeezing his fists until his knuckles were white. She had no idea, he finally said, just how painful it could get. He wanted to come with her.

"Let me help you, Laura. I'm afraid for you. I don't want you to do this alone."

But she had been adamant. It was her business. It was her problem. These people were her friends. Rob was her responsibility.

"Laura, you can't take on that kind of responsibility," he'd cried, rubbing his hands over his face as if he were trying to rub away the emotion and agony that showed in every shadowy line.

The plane lurched and yawed and climbed, and still it remained in the blinding clouds.

An intense light was glowing on the leading edge of the silver wing; the plane topped out over the clouds into the brilliant sunshine. With a sigh, the engines settled back, and they turned south toward Seattle.

Laura remembered the exact instant when Rob learned Shirley was leaving Jack. She could see him wince under the crushing blow. She heard the defensive childish comeback as he saw his last chance for motherly love slip away. "Have a nice trip."

The clouds under them were moving rapidly; the plane cut diagonally across them. Laura put her head down and closed her eyes. Rob Towne, with his delicate girl-boy face, was lost.

"Miss Jordan—Miss Laura Jordan?" he inquired.

"Yes," she replied, looking up.

The copilot was bald, his uniform wrinkled. "I didn't know you got on until I looked at the passenger list," he said.

"Well, here I am."

"My wife watches you all the time. No kidding, she never misses *Family Line*. She really worships you. Thinks you've got the last word on everything."

Laura tried to smile, but felt the tension pulling against her normal reflexes. "Well, not everything."

"I was wondering if you could sign something? It would mean a lot to her."

"Sure, what do you want me to sign?"

"You could put your name in the flight log here, and then I could copy it and give it to her."

Laura shrugged, took the offered pen and signed. "All my best to . . ."

"What's your wife's name?"

"Kay. Oh, that would be nice, using her real name and everything."

". . . to Kay. Best wishes, Laura Jordan."

"Gee, thanks," the copilot said, his fifty-year-old battered face glowing with boyish enthusiasm.

"You're welcome," she said, and may God have mercy on all of us, she thought, staring out the window at the dizzying slip of the cloud stream.

They landed in a driving rainstorm and had to walk to the main terminal, picking their way around huge jetliners parked and silent on the broad cement apron, bright yellow chalks against the massive tires.

Barbara Adams met her at the gate, and during their long embrace, Laura wished she could hang on to this solid woman who smelled of roses forever.

"You're soaking wet," Barb admonished her.

"It doesn't matter. Is there any word?"

"No, they're still searching. I heard that on the radio."

"Did you get my stuff?"

"Near as I could tell, Laura. I'm no skier."
"That's OK."
They talked as they hurried down the escalator to the parking area. "Pardon me for saying so, Laura, but you look beat. Why don't you let me come with you?"
Laura quickened her pace. "Thanks, but I'm fine, Barb. You take a cab back to the office. I've got to face this one alone."
The older woman caught her arm as they crossed through glass doors that opened automatically with a hiss of compressed air.
"Don't be a martyr, Laura, just because you feel a sense of responsibility."
Their heels clicked in the silent parking garage under dim fluorescent lights. Rain dripped across the open sides and ran in streams across the floor.
"I'm not being a martyr. I'm involved with these people. I have an obligation to stand by them, and I'm going to do it."
They found Laura's Volvo parked in a corner. Her skis were inside sitting across the back seat and poking into the front. "I'm sorry, I didn't know how to use the darn ski rack. I'm not very mechanical," Barb apologized.
"That's fine. Barb, I love you. It's going to be all right. Like my dad says, when the going gets tough, the tough get going."
"This is not a game, Laura."
"Oh God, Barb," she said, hugging her tightly, "I wish it were."
Laura had driven the Snoqualimie Pass Highway hundreds of times in all kinds of conditions. In the summer when the hills were brilliant green, you could see the steep snow-clad peaks of the North Cascades as pretty as anything in Switzerland or anywhere in the world. She had driven through blizzards, creeping along behind big trucks, their red marker lights blazing like an airfield. She had driven it tired and hungry after an exhausting day on the slopes. She had driven it when they were the first car up in the deep untouched snow that sparkled like sugar. But she had never driven it faster or with more grim determination than she

drove it that morning.

The rain slashed and pounded against the windshield and surprise gusts of wind bounced her from lane-to-lane all the way to North Bend, where it started to snow. At first the flakes were as big as quarters and burst on impact like tiny balloons full of water, but soon they hardened, piling up under the windshield wipers, narrowing her field of vision until it was reduced to a pie wedge directly in front of the steering wheel. The head wind grew stronger the higher she went, and by the time she crossed the Denny Creek Bridge, the Volvo was down in second gear and laboring.

Her hands were numb on the wheel as she listened to the morning chatter on the radio: traffic advisories for Seattle freeways; a doctor giving advice on emergency measures for bee stings; a stock market report. "The market opened mixed this morning with the Dow Jones showing gainers slightly outnumbering losers." The stock market always opened mixed, she thought, maneuvering around a Greyhound bus and fighting the swerve on the snow-covered road as she jumped out of the plowed rut.

The city was getting more electric trolleys; the price of gas was going up; a couple carrying a sawed-off shotgun and wearing Halloween masks had robbed a bank; a seventy-nine-year-old woman who taught Jacques Cousteau's children to swim would be interviewed at noon; and Rob Towne a seventeen-year-old high school junior from West Seattle was still missing from Snowcrest Resort. Towne, reported to have been skiing outside the controlled boundaries on Silver Star Mountain, was reported missing at ten last night by a skiing companion, William Blue, also a student. State Emergency Services coordinator George Simmons, who is in charge of the search, termed Towne's chances for survival growing slimmer by the hour. The near-zero visibility on Silver Star Mountain was hampering the search. Helicopters were standing by at Gray Army Airfield in Tacoma, but so far had not been able to get off the ground.

The only way to fly to Reno-Las Vegas, the announcer confided, was by taking the Sun Run Aviation Charter

Gamblers Special that left Seattle-Tacoma each weekend. "It's your ticket for the brass ring and a mighty good time," he said.

Laura floored the Volvo in second gear and felt the rear end lurch sideways. She held the wheel steady, resisting the temptation to spin it the opposite way and waited for the skid to end. When it did, she jammed the car into low gear and took the Snowcrest turnoff, peering into the snowstorm that was making the morning night.

Jack sounded so alone when he called, his voice barely audible. "I wouldn't bother you for the world, Laura, and I'll understand if you say no, I really will, but if you could come, that would mean a great deal to me. I've got a lot of faith in that boy, but it doesn't look good."

It did not look good at all, not for any of them. The parking lot was full of four-wheel-drive vehicles and several ambulances. As she got out into the knee-deep snow, she wondered where Shirley was and what she was doing.

The searchers had taken over the main lodge, piles of gear—sleeping bags, backpacks, skis, snowshoes—were everywhere. Two German shepherds slept in the corner; the tables were littered with Styrofoam cups and napkins; a large terrain map was tacked to the far wall; a low fire sputtered in the big stone fireplace. Jack Towne took her hand in his. The fleshy hand was cold and shaking.

"Thank God you've come, Laura. I prayed you'd come."

His face was pasty, and he was sweating. They looked at each other, neither speaking, and finally Laura moved into his arms, hugging him. She couldn't think of anything to say, no words of comfort, hope, or encouragement.

"Come here," he finally said, disengaging himself. "I want you to meet the fella in charge. He's a wonderful man, a real expert. He's doing a magnificent job. Everybody up here's doing their best, everybody."

She followed him over toward a long table under a terrain map. She noticed Jack was limping badly from the old injury to his knee. A small, bent, delicate man, wearing a rough alpine sweater, looked up as they approached. He was smoking a cigarette and listening to the chatter of the bank of radios in front of him while he made X's with a grease pencil on a small map mounted on a clipboard. Jack introduced him as George Simmons. Laura shook his hand. It was a woman's hand, soft and long-fingered, but with a firm grip.

"I've been talking to the party over on the south side of the mountain," he told Jack, the cigarette poised in a feminine sort of way between two perfectly straight fingers. "They haven't found anything. I'm going to have to call them back. It's getting too dangerous over there; the whole area's an avalanche zone."

"You've got to do what you've got to do," Jack said with understanding.

Laura tried to imagine what Rob might have done. He could have become lost in the storm and skied down one of the valleys, following the slope of the creek drainages. He could still be skiing out there somewhere, or he could have dug in to wait out the storm. It was possible. Or he could have fallen and broken his leg. He might be freezing. She forced her hands into her pockets. She should never have taken him down Nationale when it was closed. She was an adult. There were reasons for the closure rules. She was responsible.

"Are you a skier—Miss Jordan, was it?" Simmons asked her. He seemed perfectly calm and composed as only somebody can be who is not personally involved in a tragedy, Laura thought.

"Yes, in fact, I've skied with the boy up here. I skied with him only last week."

"Oh," he said, blowing a little cloud of smoke into the air. George Simmons did not inhale his cigarette. "And where was that?"

"Nationale," she admitted.

He arched his eyebrows. "That's been closed for a month. Avalanche danger among other things. This is a dangerous mountain, Miss Jordan."

"Yes, I know." At least he hadn't recognized her.

"Hmmm," he mused, pursing his lips until they stood out

like little red cherries from his face, "we might try another sweep up there. If he got off the track, it's conceivable he might be holed up in the trees, or—" he ran a long finger down the trail map—"if he got into one of these chutes, it could have avalanched on him."

"Do you think so?" Jack asked eagerly. "I mean he might be up in the trees?" His hands were trembling, his face was clown white.

"It's a possibility," George Simmons said carefully, eyeing Jack over the top of the map. "Are you all right, Mr. Towne? You look a little shaky."

"Oh, it's nothing. It doesn't matter. It's just a little angina."

Laura caught his arm. "Angina? What are you talking about?"

"Oh, the pressure I guess. I went to see my doctor yesterday morning, as a matter of fact. He said not to worry. It's the Early Winters thing and Shirley. Now this."

"Come over here and sit down," she said. "Right now." He leaned heavily against her.

"Let's have a doctor look at you, Mr. Towne," Simmons said crisply. "Fortunately, we have plenty of those. Dr. Thomas, say, Dr. Thomas?"

A portly man in a knee-length blue parka got up from his place by the fire. Laura eased Jack onto a steel folding chair.

"You shouldn't even be up here," she said.

"I had to come, Laura."

"Excuse me, young lady, may I look at this gentleman?" Dr. Thomas asked politely. Laura stood back.

As she watched Dr. Thomas probing Jack's chest, she saw George Simmons waving at her and went over to his table. "I didn't want to ask you when Mr. Towne was here, but was young Rob in the habit of skiing out-of-bounds? I mean was this something he did regularly?"

"I don't know," she admitted. "We did that night."

"People never believe what the mountain can do to them," he said sadly, fixing her with his surprisingly hard penetrating eyes. "Man always thinks he can outsmart a pile of rock and ice, especially a young man."

"You talk like there's no hope at all," she said, rousing herself. "There's always hope. He's young and strong and brave."

His eyes held her. They were the eyes of a fierce hawk. It was a shock to find them in such a strange little body. "Of course, there is, but the chances of us finding this boy alive are not good at all, Miss Jordan. Not good at all."

She glanced at Jack. He was leaning back, his eyes closed, his chest bared to the doctor. "I've skied this mountain. There're places to get out of the weather. Places to hole up."

"Oh, yes, Miss Jordan. I'm aware of that. But when you push your luck and your skill, it can also be a very unforgiving place."

"Aren't you being a little smug sitting down here, Mr. Simmons? Why don't you quit philosophizing and get some people up on Nationale and do another search off to the side. As a matter of fact, I'd like to go up there with them, if you don't mind."

He smiled at her, looking up from his hunched position at the table. "I'm afraid that's against the rules. I realize the boy is special to you, in fact, he's special to all of us. We don't take this casually, not at all. But it's best to follow procedure, not take chances by adding new, untried people to a search team." He folded his hands neatly in front of him. "I'm sorry."

"The hell with your rules," she said suddenly, coming over the table at him. "I'm going up there with or without your bloody permission. I'm not afraid, Mr. Simmons."

He sighed. "Excuse me," he said, and responded to a call from Search Team Alfa, reporting they were at the base of Silver Star and starting back along the cat track.

The doctor was kneeling in front of Jack, explaining something to him, motioning with his hands. Across the room, Laura caught the hard eyes of William Blue staring at her. He was sitting jammed in a corner in his blue racing suit, squatting on his haunches like a cornered animal.

"I realize you're not afraid, Miss Jordan," he said, after terminating the call, "and I'll see if Bravo Team leader will consider taking you. After all, you know the boy's habits. It might be useful."

He stood behind the chair, a hunched man, even more misshapen than he appeared when sitting. She was shocked to see his legs and spine were so twisted he could barely walk.

"I would gladly go myself," he explained, his hawk eyes on her. "I was strong and brave once, but I slipped. A technical climbing error, a stupidity,—my reach exceeded my grasp. It was in the Grand Tetons a long time ago when I was very young and foolish."

She watched him hobble over to the group of ski patrolmen. A young man detached himself and came toward her. He was wearing a T-shirt that said "Give me Rossinol or Give Me Head," and his hair stuck out like a fright wig. "You can come, lady, providing you remember I'm the honcho of this outfit. If I say we get off the mountain, that's what we do."

"All right," she said.

"Personally, I don't mind risking my ass for some stupid kid, but my team over there, they've got families, and I don't want to feel guilty about losing them. You understand where I'm coming from?" His lips pulled into a confident sneer.

"I think so."

"Good. You better get your stuff together because we're moving."

On her way out, Laura went over to Jack. "How's the patient?" she asked the doctor.

"Nothing serious, only fatigue, I think. But we need to be sure. I can't seem to persuade him to leave. He really should have a complete checkup."

"Now now," Jack said stubbornly.

People were up and moving out of the room. "Jack, I'm going up with them," she explained.

He nodded. An eager young girl in a very expensive ski outfit stepped up next to Jack. "Are you Mr. Towne?"

"Yes, I am."

"I'm Katherine Weiss with the *Seattle Times*. I'm sorry to

intrude, but I'd like to get some background on your son."

"That's all right," he said. "What can I tell you?"

"I'll see you when I get back, Jack. You take it easy," Laura said.

"Oh sure, you be careful, Laura," he replied buttoning his shirt. The doctor stood by. "Now, ah, Miss Weiss, what can I tell you about Rob? I can say this. A man couldn't have a better son."

Laura picked up her skis and started for the door. She felt William Blue's eyes on her, and she turned deliberately and went over to him. He remained crouched in his corner.

"Hello, Blue," she said.

"You meddling bitch," he hissed, "you meddling stupid bitch. Now look what you've done."

She stared down at him, feeling the animalistic hatred, and then turned for the door without answering.

They got on the chair lift under the glow of the nightlights even though it was approaching noon. The attendant, bundled to his chin, helped them on, and Laura felt the chair start up the hill. She hung onto the center post as it swayed in the high wind.

"You'd never know it's spring," her seatmate grumbled, his purple goggles reflecting her own similarly masked face.

At the top, they grouped next to the lift tower in waist-deep snow out of the wind.

"OK, first we're gonna look at the Dutchman's Fall, the chute on the left," the leader shouted over the wind. "We're gonna come in high, far apart, and if it hasn't avalanched, I don't want anybody going out there because sure as hell it will."

Laura felt her heart pounding. Please God, she prayed, let us find him in the trees. Let Rob Towne have another chance. He had such lousy luck before. He's so young, don't take him so soon. "And you, stay in line, goddammit!"

Laura nodded. They dropped down past the barrier, crossed the top of Nationale and struggled through a tight stand of alpine firs, their ski tips barely showing above the snow. It was difficult to feel the slope of the hill in the deep snow, and Laura found herself lurching sideways, off balance. Abruptly, she stumbled over the man in front of her. The line had stopped.

"Georgie," the leader called on his walkie-talkie, "Georgie?"

A hail of static came back and a small voice three thousand feet below them answered. It was from another world with light and fire and heat. She felt William Blue's eyes again, the accusing vicious eyes. "You meddling bitch."

Laura leaned on her poles and stared into the falling snow. He had to be out there somewhere.

"We're crossing to the Dutchman. I'll be back with you in about one zero."

George Simmons squeaked something back. He was like a crippled bug, she thought. There was no second chance up here.

As they moved toward the top of the chute that cut from the summit of Silver Star to the base, the snow got deeper until it was well above her waist, and she was sweating and panting to keep up. The upper part of the chute was too steep to ski, and Laura had seen the lower stretches still filled with snow into late July or August. Pink and yellow and magenta wild flowers grew around the tongue of snow at the base then.

The man in front of her faded and popped into focus with each gust of wind. It tore at them, forcing them into the steep hill. The treetops were gone. Above them, hidden in the snowstorm, was the 10,000-foot summit of Silver Star, an angry vertical spike driven into the sky.

Where tons of snow should have been in Dutchman's Fall, there was nothing but black rock and streaks of dirty ice. A massive avalanche had swept it clean; and balancing precariously over a crevice just in front of them was a red-white-and-blue candy striped racing pole that belonged to Rob Towne.

"That's his!" she shouted, fear in her voice.

"I see it," the leader snapped back. "We're going down the

side, and take it easy."

As she turned and moved down the hill, she heard him calling George Simmons to report the pole. Laura realized she should have insisted that Jack check into the nearest hospital. When he heard about the ski pole, it would be a terrible shock.

Somewhere down the hill, Laura knew they would find the main slide, but she was not prepared for the massive pile of snow and uprooted trees that was there. Above them, a load of rock broke free and came roaring down Dutchman's Fall like a locomotive running loose. Boulders the size of automobiles came end over end and slammed into the pile of snow as they watched from the side.

"If he's out there, we'll find him in the spring," the Bravo Team leader announced to them. "We're not crossing. We'll take a quick probe down this side up high here and then go back to the barn."

Laura was in a daze. Her strength was gone. A relentless force was pulling her in toward something terrible. Each movement became agonizingly slow and hopeless. The wand probe in her hand went down into the snow without a sound. Time after time, it hit nothing. All around her, the probes went up and down, the needled pistons of the methodical search and rescue machine.

The cry beside her was so startling she dropped the wand and almost fell. "I found something!" somebody yelled in her ear. The sound was harsh and shattering.

Oh God, she thought. The ski sticking out of the snow was Rob's favorite, a Roc Comp. It pointed away from the slide toward the trees. He made it, she thought, with a wild reckless burst of hope in a miracle. He stayed on top even without a pole, and he made it. He's in the trees someplace near us, waiting.

"Rob!" she screamed, "Rob!" The wind blew her words away. "Oh, Rob," she cried to herself. "Please, Rob."

They were pulling on the ski, and it wouldn't budge so the leader got out his portable aluminum shovel and dug down through the hard crust of the slide that had frozen as solid as a skating rink. His shovel made a pitiful clink each time he rammed it down. Finally the ski wiggled.

"Oh, please," Laura whimpered, holding herself together in a crouch as she watched. When she saw the white Scott boot still in the binding, she knew.

"I'm sorry, miss," the leader said, putting a mittened hand on her shoulder. She turned away while they hacked and dug and called on the radio. When it was done, she willed herself to turn and look.

His body looked natural in the dirty stretch pants and the down vest. But his beautiful face was distorted into a frozen mask of horror by globs of ice that jammed his nostrils and filled his mouth.

Rob Towne had suffocated under a foot of snow as thick and hard and unforgiving as cement.

Chapter 20

No matter how hard she tried, the picture would not fade. It was there in the quiet, empty dark hours when she woke up suddenly. It stabbed into her consciousness in those moments of fatigue during the day when she would sit back and stare at nothing. The ski poking out of the snow, the rush of false hope, the frozen horror stamped on his face by that final, gasping desperate reach for life. Rob Towne never had a chance.

The sun was shining and the cherry blossoms were out. A jet plane boomed overhead; three teenage boys, long hair slicked back, unable to hide their youthful swagger beneath blue suits, moved into the first row of brown steel folding chairs directly in front of the open coffin.

Laura Jordan sat in the back row. Jim McClay offered to come, but this was something she had to do alone. Late Friday afternoon traffic hummed on the freeway that wrapped around the cemetery like a question mark. From the rise where the mourners gathered under the rose-colored canopy, there was a good view of the snow-covered Cascade Mountains shimmering in the distance.

All in all, she thought, blinking back the tears, it was not such a bad place. Laura twisted the white linen handkerchief over and over in her hands, trying not to look at the coffin where his delicate face was so much more peaceful in death than it had been in life. Emotion overwhelmed her, a helpless grieving for a loss that was so unfair, so unjust.

Jack and Shirley arrived in a silver Cadillac limousine. They got out, stood stiffly apart by the open door for a moment, and started up the low steps. Jack limping badly, his face unnaturally red, constantly looked behind him as if he'd forgotten something important.

Chris, Wendy, and Ruth solemnly mounted the steps after them, Wendy so pale and weak, her younger sister had to help her walk. Ruth Curtis, her black dress drawn tight over her sausage shape, left the harsh cutting smell of liquor trailing behind her in the fresh spring air as she swayed by, on her way to the coffin.

There were others Laura didn't recognize. William Blue was not there. The organ began playing, weak and out of tune in the open air. White rows of clouds marched across the blue sky from west to east at different speeds, making huge drifting piles on the horizon.

Shirley and Jack were on one side of the coffin. Ruth, Wendy, and Chris sat on the other. A thin bald man in a dark suit stood up as the music faded, the last notes going flat.

"We are here," he announced formally, "to commemorate Robert Louis Towne, an outstanding young man who was taken from us by the grace of God. At the family's request," he nodded in the direction of the coffin, "the service will consist of a eulogy delivered by his beloved sister, Christina."

Chris stepped forward, a folded piece of ruled school paper in one hand. Jack looked quickly at his daughter in her dark-blue suit, and then turned away, fidgeting with the gold ring on his left hand.

Chris glanced down at her notes and then up toward the mountains in the distance. "My brother Rob," she said and stopped. "My brother Rob," she started again, glancing down at the paper. Shirley buried her face in her hands. "Rob was a wonderful brother. The first time I remember ever seeing him was in Arizona, and he was running across the lawn through a sprinkler." Her voice grew stronger, and she put the notes behind her. "I thought he was the prettiest baby I'd ever seen and certainly the liveliest." She smiled at them, her clear blue eyes steady and tearless. "He would charge through that sprinkler again and again," she recited, "until

Mom finally came out and made him stop."

Ruth Curtis bowed her blond head, clutching Wendy who looked ahead at nothing, her waxy face blank.

"And I can remember where we lived in Colorado when he was older. We had a big house there, and Rob liked to climb up on the roof in the summer and jump off, pretending he was a bird. I would get so upset because I thought he'd hurt himself—but he never did. It was like he had springs in his legs, and I knew then that he had the great natural coordination of an athlete.

"I took care of Rob a lot because Mother had to work, and we got to be good friends. Sometimes, we'd make chocolate chip cookies, and Rob would help." She laughed to herself. "Actually I made the cookies, and he ate the chocolate chips."

Jack Towne fiddled with the big gold ring. He twisted it this way and that and pulled it off and on.

"And at night, we'd make popcorn and sit in front of the TV in our pajamas. Wendy was there sometimes, and we'd pretend Rob was our little boy because he was the kind of little boy we all wanted when we grew up.

"I remember he came home one day from school, and he'd been in a fight. That was in Colorado too. We were new in the neighborhood, and a bunch of boys picked on him. They beat him up on the way home from school. He was a terrible mess. He had a bloody nose, and he was crying. But he was mad too.

"Rob didn't have a big brother; all he had was a couple of sisters. And so after I got him cleaned up, Wendy and I and Rob went back to the bus stop to find them. I don't really know what we intended to do, but when they saw us coming, they ran away and never bothered him again.

"And Rob used to say to me that having big sisters was better than having big brothers anytime. And that's the way I always felt about it too—having Rob for a little brother was better than a little sister. I wouldn't have traded him for anything or anyone in the world."

She glanced down at the notes, the paper jumping in her

hand and took a deep breath. Angry horns sounded on the freeway. A gust of wind rattled the canopy. "When I think of Rob, I think of that little boy jumping off the roof over and over again. And I think of him skiing, which is something else we liked to do together. In his heart, Rob was a skier. He loved the freedom. He loved the feeling of jumping off a big mogul like a bird. And he liked to go higher and farther than other people went.

"I don't think it's a bad thing to say that Rob was just a skier. He didn't have time to be anything else. I don't know what he might have become. Whatever it was, I know he would have always kept his love of the mountains.

"Rob was a little reckless, a little wild, but he was a good boy, and he never hurt anyone intentionally. He did his best to do the right thing. He's gone away, but wherever he is, I know it will be a better place. It will be a place where he can be wild and run free like a boy should be able to and never fall." Chris Towne crumpled the paper tightly in her fist and turned to the coffin. "So go, little brother, try your new wings. Run high and run free."

It was over quickly. The thin bald man and two assistants secured the lid on the coffin, and the bier was lowered with a soft whine into the grave. Jack limped forward and dropped a handful of dirt, his great bulk overwhelming those around him. He looked over his shoulder again. It was a quick nervous gesture. He seemed to be confused, and Laura wondered if his heart was bothering him. He turned to the thin man and shook his hand awkwardly.

As Laura stood up to go, she realized Shirley was coming down the aisle, looking directly at her.

"Shirley," she said, stepping out to meet her.

"Laura, so nice of you to come." Shirley stopped, leaving a gap between them.

"I didn't know if I should."

"You belong here as much as I do. I'm glad you did."

"I felt I should be here."

"Rob would have wanted it. I know he would have." Her eyes were red. Laura thought she was being very brave. "He admired you, Laura. You were much closer to him than I ever was."

"How are you, Shirley?"

"I'm fine. How are you? Come and walk with me for a minute."

The two women moved out from under the canopy into the sun.

"You look tired, Laura," Shirley said, holding out a white-gloved hand.

Laura took it, and they strolled along the rise, walking carefully so their high heels wouldn't catch in the loose gravel on the path.

"Jack told me you went up to look for Rob yourself."

Laura felt Shirley squeezing her hand. "I would have done anything, Shirley, anything . . ." Laura had to pull her hand away to cover her face.

"I know. I know what you must have been going through."

Laura tried to speak, but couldn't get the words out. She cleared her throat. "I'm sorry," she finally said. "So sorry."

"There's nothing to be sorry for, Laura. I mean that."

Laura found the handkerchief in her purse and blew her nose. "We'd better go back."

They turned, retracing their steps to the grave site. Workmen in green overalls were folding up the chairs, and Laura smelled the sweetness of the cherry blossoms on the trees around the cemetery. Jack was standing by the Cadillac, talking to the chauffeur while Ruth and Wendy stayed to one side.

"Jack doesn't look well," Laura remarked, noting again the redness of his face.

"I wouldn't know," Shirley said quickly, her face going taut. "He says he's having chest pains. I told him to see a doctor."

"Did he?"

"I don't know, Laura. That's really none of my concern any more."

"Shirley?" Laura stopped and took her by the arm. "This isn't a very good time to say this, but I'll probably never get another chance. Don't let what happened between Jack and me ruin everything for you. Blame me if you want, but don't blame him. Don't throw away a good relationship because of one mistake. He needs you right now more than he ever has."

Only Shirley's expressive eyes showed the agony. Her face was set and hard. "Laura, what happened between you and Jack has very little to do with my decision. I made that decision before I even knew. I guess I was naive, but I didn't know, Laura, I didn't even suspect." She turned her face away.

"I'm sorry—for everything," Laura said, feeling something important slipping away between them.

The groundsmen were stacking the flowers to one side and preparing to lower the canopy.

"Walk me down, will you Laura, please? I've got to get home, and I don't know if I can face all these people alone."

"Sure, come on."

Jack nodded to Laura as they approached, a quick nervous jerk of the head and excused himself.

"I need to talk to Ruth," he said over his shoulder.

Chris seemed fully composed. "Hello, Miss Jordan. Thank you for coming."

"I was very fond of your brother, and that was a beautiful eulogy, Chris, absolutely beautiful. I don't know how you got through it." She had Ruth's fire, her peach-smooth skin, and Jack's blue eyes. Chris smiled her serene smile. "How's school?" Laura asked her.

"Fine."

"Still going to be a doctor?"

"Yes. Mom and Wendy are going to move up with me. We're going to take care of each other while I go to school."

"Good for you. I think that's wonderful." Laura heard a cry of anger behind them.

Ruth Curtis, hands on her hips, was glaring at Jack. "I wouldn't ride with you, you son-of-a-bitch, if you were the last man on earth." She fired the words at him like bullets, spittle flying. It snaked out in a slow moving arc and struck him across the face.

Slowly, he pulled a white handkerchief out of his breast pocket and wiped it away. "I'm sorry you feel that way, Ruth," he said mechanically.

"Sorry?" she shrieked. "Sorry? You shoulda thought about being sorry before you sent this girl across the country all alone where she could get hurt. You shoulda left her home with her sister where she was safe, where she wanted to be!" Several departing mourners turned to watch. Laura, Shirley, and Chris stood frozen by the outburst. The Cadillac chauffeur rubbed his chin and waited.

"Ruth, please. Wendy wanted to go see her grandfather. I . . ."

"That's not what she told me." Ruth cut him off, her puffy face white with anger. "She told me you made her go."

Wendy cringed and moved behind her mother.

"Now, Ruth." Jack stepped toward her.

"Get away!" she screamed, waving her arms wildly, "you killed my boy!" Jack Towne stopped as if she'd struck him across the face.

"Madam, may I help you?" The chauffeur stepped forward, formally offering his arm.

"Don't touch me." But it was a cry for help rather than a warning.

Ruth Curtis was done. Her breath came in shallow gasps. She shook with the effort, tears streamed through the heavy makeup on her ruined face. "Keep him away—please," she whined, leaning heavily on the chauffeur's arm.

Laura felt the cold dampness of evening settling over them.

Jack Towne didn't move. "Would you please take them home?" he asked the driver, his voice flat and expressionless. He turned to Shirley. "Why don't you go with them."

"But what about you, Jack?"

"Oh, I have friends; I'll be all right." He waved vaguely toward the parking lot. "Not to worry."

Shirley turned to Laura, her lips were quivering. "Well," she said, touching her lightly on the shoulder, "goodbye." The door closed, and she was gone.

Jack waited at the curb, making a show of glancing at his watch. Laura thought it was such a sad hopeless gesture. There was no hurry about anything now.

Laura's feet ached from the high heels she wasn't used to wearing; the dress tugged at her. The silver limousine's red tail lights winked in the gathering dusk.

For a brief moment in the San Juans, lying next to Jim McClay in the night, listening to the soothing movement of the water against the sides of the boat, she thought it was possible to escape her share of the responsibility. For the moment, it became an isolated incident in her life, a mistake, a painful experience that would fade with time. But the midnight call about Rob Towne shattered that illusion forever.

Jack and Laura were alone. She searched her purse for the car keys. There was only one solution for her—to withdraw from her practice, the television show, and everything else connected with counseling. She was going to pull back within herself until she was ready to emerge and go in a new direction.

"I don't suppose you're going my way?" Jack said to her. The crimson color in his face had miraculously faded. The blue eyes were suddenly alert, deep in their recessed sockets.

"I might be. Where are you going?"

"Downtown."

There was no decent way to say no and, besides, she thought, what did it matter?

"Come on," Laura said, leading the way to her car sitting alone in the empty parking lot. She knew there were no friends waiting for Jack and never had been.

"I felt it was better for them to go alone," he explained carefully.

"Of course. Ruth made quite a scene back there."

"That's not her fault. She does that when she drinks."

Laura opened the passenger side with a snap and went around the car. "She blames you."

"Yes."

Laura started the Volvo and backed it out of the parking space. "Chris looks good. She told me Wendy and Ruth were going to live with her."

"Really?" He seemed genuinely surprised.

"That's what she said. She's such an incredibly strong girl."

"Yes, she is."

Laura drove without saying anything more. She turned on the headlights and got into the outside lane of the freeway. Finally, she turned on the radio. There was so much she wanted to ask him, but the right time was long past.

"Where are you going?" she finally asked.

"Oh, the bar at the Washington Plaza will be fine."

"Don't you think you ought to go home?"

"No, I don't," he said, looking straight ahead.

The tires hummed over a lane marker as she moved to avoid a slow-moving VW van. "Did you ever see a doctor about your heart?"

"No, I never did. It doesn't bother me now."

"Goddammit, Jack," she said mildly, "see a doctor."

Laura turned up the radio. They were discussing professional basketball and the college draft. "Hendricks has got all the moves, and his transition game is unreal. I mean he's like a man from outer space."

"It was a nice service," she said over the radio chatter.

"Yes, it was, wasn't it? I was disappointed my dad didn't make it."

"Kentucky is a long way."

"That's no damn excuse," Jack shot back. "I'm sorry, but it isn't. He's insensitive. It was like that with Mom; he never saw the value of gestures. Sure, I know it won't make any difference to Rob—not now—but he should have come—for me. It's not that far."

"Don't be so hard on him, Jack."

"I guess I'm at the end of my rope, Laura. You're right. He did send some flowers; they were nice."

"That's a gesture, Jack. I'm sure he meant well."

"You're right, Laura, as usual. Damn it all, you're good for me. You won't let a fella feel sorry for himself," he said hopefully.

She downshifted with a jerk to avoid ramming a bus. "You got my note, right?" she said quickly. "The one I sent before I ran away to the San Juans."

"Oh, sure. I didn't mean that. I meant it's good to see you."

"Well, it's good to see you too. I hope we can always be friends, but the rest of it's over, Jack."

"I understand, I understand. Listen, why don't you stop at the Plaza with me and have a drink for old times' sake. It would mean a lot to me, expecially tonight. It's a bad time to be alone."

She glanced over at his bearlike figure hunched against the door. "Yes, it is," she said.

"How about it, Laura? Do me this one favor."

Laura could think of a lot of reasons she shouldn't. "OK, one, no more."

"Just one. Scouts' honor," Jack Towne said cheerfully.

Chapter 21

It was hot and noisy and crowded in the Lion O'Malley Room on top of the Washington Plaza Hotel, and Laura found herself holding on to Jack Towne's shoulder as they moved through the smoke and drinkers standing three deep at the bar billed as "Seattle's Best Irish" in pink flashing neon.

The band, sitting in a horseshoe in the middle of the room, played "Shadows in the Moonlight"; and their lead singer, a handsome dark woman whose face ran with sweat under the spotlights, overrode the shouted conversations with her hoarse throaty voice.

"Oh, hi, Jack. You want a table by the window?" the cocktail waitress asked him. Laura noted her satin briefs pulled up so tight they disappeared into her crotch. White flanks switching in the blue haze, she led them to the only table available. Jack pressed a bill into her hand. She smiled. "The usual?"

"Yes," he said, helping Laura get seated. "Laura?"

"Perrier."

"Oh, come on, Laura, if we're going to have a wake let's have one," he shouted over the din.

"All right, bring me a Scotch and soda, J&B."

She nodded and was off, scooping up empty glasses as she went. Lion O'Malley's was a bar in the round that matched the circular shape of the hotel. The floor-to-ceiling amber-tinted windows gave Laura the feeling of being in a darkened lighthouse that looked over the lake on one side and Puget Sound on the other.

"They know you," Laura said loudly, leaning close to be heard.

"Yeah, this is my office away from the office."

It was a rowdy Friday night and watching the young men, ties askew, Samsonite briefcases stacked against the wall, gesturing and pounding one another on the back, reminded Laura of Happy Hour at the Officers' Club before Jim went to Viet Nam. These young stockbrokers and management trainees looked remarkably similar to army lieutenants out of uniform. The difference was these men would get home, whereas many of Jim's classmates never came back at all.

Their drinks arrived and Jack raised his glass, a snifter full of pink liquid and proposed a toast. "To better days."

"To the memory of Rob Towne," she added, surprised at herself for bringing it up.

"Yes," he said, touching her glass and taking a long drink.

Laura sipped the Scotch. It was strong. It seemed the lady in satin had mixed her a double. It didn't matter. And she supposed it didn't matter if they had a drink in Rob's memory either. The Irish did it; they were in an Irish drinking establishment; it was a rather nice custom.

The band swung into "New Old Blues." The singer's white teeth flashed; she winked at Jack. He raised a hand.

"I think she likes your style, Jack," Laura said, putting a hand on his arm.

He shrugged. "Not really," he said, sitting back. "She's putting on an act, but it's a good one, isn't it?"

He seemed to come alive in the dark. He sat back in the chair, comfortably inert, his oversize head resting against the window, a shadowy prince in his element. The heavy gold ring flashed as he brought it up to his face. She knew the electric blue eyes were watching her.

"What I can't figure out," he said, "is what he was doing up there, you know?"

"I'm not sure," she said, taking another sip of her drink. It was only partly a lie. She wasn't sure.

He shrugged. "I wonder why he wasn't skiing on the regular hill?"

She finished the drink, tipping it up until all the Scotch drained off the ice cubes. It's the same thing as being put under with sodium pentothal, she thought, feeling the numbing sensation in her face and shoulders, only cheaper. She didn't want to talk about it. Not now, not ever again. He put up his hand to order another drink. Laura noticed the cocktail waitress hovering near.

"She takes good care of you."

"You spend a lot of money, they take good care of you," he replied casually. "Hey, Maggie, did I ever tell you you're a real doll?" he asked the waitress.

Her creamy breasts were close to spilling out of the skimpy top as she leaned down to get the order. "Yes, Jack, you did."

"I guess I'd better get a new scriptwriter," he kidded her.

Maggie the cocktail waitress gave him a hard smile. "Maybe," she said. "Enjoy yourself."

The band was taking a break. Laura looked at the city lights spread below them in geometric patterns. It all looks so unreal, she thought, like a toy city.

"Anyway," he went on, "I don't suppose we'll ever know why he went up there."

Bringing it up now, she thought, won't solve anything. "I don't think so, Jack."

Their new drinks arrived, and Laura tried hers immediately. It was even stronger than the first one. She took two quick gulps.

She should have seen the avalanche poised and, at the very least, showed Rob Towne how to get out of the way.

"I wonder if something was bothering him," he went on in a detached voice, "you know? I'd hate to think it was something I said or did inadvertently." He looked around the room as he talked. It was the same preoccupation he'd displayed at the funeral.

"I don't think so." He was lighting a cigarette with a chrome Zippo. The flame emphasized the scars on his face before he snapped it shut. "I didn't know you smoked, Jack."

"I don't. Only when I'm nervous."

"Are you nervous now?"

"Yes," he said, sweeping the room again, "I guess I am."

"There's a call for you, Jack. You can take it at the bar."

He was up on his feet before the waitress finished delivering the message. "Excuse me," he told Laura hurriedly, "this could be important."

He was gone only a minute. She saw him make his way through the crowd, pick up the red telephone receiver, nod twice, and hand it to the bartender.

When he came back to the table, he was in a hurry. So much of a hurry, Laura noticed, that his limp was gone. "T.R. Timberlake's here," he said quickly, hitching up his pants before sitting down. "He just got in. He's coming up for a drink."

"Jack, I've got to go," she said. Laura didn't like the sound of his explanation. It had all the marks of a rehearsed line.

"Oh, no, please stay," he said hurriedly, holding her by the arm. "He's dying to meet you, really, Laura. Listen, please stay a minute."

"Jack," she said, "I wish you all the luck in the world, but I don't want to get involved again."

He kept a firm grip on her arm. "Please, say hello—for me. You'll like him."

"You're in an awfully persuasive mood tonight, Jack," she said, pulling his hand off her arm.

Jack Towne was so preoccupied he didn't sense her anger. "Great, that's great. Listen, Laura, if I can get him to put up some money, my partners think they can get this mess with the permit ironed out. Those people at the hearing don't represent the public over there; they're against progress, don't you see?"

"I really don't know, Jack. Look, you've got business to talk over."

"Fifty thousand dollars, Laura. That's all he's got to risk. We can get the damn permit, and Early Winters will be back on schedule."

"Jack, I'm not a promoter," she protested. It was as polite as she could be under the circumstances. Jack was manipulating her; he wanted to use her as window dressing.

"So this is the famous Laura of Laura's Second Landing," he said, taking off his cowboy hat. "T.R. Timberlake, darlin'."

He was nothing like she imagined he would be. T.R. Timberlake the Potato King was a little squatty owl of a man, much shorter than she. His close-cropped brown hair was thinning; his cowboy shirt wasn't cut well for his square shape. In fact, with the exception of a diamond the size of a walnut on his pinky finger, he was a very ordinary-looking man.

"I'm pleased to meet you," she said, holding out her hand while she planned her exit.

"Likewise, I'm sure." He smiled with unmistakable shyness. T.R. Timberlake had jolly little eyes. The Potato King would make a good Santa Claus, Laura thought.

"Well, if I'd known this lady was so pretty I woulda come over here before, Jack. You been holdin' out on me."

"Isn't she everything I told you she was?" Jack looked supremely happy.

"Are you in town on business, Mr. Timberlake?" she asked him, leaning in front of Jack. This, she knew, was definitely not a chance encounter. "Or did you happen to drop by?"

He laughed. "I'm always on business, darlin'. Came to meet you among other things. Also to buy carloads of this and that. Look, Miss Jordan, I'm no good at beating around the bush. I'm a country boy, a graduate of the Missouri School of Mines, trying to run a business that's getting way beyond me. Jack here thinks you've got real marketing talent. I need a lot of that, whether this Early Winters mess ever gets untangled or not."

Maggie was back. "Get us a bottle of whiskey, will ya, sweetheart?" T.R. Timberlake asked her. "We're gonna celebrate."

"I'm sorry, sir, we can't put a bottle on the table."

"Hell's bells, put it under the table, put it in a decanter, I don't care. Long as it's not those itty-bitty glasses. You see what you can do, OK?"

She winked at him and retreated. The band was forming

up behind them again. "Now how about it, Miss Jordan, what d'ya say?"

"Oh, please call me Laura, Mr. Timberlake," she said sarcastically with a hard edge on her voice, "and the answer is an unequivocal no. You guys have really got your nerve. You got me up here under false pretenses."

Jack laughed uncomfortably. He finished his cigarette and paid a great deal of attention to putting it out.

"We did?" T.R. Timberlake asked her, seeming to be genuinely surprised. "You call me Teddy. Heck, Laura, I thought Jack here had explained my little proposition."

"I didn't get time," Jack said lamely. "I was working up to it. We were preoccupied. My boy's funeral was today."

"You never said anything about that," T.R. Timberlake came halfway out of his chair. "Doggone it, you shouldn't even be here, Jack. What a hell of a thing."

Laura was beginning to like T.R. Timberlake in spite of herself. He seemed to be a fairly decent little man. It was Jack Towne that made her angry.

"I didn't want to let you down again, T.R."

"Jack, my boy, I live and breathe business. I even dream business, but it never comes before your family. Hell, I'd give you this doggone shirt right here if I could bring that boy back for you, and that's no lie. Avalanche was it? Terrible thing, terrible."

"It was one of those chance occurrences, T.R. Nobody could have predicted it," Jack explained seriously. "God only knows why he happened to be there at that particular time. Fate, I guess."

Laura had made up her mind. She couldn't go through another discussion of Rob with Jack or anybody else.

"Bad luck, I call it. Darn bad luck, and I'm as sorry as I can be, Jack. We didn't need to do this today, not at all."

"I have got some good news for you, T.R.," Jack said eagerly. He acted much younger in front of this squatty little millionaire.

"If you gentlemen will excuse me." Laura got up to leave.

"Whoa there, whoa there, hold on a minute." T.R.

Timberlake stood up with her. "Don't go runnin' off when we get to the good part. I like pretty girls. I like smart ones even more. I want you to listen to this. You tell me if Jack can pull this deal off. You listen, pretty lady, and I'll still name that damn restaurant after you."

She gave him a tight polite smile. "Thanks, but no. I come and go as I please, and right now I choose to go. I don't like being conned, and I don't like being used."

"Conned? Used?" he snorted, taking her hand so she couldn't leave. "Hell, we need you, woman. This deal's way beyond me, and I have a feeling it went over Jack's head some time ago. Please stay, Laura, I want your considered opinion." He kept his grip on her.

"For a minute," she said. His fingers were broad and strong, the nails flat and sliced off square.

"Thank you," he said, removing his hand and sitting down.

The drinks arrived in oversize bar glasses. "First cabin, that's what the doctor ordered." T.R. Timberlake gave Maggie a fifty-dollar bill. "No change," he said, sending her on her way with a firm hand on the rear end.

"Here's to Early Winters." Timberlake raised his glass. They all drank, Laura barely sipping hers. T.R. Timberlake made her feel better; he seemed to be honest. But she was still furious with Jack Towne for his deception.

"OK, Jack," he said, smacking his lips, "what's the news? And believe me, boy, this better be good."

Slowly, and with a flair that surprised Laura under the circumstances, Jack Towne explained how, in the minority partners' considered opinion, a carefully orchestrated public relations campaign aimed partly at the citizens of Wilson, Idaho, but mostly at several key politicians in Washington, could reverse the setback that occurred during the initial hearings.

The minority partners—State Senator Greenway and State Representative Howland—felt they had, Jack explained, more than demonstrated their confidence in this scheme by putting up all the money so far. But it wasn't enough, and what they needed, and needed now, was a financial push from Teddy Timberlake to get them over the top.

Timberlake listened, nodding now and then like a sleepy bullfrog, his wide fleshy neck folding down over his open-necked shirt. He was older than she had guessed. It was his enthusiastic approach to everything that made him seem younger. He blinked and rocked while Jack talked on and on. The band started up again. Jack said it was simply a matter of a well-targeted publicity campaign designed to demonstrate that Early Winters was good for the town of Wilson and the states of Idaho and Wyoming, whose borders it straddled.

"What do you think, Laura?" the Potato King said quietly when he was done.

"What do I think about what?"

"Do you think the place is worth it, or am I throwing money down a rat hole?"

"I don't know anything about the finances of a big ski resort, Teddy."

"I'm not asking you about finances. I'm asking you what you think of the place, the terrain, the snow, as a skier."

"I think it's got more snow than any resort in the United States. I think it comes earlier and stays later. I think it's got the finest powder skiing in the world—or at least any place I ever skied."

"So do I," he said. "How much?" T.R. Timberlake asked Jack.

Startled, Jack Towne shook his head. "Pardon me, T.R.?"

"How much do you and your little band of pirates think they need to pull this off? Laura and I want to ski down that damn Barrier Mountain up there next winter." He smiled and nodded at her.

"Fifty thousand dollars."

T.R. Timberlake grunted, took out a checkbook and started writing. When he was finished, he tore out the check and tossed it across the table. "And if that isn't enough, Jack, we're finished. That's positively the first and last dime I'm gonna put into this thing." He chuckled to himself and shook his head. "And that's a pretty good deal, considering you promised me it wasn't going to cost me a cent until we had that permit in our hands."

The crowd in Lion O'Malley's had thinned to a single line along the bar, and T.R. Timberlake led them out by being faster on his feet and more aggressive than either Jack or Laura. He waddled, but it was a quick waddle, and they had to hurry to catch him in the carpeted lobby in front of the elevator.

"You get those hotshot politicians of yours on the scent right quick," he said, pushing the elevator button. "I want to see the fur fly."

"I will, T.R., I will." Jack had to bow from the waist to get at eye level with the Potato King.

"And you come over to Boise and stay with us," he said, turning to Laura.

She shook her long blond hair over her shoulder. "Thanks, Teddy, maybe some other time."

The elevator doors parted silently, and they stepped into the padded interior. Muzak played softly from recessed speakers. The ceiling was in an egg-crate pattern of reflecting chrome to make the space look bigger.

"You come for sure. None of this 'thanks' stuff," he told her as they dropped down. "My wife's a tall woman too. Not as tall as you, of course, but you'd like her."

The elevator stopped at T.R. Timberlake's floor, and he held the doors open by placing his hand over the electric eye.

"She's read your book. She thinks you're the greatest thing since Mary Baker Eddy," he said, and stepped off the elevator.

They made the rest of the trip in silence. Jack stepped out first on the ground floor and held the door for her, a completely unnecessary gesture, Laura thought.

"Well," she said, eyeing the long line of taxis, "you won't have any trouble getting a ride home this time, Jack."

They walked out the automatic doors into the chilly night. Laura thought the downtown area was much prettier when there were no people, only quiet lighted buildings.

"You're mad, aren't you?" he said.

"Yes. I'm beginning to get a very bad feeling about you, Jack."

"I didn't know how else to do it. You could have said no to the drink." He examined the tips of his shoes.

"But you knew he was coming. You told him I was interested in a job, didn't you?"

"Yes," he admitted, looking up at her, the blue electricity pulsing steadily in his eyes.

"How could you do that, Jack? How could you lie to me like that?"

"It wasn't exactly a lie," he said miserably. "I didn't know how to get you to come with me."

"You could have asked. You could have asked me to come along and dazzle good old T.R. I could have worn another dress," she went on angrily, "something that shows more tit!" The black doorman dressed in a waistcoat and tophat glanced at them. "The trouble is," Laura said, "I was under the impression I was going to a funeral. For the life of me, Jack, I'll never understand why you chose to do this on this particular day."

He shuffled his feet and looked back at the doorman. "It wasn't like that," he said quietly.

Laura wanted to hit him, and she wanted to cry. "Well, what was it like? Tell me, dammit! Tell me why! My God, Jack I don't understand you at all."

His face was pale. He looked shocked, but his voice was calm. It was as if he couldn't make the connection between his action and her anger. "Oh, I didn't choose the day. It just happened that way. I—I—I couldn't do anything about it. And I didn't explain it because I didn't think you'd understand out there at the funeral."

"You're one hundred percent right about that. Just like I don't understand how you could walk out on Shirley while she was in the hospital. You're damn right, I don't understand."

"Oh, that," he said plaintively, turning the palms of his hands up and looking at them.

"Yes, that," she shot back at him. "It's none of my business, but, frankly, I'd sure like to know how you could do something like that."

"I didn't leave her," he said too eagerly. "Well, only for a minute. I had to go over to my office to make a phone call. It was important, and when I got back, she was gone. Gone. It was a terrible misunderstanding."

It occurred to her that nothing seemed to fit quite right any more. He was talking like a child explaining a childish mistake.

"A misunderstanding, Jack?"

"It was about Early Winters just like tonight," he said quickly, ignoring her remark. "I did it for Rob. He loved the idea of Early Winters. T.R. might have said tomorrow or the next day would be all right, but the truth is, he'd have gone on to something else, and a dream, a dream Rob and I shared, would have been gone forever."

"Oh, God, Jack, leave Rob out of this. Please leave him out of this."

She looked at the long line of cabs all neatly arranged one behind the other, but she was seeing Jack's Lincoln Continental and Jack standing beside it in the winter rain, waiting for her in front of the houseboat. There was a certain element in that scene she'd never examined closely before. It was like a theater setting, and Jack was in center stage delivering his well-rehearsed lines.

"I know I've made you angry, Laura, that I've hurt you, but I want you to be my friend. More than anything else in the world, I want you to be my friend."

"Oh, for chrissake, Jack," she cried, exasperated.

"It will work!" he said, his craggy face lighting up. "I know it will. The check will make it work. I had to do it. Please don't be angry with me, Laura. I'll do anything to make it up to you." He reached out to put his hand on her.

She stepped back out of range. He was not going to use her again. With a flush of shame, Laura realized she had not seduced Jack Towne. It was the other way around.

"Do you really want to make it up to me, Jack, really?" she asked him sharply.

"Of course," he replied resolutely.

"If you really want to do something for me, you'd get in a

taxi over there and go back to Shirley. Ask her, beg her, plead with her to forgive you. She's the best woman you'll ever find, Jack. She's got all of the good qualities and none of the bad."

"I don't think it would do any good," he said dubiously, looking at the line of cabs. The doorman waited for his signal to send one forward.

"It would mean a lot to me, Jack. I did a terrible thing to Shirley, and if you want to know the truth, I feel awful about it. And if you and Shirley could put that family back together somehow, it would relieve me of a lifetime of guilt. That's how much it means to me."

"I'll do my best," he said tentatively.

"Do better than that, Jack. Prove to me you really are what I always thought you were—an exciting sensitive man who cares about people and their dreams. Prove to me you can make it where it really counts, in a relationship with another person. Don't let this one go."

"Do you think she—she still loves me?" he asked hopefully.

"I don't know. Why don't you find out?"

He stood uncertainly, glancing first at the cabs and then at Laura. Suddenly, he was next to her, signaling for a cab and kissing her on the cheek.

"I'll do it," he said. "By God, I'll do it for you."

The cab pulled up and the driver swung the back door open by leaning over the seat. "Do it for Shirley, Jack. She's a good woman. She deserves better than this."

He got in. "If I could get Shirley back and close the Early Winters deal," he said, more to himself than to her, "it would be the best year of my life."

Before she could reply, the door swung shut. Laura saw him giving directions to the cab driver, gesturing, creating a map of his destination in the air.

And then Jack Towne was gone.

Chapter 22

She remembered the voice, the plaintive, halting, beaten voice. "I don't know what's happening to me, Laura. I can't seem to get out of the house anymore. I get dressed, and I go out to the garage and open the car door, but I freeze. I can't make myself get in. I go back inside and look in the mirror, and I don't know who it is. Have you ever had anything like that happen to you?"

Slumped in the chair, the running suit damp and smelling of sweat, Laura watched herself in color on the wide screen in her father's den. She watched as the camera swept the attentive faces in the audience, heard her own voice vibrant with self-confidence.

"Of course, I have. Growing old is especially difficult for a woman. We're not prized for our rugged good looks as we age. But tell me, did this happen suddenly? You indicated you never had trouble like this before."

"Yes, as a matter of fact, it did come on very suddenly," the woman answered.

Laura Jordan marveled at her astute analysis, her calm poise under the lights, the perfect control she seemed to have over the situation unfolding before the studio audience.

"One day I was fine," the woman said, "and the next day I wasn't. It was that quick. I couldn't cope anymore. I know I should get outside and do things, but I can't get out of the house."

"I see," the television Laura Jordan said.

But she hadn't seen at all. Yes, she cared about the woman.

Yes, she wanted to help. But no, she had no comprehension of what the woman was really going through, none at all.

But now she knew. Long after the "Family Line" program she was watching on the cassette had been recorded, Laura finally understood what it was actually like to find that one morning you could no longer face the world.

It had happened to her the morning after Rob Towne's funeral. She got up early, determined to put her affairs in order, one way or the other. Either to push on with her counseling service or get rid of it; to write another book or never write another book; to continue "Family Line" or cancel it; to conduct communication seminars for business and industry or do something else.

She made herself a big breakfast, fed the cats, opened the curtains to find spring was still hidden behind a layer of ominous clouds. She laid out pencil and paper and started a list. She labeled the list: Reasonable Options, Pro and Con.

Laura always advised her clients to make lists, to get the problem down in writing. But now she couldn't write. She could not move forward. She was trapped in the past. The scene in the parking lot starring Jack Towne played over and over in her mind.

The rain fell; he was drunk; there was blood splattered down the front of his white-on-white shirt.

"Sorry to disturb you at this late hour, Laura, but I was in the neighborhood," he said, holding his arms wide.

"My God, Jack, what happened to you?"

"I had a little setback."

Try as she might, Laura could not move the figures to find out what happened next; the lines played over and over. "Sorry to disturb you . . ." There was something vital buried in the past, but she couldn't bring it out. What had happened next? "What?" she wrote in block letters, but got no further.

When Barb Adams came to work shortly after eight o'clock, Laura turned the blank list over so her secretary wouldn't see her unanswered question.

"Well," she said with forced cheerfulness, "what's on the agenda this morning?"

Barb laughed. "A better question is what isn't on the agenda this morning, Laura. If you don't get moving, we're going to have to move out of the building, or we'll be smothered by urgent messages. Look at this stuff. You've got to get yourself in gear, sister."

"I don't know whether I'll ever get myself in gear again," she said.

But Barb Adams was having none of that. "The thing to do, Laura, is get off your rear end and do something. Call your agent then your producer, he's been screaming at me for days. After that, I've got a list of clients three blocks long."

Weary but game, Laura gave it her best. First, she called Terry Blake in Laguna.

"We were supposed to be having a conference on your next book. You promised me a detailed outline, Laura. Come on, we've got to strike while the iron is hot. That TV show of yours is going all over the country, great name exposure, just great, but you've got to capitalize on it—now."

She apologized, and told him she would get right on it. But Laura had no outline and no subject or any interest in finding one.

The producer was even more adamant. His neck was on the block. He had personally promised clients that if they would buy into "Family Line" he and Laura Jordan would turn them out at the rate of one a week for the next six months. The sad unalterable fact was, he told her, she had failed to produce one new show in the last month and the ratings on the reruns were dropping.

"Listen," she finally had interrupted him in exasperation, "I've got problems of my own."

"Get rid of them and get down here, Laura. You're a star. Nobody will ever know. For just one hour forget them and turn on that voice for me. Lean on me, cry on my shoulder, make a recording date next weekend. What do you say?"

"I'll do my best," she told him and hung up, knowing her best wouldn't be good enough.

The clients were even more depressing, and when she came across a message from Vinters of the *Los Angeles Times* asking her to call him collect, Laura knew she could not go on.

"What does he want?" she asked Barb, remembering their bitter clash over her book.

"He's going to be in town at a convention or something. He wanted to interview you again. He's seen 'Family Line' apparently."

"No," she said, "I won't do it. I can't stand up to that horrible little man again. I won't."

"Laura, what's wrong?"

"Everything, absolutely everything. Listen, just cancel it all, and I mean all of it: clients, dates, the works."

"Laura, we can't go on running this office on a referral basis. These people call because they want to see you. I have a dozen messages from the Clairbornes. They want you to be the guest of honor at their forty-third wedding anniversary. They think you changed their lives. They're supremely happy. You really ought to go."

"I can't."

"How about calling Jim McClay then? Honestly, Laura, I can't go on talking to that boy. He's worried sick about you. Do you know you haven't called him since the Rob Towne thing? He cares about you, Laura, he loves you."

"I can't see anybody—nobody."

Barbara Adams sighed. "Can I help, Laura? Is there something I can do?"

"No, but thanks. If you can hold things together for a couple of days, I'll be all right."

Laura went to her room and sat. At two o'clock that afternoon, she finally came to a decision. She had to move. She tied her hair back and put on her jogging suit. Downstairs, she kissed Barb who was close to tears, and went outside. Without thinking where she might go, Laura started running down the lake shore.

She ran hard, keeping her pace at a high count, her breathing pegged so she could stay with it. She ran down the railroad tracks, crossed the Fremont Bridge, went along the ship canal, recrossed it at the Montlake cut, and then turned toward Lake Washington.

She ran until her clothes were soaked with sweat. She ran when the sweat no longer came. She ran until her breath was hard and short, and she began gasping. Her legs were in agony, but still she went, crossing the long floating bridge over the lake where the cars whizzed within inches of the sidewalk, and the wind blew against her, slowing her pace to a crawl.

Somewhere during the long aimless run, Laura realized she was seeking the only refuge she knew, the big house on Birch Bay. Laura had no idea how many miles she had run, but knew she was close to collapse. Weaving from side to side, her mind numb with fatigue, shoulders cramping, she began to recognize familiar landmarks—Coleman Elementary Grade School, her school; the Standard Station that had been on the corner ever since she could remember; and then she heard Rocky charging up the driveway. She fell on her knees, hanging around his furry neck. "Oh, Rocky, you big jerk, I'm so glad to see you."

He was lying at her feet now while she watched the tapes of "Family Line" her father had faithfully recorded every Sunday.

"Well, is there something in your life, some unexpected event that might have occurred recently that could have triggered this feeling you have?" her TV image asked the caller.

"Not really. My husband and I have always had a good marriage. My son went through a divorce, but that was some time ago."

"I think you might be ignoring something obvious," Laura heard her smooth voice say. Oh, yes, she thought, there was always something obvious. She had a list of obvious things: the image of Rob Towne dead in the snow; Wendy Towne, a walking ghost; Shirley's hard sad face saying goodbye; Ruth swaying toward her son's coffin; Jack wanting something from her, but what was it? "To have for once something purely beautiful happen to me." What did he mean? To possess her body? Or was it something else?

The tape continued. "I want you to tell me—without thinking—answer right away—what would make you happy?" she asked the woman. "What would the ideal be for you? What would make you feel better than you feel right now?"

"Why to have my children happy, of course," the woman replied without hesitation.

"I think it's your son that's really upsetting you. He's not happy, you see, and that must be bothering you a great deal. Have you ever discussed the divorce with him?"

"Well—no—not really. He came and stayed with us for a while, but, no, I didn't want to bother him. It seemed like he had troubles of his own. And my husband thought it would be best if we let him work it out."

Laura knew what was coming next. She shifted uncomfortably in the chair, smelling the stale sweat, the odor of desperation clinging to her. She would smoothly turn to face the studio audience and with exactly the right inflection in her voice say: "It seems to me that you love your son very much, and he's being hurt, and you feel helpless. It may not be the source of all your trouble, but I really think you ought to talk to him and tell him how you feel. Tell him you love him. I'm sure it would do both of you a great deal of good."

"Yes, I could do that." There was such hope in her voice, such trust. She had the answer from Laura Jordan.

"And I want you to call me back and tell me how it went and how you're doing. We all do. This is a program of mutual support."

How had she been able to see the problem so clearly? she wondered. How had she been able to give such helpful advice? Laura stared hard at herself on the screen as she exchanged a few casual words with the audience. She didn't look anything like she felt now, sitting in the dark, the dog beside her, panting gently in his sleep.

The program cut away with Laura sitting before the audience. The camera pulled back until they were all shadows and then abruptly went to a preview of a comedy called "The Clown Show" scheduled for later that week. Then the tape flickered, and she was watching the beginning of her next program. "Welcome to Family Line," the announcer chirped.

In the end, it was all an illusion. She could see that now. The producer was right. It was show business. The callers solved their own problems. They already knew the answers. They simply wanted someone to validate them; someone who appeared to know; someone who looked competent; someone who seemed sure. Someone like Laura Jordan.

"And here's your host, Laura Jordan." She covered her eyes so she couldn't see the naive woman staring back at her from the screen. The arrogant, self-centered naive woman who didn't have any answers at all. The dog jumped to his feet, sounded a crashing bark and ran for the door.

"Hello, in there," her father said. "Mind if I come in?" A shaft of light cut into the darkened room.

"Oh, hi, Dad. You're home early." On television, Laura was about to interview a man and his wife who had problems telling their daughter she was adopted. She stood up and turned the set off, feeling all her muscles as she moved.

"Not unless you call six o'clock early," he said, coming over to kiss her. "Hey, you smell like a gym."

He smelled wonderful. The light scent of the aftershave he'd always worn still clung to his cheek.

"I feel even worse," she said. The collie circled them, whining and wagging his tail.

"He wants me to throw his ball for him. Why don't you come outside with me and talk to your old man," he suggested, putting an arm around her shoulder. "Girl, you're soaked. I'll get a dry jacket for you."

Laura stood beside him while he threw the yellow tennis ball across the gravel patio, her hands jammed in the pockets of his college letter jacket with the leather sleeves.

Rocky was in the prime of life, and unless Gene Jordan threw the tennis ball hard, the big dog gobbled it up before it got ten feet. A cold wind was blowing off the lake; there were no stars showing through the overcast.

"Weather report says a big storm's coming in," he said, heaving the ball as hard as he could. The dog lept over a piece of lawn furniture, tore after the ball and caught it on the bounce with a tremendous jump in the air.

"Seems like winter's never over sometimes," she said.

"Here." He offered her the ball. "You throw it."

"No thanks, go ahead."

He gave the tennis ball a heave. "Your mom's really worried about you, honey. She says you're thinking of giving up your business."

"I haven't really decided," she replied.

He tugged at the saliva-covered ball. Playfully, the dog refused to give it up. "Let go, damn you." He twisted the ball loose. "It's the boy Rob, isn't it?" He gave Rocky a head fake and tossed the ball in the opposite direction, but the big collie wasn't fooled. He had it and was wheeling around in six strides.

"That's part of it."

"You think it was your fault or something?"

"It was my fault."

"What are you going to do about it?" he asked her, giving Rocky a side-arm pitch in the direction of the lake. The collie went streaking down the lawn in a tawny blur, outrunning the spotlight and disappearing in the dark.

"There's nothing I can do except see that it doesn't happen again to anyone else."

"By quitting?" he asked her, hands on hips.

"Don't give me any lectures, Dad."

"I'm not giving you a lecture," he said kindly. "I'm asking you questions because I want you to know that you're not the first person who ever made a bad mistake."

The dog was back, panting. He sent him scurrying off again. "I still feel responsible for you, honey, because I encouraged you to believe you could do anything you wanted to do. I sent you out there, and I know it's rough."

She touched his arm. "You did fine. It's just that I'm not as strong as you are, not as sure of myself. You always know what you're doing." The dog sat beside them, waiting, his long pink tongue hanging over the corner of his mouth.

"I'll tell you something, Laura. Once when you were very

small, I almost got into politics. In fact, if I'd played my cards right, I could have been a U.S. senator. That was before I was in the political job at the bank. I was managing a guy's campaign then." He tossed the ball easily down the lawn. "I was always interested in politics. I knew a lot about it, but I'd never been in the game you see? Well, I won't go into details, but I made a bad mistake. To get my candidate elected, I destroyed the reputation of a very good man. I called him a communist. Hell, I didn't have any idea whether he was or not, but I knew it would put him out of the race." The dog was back, tired but still game "Give it a rest, Rocky," he said, patting him on the head. "I thought I knew what I was doing, but I had no idea at all, not until later."

"What happened to the man?" she asked her father, not wanting to know.

"Oh, I saw him years later at a Chamber luncheon. The communist scare was over then. He was back in the good graces with the establishment, but his business was going bankrupt. For a minute, I thought I was off the hook. He seemed friendly enough. Shook my hand, no hard feelings, all that." He paused and lowered his head. "He shot himself the next day. Turned out his wife left him years before because of the publicity," he said in a low voice. "I always felt I was on the trigger. Still do."

Oh God, she thought, he knows how close to the edge I really am. Laura had only one hope now, that somehow Jack Towne would be able to persuade Shirley to give it another try.

The wind had shifted to the southwest, and it was cold. Laura shuddered, and Gene Jordan pulled her against him. The dog was quiet, waiting to go in.

"I got out of politics after that," he said, squeezing the ball in his right hand. "I never went back to it. I stayed with the bank where it was safe, where I could control things, where I knew exactly what I was doing."

"That's sort of the way I feel," she said. "Only I don't know where it's safe in my line of work. I think it's better to leave it all."

"Honey," he said, taking her hand and leading her toward the house that looked warm and secure, "I'm not so sure there is a safe place anywhere. I'll be honest with you. Sometimes I wish I'd gone ahead in spite of what happened and become a senator, taken a part in running things in this country instead of taking it easy and playing it safe. Sometimes I think your old daddy could have been a famous man. Hell, I might have even done some good, you never can tell."

As they walked toward the house, Laura saw Jim McClay's car in the driveway, and as they entered the enclosed porch, she heard his mother's voice. There was no mistaking it; it was Myra McClay's untamed Scottish brogue.

"Hey," she said, grabbing her father's arm, "what is this? What's going on?"

He gave her his inscrutable Paul Newman smile. "Don't be too hard on your mother, Laura. She set it all up, so you go in there and be nice."

"Nice?" she said stopping. "I look like a pig. I feel like hell. She had no right to ask them over here when she knew—oh, Jesus."

"Well, she did it anyway," he said, trying to restrain her. She pulled away. "She did it because she loves you," he called after her as Laura marched toward the living room, hair flying.

"Maybe we better stay out here," he said to the collie, scratching his ears.

Laura burst into the room. They all looked up simultaneously as if expecting her at any time.

"Hello, Jim," she said. "Hello, Myra." She glared at her mother. "How nice to see you all. This is like high school, isn't it?"

"We were discussing Easter. That's tomorrow, you know," her mother said mildly, her hands folded neatly in her lap. "Myra and I decided it's high time we revived the old custom of the McClays and the Jordans getting together on Easter, going to church, having a champagne dinner, like we used to."

"Oh, Mother," she said angrily, "this is really too much."

"And Laura," Myra cut in politely, her Scotch face showing not a hint of anger or astonishment at the outburst, "it's not really anything like high school at all." She patted her flaming red hair and sat forward in the chair. "When you children were in high school, we hardly ever interfered. We pretty much let you alone to do your own thing, as the young folks say." She sighed, smiling, parting her fire-engine red lips. "And the good Lord only knows what you did."

"Look, Mrs. McClay, I love you dearly, but—"

"But this is far more serious, Laura," Myra cut her off. Jim shrugged and winked at Laura. "I understand you're thinking of not continuing your television program and discontinuing your counseling service. Is that true?"

"Yes," Laura admitted, noting that her father had slipped into the room.

"You absolutely can't do that, Laura. You have far too much to give. There are too many people who believe in you and need your help. You simply cannot throw that all away."

"You people are unbelievable," Laura said. "I thought you were talking about an Easter dinner?"

"We were," her mother said. "And other things."

"I'm only the driver," Jim pointed out.

"I appreciate your concern, all of you, but I'm going to make up my own mind about what I want to do. There's nobody I have more respect for, Myra, nobody in the world. You're a wonderful woman. But with all due respect, this whole thing is nothing more than a damn smoke screen—all this about Easter and how I can't quit. It's a smokescreen to cover up your matchmaking, your dream of having me married off to your son—whom I also love dearly, incidentally." She was furious at all of them. She had come to rest and lick her wounds, and they had turned on her.

Myra McClay stood up. She sighted Laura down her long nose. "I made a promise to my Angus before he died, God rest his soul, that somehow I would see that the McClay line was carried on, young woman. My son, a fine figure of a man and an excellent lawyer, seems incapable of accomplishing that simple task on his own." Laura stood in the middle of the room, astounded at the ferocity of her attack. "And for some reason which used to be clear but is unfathomable to me at the moment, Angus was very taken with you as the woman who would see that the McClay tartan still has meaning when all of us are dead and gone."

Myra McClay was trembling. Like a wall collapsing under a relentless earthquake, Laura could see her face so full of grim resolve, giving away to the emotion behind it.

"Myra," she said.

"Oh, Laura, my darling, why not?" she cried, bursting into tears and throwing her arms around Laura. "Why not? That's what I want to know. You tell me. What's so hard about two people who love each other getting married and having children? Explain it to this old peasant lady, and I'll go away forever."

Chapter 23

Dawn came slowly to Lincoln Memorial Hospital, the pale glow of Easter morning rising through the steady rain like footlights behind the dark green hills.

"I honestly thought he might be coming to see his wife," Laura told Penelope Washburn, RN. "He was like that, always doing the unexpected at the last minute."

Nurse Washburn shifted in her chair. She still looked fresh and attentive, Laura thought, her serene youthful face retained its look of perpetual optimism. "Maybe he was."

Laura stared at the rain. There was no letup. It had been coming down all night. "I really don't believe that anymore."

Fifty miles to the east, hard against the peaks of the Cascade range, the red and white Cessna lay where it had fallen in the muddy shallows, its broken fuselage covered with a heavy coat of frozen slush. The body of the young woman was gone.

"Sometimes," the nurse said kindly, "you have to accept things and go on."

Behind them in Surgery Room Number Two, Jack Towne lay unconscious, breathing by respirator, his failing vital signs registering in bright green digital figures. The scrub nurse took the heavy gold ring she'd removed from his left hand and put it in a white envelope marked "Personal."

The harsh crash of the metal door opening startled both women. Shirley's face was chalk white in the early-morning light. Her yellow raincoat dripped water on the waxed linoleum floor.

"That's Mrs. Towne," Laura whispered to Nurse Washburn.

"Let me get the doctor for you, Mrs. Towne," the nurse said quickly.

Shirley nodded. She blinked, cleared her throat, and took a pack of cigarettes out of her raincoat pocket. She reached in the other pocket to find a lighter.

"Why don't you come over and sit down, Shirley?" Laura suggested.

"I can't stay." She bowed her head and worked the lighter. "I have to be at work in a couple of hours. I'm taking the holiday shift."

The smell of cigarette smoke filled the room. "I'm glad you came," Laura told her not knowing what else to say.

Dr. Fisher looked beaten down, Laura thought, the slump in his shoulders more pronounced than when she'd seen him earlier. He was no longer playing the role of angry young surgeon.

"I can't promise a thing, Mrs. Towne." He shook his head from side to side. "I wish I could, but the surgery does give us a fighting chance to relieve the pressure on his brain. If you'll sign there, I can proceed."

Shirley didn't read the form on the clipboard. She signed it. "This one also, Mrs. Towne, if you please." He flipped a page back. "And again."

Shirley scribbled her signature. "Everything has to be done three times," he explained. "I don't know why, I can only operate once."

"Thank you," Shirley said, turning her head to exhale smoke.

"Don't thank me, Mrs. Towne," Dr. Fisher said wearily, motioning Penelope Washburn to follow him back to the operating room. "You'd be far better off to pray for your husband."

They were alone in the waiting room, both standing apart.

"Well," Shirley Towne said, looking absently around the empty room, "I guess I'd better go."

"Stay with me for a minute, Shirley," Laura said urgently. "I want to talk to you." If there was any brightness is this Easter morning it was far away, beyond the low dark clouds and steady pounding rain. The muddy gray water ran deep in the gutters, overflowing the cement sidewalks.

"I can't, Laura. I'm sorry."

"Please, I—we—need to talk."

"There's nothing to say, is there?" Shirley found an ashtray and stabbed the cigarette out.

"Give me a chance, Shirley. I need to understand what's going on."

"Oh, Laura, it's so hard to talk about it."

"I know, but let's try. We've got to try."

Wearily, Shirley Towne circled to the window and stood, looking down the street flanked by deserted office buildings, their yellow lights glowing weakly in the pale dawn.

"I don't know where to begin."

Laura watched her. "I don't either. Did Jack ever come and see you after the funeral?"

"No, why?" She stared at the floor.

Because I asked him to, Laura thought. "I just wondered. I hoped he might."

"Why would he do that?" she asked, turning to face Laura. The black circles were permanently etched under her eyes now. She looked exhausted.

"Because he cared."

Shirley Towne snapped her head up. She took in a deep breath and came over to Laura.

"Let's sit down," she said.

The two women sat, facing each other. Shirley Towne lit another cigarette and coughed lightly as she drew in.

"That's just it, Laura," she said, exhaling smoke, "he didn't care. He never cared. Not about you, me, the kids, or anyone but himself."

"Don't say never," she protested weakly.

"Never!" Shirley insisted, reaching out for Laura. "None of us could understand. Because we cared, don't you see? That's what makes it so hard." She touched Laura on the arm and then withdrew her hand.

Laura sat back, closing her eyes, giving the truth a chance to slip away unnoticed.

"He didn't want my love, but I gave it to him. He didn't

want your help, Laura, but you tried to help him." Her voice broke. "Excuse me," she said, leaning forward, pressing a Kleenex to her mouth.

"Are you all right, Shirley?"

"He didn't care about things that were important to me, Laura: a family, a child of my own. He wanted me to take care of his children. To keep them out of his way. He wanted my money. My support. And when I needed him, he wasn't there. He was never there." She lowered her head and coughed heavily.

Laura stared numbly at her. Was it possible she had been so blind? Was it possible she had been such a fool? She knew it was and much, much more.

Shirley put the soggy Kleenex down and picked up her smoldering cigarette. "I found out some things, Laura, since filing for divorce. Some things you ought to know about."

She paused and drew heavily on the cigarette. "For one thing, I paid all the bills, including Jack's office rent, over five hundred dollars a month. But there was no office, Laura. He moved out right after we got married. There was only an answering service."

"But where was he? Where did he work?" she asked, knowing the answer. Maggie with the overflowing breasts. Maggie, the cocktail waitress at Lion O'Malley's, with her satin drawers climbing her crotch. "My office away from the office."

"I also found out he was getting over fifteen hundred dollars a month from one of his accounts, The Happy Hot Dog. They paid him up until about a month ago. Fifteen hundred dollars, Laura, and I never saw a penny of it. I couldn't get my car fixed because we didn't have the money. And this is a man with his daughter working eight hours a day while she's trying to go to school."

"I can't believe it," Laura said without conviction. She knew it must be true.

Shirley Towne took two quick puffs on her cigarette without taking it from her lips. "I couldn't either, Laura, but I had to face it when he left me in the hospital. I had to face the fact he was never there in a crisis—never. Not when his kids needed him, not when I needed him. He was always somewhere else—in Boise or 'at the office'."

"But he tried," Laura protested.

It was a lie, all of it; what a sham she was trying to uphold. Jack Towne had seduced her too. The stage play he set up in her parking lot moved forward. She felt the touch of his flesh against hers. The plot was coming clear.

Shirley's cigarette burned, forgotten in her hand. "What he did, Laura, was use us, all of us, for his own purpose. You know, Laura, now that I look back on it, I can see that the idea of me coming to you for counseling, you know, scared him. It was going to ruin his arrangement. That's why he persuaded me we should send Wendy instead."

Laura shook her head to deny the obvious. She shook it back and forth rhythmically.

"And then when it turned out you might help Wendy after that first session, he got her out of the way too by sending her to Kentucky. Chris told me she never wanted to go. What Ruth said at the funeral was true. Jack made her go. Apparently, Wendy got off the bus; she was trying to hitchhike home when she was attacked."

"But why? Why would he send her away like that? Wendy's no threat to anyone; she never was."

Shirley flicked off a long piece of ash. "Because he wanted to get at you, Laura." Her dark eyes were steady. The doelike quality Laura first noticed at Sun Valley had hardened.

"It wasn't like that, Shirley."

"Oh, Laura, I wish it wasn't." The tears ran down her cheeks. "He'd taken everything I had. He needed somebody better, somebody with a name who could help him."

Laura Jordan went to her, sat down and put an arm around her shoulder. She remembered the first time they met at Sun Valley and how easily she offered Shirley advice and help, how sure she was of herself. Shirley cried silently. Those were innocent days, Laura thought, when she was so full of confidence and daring, willing to take any risk, plunge down the steepest hill, trusting to her nerve and ability. But it wasn't enough. Not for this.

"When you came and told me you'd been to bed with him

right after I had the abortion, I knew I would go absolutely crazy," Shirley sniffed, sitting up straight in the chair. "He planned it that way, Laura, to get rid of me. I was no good to him any more."

"No," Laura said firmly, removing her hands, "he wouldn't do that intentionally. He couldn't."

Shirley Towne took a deep breath and picked up her cigarette from the ashtray, looked at it, and ground it out.

"Yes, he could," she said firmly, wiping her eyes with the Kleenex. "There's something terribly wrong with him, Laura. He has no honest relationships with other people. They're objects to him. He destroys them."

Laura stood up. Her head felt like it was drifting off her neck. "Rob and Wendy were so vulnerable," she said absently.

"Yes, and don't forget Ruth. She was another woman he used. Everybody but Chris."

"She's so incredibly strong."

Shirley Towne stood up and came to Laura. "Yes, and it's very fortunate she is because she has so much to give. He wanted to share her glory as an Olympic star. That's why he was so concerned about protecting her. You remember? We talked about that once."

"Yes," Laura said, "I do remember."

"She turned the tables on him. She was the only one. She saw him for what he was, and she did her best to protect Rob and Wendy."

"Yes, she did. Oh God, Shirley, I hope you can forgive me."

Shirley Towne put her cigarettes in her purse. "There's nothing to forgive, Laura. Maybe some day when this is over, we can talk again."

"Yes, I'd like that."

"But right now, I have to get out of here. I can't stay anymore. I know exactly how Ruth felt. I have to leave." Shirley fastened the snaps on her raincoat from the bottom up.

"I understand, Shirley. Did you know something happened at Early Winters? The FBI called earlier."

"Yes," Shirley said quietly, "it's all over the morning paper.

It's very ugly."

"I'll call you sometime," Laura said, but she knew they would probably never see each other again.

"I'd like that." Shirley Towne kissed her lightly on the cheek.

Laura kept her hand on her cheek and watched Shirley go down the front walk into the rain, a small lonely figure in a yellow raincoat.

The headline read: SKISCAM SUSPECT CRASHES

> Seattle—An airplane flown by a Seattle man, sought along with three others, including two prominent state politicians and an Idaho finanacier, on criminal charges, crashed early this morning while trying to elude federal authorities near Cougar Lake in Chelan County. The pilot, Jack Towne, forty-two, of 10221 N.E. Heather Terrace Drive in West Seattle, is in critical condition at Lincoln Memorial Hospital. A passenger, Mrs. Joetta McFarland, thirty-seven, Boise, Idaho, died in that crash. Towne, president of Jack Towne and Associates, a local public relations firm, was being sought in connection with an alleged attempt to bribe a highly placed federal official in order to secure a U.S. Forest Service permit for a ski resort where he and his partners, according to Bureau officials, intended to conduct illegal gambling activities.
>
> Also arrested on those charges were: Washington State Senator Jack Howland, fifty-one (D), and State Senator Frank Greenway, forty-five (D), along with T.R. Timberlake, sixty-three, Idaho potato dealer and real estate investor. Howland and Greenway were arrested by federal agents in their Seattle homes and released on their own recognizance by U.S. Judge Andrew Tobias after arraignment in federal court here. Timberlake turned himself in to federal authorities in Idaho and will be arraigned this morning in Boise. He is the registered owner of the Cessna flown by Towne.
>
> Federal authorities say the arrests came after a three-month investigation involving the use of undercover agents who posed as gamblers with Mafia connections interested in setting up an illegal fly-in international gambling club at the Early Winters Resort, located on the

Idaho-Wyoming border near Wilson, Idaho.

According to the affidavit filed in federal court here, Howland and Greenway passed $50,000 to Under Secretary of the Interior William Nickelson in order to secure an operating permit which had been denied at a preliminary hearing in Idaho last month. Nickelson, notified in advance of the bribery attempt by federal officers, cooperated fully in the investigation, the FBI said.

According to FAA investigators at the scene of the crash, the Cessna 125 piloted by Towne was out of gas at the time of the crash, and the pilot was not licensed. Visibility in the vicinity was near zero, according to Ron Olsen, FAA investigator. "We can't find any evidence Mr. Towne was qualified to fly an airplane or had an instrument rating, although the plane was equipped with sophisticated navigational equipment," Olsen said in a telephone interview. "At this point we just don't know what he was doing."

Federal agents sent to arrest Towne in Seattle late yesterday were told he was on business in Boise, Idaho. When local agents there checked his hotel, they found he'd checked out only moments before and left his luggage in his room. Howland is a former Speaker of the House. Greenway is a freshman Senator from Manitou Beach. T.R. Timberlake is reputed to be one of the richest men in Idaho.

Mrs. McFarland, the dead passenger, was employed as a cocktail waitress at the Outlaw Inn, in Boise, Idaho, where Jack Towne was registered as a guest.

She left the newspaper on top of the scarred metal distribution box and followed the tangle of blue, red, and green lines that ran down the center of the corridor. She remembered them from physical examinations—blue was for X ray, red for blood, green for urinalysis.

Coming around a corner, she collided with a surprised hospital worker, wheeling a cart laden with breakfast trays under white plastic covers. There was a pink Easter bunny taped on each tray.

"Sorry," Laura Jordan said without stopping.

By now, her mother, father, and all the McClays would be in church wondering why she hadn't come. There would be freshly cut fir bows on the altar and a chicken-wire cross on the front lawn filled with spring flowers.

Laura knew only the Jack Towne she created in her mind: the gentle man with large dreams; a man who talked emotionally about ski resorts; a man who pulled himself up from poverty against great odds; the romantic man willing to risk and create wonderful surprises; a man with weaknesses certainly, a tendency to exaggerate, to be impractical, but a man who, in the end, could be forgiven.

But that Jack Towne was a complete and total illusion, a self-created fraud. Laura walked under a white and pink banner declaring Happy Easter. "Dr. Mason, Dr. Mason to the OR," a loud-speaker crackled.

What she didn't understand was why Jack Towne had done these things. To what end and for what purpose?

The door to the Emergency Room seemed heavy, and Laura had to brace to get it open. The shocking blue eyes were set in the same massive skull. He had Jack's size, but none of his bulk. He was sitting with Chris, leaning on a hickory cane, dressed in a worn blue suit. He stood up as she came toward them.

"Miss Jordan, this is my Grandpa Bill."

She offered her hand. His was hard and calloused, the fingers twisted with arthritis.

"Laura is a friend of ours, a counselor," Chris explained.

"Oh, yes," he said with a faint hill twang, "your lady called me about a month ago."

"Yes, Barb. How's Jack doing?"

"He's in surgery. They say it's a long shot." His voice was calm and resigned. "You'll have to excuse me, I'm not used to flyin'. I need to sit down."

"Of course." He was bald except for long white individual hairs along the side of his head that were carefully combed back.

"Grandpa, I've got to go study. I'll be back in about an hour," Chris told him.

"Sure, you go on. I'll be all right." He sat down heavily.

Chris collected a pile of books off the formica table, and Laura walked her to the door. "I'm so sorry about your dad,

Chris."

"Yes." The blond hair framed her serene face. The skin was still flawless. The only sign of emotion was the steady clenching and unclenching of her jaw muscles.

The hardness built up over the years could withstand anything, Laura realized. Chris Towne was going to study her way right through this crisis.

"If there's anything I can do, please let me know," she offered clumsily, wishing she could comfort the girl in some way.

"Once Dad's stabilized, once we know, I'm going to take Grandpa to my place to have Easter dinner with us—Mom and Wendy and me," Chris said, not responding to the offer.

"How is Wendy?"

Chris stopped in front of the door. "Not good." She put on an orange parka and zipped it up. "She's going to be committed, Miss Jordan, if she doesn't get better. Committed to a mental hospital. That will kill my mother. It will kill her."

"You love your mother very much, don't you, Chris?"

There were tears in her eyes. "My mother was a beautiful and kind woman."

"I know, Chris."

"Do you?" the girl asked her, one single tear breaking away from the corner of her eye and rolling free down her cheek. She pulled her rain hood up, crying silently. "She tried, Miss Jordan, she did her best, but it wasn't good enough."

"I think I understand about your mother, Chris," Laura said, wanting to reach out and hold her.

"I've got to go," Chris said abruptly, shaking her head. "I've got to study. I have a big test Monday morning. It's my first big test in college."

Laura put her hand on Chris Towne's shoulder. "How are you getting along, Chris?"

"OK. Miss Jordan, did you have fun in high school? Did you get to ride around in cars and go to dances?" the girl asked her suddenly.

"Yes, I did have fun," Laura told her, startled by the intensity of the question. "I did those things."

"I missed all that; I feel grown up. I've felt that way ever since my mother left. Is there something wrong with me?"

Laura moved her arm around Chris. "No," she said firmly, "there's nothing wrong with you at all, Chris."

"But I don't even have a boy friend."

"Oh, you will, Chris, you will. Give it some time." Laura hugged her, pleased to feel the anxiety coming to the surface in Chris, happy to see that under the hard-driving adult there was still a high school girl with most of her emotions intact.

Laura walked her out the door into the damp air where the rainwater dripped off the gutters and splattered on the cement sidewalk.

"I'm going to go in and talk to your grandpa for a while, Chris. I'll see you soon."

Bill Towne waited patiently, his hands folded over the hickory cane, gnarled veins running like pale worms across his wrinkled skin. He watched the clock on the wall. It was almost noon. Jack had been in surgery for two hours.

"You have a fantastic granddaughter, Mr. Towne," she said, sitting down next to him. "But I suppose you know that."

"She reminds me of my Edna. Edna was like that, full of spunk." He smiled.

"That was your wife?"

"Yep. She died, oh, fifteen, twenty years ago. More like twenty. I sure hated to lose that woman, Miss Jordan. My whole life changed when she died. Hasn't been the same since."

"Why don't you call me Laura."

"All right, Laura, if you call me Bill. You married?"

"No."

"Well, if you ever find the right person, you hang on to him. You never know what it means until they go—least it was like that with me and Edna."

"That's good advice, Bill. Do you mind if I ask you something about Jack?"

"Nope," he said, still looking at the clock. "There's damn little I don't know on that subject."

"Were you aware the FBI was looking for him? That he's involved in some sort of attempt to bribe government people over this ski resort he was promoting?"

"Yeah, I know that. They were waitin' at the airport. Nice young fella, can't remember his name. Told 'im I don't know a damn thing. But it don't surprise me none neither."

"It doesn't surprise you?" she asked him, held by the burning blue intensity of his eyes. They pulled her in. It was like staring into a fire, she thought.

"No. Jack flew in to see me right after Rob's funeral. When he comes to see me, Jack's in trouble. Always been that way, always will, I guess."

"What did he want?" she asked.

He broke the contact and let his eyes wander around the room. "What does he always want?" he said to himself. "Money. Jack's trouble is always money trouble. But this time I told him it was no go. I'd just paid for the boy's funeral, and I didn't have the cash. Loaned him the plane fare back, but that was the best I could do."

"You paid for the funeral?" she asked in disbelief, repeating his statement to establish the fact.

"Sure. How well did you know Jack, young lady?" He turned the eyes back on her.

"Pretty well—I thought."

"That's what I figured. I'm gonna tell you something about Jack, Laura, and I figure I got a right. It's not like I'm goin' against him or nuthin' cause I never turned that boy down. I done it for Edna; she wanted it that way."

He refolded his hands over the cane, flexing them slowly. "I always knew what I was. I was a workin' man; I worked with these." He lifted one hand and held it out for her inspection. It was old and wrinkled. Two knuckles were smashed flat.

"But somehow, I don't rightly know why, Jack could never accept what he was. He always had to make up somethin' better for himself, somethin' big, somethin' special like he was ashamed of his real true self. See what I mean?"

Laura nodded in agreement. Desperately, she looked for some sign of bitterness or hatred in Bill Towne's face, some indication he carried a grudge or had reason to discredit his son. She could find none.

"In high school, he talked about playin' professional football, but he never wanted to work hard enough to make the high school team."

"But he was injured," she protested.

"Not so's you could notice. He got banged up a little and he quit. I wanted him to go back, but he hung on to this injury thing like it was real. There's nothin' wrong with that knee, Laura, I know. I sat right there while the doctor looked it over."

She leaned forward. This old man knew. He was showing her the wires and ropes behind the stage, the structure of the illusion. The rain outside had stopped. The air was misty as the heat of the day warmed the wet ground.

"He wanted to be a college boy. It was his mother's fondest wish, but he quit that too." Bill Towne went on, lost in a world of his own, not talking to her but rather reciting a story he'd been waiting a long time to tell. "Took every last nickel I'd saved. I was gonna take Edna to Hawaii."

Penelope Washburn had gone off duty. In her place, a thin woman with close-cropped hair attacked a pile of forms angrily, her pencil checking and slashing as she flipped them from her left to her right.

The old man sighed. "Edna, she wanted to go to Hawaii more than anything in this world." When he said her name, there was a quaver in his voice. "Didn't make no difference to me, but I sure wanted to take her. Damn, I sure did want to take her." He paused, the blue eyes misting over. "She was a good woman, Laura, and she wanted that boy to go to college instead, so I sent him. I took the Hawaii money and sent him to Kentucky State Teachers College. It was the best I could do." He looked down at his hands. "Damn shame. He quit that like he quit everythin' else. Said it wasn't good enough for him. Said he wanted to go to Harvard or one of them places. Truth was, he couldn't cut it." Laura rubbed her eyes. The nurse's pencil scratched on, one pile of forms growing, the other diminishing. A horn sounded somewhere in the city. "There was always somethin' missin' in Jack, and I never for the life of me could figure it out. He was a smart enough kid and had ideas."

"Yes," Laura said, seeing Jack creating Early Winters that rainy night in her houseboat, the lifts, the lodge, and Laura's Second Landing. "He was an exciting man. He could make you believe in things that weren't there."

"Yep," Bill agreed, settling his intense blue eyes on her, "and he would get people to go along with him too. That was the bad part."

"He had an enthusiasm, a hope that everything would be all right; that success was just around the corner."

The eyes narrowed and burned into her. "Trouble was, what he left behind him was a lot of people he hurt. Ruthie wasn't a bad girl. I kinda liked her, pretty woman. I never met his second wife."

"You would have liked her too, Bill. Shirley's an exceptional person."

He dropped his eyes. "Jack broke Edna's heart. God, how she loved that boy, put everything she had into him, and it wasn't enough." He stopped, searching for the right words. "We had a good life, the three of us. There was always food on the table—enough food. And love—there was love. It was like a piece of Jack was never there no matter what we did. The part that tells right from wrong and truth from lies. The part that shows you how to care for the other people."

At that moment, Laura realized the turmoil inside each person is never penetrated by an outsider without permission, that whatever drove someone to do certain things and act certain ways was beyond knowing unless that person wanted to reveal their secret.

"The only thing I regret," the old man said, his voice low and husky with emotion, "was not coming to get the kids. I shoulda come and got the kids. I was a fool not to. They always liked it in Kentucky. We got a horseshoe pit there. Robbie was a fair player. So was Wendy. But it's too late now. There's Chris, but she don't need me."

"Yes, she does, Bill, and so does Wendy. They need you more than ever."

"Think so?"

"Yes."

There was a calm silence between them. Laura had found

out what she wanted to know, and Bill Towne had told the story he'd been holding inside for a lifetime.

"Maybe you're right," he finally said.

A door banged loudly in back of the nurse's station. Laura could hear the *click, click* of footsteps coming down the corridor. They both sat up, alert.

The doctor was in street clothes, and his face was set. Bill Towne stood with effort, but as Laura moved to help him, he steadied on his feet. "Mr. Towne, I'm Dr. Fisher. I operated on your son. We're not going to know anything about Jack's condition for at least twenty-four hours. We may not know anything for days. Or it's quite possible he may remain in a coma indefinitely. I can't say."

Bill Towne blinked rapidly and didn't reply.

"How's his heart holding up?" Laura asked him impulsively, not sure whether it was concern or an obsession to establish one solid reality about Jack Towne.

"Heart?" He looked annoyed. "There's nothing wrong with his heart; there never has been. This is a head injury."

"I see."

Dr. Fisher turned to Bill Towne. "The operation was a success. We've saved his life. But we know very little about the human brain. We know even less about how injuries affect it and how to repair those injuries." He cleared his throat. "I wish I could be more hopeful, more definitive, but it would be nothing more than a guess."

Laura knew he was trying to cushion the tragic reality with neutral words.

"Can I see him?" the old man asked.

"Yes. It will be a few minutes. We have to move him into intensive care in the neurological unit."

Dr. Fisher took Bill Towne's arm. "I did the best I could, sir. I did everything I know how to do."

"Thank you," he said. "I know you did, and I appreciate it, Doc. You oughtta go home and get some rest."

Dr. Fisher gave his arm a pat. "I will. The nurse will let you know when you can go in. Incidentally, here's the ring. I thought you might want to have it. We've locked up the rest of his personal effects."

He handed Bill Towne a white envelope, shook his hand and left. The old man sat down and opened it. It was the same heavy gold ring Laura noticed so many times on Jack's left hand. The old man held it up. He squinted at it, turning it over in his hand.

"I haven't got my specs, Laura, what does all that writing say?"

He handed it to her. It was as heavy as it looked. "It's in Latin, Bill. I don't read Latin very well.'

"It's not all Latin, is it?"

"No," she said, handing the ring back.

"Well, what's it say?" he demanded.

"It says Harvard University, class of 1961."

Laura was absolutely sure Jack Towne had never told her he attended Harvard. It must have been another play, she thought sadly, another production for some other purpose with someone else. Bill Towne was shaking his head from side to side.

"Mr. Towne," the nurse called, "you may go in now."

"Bill, let me go with you."

He got up, bracing himself with the cane. "No," he said, "I've been takin' care of Jack for years. Guess I always will."

"But let me stay with you until Chris gets back. I don't want you to do this alone, Bill."

He took her hand. "Do you have a family, young lady, people who love you?"

"Yes."

"Go home to your family. Go home to people who care. Don't waste your time here no more," he said.

Chapter 24

By the time Laura got to the Lake Washington floating bridge, Easter afternoon traffic was light. Wind pushed the Volvo from side to side. She was in a hurry; the McClays and Jordans would be back from church by now, ready for dinner.

A red catamaran, high on one pontoon, raced along the bridge railing where the water sparkled in shafts of sun that came down like spotlights. The boy sailing it, hiked out over the side on a cable trapeze, waved at her as she drew abreast and passed him. He looked a lot like Rob with his tangled blond hair. She watched him in the rearview mirror as the boat skipped over the wave tops, the rainbow sail stretched tight.

Bill Towne was right. It was time for her to leave, time for her to get back to those who cared. They had all done their best—Ruth, Shirley, Bill—even Doctor Fisher—but it was out of their hands.

She turned down the familiar driveway. Rocky met her halfway, the big collie leaping and barking as she pulled in behind Jim's silver Porsche.

"You smell like a dog, dog." She laughed as his hot tongue scraped across her face. She pushed him down and headed for the house.

Laura was finally convinced that no matter what she had done or how hard she'd tried, she could never have saved the Towne family. It was not her blundering that destroyed them—it was Jack Towne.

"Hello," she called, opening the door.

"We're in here," her father called back.

And although she had misjudged him badly, totally misread his motives, she would not quit because of a mistake, no matter how terrible and costly. There were others who wanted and needed her help.

And there would always be those special people who did care. That was the most important part. Bill Towne understood it. So did her mother. And Mary Kay Jordan had been right about Jim McClay all along.

"Hello, everybody," she greeted them, conscious of the hot flush on her face. "Am I late?"

She knew from her father's look he'd been worried about her. "That all depends on what you had in mind." He held his electric knife poised over the roast beef.

"To make a toast."

"You're just in time."

"Good." Laura went over and kissed Jim on the lips, then did the same to Myra McClay who enthusiastically pulled her close. The old Scotswoman smelled of lavender.

"My God in heaven, Laura Jordan, you never looked so good."

"I feel pretty good, Myra. Better than I have for quite a while."

She bent to kiss her mother and asked her father to pour champagne. When the glasses were filled, Laura stood beside him at the head of the table, holding her glass.

"Well," she said, her voice cracking, "here we all are at last." She cleared her throat.

"Were you going to say something else, dear?" her mother prompted her.

"Yes."

"The floor's all yours, Laura." Her father stood beside her. Gene Jordan had no idea what was coming next, but he wanted to be part of it.

"I'm sorry I couldn't join you all for church this morning," she said slowly, looking out the window to the lake and to the city beyond with its black glass buildings flashing like thousands of signal mirrors in the afternoon sun. "I had to take care of something, see it through. Finish it, actually. And now it's done." She searched along the bridge for the boy running free on his catamaran, but he was lost in the dazzle of water. "I had a speech all planned, but I can't remember it." Laura knew she was going to cry. "Oh, damn," she said, "I swore I wouldn't do this." She stopped, unable to go on, the room blurring. Her father hugged her.

"Is that all?" he asked. "When do we get to drink this stuff?"

"Almost," she said. She felt Jim McClay waiting intently, the hazel eyes watchful, his hard lean hands resting on the table in front of him.

"There's only a little more," she assured them all, pulling herself together. "On Monday, I'm going back to work, a lot smarter and a little more humble—actually a lot more humble. But that's not the important part." And without waiting to think or allow her hands to move, she said it, looking straight at Myra McClay. "Myra, I'm going to marry your son if he'll have me, so the McClay clan will never die, and that stubborn husband of yours won't be around to haunt me in my old age."

The Scotswoman put her head in her hands and cried.

"Well," Laura said, raising her glass to the stunned assemblage, "what do you say, Jim-boy?"

"I do," he replied, raising his glass back.

"Good," Laura Jordan said, "everyone drink your champagne quick. I'm starving."